CW01187630

Also by E.H. Demeter

Books
Musings From Wünderland: A book of Poetry and Prose

Anthologies
Cancer Sucks!
Nightmares: In Writer's Retreat
Hugs & Kisses: A Writer's Retreat Romance Anthology

Secrets

Book one of The Rune Trilogy

E.H. Demeter

SECRETS
ISBN-13: 978-1533202307
ISBN-10: 1533202303

Copyright © 2016 by E.H. Demeter.

First Printing 2015

SECRETS
Copyright © 2015 by E.H. Demeter.

Cover design by The Dust Jacket Cover Designs
Edited by Adele Harper
Book design by Foundation Formatting
Artwork by Cristy Upchurch
Author photograph by Liz Hammond Photography

All rights reserved. No part of this book may be reproduced in any written, electronic, recording, or photocopying without written permission of the publisher or author. The exception would be in the case of brief quotations embodied in the critical articles or reviews and pages where permission is specifically granted by the publisher or author.

This is a work of fiction. Names, characters, businesses, places, events and incidents are either the products of the author's imagination or used in a fictitious manner. Any resemblance to actual persons, living or dead, or actual events is purely coincidental.

This book is dedicated to my father, Kenneth Hahn.
For always believing in me, and teaching me to reach for the moon.
I love you, Dad.
Always and forever, to the moon and back.

CHAPTER ONE

"*Oh Anthony. I love you.*"
"*I love you too, Ramona. From the moment I saw you, I knew you were the one.*"

"Oh, come on! Ramona, don't buy his crap!" I frowned at the gorgeous brunette gracing my TV. Like she'd even listen to me.

Sticking my chopsticks into the box of Lo Mein I held, I shoveled the noodles into mouth with little grace, momentarily grateful no one else was around to see me and worry about my state of mind.

"And you know why you're not going to listen to me?" I asked with my mouth full. "Because you're fake and your life is a script."

As the music swelled and the peak of the romance flick played out in predictable, cliché fashion, I threw a pillow at the TV and sighed "And now you'll go on to get married and live happily ever after and never have to worry about him leaving you for someone blonde..."

Of course she would. Because her life was perfect, and she was in love. Unlike me.

Here I was, sitting alone on my couch on a Friday night in my favorite pajamas, talking to her like she actually existed. I sighed and dropped the box of noodles back onto the coffee table, snatching up my glass of wine in the process and gazing out the window. The night was vapid and depressing and with the way things had been going for me lately, why should I have expected anything else?

Pursing my lips, I blew out a long breath, causing my lips to vibrate together as I studied the glittering view of Portland. I was sure there were parties happening right outside my window—

Okay, maybe not *right* outside, but parties were happening! I mean, it *was* Friday night.

I really shouldn't have been so bitter toward the couple. One, because they were fictional, and two, it wasn't *their* fault my life had been going downhill lately. If I really stopped to think about it, I did have a lot of things to be grateful for. I had an apartment, a job, and, for the moment, a car.

Heartbreak, however, made me forget those things. And my heart was broken. Shattered. The pieces scattered to the wind like discarded bits of paper.

Heaving another sigh, I reached for my phone and stopped as I stared at the image on the screen I couldn't bring myself to change. Tommy, my *ex*-fiancé, and I smiled brightly at the camera, the shimmering blue water and iconic red rust Golden Gate Bridge serving as our background.

Bittersweet memories of that day flooded my mind without permission. The photo had been taken just after he proposed. It had taken me completely by

Secrets

surprise—so much so that I had literally jumped up and down and screamed in excitement. If I closed my eyes, I could still remember the way he laughed ...

The phone trilled in my palm, scaring the crap out of me. With a cry, I jumped and sloshed wine all over my lap.

"Oh, really?" I grumbled, grimacing as I surveyed the damage and felt the crimson drink permeate the fibers of my pajama pants.

Much to my annoyance, the ringer continued to pierce the air despite my unfortunate condition, and I thumbed the slider to answer the call. "Hello?"

My sister's concerned voice reverberated in my ear, "Juliet? Are you okay?"

It seemed that since my sister had become a mother, she was incapable of beginning a conversation without tacking on, "Are you okay?"

"Well hello, Beatrice," I replied, sighing at my wine stained pants. "I'm fine, how are you?" I looked around for something to mop up the wine now seeping into my couch, but found nothing, so I rose from the sofa and walked toward my room, the phone pressed to my ear.

"Are you sure? You don't sound fine."

"Bea, I'm *fine*." *As fine as someone whose heart has been smashed by a sledgehammer can be anyway,* I thought. "I just had a lap full of wine when you called."

Shifting the phone so I could hold it between my cheek and shoulder, I shimmied out of my PJ bottoms, riffling through my drawers for replacements.

"Oh, well, what are you doing tonight?"

Her tone was optimistically hopeful, a tone I knew all too well. It was the tone she used when she wanted to persuade me to do something I wouldn't want to do. I could almost see the million-dollar smile stretching her lips, white teeth flashing.

"I have plans, Bea."

"Oh, really? And do these plans involve something more than takeout, wine, and staring at old photos?"

I stuck my tongue out at the sarcasm in her tone, and tugged on a pair of yoga pants I had acquired during my health nut period. "Yes?" I replied, my voice upturned.

Beatrice snorted and mumbled, "Liar."

"Yeah, okay. So what if they don't? Who am I hurting?"

"You mean besides yourself? No one. But I don't see why you're wasting another moment on that sleezeball."

"Bea," I whined, closing my eyes and lying back on the soft handmade quilt that covered the bed. I had fallen in love with the sky blue ring pattern on the cream backdrop and bought it on impulse. My bank account hadn't liked the cost, but I loved it. "He's not..."

"Don't defend him, Jules. He *is* a sleezeball! What else do you call someone who cheats, and breaks off an engagement?"

I pressed my fingers to my eyes, feeling my throat tighten at her question. I didn't like talking about it. It was so much easier to box up all the hurt and pain and shove it aside.

"He just ... had some things to work through," I forced out, feeling like a vice was clamped around my vocal cords. *Like his need to be with another woman while I ignorantly planned our wedding.*

Beatrice scoffed, then inhaled deeply before speaking in a softer tone. "Come out with me and Bill tonight, Jules. We've got a sitter and everything."

She sounded so hopeful that I almost agreed on the spot, but at this point, even getting up off my bed seemed like more effort than it was worth.

"Maybe next time, Bea. I'm really tired. You and Bill have a great time, though."

Beatrice sighed. I could hear her muffle the phone as she spoke to someone else, presumably Bill. I waited, staring at the ceiling until she came back on the line.

"Okay, well … if you're sure. We miss you."

"Miss you too, Bea. 'Night."

I pushed the end button and dropped the phone onto the bed. Twisting around, I peered at the clock on the nightstand. Was eight o'clock too early to go to bed? Maybe not if you were eighty, but I since I was only twenty-seven, I figured it was.

But I was so tired—of hurting, of thinking, of remembering. Of wishing for a life I would never have. Wishing for a love that wasn't to be. Rolling onto my side, I pushed the home button on my phone, calling up the image of Tommy and myself once more.

I trailed my finger along his digitized face, squeezing my eyes closed against the press of tears. Beatrice was right, though I was reluctant to admit it. I needed to stop torturing myself.

Tomorrow. I would remove the image tomorrow.

"I miss you," I whispered, curling myself around the phone, letting oblivion claim me.

E.H. Demeter

THE DAYS CONTINUED to pass as they had before, but not nearly swiftly enough for my liking. It was as if time had purposely slowed down, begging me to wallow in self-pity. The same questions ran repeatedly through my mind: Why did he leave me? What did I do wrong? How could I have made it better? And why had he suddenly decided he liked blondes over redheads?

He had always told me my hair was one of the things he loved most. I was his red-haired, green-eyed beauty. Apparently not beautiful *enough* ...

Some part of me knew how foolish those questions were, but I couldn't seem to stop them. I did the best I could to push through the day, throwing my focus onto work. Luckily for me, that was easy to do, as I loved my job. I'd been working at Rose Village Assisted Living for the past three years and couldn't imagine working anywhere else.

After tugging my scrub top down over my head before work one morning a week later, my eyes once more found the image on my phone that I had yet to change.

"Enough's enough, Juliet," I chided myself. "He's not coming back." I leaned down and scooped up the device. My finger hovered over the settings icon, but I couldn't bring myself to push it.

Coward.

Closing my eyes in defeat, I shoved the phone into my purse and strode to the door. *I'll do it at lunch*, I promised myself as I locked it behind myself.

The morning was crisp and cool, not unusual for May in Portland. It made me wish I hadn't forgotten my jacket. I scurried to my car as the air nipped at my body heat, stopping dead in my tracks when I saw the bright yellow envelope on the windshield.

"Oh, come on!" I growled, snatching the envelope off the glass and shoving it in my purse. I didn't need to read it. I'd gotten one just like it last week.

'Dear Miss Adams,' I thought with a scowl, *'please make your payment or we will be forced into legal action.'*

"Forced into legal action" was a nice way of saying, "We'll repossess your car." The problem was, I didn't have the $6,700 I needed to make the payment, and I wouldn't for some time the way my hours were going. Six-thousand seemed like a lot. I mean, the car wasn't *that* new. But it was low on miles, and got me where I needed to go. Besides, I *liked* the little Volkswagen.

Heaving a frustrated sigh, I slid into the driver's seat, slipping the key into the ignition and starting the engine. I cranked up the fans, relishing the heat they expelled, grumbling as I caught a glimpse of the yellow envelope in my purse beside me on the passenger's seat.

It should have been a red envelope. After all, it was the cherry on my crappy life sundae.

Traffic was mercifully light and I made it to work with fifteen minutes to spare. Though a rare feat, I didn't dare dream that the tides were turning in my favor. I pulled into the staff lot and into my parking spot. The smiling daisy bobble head on the dashboard had my lips curving lightly. Maybe it wasn't all that bad.

"Morning, Stacey," I called to the receptionist as I approached the front desk. The young blonde was dressed in her usual style of clothing that was just a bit too risqué to be considered office attire. She offered me a fake, cheery smile before going back to typing.

Probably on Facebook, I thought, rolling my eyes. I nodded to a few of the other staff members on my way into the locker room. After storing my things, I clipped on my I.D. badge and headed back to the front desk to grab my charts for the day. One of them immediately caught my eye.

"Hey, Mrs. Darrow is back?" I asked Stacey as I looked over her chart.

"Yeah, she came in last night. Poor thing." Stacey clicked her tongue, tilting her head toward me, her eyes over wide and brimming with sadness as she shook her head.

"What was her daughter's excuse this time?" I sighed, flipping the chart closed. Stacey shrugged, her sadness quickly forgotten as she began rapidly typing again. I drummed up a smile. "Thanks."

"No probs."

As I started off down the hall, I decided that I would go see Mrs. Darrow first. While I was sad things hadn't worked out with her daughter, I was happy that she was back.

Mrs. Adaline Darrow was seventy-six years old and a firecracker of a woman if I had ever known one. She got away with quite a lot due to her frail appearance—she only weighed ninety-six pounds. But after having gotten to know her over the last year, I was wise to her tricks.

"Mrs. Darrow?" I called as I knocked lightly on her door, cautious in case she was sleeping. When I received no answer, I poked my head inside the room and felt the first real smile of the day pull at my lips.

There, on the floor, was Mrs. Adaline Darrow in a perfect Downward Facing Dog position. She was dressed in a canary yellow shirt and black yoga pants. Her snow-white hair was pulled back into a loose bun, and large sea shell earrings dangled from her lobes.

"You know, I never felt comfortable in that position," I commented as I walked into the room and set her chart on the tray by the bed.

Adaline gave a rough cackle, the laugh of a recovering smoker, and rose out of the position. "When you get to be my age, you look for any excuse to have your butt looked at." She winked at me before breaking out into a little boogie as she crossed toward the chair beside me. "How are you, Miss Juliet?"

"Oh, I'm all right. How have you been?" I smiled at her, doing my best to keep my voice upbeat as a fresh wave of sadness hit me. I didn't want anyone looking at my butt besides Tommy, but that wasn't going to happen anymore.

"You don't sound all right. I may be old, but I'm not deaf, you know."

I chuckled softly, pushing some hair from my eyes before nodding to her. "I know you're not deaf. You're healthy as a horse. And, you look beautiful."

Adaline gave me a penetrating gaze, as if trying to read the lies behind my words. Her pale blue eyes locked on mine and her lips pursed slightly as she stared at me.

I looked away first.

"So, umm, what brings you back to The Village?" I asked; I didn't have to fake the concern in my tone. Adaline was one of my favorite residents at Rose Village. Her presence always made things brighter.

Adaline made a face as she lowered into the burgundy chair, crossing one leg over the other. "My daughter's run off. She fancies herself in love. *Again.* Followed this one off to Vienna. I give it a month."

"Vienna? Wow." I shook my head, pulling out my blood pressure cuff. I'd never been out of the country before. Heck, I had only left the state once. "Well, that must be nice for her."

Her brow furrowed. "Nice?" she repeated with a scoff. "It's downright stupid, if you ask me. Men are nothing but trouble. And before I know it, she'll come crying to me, begging me to come home again." Adaline sighed and extended her arm toward me. "Enough to make a person go mad."

I smirked as I read the numbers off the dial. "Well, at least your blood pressure is normal. Let's listen to your heart and then I have to take your temperature."

"Not rectally, I hope."

I smiled at her as I stored my cuff away and noted her numbers in her chart. Slipping on my stethoscope, I listened as she rambled on, regaling me with tales of her daughter's many failures at finding love—a trait she seemed to pick up from her mother—as well as some of her own adventures.

"He asked me to run off to Buenos Aires with him. But I turned him down," Adaline reminisced after I pulled the thermometer from her lips.

"Why?"

"Well, he didn't want to marry me and that wasn't strictly proper in those days. He did have quite the butt, though."

Laughing, I leaned in and kissed her cheek. "Miss Adaline, you always make me laugh."

"That's good. You need someone to make you laugh. You've got far too much sadness in your eyes."

Secrets

Her observation caught me off guard. I stared at her for a moment before forcing a small laugh and smile, quickly shaking my head as I busied myself with packing up my bag.

"I'm not sad, Adaline," I insisted. "How can I be sad when I have friends like you?"

"You're a terrible liar, Juliet." She gave me a long look before waving her hand in my direction. "Go on and get. I'm feeling a nap coming on."

The rest of the morning and afternoon passed by smoothly, but Adaline's words stuck with me. I thought I was doing well, getting through each day and shoving down the pain and the hurt. But Adaline had seen right through it all. Maybe I wasn't doing as well as I'd thought.

Before I knew it, I was clocking out and saying my farewells to my co-workers. Yawning, I stepped into the locker room to collect my things. I listened quietly to the conversation around me, others making plans for the night and the coming weekend. I didn't join in. What did I have to offer? Adaline was right, I was sad. Even worse, I was mopey. And sad and mopey didn't mix well with happy people. I lifted my phone to check my messages, my heart stuttering at the image on the screen.

You've got far too much sadness in your eyes.

Inhaling deeply. I slid my thumb over the slider and punched the photos icon, calling up my gallery. A few strokes and a tap, and it was done. My beautiful nieces smiled out at me from my lock screen.

"That's better."

Slipping my purse strap onto my shoulder, I started down the hall to leave. I had only gone a few steps when I paused and decided to go back to say goodnight to Adaline.

I knocked softly on her door, not wanting to wake her if she had already gone to bed. My eyes widened as the door swung inward. Biting my lower lip, I stepped inside.

"Adaline? I don't want to wake you, but I wanted to tell you something." I whispered, looking around the dim space. I jumped as I came eye to eye with her. "Adaline! You scared me!" I gave a small laugh, pressing my hand to my racing heart.

My smile died as the realization that something was wrong dawned on me. Adaline stood in the middle of the room, her arms rigidly held to her sides. Her pale blue eyes so wide that the whites seemed to glow in the darkened room. A white mist swirled around her feet, reaching out toward me as I moved into the room, chilling me.

"Adaline?" I asked my voice strained, my gaze dropping to the ground and the unnatural mist. *What in the world? Fog?* It hadn't seemed cold enough for fog. I glanced at the window, eyes widening as I found it shut.

Adaline's sharp gasp had my gaze jerking back toward her. Heart pounding in my chest, I stopped short. Something told me not to touch her. It was then I noticed her lips moving rapidly, though I couldn't hear what she was saying. Taking a deep, steadying breath, I slipped closer and positioned my ear near her mouth.

Her breath was icy against my ear. I found that odd, but was distracted from the thought by her harsh whispering. Her words tumbled over one another, each racing to get out. Still, I couldn't hear her. I shook my head and pulled back, unable to make sense of it. "Adaline, I can't— I can't understand you. Can you hear me?"

Her lips continued to move rapidly, giving no recognition that I had spoken. Inhaling deeply, I leaned in again and pressed my ear close to her lips, shivering as the coolness of her breath washed over my skin.

"Sinking. Water rushing in, consuming me. Filling me, over powering me with its icy grasp. Pulling me down, down below the surface. Blackness, my throat closing in. I can't breathe. Oh, God. Oh *God*. I can't breathe. I'm dying. I'm dying!" And all at once, her eyes cleared, a smile over taking her as those pale blue orbs locked onto mine. "They're both coming. One to save, the other to damn."

I jerked back as her words registered. What was she talking about? Who was coming? She wasn't making any sense. "Adaline, who's coming?"

Her smile widened seconds before she gave a sharp shudder and collapsed.

"Adaline!" I gasped, my arms shooting out to catch her, "Help!" I called over my shoulder. "Someone call EMS!"

I tried to keep the panic from my voice as she shook and writhed violently in my arms. As gently as I could, I guided her to the floor and shoved my purse beneath her head. Gripping her shoulders I rolled her to the side, sweeping my fingers across her lips to make sure her airway was clear before I glanced at the clock, whispering to her. "Stay with me, Adaline."

I blinked rapidly as the lights came on and the on-call EMS team burst into the room. Strong hands gripped my shoulders, edging me away. I rose on shaking feet as I was moved aside, wrapping my arms around my body; I hugged myself tightly as I watched them cluster around Adaline.

The seizure had seemed to go on forever, but Adaline now lay unnaturally still. Heart in my throat, I watched as they lifted her from the floor and moved her onto a stretcher, calling for tests and an EKG.

"Excuse me, nurse? Can you tell me what happened?" a member of the EMS team asked me, pulling out a notepad and a pen. I jerked my gaze toward him, blinking in confusion. My eyes quickly dropped to the stitched lettering on his chest reading *Ahlström*.

"What? Oh, um, I came by to tell her goodnight and she was just standing there. I spoke to her, but she didn't respond, and she was babbling, not making sense. And she was cold ... then she started seizing."

Guilt washed over me in an icy wave, clenching my gut. It had taken me too long to stabilize her. I had been a friend before a nurse. I swallowed and looked the man straight in the eye, aware of him writing down everything I had said.

"Will she be all right?" I asked. "Do you have to take her to the hospital?"

"We'll know more soon. Why don't you take a seat, and I'll come get you in a second?" Ahlström replied, reaching out and squeezing my shoulder. His hand was warm, and his touch comforting. Blowing out a breath, I nodded, offering up a slight smile.

I sunk into the chair Adaline had occupied earlier in the day, watching as various people in different capacities entered and exited the room, each attentively

Secrets

tending to Adaline. Through the torrent of concern for Adaline's health, I replayed her odd whisperings in the silence of my mind. Despite my best efforts, it still made no sense to me. And where had the fog gone? It had disappeared with the lights, but why had there been fog at all? Closing my eyes, I pressed my fingers to my temples and rubbed. Nothing was making any sense at all.

Dusk shifted to evening before things settled down. The man who had taken my statement approached me, offering an encouraging smile.

"Hi again. So, it appears she had a grand mal seizure, as I'm sure you guessed. We're going to take her to Providence Portland, keep her overnight for observation." He paused, his smile widening slightly. "Chin up. She'll be back by tomorrow as long as nothing else happens."

Lowering my hands, I looked up into his smiling face. His eyes, I now noticed, were brown. A deep, gooey brown, like warmed chocolate. He seemed sweet without being condescending.

"Are you new? I don't recognize you," I admitted, an embarrassed smile tugging at my lips.

"Yeah, not been with the team long. I'm Robert. Your friendly neighborhood EMT."

I glanced past him as I noticed the other team members file out of the room, absently fiddling with the locket at my throat.

"Hello? Hey, you okay there?"

"Hmm? Oh! I'm sorry. I'm distracted. I mean," I rose from the chair and held out my hand to him, "I'm Juliet."

Robert smiled, his eyes on mine as he shook my

hand. Something skittered up my arm at our touch. It felt as though I'd been shocked. I gasped and jumped back, breaking the contact and rubbing my palm.

"Static electricity. Dry air," he offered with a chuckle, before reluctantly looking over his shoulder. "I should probably go, before I get yelled at," he smirked. "New guy, ya know? But ... would you want to get coffee sometime? Tomorrow, maybe? I'd love to get to know you better."

He flashed me a grin that made my knees quake and I nodded, giving a baffled laugh. "Uh, yeah. Sure. That would be great."

"Tomorrow," he beamed. "Beans Coffee? On Fifth? Eleven-thirty. Don't be late."

Stunned, I stared at the doorway, rubbing my palm as I watched Robert depart. For one ridiculous moment, I marveled at the fact that he'd been flirting with me.

Not only flirting, but also interested.

"If you don't go after that, I will."

The rough croak caught me by surprise and caused me to spin around.

"Adaline! You're awake!" I rushed to her bedside and reached for her hand, relief washing through me.

"I'm a quick healer, didn't you know that? And I meant what I said."

I stared at her, my brow furrowing in confusion. "What?"

"The young man that was working to fix me up—if you don't go after him, I will. There's something familiar about that boy."

I stared at her in disbelief before breaking out into a relieved laugh and pressing my forehead to her hand,

Secrets

feeling the choking hold of tears once more.

Adaline clucked her tongue, chiding me. "Don't you dare cry over me. I'm fitter than I look. A little fall's not gonna do me in."

"Fall?" I lifted my head and looked at her in concern. "Adaline, you didn't-"

"Excuse me, but we need to be getting her loaded up now. You can come by Providence in the morning." The lead EMT said gently, but forcefully.

"Can't I have just another-"

"You heard the man," she interrupted sharply, "it's late and I'm tired. And you need to be getting home. There's time enough tomorrow for chatter. They'll look after me."

She left me no space for argument. Sighing, I pressed a kiss to her forehead, whispered, "See you tomorrow," and stood back as they wheeled her out of the room.

THE DRIVE HOME was a blur of mingled thoughts. Adaline's words ran through my mind on replay, but I couldn't make sense of them. I kept thinking back to how she had looked when I walked into the room, still and unblinking, as if she had gone into some kind of trance.

But people don't do that, I mused as I crawled into bed. *That sort of thing only happens in the movies. Right?*

I tenderized my pillow into a suitable form and turned off the light with a sigh. Sleep wouldn't come quickly. I couldn't turn off my mind.

Who was coming? Who was dying? And what does Adaline have to do with it all?

CHAPTER TWO

I SPENT MOST of my free time over the next two weeks with Adaline. Though she insisted she was fine, I couldn't shake the feeling something more was going on. I had tried to bring up the topic of her seizure, the cryptic message she had given me, and the fog, but she shut me down each time.

For two weeks, that message had been on the forefront of my mind. It frustrated me. I knew I had to try to get her to talk about it.

Adaline and I sat outside on the small patio that was open to the residents. The day was warm with a mild breeze that kept us cool. Adaline reclined in one of the well-cushioned lounge chairs, her eyes closed and face turned upward toward the sun. She had spent most of the morning telling me about her girlhood. Her stories always left me fascinated—her life was like something out of a fairy tale.

"You really swam the English Channel?" I asked, unable to hide the disbelief from my voice.

Her eyes still closed heavenward, she smiled. "I sure did. Everyone made a big fuss about it too. Gave me all sorts of ribbons and a medal to boot. Still got it somewhere."

"Wow. Your life is so amazing! I can only hope to do half of the things you've done."

At that, Adaline looked at me. "You've got to keep your eyes open, Juliet. You never know when the adventure of your life could happen."

I smiled at her, but I didn't believe her words. Given all the truly amazing things she had told me, I just didn't have it in me to believe anything like that could ever happen to me. I had kept my eyes—and my heart—open, and what had I gained?

A lot of tears and about five extra pounds.

Drumming up my courage, I leaned toward her, keeping my voice light and casual.

"Adaline, I wanted to ask you about–"

"What ever happened with you and that boy?" Adaline interrupted. "Didn't he propose?"

She couldn't have hit on a better subject to derail me. Dropping my gaze to my hands, I fell quiet as I tried to find the words to respond.

"Well ... yes. But ... it didn't work out. We, um, broke up."

Adaline narrowed her eyes at me as I finally looked back to her. She remained like that long enough to make me feel self-conscious. Just when I was beginning to think she wasn't going to say anything, Adaline scoffed and brushed at the knee of her lime green pants.

"Idiot," she grumbled.

I blinked in shock at her statement, making a mask of my face and once more banking down on the hurt. "What?"

"That boy." She turned her eyes to me once more,

hitting me with that oddly penetrating gaze. I noticed her eyes didn't seem as pale as they had before. "It would take a pretty big fool not to see what a treasure you are. You're better off. Nothing good ever came out of tying yourself to someone so blind."

I smiled softly, touched by her words. Curiosity swirled within me. "Sounds like you're speaking from experience."

Adaline cackled, slapping her hand against my knee with enough force to make me wince. "Haven't you been listening to my stories? I sure am speaking from experience!" She winked at me and gave another laugh as she crossed her arms over her chest. "Tabitha's father was the only one I ever married."

The shift in her tone as she spoke her last thought caught my interest; I leaned toward her. "How come? I mean, why was he the only one you married?"

Adaline sat in silence for a time, appearing distant as she gazed across the lawn with the breeze ruffling her hair. She gave a small shrug, her eyes narrowing. "Well, I suppose you could say he captured a part of me no one else had."

I smiled gently at her. I couldn't help it—it sounded so romantic. After all of the amazing stories she had told me, she had always been very vague when it came to her husband.

"How romantic," I sighed dreamily.

Adaline turned her gaze to me. It seemed to take her a moment to focus on me before she gave a small smile. "Sounds that way, eh? Well, it was something. Anyway," she said, her tone changing, seeming forced, "I think I hear a nap calling my name." She once again thumped her hand on my knee and rose from the lounge chair.

"Want me to walk you to your room?" I asked. I felt bad questioning her, but it was apparent that his loss still affected her.

"I am perfectly capable of walking to my room, Juliet," she chided. "Next, you'll be asking to wipe my butt."

Adaline cackled at her own joke and walked off, leaving me staring after her in a mix of amusement and shock. I never could keep up with her moods, and there was no telling what was going to come out of her mouth from one moment to the next.

Shaking my head, I rose from my chair and tidied up the patio. That didn't take me long, and I still had an hour before I had to clock out. With a soft sigh, I resigned myself to the fact that I was going to have to tackle the paperwork I'd been neglecting for the past week.

Stacey gave me a sickly-sweet smile as I entered the office and she passed over the large stack of files requiring my attention. I tossed a fake smile her way and cradled the files, slipping off to the break room and nabbing a space at the circular table.

By the time I finished, my neck was stiff and I was more than ready to be going home.

"Goodnight, Stacey." I smiled, clocking out and making my way out of the building.

MY LIFE BECAME so monotonous, I could set my watch by it. Get up, go to work, go home and call for takeout, or zap any leftovers. I was becoming the boring homebody no one wanted to hang out with. The only thing missing from my life was a cat.

I could get a cat ...

With a rough shake of my head, I shoved the thought from my mind. The times I spent with Adaline listening to her tales were the highlights of my days. That thought gave me pause. My best friend was a seventy-six year-old woman.

I unlocked the door of my apartment, dropping my keys in the bowl by the door and hung my purse on the peg. An insane urge to yell, "I'm home!" came over me, but I didn't do it.

Heaving a sigh, I strode into the kitchen and yanked open the drawer where I housed an alarming amount of takeout menus.

Maybe Beatrice is right. I need to stop sulking and move on. Stop thinking about Tommy and what he is doing. If he is all right, if he is thinking about me...

"No," I told myself sternly, giving a sharp shake of my head and focusing on my menus. "The only thing you need to think about is Indian or pizza .... Pizza it is!"

I grabbed up my phone and placed my order. Pizza would ensure me lunch tomorrow, and maybe even dinner. It would also allow me to put off going to the grocery store for another day.

Trudging toward the fridge, I pulled open the door and looked over the meager contents.

Maybe I'd better do some shopping first thing in the morning, I thought, grabbing my last bottle of wine. Prepared to wait for my food, I popped in the movie I'd rented before dropping onto the couch and opening the wine.

"Thank God for twist offs, huh?" I asked the TV as I took a grateful sip.

Secrets

Forty-five minutes later, I was halfway through *Much Ado About Nothing* and had made a decent dent on both the pizza and the wine. My head was buzzing nicely and the movie was suddenly much funnier than it had been. I giggled as the characters traipsed and tripped along through their comical tale.

"Oh, Benedict, you're so funny." I brought the bottle to my lips and glugged down some of the sweet nectar. As I lowered it, my gaze landed on my phone. *Beatrice would love this movie. I should call her.* Without a second thought, I swiped it off the arm of the couch and opened my contacts list.

I giggled, attempting to blink away the bleariness plaguing my eyes, and stabbed randomly at my contacts until the device began to ring.

And ring. And ring.

My wine filled brain was easily distracted and I became consumed by the movie, the ringing becoming oddly soothing.

"Hello?" a harried voice sounded in my ear, jerking me roughly to attention. Cold dread lined my stomach. I knew that voice.

My world stopped. Mouth hanging open, I ripped my phone away from my ear and stared at the call screen.

Tommy Donovan.

Oh no.

With the force of a speeding train hitting my chest, time resumed its normal speed, rocketing my pulse into orbit.

"Hello? Juliet, I know it's you." A heavy sigh followed, causing me to bring the phone back to my ear so fast I cracked myself in the head with it. Wincing,

I sat up straighter and cleared my throat.

"Oh hi, Tom. Thomas. Tommy. Hi. Hellooo. How, uh, how are you?"

Smooth, I chided myself, sinking down into the cushions and wishing the call would drop. Or that I would be hit by lightning. Either option would have been acceptable. Silence filled the void before Tommy took another deep breath.

"I'm fine. Juliet, listen, you have to stop doing this."

"Doing? I, uh, I don't–I was trying to call Beatrice and–"

"And the last time it was the pizza shop and the time before that your mother. I don't want to have to pursue this legally, so please, just ... remove my number and-"

His voice trailed off as a female purr sounded in the background, but he didn't need to say anything else. In my mind's eye, I watched my heart swell up like a balloon before shattering into a million pieces.

"You–You're right," I stammered. "I –I'm sor ... I'll do that right now." My voice was strained, my throat tight with tears.

"I have to go. Don't call me again."

Tears slipped down my cheeks as feminine laughter echoed down the phone line and reverberated in my ears. Three dull beeps signified the call had ended, but I didn't move, frozen by what had just happened. The movie played on, but I was no longer watching.

It was over. Really and truly over. He had obviously moved on and I ...

I was broken.

Secrets

I WOKE TO darkness. Rubbing my eyes, I sat up and looked around for the source of what had woken me. My yawn turned into a wince as I rubbed at a crick in my neck, making a mental note to never sleep on my couch again. My head ached from the wine. The pain was so bad, it was buzzing.

I moaned, covering my face with my hands. The buzzing seemed to get worse the more awake I became that I could even feel it in my feet.

My brow furrowed before I realized the buzzing was not in my head, but my phone. I fumbled around the cushions as I searched, frowning as I came up empty handed.

"Where is it?" I scrubbed at my eyes with the heels of my palms, willing my headache to abate. Sliding to the floor, I folded into a sitting position and looked blindly around, my fingertips searching.

The buzzing stopped.

"Oh, no. Come on. Where are you?" Getting up and turning on the light was too much effort just to find my phone. Added to that, I was pretty sure anything as bright as the lights would make my head explode. With a grunt, I flopped onto my stomach and stretched out my arm, still searching. "Come on, *come on.*"

The buzzing started again. And the phone lit up.

"Ah ha!" I shoved my hand beneath the ottoman and grabbed up the buzzing device with a triumphant grin, sliding my thumb over the surface to answer the call.

"Hello?"

"Oh, thank God! Juliet! Do you know how many

times I've called? I was about to send Bill over if you hadn't answered! Are you okay? Should I send Bill anyway?"

I winced at the loudness of her voice, then again when she screamed for her husband. Sighing, I pressed my face into the carpet, allowing it to muffle the sounds of my grumbling. Of course it was my sister. Who else would it have been?

Tommy, a tiny, hopeful voice whispered before I squashed it down.

"Hello, Bea. I'm fine, no, there's no need to send Bill. I was asleep."

Rolling over onto my back I stared at the ceiling as Beatrice continued to rant on about how worried she had been. Her voice only succeeded in making my headache worse.

"Bea! I said I was fine! I'm not dead, I was just asleep. Stop worrying about me before you give yourself an ulcer."

"I will not stop worrying about you, Juliet. You're not in a good place right now and you need someone to worry about you!"

"And what would you know about it, Beatrice? I don't remember you ever being dumped by your fiancé," I snapped, jerking into a sitting position and groaning in pain for my effort. "Ow," I whimpered, placing my hand to my head again.

"That's not fair," Beatrice said in a soft, tinny voice that instantly made me feel horrible.

"I know, I know. I'm sorry ... Just ... back off a bit, okay? You're my sister, not my mother." I forced my tone to be light and joking in hopes of fending off an emotional conversation and bringing her around to the reason she had actually called for.

"I'll try. I was actually calling to see if you had plans this weekend."

I groaned softly and stared up at my ceiling. Beatrice was nothing if she wasn't tenacious. I knew from past experience she would keep asking until I gave in.

Squeezing my eyes closed, I rubbed my brow and bit the bullet. "Ah, No. I don't have any plans this weekend. Did you have something in mind?"

I could almost hear her smile through the phone line and couldn't help but chuckle as she squealed. "I did, yes! Bill has the week off so we're packing up and going to Cannon Beach. I was hoping you would come out to the beach house with us."

"The beach house? For a week? I don't know, Bea-"

"Jules, the girls would love it."

She went there. She was pulling the niece card. How the heck was I supposed to refuse when she used my nieces against me? I sighed, because I knew I couldn't.

"All right. I'll go."

"Really? Oh, Jules! That's great. That's just ... Okay, okay, we'll pick you up at nine-thirty, so be ready. I'll see you in the morning! I'm so excited! I have to go. Go pack. I love you!"

"Bea-Beatrice. No. I'll just-" I sighed as the connection ended. "Drive," I finished and dropped my phone to the floor, looking around my dark living room. It was only ten, but it felt like an eternity had passed since I had stupidly dialed Tommy. Biting my lip, my gaze drifted slowly toward my discarded phone.

"No! Don't you dare! That path is gone and burned," I told myself firmly, shoving myself to my feet. I stumbled into my bedroom, stopping short as I spotted the full-length mirror. Without a thought, I shucked off my clothes and stood there, examining myself.

I wasn't an unattractive woman. My hair was a glossy, natural red, and long, well past my shoulders now. My skin was pale; I couldn't hold a tan, but I could burn with the best of them. My eyes were a pretty green. My grandfather had always said they were like emeralds.

I guessed I was about average height for a woman, about 5"5', and slender. Not model slender. The last few months of takeout certainly hadn't helped my waistline, but I wasn't obese.

Sighing dishearteningly, I kicked my crumpled clothes aside and flopped onto the bed, still no closer to understanding why Tommy had lost interest in me. I punched my pillow and shoved away the thought. I really needed to stop wallowing. I needed to push aside any fresh bouts of pain and hold my head up high.

I had a beach trip to pack for.

CHAPTER THREE

TRUE TO BEATRICE'S word, they arrived at nine-thirty the next morning, leaving me just enough time to call my boss, only to find out she had already spoken to Beatrice about my taking time off. My boss had said she felt that a vacation was the best thing for me. I didn't know how I felt about others deciding what I needed, but for the time being, I was trying to roll with it.

Three brisk knocks announced their arrival. I looked around as I walked toward the door, wincing at the state of my place. Clothes and old take-out containers were scattered about, and the sink and counter tops were in a sorry state, cluttered with dirty dishes.

It would be best if Bea didn't see how messy my apartment is. The last thing I need is for her to start in on me for that.

Pulling open the door, I flashed Bea a quick smile. "Hey! I'll be right down!" I announced before promptly slamming the door in her face.

Blowing out a breath, I spun on my heel and ran toward my room to grab my bags. I knew I didn't have long before the shock wore off and Beatrice started looking for my spare key.

Hauling my bags off my bed, I gave the room a frantic once-over, making sure I hadn't forgotten anything. Reasonably sure I had everything, I trudged toward the door just as it swung open.

"Juliet Leigh, I don't know what that was about, but it was very rude!" Beatrice scolded in what I commonly referred to as her, "Mommy Tone," her arms crossed over her chest, expression stern.

"Good morning," I countered, still smiling. "Have you eaten? Because I haven't and I am *starving*!"

Beatrice sputtered and laughed as I leaned in and kissed her cheek, gently edging past her and pulling the door closed behind me.

"Well, yes. I mean, the girls ate, but I'm sure we can stop somewhere. I'll tell Bill to put your bags in the van," Beatrice chirped, waving animatedly in the direction of her husband, signaling him over.

"Wait-what? I was going to drive myself."

"What?" Beatrice spun toward me so fast she almost fell over, her eyes wide in shock. "I thought we would all ride together. I have it all planned out! I have games and coloring pages! And! And, it will save on gas!"

I bit back the sigh desperately trying to escape and stooped forward to lift my bags. "Yes, it would save on gas if we all rode together, but if there's an emergency at the Village, I would have to call a cab."

Beatrice gave me a truly pitiful look as Bill arrived. I was pretty sure I saw her lower lip quivering as I handed off my bags to Bill.

I groaned. "Fine! Okay! We'll ride together."

Bill shook his head with a soft chuckle as Beatrice

threw her arms around my neck, bouncing up and down as she squeezed me.

"I love you, Jules! I'm so glad you're coming with us. You need to do more than stay in cooped up in your apartment all the time."

"Yeah, yeah," I grumbled, disentangling myself from her grip and walking toward the van. I could only imagine just how *fun* this ride was going to be. Two hours in a van with my nieces and my sister. I didn't know how Bill did it every day. "And I *do* do more. I had a date the other morning." I said smugly, throwing open the door of the van, leaving Beatrice sputtering as I was greeted by the delighted screams of my nieces.

"Auntie Jules!" they squealed.

"Hello, my beauties!" I beamed as I climbed in, pausing to kiss each girl on her forehead before flopping into the backseat. "I've missed you two."

The girls giggled and echoed "missed you too" back at me, kicking their legs against the backs of the seats before them. I chuckled and settled into the middle of the backseat behind the girls.

At least I'll have plenty of legroom, I thought with a frown, tossing my purse into the seat beside me.

"Girls, girls, don't kick the seats," Beatrice chided as she climbed into her seat and twisted around to face me. "Are you comfortable, Juliet?"

"Oh, yeah. I'm *great*."

"Wonderful!"

I rolled my eyes as the sarcasm flew right over Beatrice's head and watched her have a whispered conversation with Bill.

"Auntie Jules, look what I got!" Keegan cried, twisting around and thrusting out her hand, in which she clutched a small, vibrant blue iPod.

"Whoa! That's pretty cool, kid. What've you got on there?"

She rattled off names of bands I had never heard of, flashed me a smile and promptly inserted her earbuds into her ears. Before I knew it, she had zoned out to her music. I chuckled softly, shaking my head.

My amusement died, however, when I noted Kylie staring at me unblinkingly. I stared back, keeping my face straight. Still, she didn't blink. My eyes began to prickle as they dried out, but I continued to hold my gaze. My eyebrow began to twitch from the strain of not blinking.

I finally gave in and blinked, and Kylie dissolved into a fit of giggles, yelling, "I won! I won!"

"Yeah, yeah. Creepy little mutant," I said endearingly before casting my now watering eyes toward the front of the van, rubbing my rumbling stomach. "Hey, Bill, any way we could swing through a McDonalds?"

I knew at once I'd said the wrong thing. Kylie screamed in delight and began bouncing in her seat, her strawberry curls bouncing. "I want French fries!"

The look Beatrice shot me could have curdled milk.

"Sorry," I muttered, catching Bill's eye. I was relieved to see he was chuckling.

"Yeah, I think we can manage that. And you can have French fries, Kylie." Bill called over his shoulder as he pulled the van away from the curb.

The trip to McDonalds was blessedly quick and soon we were all occupied with eating. Soft music filtered through the vans speakers and within the hour,

Secrets

the van was silent. I smiled at a passed out Kylie, her head lolling to the side and her French fry bag held loosely in her fingertips. Keegan was staring out the window, but I couldn't tell if she was awake or not.

Shaking my head, I shifted in my seat and pressed my forehead against the glass of the window, watching the pine trees pass in a blur of green and brown. The road twisted and wound around the landscape, much like my thoughts.

There was a reason I'd been working so much. Keeping busy kept my thoughts at bay. Drinking kept my mind from wandering to ... *him*. Doing nothing for two hours gave my mind entirely too much freedom to wander where it would. Too much time for self-doubt to creep in and fill my soul.

By the time we reached the beach house, I felt wretched. My stomach churned and threatened to revolt against the double cheeseburger I had consumed. All I wanted was to be out of the van. I'm not sure who was happier when we pulled into the drive, the girls or me.

With excited squeals, the girls scampered from the van and took off, Beatrice following with shouted warnings about staying where they could be seen. Bill and I followed less enthusiastically. Stretching my arms above my head, I cast my eyes toward the overcast sky, fleetingly wondering if anyone had bothered to check the weather. I decided I didn't care.

The breeze held a chill, but the heavy salt air was invigorating. There was something about the unique briny smell that called to the most ancient parts of my soul, waking them to life.

I smiled at the girls as they charged up a small

dune and into view, hair streaming behind them like wild banners. I wondered if theirs would stay red, like mine, or darken like Beatrice's. Either way, they would be beautiful.

The screams of gulls filled the air as the girls ran through the heart of a resting flock, sending the birds crying in rage. Their wings beat furiously against the cold gray sky as they sought the safety of height.

As I watched the white and gray bodies disappearing into the clouds, I began to muse. When I was a child, I had always pretended I could fly. I had broken my leg jumping off the roof because my neighbor had promised me I would grow wings before I hit the ground.

Falling in love had been a lot like that memory.

Blindly I'd jumped, sure that I would sprout wings and soar into the sky. Reality rose up just as fast and unforgiving as the ground had, breaking me. I tried to shake off the dismal thoughts plaguing me as I moved to help Bill unload the van, but I wasn't very successful.

The beach house was a modest three-room structure painted a light gray with blue shutters. The floor plan was open—the kitchen, dining and living areas all taking up the same space while the bedrooms were relegated to the left side of the house.

Within moments of entering the residence, the girls had claimed space on the living room floor and had toys, clothes and shoes scattered everywhere. I angled my steps away from the living area, leaving Beatrice to fuss at the girls, and slipped down the hall toward the guest room. The walls were painted a calming blue. The bed was dressed with a creamy white bedspread, and an area rug in fading tones of azure

Secrets

rested on the floor.

A driftwood frame took up most of one wall and held a large print of a sunset beach scene. My sister was very literal about her decorating; she had made sure there was never a doubt that this was a beach vacation house. Dropping my bags, I stared at the print, studying the colors, the movement of the ocean. I felt frozen. Time didn't seem to matter anymore as I stared at the photograph, emotions roiling inside of me. So completely absorbed in the majesty of the art, I wasn't actually aware of Beatrice's presence until I heard her come to a stop beside me.

Arms lightly crossed over her form, she too began looking at the image. "Bill took that. Last summer," she said quietly, a soft smile curving her lips.

Her voice broke the spell, and I slowly turned my eyes to her. I knew she had spoken, but had no idea what she had said. "What?"

"Bill, he took that last summer. It's one of my favorites."

I stared at her, uncomprehending. *When did Bill become a photographer?* The print on the wall was more than a lucky catch by a novice—it was true art.

"But ..." My tone must have given away my shock because she laughed and placed a hand against my shoulder.

"It's been his hobby for a while, something to take his mind off work. He's only recently gotten more serious about it."

I nodded mutely, looking to the landscape once more, staggered by this sudden new insight into my brother in-law.

"Dinner will be here soon," Beatrice said "We

always do pizza the first night here."

"Okay," I replied, nodding and still looking at the image, only now noting the tiny black lowercase M-shape that was the silhouette of a seagull. Bill had managed to tame the beast in this image, to capture the softer side of the ocean. It stuck like a bolt to my heart, the utter peace and serenity of the scene. A peace I longed for. A peace I would never have.

"I'll call you when it's here?" Beatrice asked, heading toward the door.

"Uh-huh," I was vaguely aware of her soft laugh and the door closing. Silence filled the room as feeble sunlight fought through the clouds to warm the pane of my window.

Without ever becoming aware of when I started, I began to cry.

CHAPTER FOUR

I WAS AN outsider to an evening that was filled with laughter, pizza, and fights over what we would be watching, an interloper to their happy vacation. Fear held me back—fear that I would spoil the fun, and say something wrong. I had come on this trip to escape, but it seemed grief was not easily left behind.

The sound of my nieces' giggles and whispered conversations finally died down just after midnight. From my room, I could hear Beatrice and Bill's quiet conversation in the living room, though I couldn't make out what they were saying.

After claiming a headache, I retreated to my room fairly early in the evening. Now, I lay staring at the deeper darkness that was the ceiling, waiting for sleep to claim me.

I was beginning to regret my decision to come. I knew Beatrice had asked me out of some hope that being around family would cheer me up. But truthfully, it was only furthering my depression.

Sighing, I rolled over onto my side and began beating my fist into the pillow. A surge of emotions had awoken in me by Bill's photograph. I was feeling raw, like an exposed nerve—naked and vulnerable.

What was I doing here? I was the black cloud over this happy picnic. They would be better off with me faking a work emergency and leaving before I could ruin their fun.

Juliet: The Ruiner would be my epitaph.

With a groan, I flopped over onto my stomach, groping beside me for one of the spare throw pillows on the bed. Clutching one, I planted it over my face and held it there. I'd never before had a suicidal thought in my life, and even with things as bad as they were, they weren't *that* bad.

Yet.

I had been hoping the absolute darkness the pillow offered would help to convince my brain that now was a good time to shut off and go to sleep. However, it only made it hard to breathe. Throwing the pillow from my face, I sucked in the cool fresh air and squeezed my eyes closed and tried to *will* myself to sleep.

The night dragged on with me sleeping in fits and starts, waking from half remembered dreams, only to fall back into a troubled slumber. The screams of running girls startled me awake for the last time, and I groaned. Morning light shone through the window, announcing the beginning of the day. I was sore, exhausted, and cranky. I didn't know how much sleep I had gotten, but I knew all of it was poor. Leaving my room, only one thought filled my weary mind: Coffee.

Laughter drifted down the hall, followed closely by the smell of bacon and eggs. My stomach rumbled noisily as I stepped into the main living area, wincing at the loud voices of my nieces.

"I want pancakes!"

"I want waffles!"

"You're both getting toast," Beatrice said firmly, putting a plate before each girl and looking toward me with a smile. "Good morning, Juliet. Are you hungry?"

"Coffee," I mumbled, shuffling toward the coffee maker and inhaling the nutty aroma of the sweet nectar of life. Two cups of coffee later I was feeling mostly human. The girls ate and bolted off to explore the tide pools, dragging Beatrice along with them. I hung back, depression and doubt still making me feel like, "Juliet The Ruiner."

Lingering at the patio door, I watched the girls run over the bright white sand, bright pink pails clutched in their hands, their hair bouncing with their motion.

"Beatrice told me you liked the photograph in your room. I could print you a copy of it, if you wanted."

I looked over my shoulder toward Bill as he spoke, offering him a small smile. Taking a bracing pull of coffee, I settled my thoughts before answering.

"That's really nice, Bill. Thank you. You're pretty good with a camera, by the way. When did that happen?" I teased half-heartedly.

Bill shrugged off my praise with a chuckle, leaning against the opposite side of the doorframe and looking out toward his daughters. "It's just a hobby, but thanks all the same."

I returned my gaze to the girls, sipping my coffee as I watched them laughing and throwing sand. Bill was a good guy; I'd always thought that. Surreptitiously, I slanted my eyes toward him, noting the faint lines fanning out from his eyes, carved into his tanned skin. He had a happy face, one that made it hard to imagine him frowning. His wavy brown hair was full and thick, his eyes brown, and he kept himself in good shape. All in all, a handsome man.

He was also safe. Bill didn't rock the boat, or take risks. He was solid, dependable, and everything Beatrice had ever wanted. Everything anyone should ever want.

"Rough night?" Bill asked, pulling me from my thoughts.

"Yeah, pretty apparent, I guess, huh?" I laughed self-consciously, running a hand over my messy hair.

"I always have trouble the first night. Just takes time to get used to something new, you know?"

I gave a noncommittal sound, lifting my cup only to find that I was out of coffee. Sighing, I stared down into the empty cup.

Bill chuckled at me, shaking his head. "Well, I think I'm going to head down. You coming?"

"Huh? Oh, maybe in a bit? I think I'm going to shower first." I offered him a smile, holding out a hand for his mug. I felt silly, but I made a small show of washing out the mugs as I waited for Bill to depart.

The sound of the door closing was my cue to relax. Dropping all pretenses, I leaned against the counter and closed my eyes. I needed a shower, that wasn't a lie, but all I wanted to do was go back to bed. Dropping the towel onto the counter, I exited the kitchen and walked forlornly into my room. I stood in the doorway, staring into my room without really focusing on anything. I glanced over my shoulder, sighed, and let the comfort of the bed win out.

Secrets

The sky was darkening when I woke, the distant rumble of thunder rolled across the heavens. Lying quietly, I listened to the herald of the coming storm, the sounds of life continuing around me. Beatrice was setting the girls up in their room, probably with a movie. I could hear them giggling and playfully arguing. Unwarranted, a smile curved my lips at the innocence of them, and I found myself fervently hoping that they would never experience sadness, heartbreak.

But I knew they would.

The door to my room creaked open slightly. I didn't move, not entirely sure I wanted to be around anyone yet. Golden light spilled through the doorway, splashing across my face. I had to marshal my expression so as not to react and give myself away. After a moment, the door closed once more and soft footfalls retreated down the hallway. I counted the beats of my heart, until the numbers stopped making sense. Nothing made sense anymore. With a soft sigh, I flipped back the covers and rolled out of bed, grabbing my jacket as I stood.

The movie the girls were watching, combined with soft music playing from the living room, masked the sounds of my steps as I came down the hall. The living room was empty, the patio door open to the cool night breeze and the sounds of the approaching storm. Pulling up the zipper of my jacket, I stepped outside onto the small covered patio and looked around, my gaze drawn to the entwined form of Bill and Beatrice.

I could only just make out the sound of their whispered conversation over the crash of the waves against the shore. I knew I should look away—that it was rude to stare and that at any moment one, or both, of them could look over and catch me intruding on this intimate moment—and yet, I stood.

Transfixed, I watched as Bill pulled her tighter against him, moving his hands along her spine and up into her hair, pulling her head back ever so slightly. Their lips met; the kiss was quiet, passionate, and heartfelt.

Pressure built up in my chest as something within me broke. I tore my gaze from the couple and ran, thunder echoing the pounding of my feet against the sand.

The ocean roared to my right, its white-tipped waves angrily crashing against the shore and dying into harmless foam. I had no thought, no destination, no desire other than to get away, to remove myself from the vision of perfect love before me.

Pain flared in my side, forcing me to slow to a walk. Breath streaming in ragged pants, I clung to my ribs, cursing the pain. The sky above was an eerie steel gray, the air filled with salt and the sharp scent of ozone—tale-tell signs of the proximity of the storm. Gulls screamed and wheeled above me, as if warning me to turn back, to take cover.

I pulled my hood up in defiance against the imagined warning and looked out toward Haystack Rock. The waves brushed against the base of the rock like a lover's caress, angry and passionate at the same time.

The night had grown colder as the storm drew closer, catching me off guard. The frigidness tore through my inadequate layers, seeping into my bones.

Secrets

My mind was so far away that I didn't even realize the waves washing over my calves, chilling my feet like a greedy vampire feasting upon my warmth.

The elements were certainly reflecting my mood. I brushed a wayward lock of hair from my face, my eyes inexorably drawn to my ring finger, where a faint white circle still lingered. White-hot tears blurred my vision; a glacial fist gripped my heart and my breath once more came in ragged gasps as I sunk to my knees in the wet sand.

When would it stop? When would I just accept the loneliness and go numb? Five years. Five years of my life, gone. Wasted on someone who never really cared for me?

"Why? Why me?" I screamed. The words ripped from my lips, something between a curse and a plea. Anger welled within me, searing through my being. It burned up my throat and spewed from my mouth in a sharp series of cries that left me scalded and raw. Thunder rumbled overhead, drowning out my screams.

And then the sky opened up.

Icy rain fell from the sky like frozen bullets, kissing along my jacket with painful pops. Still I sat there, shivering, my brain screaming for me to move, to seek cover, my body not giving a damn.

The rain fell steadily from the leaden sky, soaking the sand and turning it black. Lightning ripped across the air, illuminating the world around me, turning everything monotone. The jagged bolt tore free from the heavens and struck the sand with a deafening *pop*.

Surging to my feet, I took off once more, confused and turned around, unable to discern landmarks, unaware I was cutting a suicidal path down the beach away from known shelter.

Somewhere in my mind I knew what would happen if I didn't take cover soon. The ocean was a siren, seductive, alluring and deadly. Her ghostly fingers reached for me with every pounding step, sucking the sand from beneath my feet and tripping me up, teasing me with her frigid caress.

"Come ... Come ... Come ..."

I stopped dead in my tracks, whipping my head around, searching, certain I had heard something. But there was no one there.

Thunder shook the world, making me jump and swallowing my screams like a ravenous animal. Lightning flashed, jagged fiery swords against a gray backdrop.

The crash of waves mixed with thunder, the sound raw and terrifyingly powerful. The intensity of the storm frightened me to my core.

I ran.

CHAPTER FIVE

TINY DAGGERS OF icy rain pelted my exposed skin. I ran blindly. I was lost, alone, faced with the very real possibility that I could die. Lifting my numb hands, I sluiced water from my face, struggling to focus as I squinted through the rain into the blackness before me. Lightning illuminated the sky and I saw it.

A depression in the rock.

Hope flared within me as I charged forward, my boots slapping against the sand. My only thought was shelter. I reached the depression and ducked inside as another jagged fork lit the world, rapidly followed by the deafening boom of thunder.

My relief of finding the shelter was quickly washed away by shock as I looked upon my surroundings. What I thought was a small depression in the rock was, in fact, a cave with curved walls worn smooth by wind, water, and time. I jerked back as I smoothed my hand over the wall, perplexed by the unusual warmth and faint white glow emitting from the rock. Biting my lower lip, I stepped into the cave, awed as its vastness was revealed to me. The smooth walls seemed to stretch for miles, the glow weakening toward the furthest reaches.

Fear warred with curiosity as I moved deeper into the cave, filling me with a thrilling unease. I patted my pockets in a futile search for a flashlight, only feeling the shape of the compact first aid kit I made a habit to carry.

My gaze dropped to the ground, my brow furrowing as I stumbled to a stop. Elongated marks in the sand gave the frightening impression that something had been dragged into the cave. Something large.

My pulse thrummed in my ears as panic rose, filling my chest and squeezing my heart in a vice-like grip. I wasn't alone. What if it was an animal? A hurt or scared animal that wouldn't think twice about attacking first?

My worry quickly gave way to hysteria, causing me to spin around with every intention of running, fleeing the cave for the beach. The pounding thunder stopped me in my tracks. I couldn't go back. The beach was death. For the moment, the unknown was safer.

I turned to move deeper into the cave when my foot came down on something slippery, causing me to lose my purchase. Pin wheeling my arms did nothing to restore my balance, and I came down hard, the back of my head smacking against a small, sharp rock. Pain bloomed bright white behind my eyelids; it was so encompassing that I lost the ability to think for a moment.

I sat up gingerly and touched the back of my head, wincing in anticipation. There was no warmth, no metallic stickiness indicating a wound. Holding my hand to my head, I looked for the source of my fall. Not far from my foot rested what appeared to be a pile of cloth in the color of shadows freckled with mist.

"What the ..." Rolling onto my knees, I stretched out my hand and grasped the fabric, though I wasn't certain it was. It was light as air and fluid as water. Like the stone around me, it seemed to give off its own warmth. It was like nothing I had ever seen before. Turning it over in my hands, I tried to piece together the puzzle I had stumbled upon.

What is this? How did it get here?

I stretched the odd fabric between my hands, narrowing my eyes as I looked it over. It resembled the stuff I assumed a wet suit was made from. The texture was rubbery while still somehow fluid. And so warm.

I brought it closer to my face to examine it when a soft glimmer caught my attention. Brow furrowing, I glanced down, blinking in confusion at the thick silver ring stuck in the sand. I had just picked it up when a soft, echoing sound from the back of the cave startled me.

I turned abruptly, peering into the dim light and was rewarded with the fuzzy outline of something lying adjacent to me on the floor against the far wall. My heart thundered in my chest as I stared at the figure huddled in the deeper darkness. I couldn't discern any features to tell me if what I was looking at was man or beast.

Thunder rolled across the sky, the sound oddly muffled by the walls of the cave. I shoved the fabric and ring into the inside pocket of my jacket and zipped it closed, creeping toward the back of the cave.

This is stupid. Turn around, go back to the front of the

cave and wait it out. Just turn around, Juliet ...

Keeping one hand against the wall of the cave, I walked cautiously, coming ever closer to the figure. A soft gasp escaped my lips as I found myself looking down at a man.

He was curled in the fetal position, his body marred with tiny cuts and bruises. Tangled and matted dark hair clung to his brow. A line of blood trickled from his temple and slid down the strong line of his jaw before dissolving in a puddle of water beneath his head.

My nursing instinct kicked in, overriding my fear, and I knelt down beside him, checking his pulse with a trembling hand. Relief washed through me as his pulse beat steadily against my fingertips. He was alive. I tugged off my jacket and searched the pockets until located my first aid kit.

I worked quietly, my eyes darting back to his face time and again as I saw to the worst of his wounds. Leaning over him, I brushed his hair aside and applied a butterfly bandage to the cut along his temple. He would have one heck of a headache when he woke and I had a niggling fear that he would require stitches.

Sitting back on my heels I looked him over. He was very handsome, the lines of his face classic, his black hair full and shaggy. His skin was a dusky olive, reminding me of the Mediterranean.

And he was naked.

I felt my cheeks heat as my eyes moved over his body, seeing more than his wounds now. My breath caught at the sight of the muscles of his arms and thighs. His hands were wide-palmed with long fingers. They looked rough—working man's hands.

Secrets

"Who are you?" I whispered, looking to his face once more. His brows were dark like his hair, his nose straight and long. His eyes were almond shaped and trimmed with long, inky dark lashes that kissed his cheeks.

Who *was* he? Why was he out in the storm and how did he come to be naked in this cave? Questions ran through my mind as I reached out to touch his hand. A strangled cry broke passed my lips as his hand shot out, fingers wrapping around my wrist, his grip startling. I gasped as I found myself jerked forward until our noses were all but touching. Piercing ice blue eyes bored into my own.

"Who are you? How did you find me?" His voice was rough and sudden, like the thunder that boomed outside, and just as wild. He had an accent I couldn't place, and he smelled of the sea.

I wondered if he would taste of the sea as well.

My brain worked frantically to remember how to form words. I was captivated by his gaze, the fierceness of his tone, and the strength of his grip on my wrist. Slowly, I brought a hand up and lightly brushed my fingers along his wrist.

"Please, I was just looking for shelter from the storm. You were hurt, so I ... I helped you." Lifting my fingers from his skin I pointed to his temple, experiencing a wild and momentary regret at the loss of contact.

He held my gaze, as if weighing the truth of my words. With a grunt he released me, giving me a little shove to create space between us. Wincing, he moved into a sitting position and leaned back against the cave wall, closing his eyes once more.

His nudity didn't seem to bother him, but I was left forcing myself to keep my eyes averted. His movements were fluid and graceful, every one exuding quiet confidence.

"What are you?" I blurted.

Slapping my hand over my mouth, I mentally berated myself. Had I really just asked that? Not *who* are you, like any sane person would have done, but *what*. Heat flushed through me, embarrassment gripping my stomach as I lowered my hand from my lips. I didn't know why, but the question felt *right*. I stared at him in shocked horror. I could do nothing else.

The grin that spread across his face was quick and deadly, sending unexpected desire shooting through me. I bit my lower lip, curling my hands into fists as I felt my body quicken.

Whatever this man was, he was dangerous. And I knew I would do best to remember that.

He opened his eyes, the grin still in place and pinned me with his gaze. I felt naked before him, as if he could see into my soul and was weighing my worth. It left me uncomfortable. Vulnerable. I shifted where I sat but didn't look away.

"You ask interesting questions," he leaned toward me, droplets of water clinging to his chest. The glow of the cave made them appear like fire, as if his skin were embedded with tiny crystals.

I watched the water slide down his dark skin like lines of liquid silver. Swallowing hard, I forced my gaze upward, only to drown in the white-blue depths of his eyes.

"Who *are* you?" I whispered, growing steadily

more uncomfortable with the effect this stranger was having upon me.

"I am ... Something more."

I stared at him as he offered up his reply, waiting for more. When nothing more came, I shook my head, flicking my hair out of my face.

"'Something more.' Right," I grumbled, certain he had sustained a head injury with that response. "Great. What are you doing out here?" I asked with exasperation. "And where in God's name are your clothes?"

I averted my gaze from his nude body, suddenly finding the spot just above his left shoulder very interesting. A look of confusion crossed his features, bright eyes dipping downward as he looked himself over.

"I am not certain."

Cautiously, I looked back to his face. "Not certain of what? Who you are, or why you're naked?"

"Why I am naked. I recall who I am. Though where I am remains a mystery."

I bit back the scathing retort that flung to my lips. He was alone and injured; the hit to his head could have scrambled his mind more than I had thought. Inhaling deeply, I put on my sweetest smile. "And your name is?"

"Marsh, Marsh Darrow."

Marsh Darrow.

The name washed over me like a warm wind. It rolled over in my mind, strange and yet familiar, as if I had been waiting my whole life to hear it spoken from this man.

Licking my dry lips, I met his gaze, my heart

pounding in my chest and my throat constricting. "I'm Juliet. And, um, you're in Oregon. Cannon Beach, Oregon."

"Oregon." He nodded, his dark hair dripping down over his eyes, breaking the spell.

I waited a heartbeat before shrugging out of my jacket and offering it to him. "Here."

"Thank you."

His fingers brushed over mine as he took the jacket, sending heat radiating up my arm. I jerked my hand away, looking down at my fingers, half-expecting them to be burned.

"Something wrong?"

His voice was so smooth and deep. It rolled over my senses, stimulating them in ways I hadn't known possible, leaving me frustrated.

"No …" I waved my hand airily, shifting to look around the cave, searching for any sign of his clothes. There was none, and it seemed no matter where I looked, my eyes couldn't resist drifting back toward him.

Traitors.

"What were you doing out in the storm?" I whispered, watching the movement of his form as he slipped the jacket on and settled back against the wall. Lucky for him I had a penchant for men's jackets.

"I do not recall. I was swimming. I did not hear the storm approaching and was caught by surprise."

"Swimming? You were swimming? Are you insane, or just suicidal?"

Marsh looked at me, humor lighting his eyes and features. "Yes, swimming. Is it not a common recreation here? As I said, I did not anticipate the inclement weather. Also, I am neither insane, nor suicidal."

"Uh huh." I crossed my arms over my chest, not entirely sure I believed him. Twisting, I looked back toward the entrance of the cave, relief washing through me as I realized the rain had stopped. The storm had passed.

How long had I been here? Long enough for Beatrice to realize I was gone, certainly. I sighed as the image of her frantically running through the small house screaming for me flashed in my mind's eye.

"What troubles you, Juliet?"

The way he said my name made my pulse quicken. His head was tilted to the side as he watched me, quietly studying me.

"I'm fine. I was just thinking that my sister is probably worried sick about me."

It took more effort than expected to keep my voice light and casual. Marsh smiled at me, the expression quick and easy, lending warmth to his cool eyes that made my insides puddle.

"You live nearby?"

"What? No. I'm just ... I mean, my sister has a cottage here. On the beach." My words tumbled out, tripping over my tongue and making me feel like a fool.

Get a grip!

"Oh. Well then, perhaps you would be willing to assist me?"

"Assist you? I can try ..."

"Is there any way you could bring me some clothing? I am assuming from your questions that mine are not here."

I stared at him, captivated by the strange lilt in his

voice, the casual way he laid against the stone. He was beautiful in every possible way.

Too late I realized he had stopped talking and was now staring back at me, humor in his eyes once more.

"What? Clothes! Right, of course. I'm sorry ... I bet you get that a lot."

"I can honestly say this is the first time I've found myself alone in a cave, in a state of undress with a woman."

I laughed nervously, twirling a lock of hair around my finger as I bit my lower lip. I couldn't leave him, not with a head wound. My years of training wouldn't allow it, just like they never allowed me to leave the house without the first aid kit.

But Beatrice ...

She wouldn't understand. She would question me mercilessly about this strange, naked man.

My brows rose as a thought lit like a bulb in my brain.

Assuming she found out about the strange naked man.

"Look, I'm not sure it's a good idea for me to leave you alone, considering your head injury," I noted.

Marsh lifted his brows, a smile flirting about his lips. "What would you suggest, then?"

Dropping my hands to my knees, I took a deep breath and looked him in the eye. "I think you should come with me."

CHAPTER SIX

"COME WITH YOU?"

I was pretty sure my expression echoed the disbelief in Marsh's tone. Had I really suggested that? What other choice did I have? I was less comfortable leaving him here than I was taking him with me.

"Yes. I want you to come back to the beach house with me."

"Now?" Marsh studied me, disbelief still written across his face.

"No, in two hours. Yes, now! What is so hard to understand about that?"

My voice rang against the stone surrounding us, echoing back at me and sounding shrill. I sighed in frustration as I shoved my hands through my hair. This was the strangest situation I had ever found myself in and I didn't like it one bit.

"All right. I will come with you." Marsh's voice was low, like the far-off purr of thunder.

I lowered my hands from my face, heart pounding in my chest. I needed to get away from this man before he sent me into cardiac arrest.

"You will? Great. That's ... great."

Marsh nodded, shifting and rising to his feet. Panic shot through me as he went white and swayed. I lunged forward, shoving myself under his arm and placing my hand against his chest in an effort to steady him.

"Whoa, easy there, Big Guy. Just breathe. Slow movements, okay? Let me help you."

Keeping one hand against his chest, I pressed my other to his back, slowly helping him move through the cave. I had been right in guessing he was tall. Marsh stood at least a foot over my small frame. In fact, if I just leaned closer, I was certain my head would fit perfectly in the space between his shoulders and chin ...

"Juliet?"

"Huh? What?" I jerked my head back, fighting down the blush that rushed up my neck. What the heck was wrong with me? I didn't even know this man and I was daydreaming about snuggling?

Seriously, get a grip!

"I am feeling steadier," Marsh explained. "I believe I can walk unassisted now."

Ignoring the amusement in his tone, I stepped back and looked at him critically. The black jacket looked good on him, the dark color giving his skin a warm, golden tone, though he was still paler than I liked. Thankfully, the jacket stopped at mid-thigh, keeping him modestly covered.

"Aren't you lucky I like big jackets?" I smiled, forcing myself into motion.

"I am very lucky."

I carefully picked my way toward the entrance,

glancing toward Marsh every so often to check on him.

Sound rushed back into being with terrible force as we exited the cave, causing me to stumble from the onslaught. I felt as if I'd stepped through some barrier, separating the cave from the rest of the world. I had the unnatural feeling that if I looked over my shoulder, the cave would be gone.

"Juliet?"

"I'm fine," I said quickly, wanting to waylay Marsh's obvious concern. "Just got a little light headed." I tossed him a reassuring smile, but didn't let my eyes linger. If I looked at him too long, I would begin to stare, and that was not only rude, but also embarrassing.

"I did not take you to be a maid," Marsh commented conversationally as we began to walk up the beach.

"A what?"

"A maid. A virgin, to use the current vernacular."

Heat rushed to my cheeks in a mix of embarrassment and annoyance. I was getting tired of blushing. I was thankful, however, that the darkness hid my reaction. "That's none of your business."

"You are a maid then?"

I stopped and whirled around to face him, exasperated by his line of questioning. "No, I'm not, if you must know!"

Marsh chuckled, the sound low and smooth, his eyes bright even in the darkness.

"I was simply trying to make conversation," he justified.

"Well, try asking about something else! I don't usually share personal information with strangers," I snapped, spinning around and resuming movement.

"Do you often invite strangers to your home?"

His question caught me by surprise; I froze. "What?"

Marsh gave me a cryptic smile and walked passed me, his footsteps light against the wet sand. "Are you coming?"

Silence filled the space between us as I led the way toward the cottage. The soft hiss of the waves was soothing, but the temperature was bitterly cold. We hadn't been walking long before I began to shiver. Tucking my hands beneath my arms added some warmth, but the cold was still biting.

Before long my teeth were chattering so hard I was afraid they would break. It took me a moment to realize that Marsh was no longer beside me. Fear bloomed in my chest as I whirled around, eyes searching the dark beach for him.

My brows shot up toward my hairline as I found him standing a few paces behind me, arms held wide open.

"Come here."

"What are you doing? You scared me!"

"I said, come here. You're cold, I can warm you."

I lifted my brows and shook my head, snorting at the ridiculousness of it all. "Uh huh, I'm sure you could," I mumbled. "It's not much farther, I'll be fine. Come on." Marsh didn't move, however; instead, he stubbornly kept his arms open, a determined look etched on his face.

"You're serious?" I asked, baffled. "Oh my God ... Fine! Fine, we'll hug or whatever ..." I stomped toward him, holding up a finger. "*No* groping," I warned him.

Despite the darkness, I could see the glint of amusement in Marsh's eyes, as well as a crooked smile that played about his lips. I was surprised by the dimple that winked into existence in his right cheek.

"No groping," he vowed. "You have my word."

I let out a half-hearted exhale of frustration and walked into his open arms. Warmth washed over me, penetrating me to my core. My breath caught as his scent enveloped me, invading my senses until I could breathe only him.

The strength of his arms around me, pulling me tightly against his form, made me vibrantly aware of every muscle and curve of his body. He radiated heat from head to toe; I could feel it burning through my clothes, warming me to the depths of my soul.

"Are you warm now?" Marsh's lips brushed against the top of my ear as he spoke, his low tone sending my blood pressure skyrocketing.

"Yes. Yes, I'm much warmer now." My voice was anything but steady as I pulled back out of his grasp, his warmth clinging to me like a second skin. "You're not running a fever are you? You're really hot."

Marsh shook his head, falling into step beside me. "I do not believe so."

I chewed on my lower lip as we walked in silence. In the near distance, I could see the yellow glow of the patio light shining like a beacon.

"Do you always talk like that?" I asked, slanting a glance in his direction, trying to gauge by look alone if he was burning up with fever. The heat he emitted, while appreciated, was slightly concerning.

"Do I always talk like *what*?" he asked back.

"Like all ... proper." I waved my hand, as if batting his words from the space between us.

"I suppose. Does it bother you?"

I shrugged. "I guess not." Realizing how close to the cottage we were, I lowered my tone. "Okay, shh. They might be asleep. I don't even know what time it is."

Apprehension filled my stomach like lead weights as we approached the house. I *hoped* they were asleep. How was I going to explain this to Beatrice? Her sharp eyes were not going to miss the naked man I was currently trying to sneak through her back door.

The house seemed quiet, as if everyone inside was asleep. Could I really be so lucky?

"Okay," I breathed. "I *think* everyone's asleep, so if we just slip in quietly ..." I paused, confused as I saw Marsh standing beside me, his hands at his side and his head tilted back, staring at the sky. "What are you doing?" I asked, perplexed.

"It is just after midnight," Marsh said matter-of-factly.

"How can you possibly know that?"

"The stars."

I blinked at him, looking from him to the overcast sky and back again. "There are no stars."

"There are always stars. They do not disappear simply because we cannot see them." Marsh lowered his eyes from the sky, causing my insides to squirm girlishly as he smiled at me.

"Oh. Well, thanks. Let's go."

Stepping up toward the sliding door, I braced my hands against the cool glass, easing it open. I was relieved when it slid easily open without making a

Secrets

sound. Waving my hand in signal, I led Marsh into the main room, casting my eyes around as I searched for signs of Beatrice, finding none. I reached back and slid the door closed before grabbing Marsh's hand and pulling him toward my bedroom.

I paused outside my door, sure this final step would be the moment that would betray us. Squeezing my eyes closed, I reached out and grasped the doorknob, turning and pushing the door open in one motion. A soft creak issued from the hinges, sounding loud as a gunshot in the silence. Cursing softly, I tugged Marsh into the room and shoved the door closed. I pulled him away from the door and waited in silence, counting my heavy heartbeats. By the time I had reached fifty-six, I felt we were in the clear.

"I think we're safe," I whispered, turning to face Marsh as I hastily released his hand. The heat of his flesh clung to my fingers and I fought the urge to curl my fingers into my palm to relish it.

Marsh said nothing as he looked around the small room, taking in the bed and the nonexistent personal touches. I watched as his eyes focused on the picture of the ocean, studying it as I had done the night before. Had it really been so little time? I felt as if this night had stretched on forever.

"My brother-in-law took that," I said softly as I sat on the end of the bed, curling a leg beneath me. "I didn't even know he did photography."

"It is a wonderful thing, to be able to capture beauty and preserve it in such a way. He has an eye for the art."

I studied Marsh quietly, thinking over his words and finding that I agreed with him. "Well, after the shock wears off, you can tell him so yourself."

"The shock?" Marsh asked, keeping his voice low as he came toward the bed. I looked up at him, swallowing at the sudden dryness in my throat.

"Um, yes. The shock of you being here. You didn't really expect my sister and brother-in-law to just take your sudden appearance in stride, did you?"

I attempted to add a flippant tone to my words, hoping it would hide the catch his closeness brought about. I felt like a fool; I didn't even want to think about anyone's reactions to Marsh, especially my nieces'.

Yet another stupid and impulsive decision in a lifetime of stupid and impulsive decisions.

Sighing, I dropped my head into my hands, covering my face.

"I thought nothing," Marsh admitted, "as I do not know your sister or brother. Though I see your point." His voice drew closer, the bed shifting as it accepted his weight. I could feel the heat of him brushing against my side and knew without looking he had sat beside me. "I do not wish to bring you troubles, Juliet. If I could borrow some clothes, I will be gone before the dawn."

Lowering my hands, I stared at him. Was that what I wanted? Did I want him gone?

"No," I argued softly, surprising myself. "No, not with that head injury. I told you, we'll see how you're doing in the morning."

Marsh looked at me, silence stretching between us as I once again felt as if he were weighing the worth of my soul.

"As you wish."

Secrets

He would quote a line from my favorite movie.

Pressing my lips together, I nodded, rising from the bed and crossing toward the door.

"Don't ... Don't go anywhere," I instructed. "I'll be right back."

I slipped out of my bedroom, pulling the door closed behind me. I knew I would never be able to get into Bill and Beatrice's room without waking them. My only hope was the laundry.

My steps were quick and quiet as I tiptoed down the hall toward the bi-fold doors hiding the washer and dryer. I slid the doors open and crouched down in front of the dryer. Sighing in relief, I pulled open the door to reveal a small load of clothes. Quickly picking through it, I found a shirt and pair of jeans belonging to Bill.

I closed the dryer and nimbly stepped back toward my room. My hand had just touched the knob when I heard a door creak open.

"Auntie Jules?" Keegan's sleepy voice asked.

I turned to see her standing in the doorway, scrubbing at her eyes. Her hair was a wild mess from sleep, eyes barely opened.

"Yes, it's me, sweetie. I was just going to the bathroom. Go back to bed."

I smiled at her, waiting until she had shuffled back into her room, and then shut the door. I leaned back against it, listening with closed eyes to the quiet shuffling of Keegan in her bed.

That was close.

I quickly slipped into my room and shut my door firmly behind me. To my surprise, the room was pitch black.

"Marsh?" I whispered as I edged my hand along the wall, searching for the light switch.

"I am here."

He spoke just as my fingers found the switch. Light flared, illuminating the room and searing my eyes with the sudden brightness. I blinked multiple times, cursing myself.

"Gah! Why are you sitting in the dark?" Blinking a few more times, I crossed toward him, holding out the shirt and jeans. "These were all I could find."

"I do not mind the dark. And thank you." Marsh smiled as he took the clothes from me. The sound of a zipper filled the room and my gaze was suddenly glued to naked flesh.

Beautifully bronzed and well-muscled naked flesh.

"Whoa! Okay!" I slapped a hand over my eyes to force myself to stop staring. I laughed at myself, and the night in its entirety, in exasperation. "You really have no problem with nudity, do you?"

"No. That is the body's natural form. It is how we come into this world. There is no reason to fear it."

I parted my fingers as I heard another *zip*, softer this time. It was all I could do to keep my mouth from falling open. If Marsh looked good naked, and if I was honest with myself he certainly did, he looked even better in jeans.

Bill's jeans were snug in all the right places on Marsh, sitting low on his hips in a way that made my libido want to sit up and beg. Licking my lips, I tore my eyes from him as he pulled on the plaid shirt, leaving it unbuttoned. For my viewing pleasure, I was sure.

"Are you, uh, comfortable?" I stammered.

"These will do for now. Thank you, Juliet."

Secrets

I nodded and moved toward the bed, sitting on the end of it instead of throwing myself across it face down like I wanted. I was suddenly overwhelmingly tired. All I wanted to do was sleep, but there was just one thing stopping me.

"I can see you are very tired," Marsh noted. "If you don't mind sharing a pillow and a blanket, I will let you get some sleep."

My eyebrows shot upward as I looked over at him, my overtired brain coming up with all sorts of unnecessary innuendos for his statement.

"You're *not* sharing the bed with me," I informed him rather bluntly. Though, there was a part of me that certainly wouldn't mind if he did. I squashed her down pretty quickly.

Marsh chuckled, shaking his head faintly before turning his humor-filled eyes on me. "I was not asking to. I will sleep on the floor, of course."

Blushing in embarrassment, I stood, peeling the comforter off the bed and crossing toward him, offering him the blanket and a pillow.

"Here, sleep on that. For padding. There's a few extra blankets in the closet."

Conversation died off as Marsh made his bed and I crawled into mine after turning off the overhead light. Chewing my lower lip, I listened to the sound of Marsh's breathing as the darkness settled in around us.

"Marsh?" I whispered, unsure if he was asleep or not.

"Yes, Juliet?"

"What will you do? I mean, do you have a place to go? What about money? Do you have any?" I rolled toward the edge of the bed, gasping as I came nose to nose with Marsh.

His eyes were almost luminous in the darkness of the room. His breath washed over my face, smelling faintly of mint and sea salt. My fingers itched with the sudden need to caress his face, feel the warmth of his skin...

"Your concern is appreciated," He didn't move toward me, but I wanted him to. "I have money, yes. I will just need to get to a bank. As for having a place to go, I do not currently, but I will find a place. You need not worry. Your part in this is done."

Disappointment stabbed at my heart as I nodded slowly and rolled onto my back. I stared at the ceiling, my mind spinning.

Was it? Was my part in whatever this was done? Just like that? In a few hours this man would walk out of my life. Gone. As if he had never existed. In a few hours, I could go back to my normal, boring life. Was that what I wanted?

I sure hoped not.

"Good night, Marsh."

"Sleep sweet, Juliet," came his quiet reply.

My lips curved into a smile as my eyes closed. I didn't know what tomorrow would bring, but I knew one thing:

It would be interesting.

CHAPTER SEVEN

MORNING SUNLIGHT FLOODED the guest room, rays blasting through the sheer curtains as if they weren't there. Heat seared my eyelids, rousing me from my sleep. With a groan, I pressed my face deeper into the pillow, ignoring nature's voice calling me to wake.

My head popped up from the pillow when I heard three sharp raps at my door. A strangled gag escaped my lips as my hair caught in my mouth, impeding breath.

I growled. "Who'zit?"

"Juliet? Are you awake? It's time for breakfast." Beatrice's voice made me groan, and I shoved my face back into my pillow.

Just once in my life would it kill her to let me sleep in?

"Juliet?" Beatrice repeated. "Did you hear me?"

The memory of the night before slammed into my mind with vivid recollection as I heard the doorknob turning. I threw back my blankets and leapt from the bed, flying across the room with extension to make a ballerina jealous. I slammed my hand against the door just as it began to open, visibly giving Beatrice a good startle.

"I'm up, I'm up," I breathed, hoping I sounded more sleepy than panicked. "I'm not dressed, Bea."

Beatrice glared at me through the small opening. "I see your morning manners haven't improved. Just ... come while it's hot, okay?"

"I will. Thanks."

I pushed the door closed, leaning against it with relief. Brushing my hair from my face, I shuffled toward the dresser, stopping short as I felt someone's eyes on me.

Marsh sat on his makeshift bed, looking up at me with what was becoming his signature look. He removed the shirt I gave him at some point in the night, his left arm resting casually over a bent knee, the other bracing his weight.

"Good morning,"

So ... it wasn't all a dream.

Offering a skeptical smile, I tugged at the hem of my shirt, trying desperately to make the fabric lengthen enough to cover my thighs.

"Good morning," I stammered. "Yeah, could you uh, just, turn around so I can put some pants on?"

Marsh watched me, lips curving upward before nodding once and twisting at the waist.

"No peeking!" I warned, yanking open a drawer at random and fishing around for my jeans. I tugged them on, hopping on one foot as my toes became stuck in the hemline.

"Oh, for the love of ..." I grumbled, shoving my foot through the hole and pulling up the zipper.

"Are you always so ... animated while dressing?"

"Hey!" I crossed my arms over my chest and

Secrets

glared at him. "I said no peeking!"

Marsh shrugged as he stood and stretched his arms over his head. "It was not my intention to peek—your hopping about was attention-catching."

I stopped glaring as I watched him, caught off guard by the obvious strength of his body. His skin was taut over well-defined muscles in his arms and abs, making my mouth water.

I was so caught up in watching him that I didn't hear the door until it was flying open. Tearing my eyes from Marsh, I watched as a wild haired Kylie bounded into the room. Her smile fell as her eyes locked on Marsh; her mouth widened into an O of shock and confusion and she let loose an ear-piercing banshee scream.

I grabbed for her while cursing, but I was too late. Quicker than I knew how, she spun and ran from the room, still shrieking.

The sound of footsteps pounding down the hallway laced with concerned voices soon followed. I looked desperately at Marsh, but knew there was nothing either of us could do.

With dramatic flair, Beatrice swept into the room, eyes wild. "What on Earth is going on-" She stopped mid-sentence as she looked at Marsh. "Who is *this*?" Her voice was deathly calm, sending chills of apprehension skating up and down my spine.

"Bea, this is Marsh Darrow," I answered her wrath meekly. Marsh offered Beatrice a hesitant smile as he bent to retrieve his shirt.

Beatrice watched Marsh with narrowed eyes before whipping her gaze to me. "Hallway. Now." Her tone was brisk and shaky, a peek into just how close to the surface her anger was.

I cast a quick glance at Marsh before trudging out of the room. My trudge, however, was not fast enough for Beatrice. I had barely cleared the threshold when she grabbed my arm and dragged me toward her room, slamming the door behind us.

"Jesus, Bea!" I grumbled, rubbing at my arm and trying not to glare at her.

"Don't you *dare* 'Jesus, Bea' me! How *dare* you! What were you thinking? Your nieces are right across the hall! What was your plan, Juliet? Sneak him out the door while the rest of us slept? Or maybe after breakfast? Was this your coffee date? You invited your coffee date to a family weekend?"

"No! Of course not!"

"Then who is he? *How* did you even meet him? Some Internet site?" A look of horror bloomed on her face as she ran with that last thought. "Oh my God. He's a *prostitute*!"

I crossed my arms over my chest. "Yes, Beatrice. He's a prostitute. I'm a disgusting, horrid human being and brought a prostitute into the same house as my *sister's family*!"

"Did you?"

"No!" I almost screamed. I couldn't believe that she really thought I would do something like that. It hurt more than I wanted to admit. "I found him on the beach last night. He was hurt and I didn't think it was safe for him to be alone, so I brought him here. But it's so nice to know what my sister really thinks about me."

Wrapping my arms tighter around myself, I turned my back on her and stared out the window. If I squinted through the lace curtains, I could just make out the blue ribbon of the ocean.

"Juliet ... Jules, I'm sorry. I don't ... I'm not sure where that all came from. Hormones, maybe."

The random comment was enough to draw my attention momentarily from my hurt and anger. "Hormones? I get yelled at because you're on your period?"

Beatrice looked as if she regretted mentioning it. With a sigh, she walked to the bed and sat, primly crossing her legs. "No, Juliet. Bill and I were waiting ... I'm pregnant. Due in November."

"Pregnant?" I stared at her, unable to think past that one word. Emotions roiled inside of me, fighting for dominance.

Pregnant.

Beatrice was the perfect child. College graduate, with honors. Perfect marriage, perfect family—and now another grandchild.

And then there was me. The one who struggled through college to scrape out a nursing degree. The one who couldn't hold a boyfriend, let alone a fiancé. The screw-up.

"Uh, wow. Congratulations," I mumbled, too shell-shocked to form a more convicted response.

"Thank you. We're very excited. I really didn't mean to yell at you about ... about your young man."

"He's not mine!" I snapped, cutting her off. "I *found* him last night during the storm! Don't you listen to me?"

Beatrice held her hand out to me, clearly wanting to stave off my tirade. "All right, I apologize *again*, Juliet. I just wish you'd woken me, or said something."

"I didn't get the chance." I scrubbed my hands

over my face and groaned. "He's not staying anyway. I was going to take him to the hospital this morning. I think he might have a concussion."

Beatrice rose gracefully to her feet, smoothing out her shirt before smiling at me. "How about some breakfast?" Without waiting for my response, she pulled open the door and started off down the hallway.

Blowing out a breath, I followed her, pausing at my door to get Marsh. Only, he wasn't there. With a furrowed brow, I walked into the main room to find Bill, Keegan, Kylie, and Marsh sitting at the table together, eating eggs and toast.

Bill looked up as Beatrice and I walked in. He rose from his chair, offering it to Beatrice and stepping into the kitchen to make her a plate.

"Sorry we didn't wait," he explained, "the girls were hungry."

I waved off Bill's comment, but my eyes were on Marsh. "Enjoying your toast?"

Marsh smiled sheepishly, wiping his mouth with a napkin before speaking. "They invited me," he replied.

"He looked hungry, Auntie Jules!" Keegan cried, shoving a piece of toast onto the two stacked on Marsh's plate.

"That was nice of you, Keegan." I ruffled her hair and sat down, snagging some toast for myself.

Bill smiled at me as he came around, setting a plate of fruit before Beatrice. "Are you and Juliet friends then, Marsh?"

"I bet he's her boyfriend!" Keegan declared gleefully.

I coughed, choking on my toast and grabbing for the nearest glass of water. Marsh chuckled, recovering

Secrets

much quicker than I as he thumped his hand against my back.

"I am not her boyfriend," Marsh corrected; he smiled charmingly at Keegan before looking to Bill. "We met last night during the storm."

Bill lifted his brows, looking between us in confusion. "During the storm?" he asked. "I didn't know you went out, Juliet." Bill lifted his brows, looking between us in confusion.

"Oh, yeah," I said, trying to brush it off. "I went out for a walk, and then the storm hit and I stumbled upon a cave to wait it out in."

"And Mr. Darrow just happened to find the same cave?" Beatrice challenged, her tone full of disbelief.

"Indeed I had," Marsh answered. "Though as I was apparently unconscious at the time, I did not realize it. I was lucky Juliet was there to find me." Marsh smiled at me, completely nonplussed by Beatrice's tone.

"Sounds like it," Bill said with a smile as he lifted his coffee. "Where was this cave? I'd like to see it."

The mention of an unexplored cave had set the girls off in a fit of excitement. They began to bounce in their chairs, begging and pleading to go search for the cave as well.

"About a mile and a half, maybe two down the beach. It was my plan to go back there today," Marsh said with a chuckle.

"Go back?" I hissed at Marsh, not expected that response at all.

"Yes," he confirmed. "I lost something important to me and I need to find it." Marsh's eyes locked on mine, as if trying to import some deeper meaning to

73

his words. I shook my head, breaking the connection as tingles went racing down my spine.

Bill chuckled and set down his mug, "Girls, girls! That's enough. Go get dressed and we'll all go explore."

Keegan and Kylie ran from the table so fast they upset their chairs, screaming in delight as they pounded down the hallway.

"I should go put my shoes on if we're all going," I said, rising from the table. I slipped down the hall and into my room, snagging my shoes before sitting on the bed to put them on.

I sighed. This day was going anything but how I had imagined it would. Everyone seemed to be taking to Marsh, which was weird enough, but finding out Beatrice was pregnant?

I shook my head. I knew I should be happy for her, and a part of me was. But there was a larger part—most of me, really—that was insanely jealous. I placed a hand to my abdomen. *Will I ever know what it feels like to be pregnant? Or will I always be the aunt?*

A knock sounded on the door, causing me to jerk my head up. "Yeah?" I called, yanking on the laces of my shoes to tie them.

Marsh poked his head into the room with a smile. "Bill and your nieces are ready to go," he announced. "I convinced them to wait for you."

"Oh, you didn't have to do that. Is Beatrice not coming?"

Marsh shook his head, crossing his arms over his chest. "What's wrong?" he asked,

I flashed him a fake smile. "Nothing," I said, rising from the bed and slipping past him out the door. "Why would anything be wrong?"

Behind me, I heard Marsh snort in disbelief. I really needed to be less transparent.

CHAPTER EIGHT

THE STORM HAD ravaged the beach with debris, but the chaos of it was beautiful. Thick ropes of kelp lay haphazardly, driftwood nestled safely inside. Egg white foam clung to the pale sand, tiny seashells locked in the bubbles. Gulls screamed and wheeled, fighting noisily over a sea creature buffet.

Keegan and Kylie ran ahead of us, screaming in delight as they explored. Bill followed behind, hands in his pockets while he occasionally called out warnings, leaving Marsh and me to bring up the rear.

I glanced toward Marsh for what felt like the millionth time since we left the cottage. I didn't understand it, but I couldn't stop looking at him. I hadn't even known the man for a full day, yet I found myself wanting—no, needing—to know him.

I shook my head, laughing softly at myself. I needed to get a grip before I made another bad decision.

"What is so funny?" Marsh asked, tilting his head and he looked at me.

"Huh? Oh, nothing," I replied, "I was just thinking. Do you really think you can find the cave again?"

"I do, yes. I remember how far we walk when leaving it."

"You do? Wow. Have you always been able to do that?"

Marsh chuckled and nodded, rubbing the back of his neck. "Yes, it's sort of innate. I've always been naturally good with directions."

"I'm sure that's helpful if you find yourself in a new place," I smiled at him before looking ahead to watch the girls. "What did you lose again?"

I felt Marsh looking at me, the silence heavy with the weight of question. "In the cave?" I clarified, turning my gaze back to him. "The reason we're going back? You said you lost something important."

Marsh nodded. "Oh, yes. Besides my clothes, you mean?"

"Yes, though I'm still trying to figure that out. Unless you were swimming naked?"

Marsh laughed and I was pretty sure he even blushed a little. I felt my smile widen at his laugh.

"I lost something very special to me."

"You said that, but what was it?" I looked at him, raking my hair away from my face as the wind kicked up. I licked my lips as I waited for his response, tasting salt.

Marsh looked at me, emotion passing over his face. "Something very special."

I sighed. "Did you lose your wedding ring or something? Don't want the wife to know about your midnight death swim?"

Marsh chuckled, clearly choosing to ignore my biting sarcasm.

"I don't have a wife, so it would be hard to lose a wedding ring."

"Girlfriend?" I asked, keeping my tone neutral as I scuffed my toes in the sand.

"I am currently unattached. Yourself?"

"The same," I replied, not really wanting to get into my whole sad tale at the moment. Or ever.

I was saved from further questioning by Bill as he jogged back toward us. "Is it much further?" he asked. "The girls are getting tired and want to head back."

"Why don't you and the girls go on back? Marsh and I can look a bit more?"

Bill looked from me to Marsh and back again, uncertainty on his face. "Are you sure?"

"I'm sure. We'll be fine. Go on." I patted Bill's arm and gave him a winning smile.

Still appearing tentative, Bill nodded. "Be back for lunch, okay?"

"Bill! Go!" I laughed and shoved at his arm, smiling still as I watched him go. Shaking my head, I continued down the beach, enjoying the splash of the waves and the crunch of the sand beneath my feet.

"He cares about you very much," Marsh observed softly as he walked by my side.

"Who, Bill?" I shrugged. "Yeah, I guess so. I mean, I'm his wife's sister." I closed my eyes, inhaling the briny air. "Don't you just love the beach?"

"You do not come to the beach often, do you?" Marsh observed, tucking his hands into the pockets of his jeans.

I looked toward him. "No, I don't. Do you?" I then turned my focus along the sea wall, perplexed. "I don't see the cave. Do you think it's close?"

Secrets

Marsh looked down the beach, narrowing his eyes and frowning as he scanned the perimeter. "It should be right there, but I do not see it."

Shading my eyes with my hand, I looked down the beach in the direction he had pointed, searching the landscape for a depression in the rock or a deeper shadow indicating a cave.

"Huh, I don't see it either," I remarked. "Are you sure it wasn't farther up?"

Marsh shook his head, still glowering. "No, I remember. It was *right there.*"

I scoffed. "That doesn't make sense. I mean, you hit your head pretty hard last night. Let's walk further up, just to be sure."

I coaxed him gently, giving him a small smile before taking the lead and walking farther up the beach. Marsh followed along, brooding silently.

After we had gone another half mile, I paused and sighed.

"This doesn't make any sense," I grumbled. "Caves don't just disappear!" I slapped my thigh, turning to look at Marsh. "Maybe we missed it. Passed it somehow." I turned, shielding my eyes with my hand as I looked back in the direction we came.

"We did not miss it," Marsh argued. "It was here. The question is, why did it go?"

Dropping my hand, I looked up at Marsh, a mixture of amusement and worry coursing through me. "'*Why*'? Marsh, caves don't appear at random. This is reality." I reached out to touch his temple. "Is your head hurting?"

Marsh jerked away from my hand, anger and annoyance written on his face. "Reality is not as simple as you would believe," he snapped, his eyes searching the landscape relentlessly.

"Okay, sure. But whether that's debatable or not, the cave is gone. Or, we were a *lot* further down the beach than we thought."

"No, it was right here. I do not understand."

I sighed softly, watching him as he paced. He looked so lost and confused; it tore at my heart. "I'm sorry, for whatever it was you lost. Maybe if you described it to me? I might have seen it?"

Marsh shook his head slowly before he finally looked back at me. The sheen of tears I saw in his eyes shocked me.

"Marsh-" I started, but I didn't really know what to say. He looked like he'd lost a piece of himself.

Once again, he shook his head, turning from me and stalking off down the beach. I stared after him, chewing my lower lip. I knew nothing about this man. He was a stranger to me. This could be completely normal behavior for him.

Something inside told me that just wasn't true.

Making a snap decision, I jogged after him, calling out to him, "Marsh! Marsh, wait!" I panted softly as I caught up to him. *I'm in worse shape than I thought.* "What did you lose in the cave?" I questioned softly, falling into step with him.

He was silent for so long that I stopped waiting for an answer. As it was, his reply was almost lost to the sound of the gulls and waves.

"A piece of myself."

I turned and stared at him, not understanding. He had said he'd lost something very important, but was adamant against disclosing any details.

Secrets

A piece of myself.

His confusing, elusive statement danced around in my head.

"Maybe ... Maybe someone found it and took it to the beach station?" I suggested. "We should check the lost and found before giving up all hope."

"I suppose we could try that, yes."

"Great! Let's go see what we can find, huh?"

I gave him an encouraging smile and took his hand, guiding him down the beach toward the station. I frowned as he pulled his hand away from mine, instantly missing the warmth of his fingers.

"Is it something that can be replaced?" I asked softly.

"No," was his stiff reply.

An oppressive wave of guilt and sadness washed over me—I had nothing *to* feel guilty about, but I did. I chewed my lower lip, thinking back to the previous night, about the storm and the cave. Had I seen something? I hadn't seen any clothes, and it had been too dark to see much of anything.

Wait, I did see something.

In a flash, I remembered the strange cloth that I had picked up and pocketed.

"Marsh," I breathed in excitement, "I just remembered something!"

I turned to look at him, but he was gone.

Puzzled, I froze, looking around the beach. "Marsh? Marsh!"

I received no reply except the screaming of the gulls and the crashing of the waves against the shore.

81

CHAPTER NINE

Keegan and Kylie asked about Marsh when I arrived back at the beach house alone. With a forced hug and smile, I replied, "He had to go, girls."

I ruffled Kylie's hair as both girls gave a chorus of disappointment. Beatrice gave me her signature look of curiosity and concern from across the kitchen. I shrugged in response.

What else was I going to say?

Making excuses for a relative stranger felt odd enough, but what made the situation stranger was admitting that I missed him. I missed his warmth, the humor lurking in his eyes. His easy smile. The way his gaze seemed to linger over me when he had thought I wasn't looking.

I blinked, shaking my head. I missed a man I had just met.

"Hey, Bea?" I called softly, wrapping my arms around myself as I crossed the room to her. Beatrice's back was to me, her focus on the counter she had been preparing lunch on.

"Yes?" She wiped her hands clean on a towel,

turning to face me.

"Do you think it would be okay if I stayed here for a while longer? I know you guys are leaving today, but I was hoping I could stay?"

Beatrice looked at me for a time before a soft smile came to her lips and she hugged me. "Of course you can stay. But what about a car? You rode with us."

I squeezed her with gentle relief, grateful that my ride was her only question. "Don't worry about that. I'll either rent a car or take a bus home."

Beatrice pulled away and studied me before nodding. "Okay, Jules. I'll let Bill know."

"Beatrice?" Bill called from down the hall. "Have you seen my red plaid shirt and spare jeans?"

Beatrice laughed and shook her head as she left the kitchen. Her reply was muffled as I ducked into my room and closed the door.

I felt a slight pang as my gaze landed on the crumpled blankets Marsh had used. I had known the man for less than a week, and I missed him.

What was wrong with me?

I shook my head as I crossed the room and pulled my jacket off the bed. My fingers trembled as I began to search the pockets, stopping when I felt a lump in the inside one. Taking a deep breath, I slid the zipper back and pulled out the object hidden within.

My pulse quickened as I looked down at the odd fabric. There suddenly seemed like more of it. Using both hands, I unrolled the material and stretched it out over the bed, shocked by the size. It was easily six feet long, maybe two feet wide. Big enough to be considered a blanket. Yet it had fit in my pocket. It didn't make sense.

Leaving the cloth for the moment, I reached into the pocket once more and withdrew the ring. It was definitely a man's ring; the heavy silver band was set with two flat sapphires, surrounding an emerald. I studied the ring with interest, watching the stones flash and wink in the afternoon light, as if they were alive. Turning the ring, I caught a glimpse of what appeared to be deep scratches along the inside of the band. I discovered the scratches were actually an engraving as I brought it closer to my face. Disappointment filled me when I couldn't read it.

"What is this?" I muttered to myself, sinking down onto the bed.

Is this what Marsh had been so desperate to find?

It must have been. Was it a family heirloom? It certainly looked old enough to be one.

Sighing, I leaned my head back and closed my eyes, absentmindedly running my thumb over the stones on the ring. They were warm to the touch, as if they'd been sitting in the sun for a length of time.

Marsh had been warm. Even unclothed and stranded in that mysterious cave, he had been warm. Almost hot to the touch—firm and solid ....

Stop that. He's gone.

Fantasizing about a man I would probably never see again was the last thing I needed to do.

Shifting my position, I grabbed the cloth off the bed, wanting to examine it more closely.

I'd had it the whole time, and I hadn't even known. Marsh had said it was close, but how could he have known? Was it just wishful thinking that led him to speak those words? And how was I going to return it to him?

Secrets

The bedroom door opened; my head popped up to see Beatrice step inside.

"Jules, I just wanted to-" She paused, brow furrowed as her gaze shifted to the cloth draped across my knees like an otherworldly blanket. "What in the world is that?"

A pit grew in my stomach, cool nervousness flooding my veins, just like when I was fourteen and she had caught me smoking cigarettes in the garage.

"It's nothing," I stammered. "I mean, I don't know what it is. I, um, I think this is what Marsh was looking for."

Beatrice sat down beside me, reaching out to touch the cloth. Disgust flashed across her face as she jerked her fingers back. "What in the world?"

"I know. I've never seen anything like this." My fingers trailed over the material, the ring on my thumb winking in the light.

"Where did you get that?" Beatrice asked, taking my hand to examine the ring.

I shrugged, pulling it off my finger and offering it to her. "I found it when I found the cloth. Weird, right?"

"Everything about this is weird."

Beatrice lifted the ring, looking it over closely. "It appears to be very old, but well cared for. An heirloom, I'm sure." Turning the ring between her fingers, she continued her appraisal. "Expensive. Marsh will be happy to have it back." She smiled at me and offered the piece back.

"There's something on the band," I added. "An engraving or something. I can't make it out."

Beatrice pursed her lips, studying the engraving

closely with an appraiser's eye. "I'm sorry, Jules. I don't know what it says either."

I exhaled and took the ring back, disappointed that Beatrice couldn't read the engraving either. Why had I briefly thought she would be able to? I closed my fingers around the ring, soaking up its warmth. "Thanks anyway, Bea."

"Well, I'm glad I could put my knowledge to some use. It's been a while since I've done an appraisal. Why don't you just ask Marsh if you're so curious? I'm sure he'll be very happy to hear you found his things."

There was that pang in my chest again. "He left. I don't think he's coming back either." I pulled my knees to my chest, wrapping my arms around them with a sigh. I could feel Beatrice staring at me as she laid her hand on my shoulder.

"Maybe you just misunderstood him?" she suggested in a soothing tone.

Rolling my head toward her, I gave her a deadpan look. "Beatrice, stop. I'm not a child. We were walking, I turned around and he was gone. Pretty clear to me."

I sat there, Beatrice crouched next to me, silence stretching between us. I knew she was trying to think of something to say, some way to fix it. All I wanted was to brood.

Is it even possible to have feelings for someone you just met? Or am I just crazy?

I suppose anything was possible, but to feel this bummed and depressed over a man I barely knew was strange to say the least.

Bill stuck his head into the room, breaking the silence. "Everything's loaded up, babe," he announced. "Ready to go when you are. See you next week, Jules?"

Secrets

I blinked and looked at Bill. "Next week?" I asked.

"For dinner," Beatrice reminded, patting my shoulder as she stood. "Kylie's birthday. Remember?"

"Oh, right, of course," I watched her move to Bill's side. "I'll be there." I flashed a quick smile.

Beatrice eyed me like a worried mother hen. "I'll call and remind you. Be careful out here, okay? Call if you need anything."

I pushed to my feet and moved to hug her. "You know I will," I assured. "Drive safe, you guys. Call me when you get back to Portland?"

Beatrice nodded, kissing my cheek before pulling away. Bill grinned at me before the two of them exited the room.

With a soft groan, I walked back to the bed, flopping down face first onto it and listening to my family leave the cottage.

I was alone. Again.

Everything ached. It was a pain like nothing I had felt before. Worse than the pain I had felt after Tommy left me. It was as if my soul had been ripped in two, shredded and left to blow in the wind. None of this made sense. How could I possibly feel so deeply for him so soon? Was I that desperate?

I curled into the pillows and blankets, blowing out a breath and closing my eyes, wishing Marsh was there. Wishing I wasn't alone.

My thoughts full of him, I fell asleep.

CHAPTER TEN

*M*IST. I WAS *surrounded by cold, white mist. A white haze obscured my vision. Everywhere I looked was opaque. I held my hand out before me, but even that was lost in the thick whiteness.*

"Coming ..."

I whipped around, searching for the owner of the voice. There was none. The word seemed to echo around me, bouncing off the white mist and flinging back at me. My heart raced painfully in my chest as I took a hesitant step forward.

"Hello?" I called, my voice sounding small in the vast area I inhabited. I didn't know how I knew, but I was sure this place was vast indeed.

"Searching for the lost."

Once again I spun around, only to find myself staring at that thick white wall. My heart thrummed in my chest, so hard I was sure it would break free and skip off into the whiteness beyond.

"Hello! Who's there?"

Unsurprisingly, there was no answer. I crossed my arms over my chest and shivered in the sudden cold.

Secrets

Only then did I realize I was wearing a dress. The material was thin, and felt like silk, the color the deepest blue of the ocean. The straps, if you could call them that, were golden cords. Staring down at myself in confusion, I was startled as the echoing voice spoke, louder than before.

"Danger to the lost."

I clapped my hands over my ears as the voice boomed around me, filling my head, stabbing pain through my eardrums. "Stop it!"

"Protect. Keep hidden. Protect." The voice seemed to reverberate through me, bones quaking with the force of it.

"Protect what?" I demanded of the mist, wincing as the world around me pulsed with light and force. It slammed into me, causing everything inside of me to still.

"Guardian," the voice boomed cryptically.

The cold and mist closed in around me, pressing against my skin and leeching away any warmth left. I fruitlessly shoved at it as I tried to fight it off. It swirled around me, engulfing me in its icy grip. I gasped for breath and only succeeded in drinking in the mist, chilling my insides like a kiss of death. My throat closed up and I tore at it, my nails rending deep gashes in my flesh as I struggled to breathe.

Mist all around me, encircling me. Inside of me, blotting out my vision until there was nothing left but that milky whiteness ...

I woke with a start, my heart slamming against my ribs. Sweat soaked my body and bedclothes, my teeth chattering so hard pain radiated up my jaw. I was chilled through, and for a moment, I swore I saw my breath misting before me.

Rising from bed, I grabbed my coat from the bedpost and pulled it on. It did little to ease the persistent chill, but it was a start. I walked down the dark hallway to the kitchen, rubbing my arms vigorously.

How long had I slept? It seemed all I'd done for the last few days was sleep. The world beyond the windows was cast in darkness and shadow. The clock on the stove informed me it was five after eight in the evening. Exhaling heavily, I set the coffee pot to brew and leaned against the counter, staring across the living room.

I couldn't shake the dream from my system. Never before had I dreamed anything like that. Lifting a hand and rubbed at my throat, unconsciously feeling for scratches. It had been so real, so frightening.

Three soft beeps signaled the coffee was done. The heavy nutty scent filled the air and pulled me back to the present. I poured a full mug, and left it black, sipping it as I left the kitchen. I could already feel the caffeine bolstering my system.

I slid the glass door at the end of the living room open and stepped out onto the patio. Steam rose from my mug as I looked out over the dark beach to the distant waves. The scent of rain was heavy in the air, the ocean tipped white from the wind.

Another storm growing on the horizon.

Thunder rumbled in the distance as I stepped further out onto the porch, leaving the sliding door open to the cool night air. Fingers of lightning danced across the black and purple sky, illuminating the rolling waves before plunging the world back into darkness. I frowned at the sky, drinking my coffee. I wasn't a meteorologist, but the recent storm activity seemed unusual.

Leaning against a column, I closed my eyes, breathing in the coming storm. Thunder, closer this time, filled my ears with the sound of sky and wave.

Lightning cracked across the sky as I opened my eyes, illuminating a figure striding toward me. A scream rose in my throat and the coffee cup fell from my hands, shattering at my feet and sending the hot liquid splattering across the flagstone as I scrambled backward.

Bright blue eyes shone out of the darkness as another bolt of lightning shattered the night, striking me with their familiarity.

"Marsh?" I whispered, my voice ragged from fear and shock.

Blindly I fumbled behind me for the light switch. I flicked it, illuminating the porch and blinding us both.

"I'm sorry!" I apologized. Blinking from the sudden light, I stared at the man I thought I would never see again, my heart galloping in my chest. He was dressed as he had been before, though he had added a dark brown trench coat in the time we had been apart.

My heart thumped painfully in my chest, my eyes moving hungrily over his face, as if trying to memorize every detail.

"You came back," I whispered, unable to speak any louder. I couldn't believe he was really there. Emotions ran rampant inside of me, leaving my mind muddled and confused.

"I came back," he stated simply, his accent

coloring his words. He stepped onto the porch just as the sky opened up and the rain sluiced from the heavens, pockmarking the sand with tiny craters.

"Why?" The question slipped out automatically as I stared at him, willing my heart to steady.

Marsh looked back at me, his gaze so intense that it felt as though it pierced my soul, causing my insides to squirm and my stomach to tighten. Heat filled my cheeks and I gave up all attempts to still my heart or steady my breath.

"Truthfully? I could not stay away."

My heart slammed into overdrive and my breath caught in my throat, choking me at his words. I stared at him, unable to look away as the rain fell down around us, the storm intensifying.

"I, I had a nightmare," I blurted, having no idea where the admission came from or why I was bothering to tell him.

I wasn't the only one shocked by my confession. Marsh's brows lifted as he regarded me, shifting his feet before placing his hands in his pockets.

"A nightmare?" Curiosity tinted his tone as he stepped closer still. I could touch him if only I lifted my hand. His nearness was overwhelming. The scent of him washed over me. He smelled of the sea. Of salt, and sand. Leather and something else that was uniquely him.

I nodded mutely, stepping back into the safety of the house. That small distance allowed me to breathe. Why was I reacting like this? Yes, Marsh was attractive, but I had been around attractive men before without completely losing my mind.

I cast a surreptitious glance his direction as I

moved toward the couch, curling up on the cushion before patting the one beside me in invitation. Marsh stepped in behind me, nodding before moving to close the door.

"No, leave it open. Please. I like the sound." I smiled softly at him as I tucked my legs beneath me, watching him move as he crossed the room to me. He had a graceful way of moving, his motions fluid and economical, in a way. Captivating. I found it increasingly hard to look away.

Marsh lowered his tall frame onto the couch, sitting in such a way as to be facing me, one arm stretched out along the back of the couch. "Tell me about your nightmare."

The request was quietly said and caught me off guard. I blinked at him before shrugging and dropping my gaze to my lap.

"It was a nightmare, I don't know," I hedged.

"So, you do not remember it?"

"I didn't say that."

"Then you do remember it?"

I sighed heavily and shoved my fingers through my hair. "What does it matter?"

"It could matter naught. You, however, brought it up, so I think it matters to you."

Slanting my eyes toward him I pursed my lips. He seemed genuinely curious, and he was right, I *had* brought it up. I supposed I *did* actually want to talk about it.

"It was ... strange. Very creepy and unsettling. And real. It was so real, like I was actually there. I've only ever had one other dream with such realness before."

"Tell me about it."

"Which one?"

"Both."

I rubbed at my forehead silently before exhaling slowly and dropping my hand. What would it hurt?

"Tonight, I dreamed of mist. Everything around me was white. I couldn't see. And it was cold. Really, really cold. There was this ... voice. Just a voice, no body—or at least I never saw who was talking."

"What did the voice say?" Marsh's accent was sweet, his voice soft and lulling.

I felt myself continuing without thought, as if he were pulling the words from my lips. "It was like I could only hear snippets. Like it was struggling to pass a message to me. Something's lost and searching, or something is searching for what is lost. And there was something about protecting ... and danger." I gave a self-deprecating laugh and covered my face with my hands. "I'll bet that sounds insane to you."

"Not at all."

Turning my head, I lowered my hands, regarding him in disbelief. That was not what I had been expecting. Then again, when had he been what I was expecting?

"Tell me of the other dream?" he asked.

"Oh."

I licked my lips and looked out the open door, listening to the thunder and the rain. Flashes of lightning lit the room and I waited for the roar of thunder to die off before I spoke. Marsh never moved, waiting patiently for me to find the words.

"I had them a lot when I was younger," I explained. "I think they started when I was six? They mostly stopped when I turned thirteen. In them, I was drowning. Every night, I would drown. There was water everywhere. Above and below me, I could never tell which way was up. I would just spin and twist, my throat constricting tighter and tighter. Just before I woke up, I would always see this weird blue light …" I shook off the chill that ran through me at retelling that particular secret. "You know, my sister is the only other person I've ever told that to."

Lightning flared, brightening the room and lighting one side of Marsh's face. It was brief, the light there and gone so quickly that I was sure I imagined the look of shock and disbelief that crossed his features.

Now he probably thought I was crazy.

"I am honored you would confide in me, Juliet," Marsh instead said. "To be honest, I do not envy you your nightmares."

I laughed, shaking my head before looking at him. "I don't envy me either. But like I said, I haven't dreamt about drowning since I was a kid."

"That is a good thing. Had it persisted you might not have come to the beach. You saved my life, you know."

Marsh smiled at me, reaching out to take my hand in his. His flesh was warm, it spread through me, chasing away the chill that had plagued me since waking from my nightmare. I curled my fingers around his and met his gaze, this time preparing myself for the kick my heart gave the moment our eyes met.

"I'm glad you came back. When I turned around on the beach and you were gone …" I shrugged, looking down at our joined hands. His were so much larger than mine. And tan. His skin held the color of someone who was accustomed to being outdoors. Heat filled my cheeks as a small voice reminded me that he had been tan *everywhere*.

"What are you thinking?" Marsh asked, a smile in his voice. His question only made me blush harder.

"Nothing. I'm not thinking anything," I lied, pulling my hand from his. Marsh chuckled as he rested his hand on his thigh, his eyes never leaving me.

"Of course you're not. I apologize, for leaving without giving any warning."

Thankful for the topic change, I willed the heat from my cheeks and cleared my throat. "Why did you?"

Marsh sighed and ran his fingers through his hair, leaving it deliciously tousled. "I went back to the cave."

"It was there?" I asked in shock, leaning toward him.

Marsh shook his head and lowered his hand. "No. It is still locked to me. I could feel its energy, but I could not access it."

His frustration was palpable, and I empathized with him. Still, his choice of words left me worried for his sanity. I blew out a breath and sagged back against the couch, twirling the chain of my locket around my index finger. "Where are you from? I can't quite place your accent."

"I was born in Ireland. I lived there until I was eighteen."

"Why did you leave? I've always wanted to travel there. It always looks so peaceful and picturesque."

Marsh chuckled and nodded. "Aye, it can be that. I was born in Killarney, in County Kerry."

I watched him, smiling softly at the love I heard in

his voice. "Why would you leave?"

Marsh shifted in his seat and sighed. "My family had ... issues ... with another family. My grandmother thought it would be best if I left for a time. I went to Victoria, Canada for a short time before traveling to Aberdeen, Washington to stay with distant family there."

"So, you live in Washington?"

Marsh touched a fingertip to his temple, wincing slightly before nodding. "Yes, I lived in Aberdeen."

"But you don't anymore?"

"No."

I nodded, pursing my lips. "How did you get all the way down here, then?"

He shook his head and grinned at me. "That, I do not remember."

I frowned and dropped my hand from my locket, blowing out another breath. "Your grandmother, did you live with her?"

"For a time I did, before the feud became too much."

"What are your families fighting about?" It seemed absurd to me that two families could be feuding over something. It was almost archaic.

"Lands," Marsh sighed and closed his eyes, rubbing at the bridge of his nose.

Biting off a shocked laugh I shook my head and muttered, "Hatfield's and McCoy's."

"What?"

I frowned at the tenseness of his tone, leaning toward him to study his face. Even in the darkness I could see the signs of pain. "Does it hurt to remember? I bet it does, I'm sorry. I shouldn't push you."

Marsh lowered his hand and shook his head slightly before smiling at me, though it was strained. "It hurts a bit. It is only natural for you to be curious about me. As I am about you."

I laughed softly, "Me? There's nothing intriguing about me. I wasn't the one found naked in a cave with a patchy memory."

Marsh chuckled, his eyes glowing in the half-light. "True. But I did see you for the first time in that cave. Your hair dripping and skin glowing." His voice softened as he reached out and touched my hair with his fingertips.

I blushed deeply at his words and touch, wetting my lips with my tongue before clearing my throat. "I was soaked to the bone. I'm not sure how much glowing I was doing."

Smiling lightly at him, I pulled away from his touch and looked toward the patio. "The storm stopped."

"So it did," Marsh answered, his tone distracted.

Looking back toward him, I was surprised to find his eyes had not left me. I shifted on the couch, very aware of how close his fingers were to my shoulder. It was as if he radiated heat. I could feel it against my skin through my jacket and shirt.

I pushed myself off the couch and crossed the room, needing to distance myself from him and his unexplainable heat.

"Are you all right?" he asked.

"I'm fine. Just tired. Oh, man. It just hit me, you know?" I faked a yawn and stretched before clapping my hands together and plastering a smile on my face. I was certain I looked like a fool.

Marsh eyed me warily as he rose slowly from the couch. Surely any previous notions he might have harbored about my sanity were resurfacing. "Yes, it has been a long day. You should sleep, I will go."

"Go? What? No. No. You'll stay here."

Marsh lifted his brows as he regarded me before casting his gaze around the empty room. "Your family has gone?"

"Yes."

"Yet you wish me to remain?"

I could hear Beatrice's voice running through my head, tossing out warnings. He was a stranger. I had no idea what his intentions were or even if he *had* any intentions toward me. It would be better if he left. Safer if he left.

I had never felt safer in my life.

Tucking that stray thought away for later, I smiled at him, "Yes, I want you to stay with me. Please."

I looked up at him, the differences in our height causing me to tip my head back so I wasn't staring at his chest. Marsh crossed the room, stopping before me. He leaned toward me until only inches separated our bodies.

My heart rioted in my chest like a caged bird fighting for freedom. I stared up at him, enraptured by his gaze and the hint of a smile playing about his lips. My breath caught in my throat as he leaned closer still, his lips dangerously close to mine.

"Then I shall stay," he closed the patio door and pulled away from me.

I stood statue still, my brain desperately trying to quiet my rampant hormones and make sense of what had just happened. Blinking rapidly, I closed my parted lips and stared at him.

"What?" I managed finally.

"I said, I will stay."

Lifting my hands to my face I shook my head, utterly baffled by what had just transpired. "Umm, okay. Great. I'll just, um, move my stuff into the master bedroom."

I turned to leave the room, my body screaming in protest at each step I took away from Marsh. It took everything within me not to run down the hallway and slam the door. I had never felt attraction like this before. It was as if something were pulling me to him—a living force. But that made no sense.

Blowing out a frustrated breath, I pushed away from the door and crossed to the dresser, pulling out what I would need for the night.

I tried to convince my hormones that I was a responsible adult and not a reckless teenager who necked on the couch, but they were having none of that. Pressing my hand to my racing heart, I turned to toss my things on the bed and screamed.

Marsh threw his hands out before him and moved forward slowly, his face full of apology. "It's only me. I'm sorry I frightened you."

"What are you doing in here?" I demanded, stomping my foot. My body couldn't take much more tonight. I certainly wasn't thinking about a romp in the sheets now. Fear was a crappy way to sober up.

"I wanted to apologize."

"For scaring me?"

"No. Well, yes. I wished also to apologize for my actions in the front room. I should not have gotten so close. I made you uncomfortable and I apologize."

Secrets

I stared up at him, my lips forming a small 'o' of shock. He'd made me uncomfortable?

That is one way of putting it, I suppose.

Rubbing my brow, I laughed to myself as I bent to retrieve my clothes from the floor. "It's fine. No harm, no foul."

Marsh nodded and slid his hands into his pockets as I crossed to the bed and grabbed my pillow. I did my best to ignore the feel of his eyes on me as I moved.

"I'm just going to grab that ... and going to bed now." I had no idea why I was giving him a play by play of my actions. He was wondering the same thing if his expression could be believed.

Ducking my head to hide my flush, I pressed my clothes and pillow to my chest and made my way swiftly toward the door. Could this night get anymore weird or embarrassing? First the creepy nightmare, then Marsh returning out of the storm, which had brought about all sorts of unexplainable feelings, and, to finish the evening, he'd scared me half to death. All I wanted to do was crawl into bed and pretend the last few hours never happened.

"Juliet?"

I stopped just outside the doorway as he spoke my name. It was as if a warm breeze washed over me, causing pinpricks of delight to dance across my spine. I turned slowly, schooling my features into a look of curiosity to conceal the tumultuous feelings he was causing within me.

"You dropped these."

My face turned so red I was sure I rivaled a tomato as I found his long fingers extended toward me, a lacy, sky blue thong dangling from them.

"Thank you," I squeaked, ripping the underwear from his hand and stuffing it inside my pillowcase.

Lesson learned. It can *always* get worse.

"Goodnight, Juliet." Marsh's eyes were bright with humor as I backed out of the room, muttering something unintelligible that sounded like goodnight.

I walked into the master bedroom, clinging to whatever shred of dignity I had left as I flopped onto the bed and let loose a muffled scream. Tonight, I had run the gamut of emotions. I had been depressed, surprised, turned on, scared, and mortified. I couldn't help but wonder if they handed out ribbons for most emotions felt in a two-hour timespan.

Rolling onto my back, I inhaled and said a quick prayer that tonight was not a foretelling of how any future encounters with Marsh would play out.

CHAPTER ELEVEN

MARSH AND I spent most of the morning alternately ignoring one another. After the incident the previous night, what I'd deemed the "almost" kiss, I didn't know how to face him.

After spending a good portion of the morning closed up in my room, I was at my breaking point. I needed to grab a change of clothes, and my stomach was loudly declaring a need of its own. Opening the door slowly, I peeked out into the hallway.

No sign of Marsh, and his door was closed.

I tiptoed past his door and made a beeline for the kitchen, desperate for coffee.

I was so ready for that sweet, dark nectar that it took me a moment to realize I wasn't imagining the heady scent wafting toward me.

Marsh turned as I stepped into the kitchen and stopped short. His smile was warm and inviting, "She wakes," he said warmly. "I was just about to bring you a cup when I realized I never asked how you take it."

I stared at him, my brain scrambling for a response as I waited for the rush of embarrassment I was sure was coming. Except, it didn't come.

"Ah, three sugars. Thanks."

Crossing my arms over my chest, I leaned against the counter watching him warily. I searched his features for signs of weirdness, or any reaction from the night's happenings. I was out of luck, as the smile never left his lips.

He added three sugars to a mug before he passed it to me.

"Thank you," I said again, sipping from the coffee as I watched him over the rim. Taking up his own cup, he leaned back against the opposite counter and watched me back.

"Did you sleep well?" he asked.

I lifted my finger as I took a bracing sip of coffee.

I would be cool. I could do this, I could be just as nonchalant as he.

Swallowing, I flashed him a smile. "Oh, yeah. I slept like a baby."

Exactly like a baby. Up every two hours.

Marsh smirked. "That's good then."

Not knowing what else to say, I took a gulp of the coffee. The heat shocked me and I swallowed hastily, scalding my throat and choking. Mortified, I turned away from him until I regained control.

When I spoke, my voice rivaled a five pack a day smoker, "Did you?"

Marsh nodded as he set down his cup. "Are you all right?"

"I'm fine. So, did you sleep all right?"

"I did. The bed was very comfortable. Thank you."

Silence stretched between us as I thought frantically about something to say. I was saved the trouble, Marsh interrupting my panic.

"I do not wish to hold you from any plans you might have had for today," he noted.

"Plans?" I shook my head. "I, no, I mean I didn't really have anything ... We should go shopping! Get you more clothes."

Marsh lifted his brows before looking down at himself. "What are wrong with these clothes?"

"You can't wear the same clothes every day, Marsh."

"I have no money though."

I waved my hand, seizing on the idea. "Don't worry about that. I'll get you a few things."

"Juliet-" Marsh began.

"I said I'd get them, okay?" I interrupted, my tone brooking no argument.

Marsh looked at me for a long moment before nodding and pushing away from the counter. "Okay."

His lowered voice had fingers of delight dancing along my spine. Gulping down the remnants of my coffee, I sidestepped around him.

"I'll be right back!" I called over my shoulder as I hurried down the hallway. I scampered across the guest room before yanking open the drawers and pulling out my clothes, thankful that I hadn't brought many. Casting a quick glance over my shoulder, I stepped out of my sleeping shorts and pulled on a pair of jeans. I tugged off my tank top and donned a bra and shirt.

I was just tugging my shirt down over my head when I heard the floorboards creak. Spinning around, I saw Marsh standing in the doorway.

"Marsh!" I gasped. "Changing!"

"Oh! Uh, Sorry!" Marsh whirled around, turning

his back to me and shaking his head.

"How long have you been standing there?" I demanded, horrified.

"Only a moment. I didn't see anything!" Marsh defended, his tone embarrassed.

"I don't know what it's like in Ireland, but here it's considered rude to spy on someone while they're changing!"

Marsh shook his head violently, keeping his back to me. "I didn't know where you went, and you left the door open. I was just trying to find you. Besides, you've seen me in states of undress."

"Oh, so because I've seen you naked I should return the favor?"

Marsh shifted so he could look at me. "If you wish. I would offer no complaints."

The smile that grew upon his lips was slow and teasing, and more than a little sexy. It lit his eyes with an inner heat.

I licked my lips, my mouth suddenly dryer than the desert. "Aren't you supposed to be a gentleman or something?"

Marsh chuckled low and deep, his eyes never leaving me. It was telling that I was becoming used to his stare. "Yes, I am. However, I am still a man. And you are beautiful."

I lowered my eyes as heat filled my cheeks. Beautiful? He thought I was beautiful? Or was he just saying that because he'd seen me topless?

"Thank you," I said, looking everywhere but at him.

Marsh nodded, running his fingers through his hair. "Shall we go? Shopping, I mean?"

I nodded, taking care not to brush against him as I marched past him, stopping only long enough to grab my purse off the kitchen counter before stepping outside.

It was a warm day, a blessed break from the chilly weather the storms had brought. Closing my eyes, I tipped my head back and breathed in the air in a desperate attempt to calm myself.

What *was* it about this man that turned me into a bumbling fool? How was it possible he could turn my insides to jelly with just a look? I didn't understand it, but I couldn't deny that was exactly what he did.

"Juliet?"

"Are you ready?"

Marsh nodded and I turned, waiting for him to fall into step with me as I started off toward town.

"Where did you get the coat, anyway? And the shoes?" I asked after a while, tucking my hair behind my ear as I glanced his way.

"Oh, I found them," Marsh replied casually.

"You found them? A perfectly good coat and pair of shoes? In your exact size?"

"Yes, I found them." Marsh looked at me, his brows lifted. "Is that so strange?"

"I'm just trying to decide if your definition of 'found' and mine of 'stealing' are the same."

Marsh chuckled, slipping his hands into his pockets as the sea breeze ruffled his dark hair. My fingers itched to run through those black curls, feel their softness against my skin. I quickly cast away the thought and cleared my throat, focusing on where I was walking.

The sand slipped beneath my feet as I walked,

gulls wheeling and screaming overhead. The sun played peek-a-boo with the clouds. All in all, it was a perfect day for the beach. And here I was, walking along with this man I barely knew.

I looked toward him. "Do you remember anything more of your life? I know memory can come back in flashes."

"I am remembering more, yes," he confirmed. "Though some things are still a bit hazy. Was there something specific you were curious about?"

"No, nothing specific. Just, you in general. I mean, it's not every day you find a man in a cave on a trip to the beach."

"That's probably a good thing, or else I'm sure many single women would flock to the caves."

"Could be a decent tourism boost," I shrugged, flashing him a grin.

I was rewarded with a deep laugh. I liked his laugh. It was real and gave you no doubt he found what you had said or done humorous.

"Could be," Marsh agreed, looking down at me with a smile. The light reflected in his eyes, making them fire like polished stones.

"You have the most incredible eyes," I blurted. Heat filled my cheeks rapidly and I tore my gaze from his.

"Thank you. Yours are quite beautiful as well."

His words insured that my blush would be staying for a while, and this time I didn't have the cover of darkness to hide behind. Ducking my head I tried to arrange my hair to hide my burning cheeks, but soon felt like a fool. Sighing, I shook my locks back and glanced his way.

Secrets

"What were you doing?" he asked, clearly puzzled.

"Huh?"

"With your hair, what were you doing?"

"Nothing," I assured with an awkward smile, "don't worry about it. So, um, do you have anyone who would be looking for you?"

Marsh lifted his brow at my obvious topic change, keeping his face lifted up to the breeze and closing his eyes as the wind washed over him. He really was a man who enjoyed being outdoors. And he fit well in the setting—I could easily imagine him piloting some boat over the rolling waters of the ocean.

"No. I have some friends in Washington, but they knew I was going to be gone for a while, so they would not be worried yet."

"What about your grandmother? Won't she worry?"

"She is not really the worrying type," Marsh chuckled, smiling down at me. I couldn't help but feel like I was missing out on a private joke.

"If you say so." I shrugged before pausing, looking around to gauge our location. I spied the street sign that declared Hemlock Street. "This is Hemlock," I noted. "It's the main road. If we stay on it, we'll end up right in the heart of town."

Marsh extended a hand before him. "Lead the way," he said, lips twitching.

Cars rolled lazily by, honking politely to let us know they were there. I lifted my hand to a few, recognizing their presence, but the man walking beside me was a source of distraction.

None of it made sense. It was like something out of a movie or a book. Tall, good-looking men didn't just appear before you. Tall, good-looking men who were even remotely interested in you were an even rarer find.

The town spread out before us, a cute little cluster of buildings clinging to a different era. Red brick set in alternating diagonal patterns lined the sidewalks and filled the areas between the buildings. The architecture of the buildings was simple, homey and welcoming. Wide storefronts beckoned shoppers to come inside and browse their wares. Brightly colored signs drew the eye and caught the attention of the tourists.

"Clothes, clothes, what about Cannon Beach Clothing Company?" I offered, glancing between Marsh and the store entrance. "We should be able to find you something there I think."

"I leave myself in your hands, Juliet," Marsh assured. "You know this place better than I."

I snorted softly and shrugged, leading the way toward the store. "I guess so. I haven't been up here in a while, but Beatrice loves it, so here I am."

"It is a beautiful place."

I risked another glance at him and felt a smile tug at my lips. "You really are in your element, aren't you?"

Marsh remained quiet for a bit before nodding and looking down at me with a smile. "I suppose I am."

I smiled back, keeping my eyes on him, heedless of anything I could walk into.

"Juliet?" a voice behind me called.

I stopped short, my heart stilling in my chest.

No, no. Not here. Not now.

Taking a deep breath, I turned my head toward the voice, my smile tightening. "Hello, Tommy," I managed.

Tommy Donovan shook his head in disbelief, chuckling. "Wow, small world, huh?"

"Smaller than most think,"

I smirked at Marsh. My humor was short lived, though, when Tommy replied. "Who's this? New boyfriend?" he asked with an upward sneer. Tommy was shorter and slimmer than Marsh, but he didn't let that stop him from trying to intimidate him.

I whipped my head around, staring at Tommy with a slack jaw. I blinked in shock, struggling for words.

Boyfriend? Does he really think I could move on so quickly?

Though I suppose the question wasn't so shocking, considering he had.

Marsh and I spoke at the same time:

"No, he's not."

"Yes, I am."

I blinked at Marsh, not sure where that had come from at all.

Tommy chuckled, looking between the two of us with lifted brows. "Well, is he or isn't he?"

"Uh, um ... He ..." I stuttered, fumbling once more for words.

Marsh saved me from having to answer by slipping his arm around me and pulling me close to him.

"I am," Marsh replied to Tommy. "Though it's new, so we're not telling many people."

My heart stopped in my chest. I found some satisfaction in Tommy's shocked expression as he looked between us before giving a derisive snort of laughter.

"Wow," he muttered. "Moved right along, didn't

you Jules?"

I swallowed, a huge lump forming in my throat at his accusation. Marsh tightened his hold on me. I could feel his body tense, as if he was preparing for a fight. But why? Why would he be willing to fight for me? I gave myself a mental shake and pressed my hand to Marsh's chest.

"Yes, I have moved on," I replied. "Just as you did." I smiled tightly at Tommy, enjoying the annoyance that flashed in his eyes.

Sleezeball.

"Well, uh, you two enjoy the rest of your day," Tommy smiled at me, though it didn't reach his eyes. Glaring at Marsh, he stepped around us and went on his way.

As soon as Tommy was gone, I blew out a breath I didn't know I'd been holding. I closed my eyes, forcing my body to relax.

"That was awful," I groaned. "Thank you, for helping me." I smiled up at Marsh and gently extracted myself from his hold.

Marsh nodded, letting his arm fall to his side. "Of course. You've done so much for me, it was the least I could do."

I nodded, absently rubbing at my arm. The warmth of him clung to my skin, and I wondered how he was always so warm. I grinned, "So, shall we then?"

Marsh nodded and I led him into the clothing store. It wasn't crowded, luckily. I wasn't particularly fond of crowds, so this was a boon for me. I strode toward the first rack of men's clothes I saw and began pawing through it.

"What's your size again? I know that Bill's things

aren't fitting you well."

I frowned as I was met with silence. Turning from the rack, I saw Marsh standing in the doorway, looking around in confusion. With a frown, I walked toward him, releasing the shirt I had been holding.

"Hey, are you okay?" I asked. Marsh jerked as if he was startled, his whole body shaking. Worry ran through me like shards of ice and I reached out to touch his arm. "Hey, what's wrong?"

"This place, it reminded me of a shop in Ireland. My mother used to take me there. Just a memory I wasn't expecting to have." Marsh's expression was one of attempted assurance to waylay my concern.

"You haven't mentioned your parents before. Are they still alive?" I asked softly, watching his face.

"No. They're not."

"I'm so sorry."

Curiosity bloomed within me but I slammed the lid on it. Now was not the time or place to be questioning him about his parents. That could come later.

"Did you still want to shop?"

As soon as I'd asked the question I wished I could take it back. How selfish and materialistic did I sound?

Marsh nodded, his smile more real this time as he covered my hand with his own. "Yes, and thank you for your concern."

I smiled at Marsh before lowering my hand and stepping away. Marsh was easy to shop with, unlike many other men I'd known. He was quiet and didn't complain as we looked through the racks, nodding to me when I showed him something he liked or shaking his head when he didn't. Before long, we had three pairs of jeans and an armful of shirts.

"There. That wasn't so hard, was it?" I asked with a smile as we stepped out of the store.

"Not at all. I will pay you back. As soon as I remember which bank I use." Marsh chuckled softly before his brow furrowed.

"Hey, don't worry about it. It'll come, in time." I tapped my temple and looked up at him. "Your memory."

Marsh nodded. "It will. Sooner would be better, however."

"And here I thought you were so patient," I teased, bumping him with my shoulder.

"I am very patient," he said. "Just not when it comes to my memory returning." Marsh sighed, lifting his hand and rubbing his forehead. "I hate not knowing."

"Hey, why don't we get something to eat?" I offered, smiling encouragingly at him. Marsh nodded and I looked up and down the street, searching. I smiled brightly as my eyes landed on a familiar sign. "There! The *Lazy Susan Cafe*. They have great breakfasts. Come on."

I reached out and took his hand, entwining my fingers with his as I led him toward the cafe.

We chatted over stacks of pancakes and scrambled eggs. Our talk wasn't serious, but it was nice. Simple things, like our favorite colors and childhood memories. I was surprised by how much of his childhood Marsh remembered. His parents had died while he was still young, leaving him in the care of his grandmother.

"She's been my whole world since I was ten,"

Secrets

Marsh said softly later as we walked along the beach after dropping off the shopping bags at the cottage.

"What was it like?"

Marsh shrugged, a nostalgic smile flirting about his lips. "At first it was every kid's dream. She was worried about how I was coping, so she overcompensated. I had brownies for breakfast and ice cream for dinner. But after a while, we just found our rhythm. She didn't hide her grief from me, and encouraged me to do the same. We cried together."

I smiled up at him, crossing my arms over my chest as a sea breeze kicked up, chilling me. "You miss her."

"I do. Very much so." Marsh looked down at me and smiled. "But being with you is lessening that."

I looked away, heat filling my cheeks. He spoke so easily the words that set my heart to racing and my blood warming. Did he even know the affect he had on me? I doubted it.

I smiled softly at him as we continued our path down the beach, falling once more into companionable silence.

I knew I was hiding behind that fact, and growing more and more worried it was nothing more than a flimsy excuse. One made of such thin material that a strong breeze would tear it to shreds. But deciphering my feelings for the man borne of the sea was something I would have to deal with another day.

CHAPTER TWELVE

THE NEXT TWO days passed by in a blur of beach walks and late-night talks. I loved every moment of it, learning more and more about Marsh and hearing about his life in Ireland. His tales fed my growing travel bug, and I mentally began to calculate just how much it would cost me to go there. It would probably be a small fortune, but I didn't care.

"I can't imagine leaving such a beautiful place," I sighed, curling my legs beneath me as I sat on the couch before passing a bowl of noodles to Marsh.

"Thank you," Marsh replied. "It was a hard choice, but one of necessity."

I nodded, stirring my soup. "I have to go back to the city tomorrow," I said softly, spooning up some noodles but not eating. I didn't want to go back to my real life. I wasn't ready to let go of this fantasy life I had found myself in.

"I am sure your parents will be happy for your return."

I snorted. "I doubt it. We don't really get along."

"I am sorry to hear that. Family is important."

I shrugged, setting aside my bowl and looking at

Secrets

Marsh. I had given up trying to keep my eyes off of him. It was nearly impossible to look anywhere but at him when he was around.

Marsh shifted in his seat. "That man from the other day, he was your boyfriend?"

"Ex-fiancé, actually." I exhaled. I had hoped we could avoid this little chat, but he deserved an explanation. "He left me for another woman."

Marsh looked at me, his gaze hot. "He is a fool. He would have to be to let go of someone like you."

My cheeks burned as my heart raced in my chest, banging against my ribs with such a clamor I was sure he would hear it.

"We just wanted different things, I guess," I mumbled, my throat tight with emotion.

Marsh leaned toward me, resting his hand on my knee and sending my pulse skyrocketing. "Juliet, I wanted to-"

"Ah, I'll just take these into the kitchen."

I scrambled off the couch, grabbing the bowls as I rushed off. In the safety of the kitchen, I blew out a breath and leaned against the counter, covering my face with my hands.

What was wrong with me?

The man is gorgeous.

And unless I was wrong, he was interested in me. *Me. Juliet Adams.*

I lowered my hands and turned as the floor creaked. Marsh stood in front of me, shoulders hunched and hands hidden in his pockets. He looked awkward and unsure of himself, with his dark hair falling into his eyes. He was undeniably sexy, and I could no longer deny the attraction I felt for him.

"Juliet." His soft tones washed over me, freeing me from my fear. And all he had done was speak my name. He stepped closer to me, his eyes once more on mine. "I seem to keep doing the wrong thing when it comes to you."

I shook my head, shoving my hair from my face and gripping it before sighing, letting my hands fall to my sides.

"No, it's not you," I insisted. "I'm just a bit ... skittish. Tommy accusing me of moving on and all." I gestured with my hand lamely before dropping it against my thigh.

Marsh nodded, once more holding me with the penetrating stare. "And you have not moved on?"

"I have."

"Then what is the problem?"

"I don't ... I don't know."

"Perhaps then there is no problem."

I bit my lower lip, watching him stalk closer to me. I had grown used to the rapid pace my heart found when he looked at me like that. Shivers ran up and down my spine. The tiny hairs on my arms and the back of my neck rose as if the room had become statically charged.

I couldn't look away. I was powerless to move as Marsh closed the distance between us, stopping inches from me. His chest brushed against mine and I inhaled sharply, swallowing the scent of him. It exploded through me like a drug in my veins, going straight to my head and making me dizzy with desire.

"You are an incredible creature," Marsh whispered, his voice low and husky, sending darts of pleasure to my most private depths.

Secrets

Lifting his hand, he cupped my cheek, his ice blue eyes staying on mine as he brought his lips toward mine. He was so close, the insane warmth of his skin and the mind-numbing scent of him had me panting. I was confident I would turn into a puddle of desire if he came any closer.

The level of attraction I felt for him was extraordinary. I was sure it went beyond simple human bounds—I couldn't imagine another man ever making me feel the way this man did with just a look.

"What are you?" I whispered heedlessly, my eyes all but closed, his lips so close I could taste him.

I waited anxiously for that press of flesh against flesh. Yearned for it. But it never came. Slowly, I opened my eyes and blinked in confusion as I found him staring at me eyes wide.

"Marsh?"

"I have to go," he declared abruptly, withdrawing his hands from me as if I burned him.

As always, the heat of him lingered, but it only added to the muddling of my mind.

"Go? Now? But-But I thought..." I shook my head, more than a little confused by the abrupt change of direction and doing my darndest to think around my screaming hormones.

"Forgive me." He looked as if he wanted to say more. Instead, he turned and strode down the hall. A moment later he returned, dressed in his coat with the bag full of clothes I'd bought him slung over his shoulder.

"Be well, Juliet," he said, lingering near the doorway.

I urged him to speak what was on the tip of his

tongue that he refused to, screaming in my head for him to say *something*. Offer some sort of explanation. But the sudden shift in mood had robbed me of my voice, leaving me staring after him in silent plea.

Marsh glanced at me, a sad smile twitching up his lips before he turned.

The door opened, closed, and he was gone.

CHAPTER THIRTEEN

THE DULL BEEPING of the monitor filled the background, but he ignored it. He had become all too used to the electronic sounds of the machines. The room was cast in darkness, the only sounds the monotonous beeping and soft, rhythmic breathing of the woman.

Her white hair seemed to glow in the moonlight that fell through the open window, lending her an otherworldly phosphorescence. He chuckled at the thought and shifted in the chair he occupied.

Deep in his pocket, he felt a vibration. He pulled out his phone and viewed the screen. The message on it was short and to the point:

DOES SHE LIVE?

With a grim smile, he responded with one word:

YES.

Holding the phone lightly in his hand, he looked back to the sleeping woman, ignoring the buzzing of the phone. It sounded angry, as if it were channeling the emotions of the sender. He grinned, sinking back into his chair and tapping the phone against his knee.

It furiously buzzed again, drawing forth another hushed chuckle.

"Dream sweet, Adaline."

CHAPTER FOURTEEN

I SMILED SOFTLY as I slid out of the cab, leaning back in to pay the driver. Shouldering my bag, I looked up at my building and sighed.

"Home sweet home," I muttered, walking up the steps and struggling a bit with the door. After coming up with some rather inventive curses in my head, I finally made it through the door and up the stairs to my apartment. I unlocked the door and stepped in, letting my bag drop to the floor.

"Honey, I'm home!" I called to the empty space. Deafening silence hit me like a ton of bricks. What had I been expecting—Marsh to be waiting on my doorstep when I arrived? I frowned as I realized that was exactly what I'd been expecting.

"Idiot," I mumbled, stooping down and scooping my bag up from the floor. I kicked aside a takeout box as I marched toward my room, the putrid scent that wafted up from it making me gag. I needed to clean house. Badly.

With a huff, I dropped my bag onto my bed and yanked open the zipper. I stood there, staring at my clothes, not knowing what to do. My heart clenched in my chest as thoughts of Marsh tried to creep into my mind. I gritted my teeth, shaking my head violently as I shoved away the thoughts of him ... of his warmth, the roughness of his hands, and the blue of his eyes ...

"Stop it, Juliet!" I scolded myself. Grabbing an armful of clothes, I marched across the room and shoved them into the overfull basket. I straightened up, slapping my hair back. My place was a sty. How had I lived like this for so long? Shuddering, I grabbed a hair band off my dresser and pulled back my red locks. Enough was enough.

After a few hours of hard cleaning, my apartment was all but literally sparkling. It smelled strongly of cleaner, but I liked that. I peered at the three trash bags, trying to decide if I wanted to take them down now or later.

With a sigh, I grabbed the three bags and ran them down to the shoot, shoving them into the opening and slamming the door closed. I raced back to my apartment and closed the door behind myself, shutting my eyes and exhaling. The trash shoot scared me. It was an illogical fear, and I knew that. It didn't stop me from being afraid, though.

Pushing away from the door I walked into the kitchen. My stomach growled loudly and I frowned as I peered into my empty fridge.

Crap. Looks like it's takeout again.

I pulled open the takeout drawer and removed the menus, spreading them out on the counter. I tapped my lower lip as I pondered what I was hungry for. Across from me, a blinking red light caught my attention.

A message?

Secrets

My stomach sank as I thought of all the possibilities, none of them good.

They're going to take my car.

I groaned, sliding toward the phone. With a wince, I stabbed at the voicemail button, fear settling in my stomach like a lead weight.

"You have one new message," the automated voice informed me. I curled my fingers into my palms, waiting for the proverbial other shoe to drop.

"Juliet. Hi. This is Robert. I hadn't heard from you in a few days, so I just wanted to see if you were doing well. If you're not busy, would you like to grab dinner on Saturday? Call me back and let me know."

My eyes flew open and I scrambled for a pen and paper, scribbling down his number before the voicemail ended.

The pen dropped numbly from my fingers. I couldn't believe he had actually called. He not only wanted to check up on me, but he wanted to see me again.

All thoughts of food forgotten, I grabbed up my phone and keyed the speed dial for Rose Village.

"Rose Village Assisted Living," I heard on the other end. "Karen speaking. How may I direct your call?"

"Karen, it's Juliet!" I exclaimed, breathless with nervous excitement. "Can you tell me if I'm working this Saturday?"

"Uh, sure. Hang on." Karen's tone did nothing to hide her confusion.

Muzak filled the line and I drummed my fingers

against the counter as I waited for her to check the schedule. The line crackled as the muzak cut off and Karen's voice replaced it.

"Still there?" she asked. "It looks like you're off this Saturday, but you have the overnight shift Sunday."

"Great, thank you!"

I hung up before she could say anything more, clutching the phone to my chest. I felt like a crazy person. I had spent the better part of a year moping over Tommy, and suddenly I had two men vying for my attention.

They're both coming. One to save, the other to damn...

I pushed the thought away and looked at Robert's number, tapping the top of the phone against my chin.

Should I call him now? Would that be too soon?

I didn't want to sound needy—or worse, desperate.

You're being an idiot. Just call the man already!

Exhaling, I rolled my neck, shaking out my limps like a fighter about to go into the ring and willed myself to relax. I could do this. It was nothing. Just a simple phone call.

Licking my lips, I dialed the number and brought the phone to my ear.

It rang.

And rang. And rang.

My heart sinking, I was just about to hang up when a harried voice came across the line.

"Hello? Hello? Is anyone there?"

"Robert? Hi. It's Juliet."

I made a face at the horrible squeak that my voice had become. I sounded like I had swallowed a rubber

Secrets

duck. Clearing my throat, I began to pace the kitchen. "I got your message. Thank you, by the way. It was really sweet of you to want to call and check up on me."

"Juliet, hi. Yeah. I had such a great time on our date; I thought we might do it again. Are you free on Saturday?"

"I am. Yeah. Yup. Totally free. Nothing planned."

I squeezed my eyes closed and pinched my nose. What was wrong with me? Clamping my jaw closed, I breathed out through my nose.

Shut up, for the love of God, shut up.

Robert chuckled, his smooth voice rolling across the line and skating down my spine. "That's great. Would you like to go to dinner with me?"

"Yes, I would like that," I breathed, dropping my hand from my face.

"Wonderful. I'll pick you up at seven?"

"Seven sounds great. I'll see you then."

"See you. Goodbye."

I clicked off the phone and set it on the counter with exaggerated care. I stood quietly, eyes wide, letting it all sink in. Without warning, a loud whoop escaped my lips. I threw my hands in the air, letting go another excited yip as I began to sway my hips side to side and dance around my kitchen.

"Oh yeah! Go me! I've still got it! I've got it! I'm hot and men still want to date me!" I sang, slapping my hands on my hips and thrusting them forward.

The momentum carried me forward and I grunted as I awkwardly pin wheeled my arms, trying to catch my balance and save my face from being crushed. Blinking, I straightened, thankful I lived alone and there was no one to see my blunder.

I couldn't stop smiling. It had started off small, just a twitching of my lips, but as I perused the takeout menus, it grew into a full-blown, "cat that ate the canary" grin.

Tommy really was a fool, as Marsh had said.

Marsh.

There it was again, thoughts of him invading my brain and my heart. Pushing them aside, I grabbed a menu at random and looked it over. I snagged up the phone and dialed the number, placing my order.

After I hung up the phone, I glanced around for my purse. I didn't see it in the kitchen, which meant I had left it in my room. Groaning, I trudged into the bedroom, sifting through the items on my bed. No luck.

Panic set in as I flew about the room in search. I knew I'd had it when I had arrived home—after all, I had paid the cab driver and come straight up.

So it has to be in here somewhere.

Swallowing down the lump of fear that lodged in my throat, I turned my bag over, shaking out the contents. A few socks and some spare change rolled out, but no purse.

"Crap!" I snapped as I flew to my laundry basket, knocking it over and spilling the clothes across the floor. As I frantically sorted through them, my fingers brushed against a patch of rough cloth and I whooped in delight, extracting my purse from beneath a pile of panties.

"Thank God," I muttered, hugging my purse to my chest. Fear gone, I looked around in dismay at the mess I had made. Blowing out a breath that fluttered my hair, I tossed my purse onto my bed and got to work relocating the clothes into the basket.

Tomorrow would definitely be laundry day.

I frowned as I saw a shirt lying haphazardly at the bottom of the bed. Striding toward it, I hissed in pain as my foot came down on something sharp. Leaping back, I looked down, my brow furrowing. I crouched down to pick up the offending object.

It was the ring. The one I believed to be Marsh's.

I had forgotten all about it in the excitement of his return. I licked my lips as I turned the silver circle around and around my finger, watching it wink in the light. It was warm. I narrowed my eyes at the oddness of it. How could it possibly be warm? It had been shoved in my bag, with nothing in there to conduct heat. And it certainly wasn't hot enough in my apartment to have warmed the ring to this degree.

I twisted around to look for the strange material, wondering if I had managed to bring it along with me as well. After a quick scan of my bedroom, I spotted it lying on the floor just behind my laundry basket.

I scooped it up, shivering at the odd feeling it brought. It flowed against my hand like water. I sat back down on the bed as I stared at the supple material.

Was it even material? I had been calling it that, but now I wasn't sure. I peered at it, trying to figure it out.

Could it be some sort of hide?

Wrinkling my nose, I laughed at myself.

A hide? From what sort of creature?

I had never heard of anything having skin like this. And it was perfectly shaped, with no jagged edges. Even if it had been from an animal, it was highly unlikely it had just fallen off.

Did both of these things belong to Marsh? What

did the engraving on the ring say? What the heck *was* the cloth *really*? And why did the one person who could give me the answers have to disappear so abruptly?

My head jerked up as the buzzer sounded, announcing I had a visitor. Dropping the strange cloth onto the bed, I ran toward the door and pressed the button to release the outer door. Three brisk knocks sounded as I was walking back with my wallet.

"Coming, I'm coming," I called, counting out the bill plus tip. I dropped my wallet on the counter and pulled open the door, offering a wide smile to the delivery boy and exchanging the cash for pizza.

Thanking him, I closed the door and set the pizza on the counter. My eyes kept drifting toward my doorway as I helped myself to it, my thoughts consumed by the strange cloth. I knew it had something to do with Marsh. I had no idea how I knew, but I did. I was as sure of it as I had ever been of anything in my life.

I wanted to ask him about it, to question him. But I had no way of getting in touch with him.

Sighing in frustration, I strode toward the couch, plopping down with every intention of enjoying a sappy romantic comedy with my meal. Still, I couldn't let go of the questions.

CHAPTER FIFTEEN

I YAWNED AS I walked down the steps of my building the next morning, my mind solely focused on coffee. The scathing red paper I spotted tucked beneath my wiper stopped me cold.

"Damn it," I growled as I jerked the paper off my windshield and threw myself into the car. It was too early for this crap.

I will get you your payment and then you can stop harassing me!

When I arrived at Rose Village, I raced into the building, ducking behind an orderly to escape the sharp eyes of the morning receptionist. Grinning to myself, I went into the locker room and stowed my purse. I slid on my name badge on my way to checking the roster. My grin widened when I saw I was on Adaline's rotation.

"Good morning, Adaline!" I sang as I walked into her room. I stopped short as I found her curled up on the bed, still asleep. I crossed to the foot of her bed and pulled out her chart, looking it over as worry filled me.

"That paper isn't going to tell you a thing."

I jerked my head up, catching myself before I dropped the clipboard.

"Adaline, you scared me." I shook my head and crossed toward her. "What are you still doing in bed?"

Adaline grunted and rolled onto her back, smiling at me. "Just a stomach bug," she muttered with a wave of her hand, sitting up in the bed. Her snow-white hair draped over her shoulders was tousled from sleep.

"A stomach bug? How are you feeling now?" I pulled out my blood pressure cuff and walked toward her, placing it on her arm.

"Oh fine, fine. They said I was dehydrated. Been pumping me so full of liquid, I can't take it. I don't think I've peed this much since I was a babe."

I snorted, noting her blood pressure on the chart and replacing my cuff in my pocket. "Your numbers are good. I'm glad you're feeling better. I missed you."

"I missed you too, honey. I heard you went off to the beach." Adaline shifted on the bed, her faded blue eyes honing in on me.

I nodded, a smile flirting about my lips. "I did, yeah."

Adaline cackled and pushed at my arm. "Had you a good time, did you?"

I ducked my head, feeling my cheeks heat as I looked down at her chart, pretending to be focused on reading it. As always with Adaline, it was as if she could see right through me, into the heart of me.

"I'll get it out of you one way or another," she laughed, her tone teasingly threatening.

"Okay, okay! I did have a good time, yes. It was ... interesting."

Adaline lifted her brows, her pale eyes brightening

with interest. "What made it interesting, dear?"

I licked my lips, not sure how much to tell. I was still sorting through my weeks at the beach. I should have known Adaline would pry—it was how she was. I didn't mind it so much, but I hadn't decided how much I wanted to share.

"You met a man," she concluded, brows shooting up.

"Yes," I laughed, shaking my head and looking back to her. "I met a man. But it ... it didn't work out."

Adaline snorted and leaned back on her pillows. "Oh honey, there's nothing wrong with a little beach fling. Was he hung?"

"Adaline!" I cried, scarlet flaring in my cheeks. I nervously laughed at the audacity of her question.

"What? Can't humor an old lady?" Adaline grinned cheekily at me, attempting to pull an innocent look and failing miserably.

"I should have known you would ask me that," I chuckled, shaking my head and pushing my hair back.

"It's a pertinent question."

My eyes narrowed as she shrugged, her grin belying any innocence she might have been trying to play off.

"No, we didn't have ... We just talked. A lot. And ... almost kissed. But that was it."

Adaline looked at me, brows pulling together in a look of disbelief. "Was he blind?"

"No, why?"

"He must have been to not have tried to get a piece of you."

"Ha ha." I blushed, heat flowing down my neck. "You're horrible."

Adaline cackled, her pale eyes bright with their ever-present mischief. "Anything new happening besides the beach stud?"

I bit my lower lip with a nod, unable to hide my smile. "Yes. Robert asked me out again."

"Woo! Look at you. Showing those idiot boys up left and right. Is he taking you somewhere nice?"

I shrugged. "I don't know. He didn't say, and I didn't ask." I looked back to her. Now that she mentioned it, I hadn't really even thought of asking.

"Well, if he don't take you somewhere nice, you send him here. I'll straighten him out." She nodded, and then winked at me.

"I'll be sure to do that. You get some rest now." I leaned over her, pressing my lips to her forehead. "I'll come check on you in a little bit."

Adaline patted my cheek, smiling up at me. "You're a good girl, Juliet. More special than you know."

I looked down at her with a soft smile, feeling confused. "Thank you, Adaline."

Adaline grunted and dropped back onto her pillows. "All these naps, like I'm a child or something."

I smirked as I walked out of the room, hovering in the doorway until her breathing leveled out. Closing the door with care, I walked down the hall to the lounge. I smiled at Karen before crossing to the coffee machine.

"Hey, Juliet," Karen greeted me. "How was the beach?"

Snagging a muffin from the basket, I carried my cup toward her table and sat with a smile. "It was stormy," I replied. "Was it storming here?"

Secrets

Karen shook her head, setting down her e-reader. "No, it was pretty dry last week."

I nodded, an awkward silence stretched between us. Karen picked up her e-reader and went back to reading as I devoured my muffin and drained my mug. Rising from my chair, I made myself another cup of coffee.

"Hey, Karen—do you know how long Adaline has been sick?"

Glancing over my shoulder, I saw Karen shake her head as she leaned back in her chair. "Not long, she only started complaining of stomach pains yesterday."

I frowned and nodded, sipping the hot coffee. "Has she had anymore seizures?"

Karen sighed, setting her book down once more. "Why don't you read her chart and find out?"

I blew out a slow breath. Would it kill her to share information with me? Grabbing another muffin from the basket, I walked out of the lounge to the computer, leaving Karen to her reading.

With a few keyboard strokes, I logged in and pulled up Adaline's medical file. Pursing my lips, I scanned the screen as I examined the notations.

"No more seizures. No tests, no abnormalities," I muttered, tapping the screen. That was good news but for some reason, it brought me little peace.

I worked on the computer for the next couple of hours, until my back was aching from the hunched position I had been in. I groaned and straightened, checking my watch.

Time to log off.

I gathered my files, grabbing the records for the next two patients I needed to see. On my way to them,

I paused outside Adaline's room, warring with the decision to pop in on her. I hoped she had slept well and was feeling better.

An alarm blared with sudden urgency, causing those of us in the hall to jump in response. I heard a clamor rising behind me as the crash team approached.

"We have a code blue in room 46-A!" one of the team members frantically pushing the crash cart explained. "Call Doctor Robins!"

Instant fear gripped my heart, chilling me though as I watched the unit disappear into the room.

Adaline's room.

Gasping for breath, I shoved into the room, knocking aside a nurse exiting the room.

"Resume chest compressions! Where's that epi?" the crash nurse called, straddling Adaline as she pumped on her chest.

"No. No, no no no!" I screamed, stumbling into the room, my legs going numb. I bit my lower lip until pain shot through my body, my eyes locked onto the limp form of Adaline.

"Move out of the way!"

The gruff voice of Doctor Robins sounded in my ear as he pushed me aside. I stumbled and fell into the chair most often used by visitors. My heart lodged in my throat as he moved in, consulting with the crash team. With a shiver, I curled up in the chair and watched the heart monitor. The steady monotone sound that soon followed filled me with dread.

Flatline.

No. No! She is not dead!

Seconds crawled by as I stared at the heart monitor, willing the line to move, to peak.

Secrets

"Beat!" I ordered, not realizing until a moment after that I had spoken aloud. It didn't matter—no one seemed to notice anyway. Tears slid down my cheeks as I looked at Adaline's slack face. "Don't leave me," I whispered desperately.

Beep. Beep.

The line peaked once, then again. And again after that.

"We have sinus rhythm!" the charge nurse cried.

A rush of hope flared within me. Scooting to the edge of the chair, I looked at Adaline, willing her to open her eyes, to be okay.

Adaline coughed violently before coming awake, her arms flailing as she slapped at the nurses and doctor surrounding her. I shoved off my chair and ran to her side.

"Adaline!" I called in assurance. "Adaline, calm down! They're just trying to help you." Without thinking, I grabbed her flailing hand and pressed it to my chest, just above my racing heart. She stopped flailing almost immediately, her eyes blazing as they locked on mine. I held her stare, not caring that I was openly crying in front of everyone.

"Juliet, you came back," she slurred, her lips turning up into a crooked grin. Twisting, she placed her hand against mine. Her paper-thin skin was cold, sending chills down my spine.

"Don't ever do that to me again, okay?" I whispered to her, sniffling. I heard Doctor Robins call to me; I stepped away from Adaline, reluctant to leave her side.

"Are you the nurse on her rotation?" the doctor asked as I faced him, looking at me over the rims of his spectacles.

"Yes, sir. I am. I was just coming to check on her. I don't know what happened."

"Yes, well, I want you to stay in this room with her until your shift is over. She needs to be watched for the next twenty-four hours. I'm going to order a few tests and another EKG."

I nodded, standing there dumbly as Doctor Robins repeated his instructions to the charge nurse and left.

Once everyone was gone, I moved to Adaline's bedside, sitting on the edge of the mattress.

"What happened?" I asked as I looked down at her. Worry filled me, tearing at my gut as I scanned her pale face. For the first time since meeting her, she seemed very much her age.

Adaline shook her head, waving me off. "Just a little hiccup," she insisted. "I'm fine." Her eyes narrowed. "Don't look at me like that, child. I told you it would take more than this to kill me."

She sounded so confident, her wan smile smug. I couldn't help but laugh, though it held little humor.

"You really are a stubborn thing, aren't you?"

Adaline smiled and took my hand in both of hers. "You have no idea."

We sat quietly for a time, Adaline holding onto my hand. I was content to let her do so, needing the comfort of her touch. She dozed off and on, each time sending me into a slight panic until her eyelid would twitch or she would let go a rough snore.

I wondered if she knew how much she had come to mean to me. In the last year, this old woman had become my best friend. I would be lost without her cheeky smile, her sharp wit and sarcastic mind.

"Tell me, about the beach stud."

The whispered request broke me of my thoughts. Blinking, I looked down to find her smiling up at me. I smiled in return and squeezed her hand.

"All right, what do you want to know?"

"What was his name?"

"His name was Marsh. Marsh Darrow." I frowned, glancing at her as I realized they had the same last name. "Wait—"

Adaline's eyes widened, her lips parting in shock. A cool wave of worry filled me, my stomach clenching.

"Adaline? What's wrong? Are you having another episode?" I quickly looked toward the monitor, searching the screen for signs of distress.

Adaline shook her head, covering her mouth as she coughed. "No, no. Nothing like that. I told you, I'm fine, child."

I clasped her hand, settling back on the bed. "Then, what happened? You looked scared."

Adaline's expression was drawn and serious. "I was not expecting to hear you speak that name."

You know him, don't you? You know Marsh."

She nodded solemnly, her eyes holding mine. "Yes, child. I do."

I couldn't believe it. It was the last thing I had ever expected to hear from her. How could she know Marsh? Nothing was making sense today. I rubbed at my brow, wincing at the building headache.

"Adaline, I don't-I don't understand. How?"

Adaline sighed, shifting to sit up a bit straighter. She casually reached for the water on the bedside table and took a long drink, all the while my heart pounding in my chest. With all the scares I had over the last month, I was certain it had indented my ribs permanently.

"Adaline, how do you know Marsh?" I demanded, unable to wait any longer.

She sighed, looking toward me. Her eyes seemed brighter, less faded than before. It was unnerving.

Licking her lips, she nodded.

"Marsh Darrow is my grandson."

My whole world stopped as I stared at her. I felt paralyzed, unable to move or even think past that revelation. Her grandson? I shook my head, letting go a soft laugh of derision.

"That's not funny, Adaline."

"Do I look like I'm joking, child?" Adaline scoffed and narrowed her eyes at me. "A tall young man, with black hair and blue eyes, and a scar just under his right eye, yes?"

Her words washed over me, echoing over and over again in my mind. She described him perfectly, down to the scar I had longed to touch. Was the world really so small, as Marsh had joked? How could I have possibly met grandmother and grandson with no knowledge that there was a connection?

"Yes," I whispered, my throat tight. I struggled to breathe, my brain working overtime to sort everything out. It was strange, but why had she looked so frightened?

Adaline lay back on the pillows with an elongated sigh. "How exactly did you two meet at the beach?"

Even exhaustion and near death could not dull the sharpness of this woman. The faded blue depths of her eyes were brighter than ever, one brow quirked upward slightly. She was doing her best to appear disinterested, but for the first time, I saw through her guise.

"We met during a storm. I-I found him in a cave. He'd hurt his head, so I treated him."

I opened my mouth to ask her a question when she jerked up and gripped my forearms with surprising strength.

"What cave? What state was he in?" she demanded.

"He ... was knocked out. I don't know. It was a cave along the shoreline at Cannon Beach." I stared at her, wincing at her grip and her intensity. "Adaline, what is going on?"

"He hurt his head you said?" she demanded, ignoring my question.

"Yes. But I treated the wound. He didn't even need stitches. Adaline, you're hurting me."

She released me and jerked her hands away, staring down at them as if they were alien. She was shaking like a leaf in a strong wind. I moistened my lips, rubbing at my arms where she had grabbed me.

"I am sorry, child," she sighed. "I got carried away with worry. I have not seen my grandson in some time. Was he well?"

I nodded, still unsure of what to make of the situation. Her reaction had been far more than worry.

She had been scared. But of what?

Somehow, I knew that I would not get the answer.

"Yes, he was fine. Are you sure you're all right?"

Adaline nodded, patting my knee and offering a forced smile. "Yes, yes I'm well. Just tired. I'm going to rest now, Juliet. I've had enough excitement for the day I think."

Without giving me any space to object, Adaline turned her back on me. I didn't move, but within moments she was snoring softly. I narrowed my eyes at her, not convinced she was actually asleep. I remained on the bed until she let go a rather loud snore.

Defeated, I rose from the bed and left, stopping in the doorway to look back at her for a brief moment.

She was hiding something from me—something about Marsh. And I intended to find out what it was.

CHAPTER SIXTEEN

SATURDAY EVENING ARRIVED with a bang. I had spent the whole day puttering away, wasting time and now I was down to the wire. It was time to get ready. Rushing into my room, I pulled off my Tardis blue Doctor Who shirt and shimmied out of my jeans, leaving them in piles on the floor as I strode through the room. The wink of light reflecting off a surface stopped me in my tracks.

I stared at the silver ring resting on my nightstand. I had spent the whole week puzzling over the new information I received from Adaline and I still couldn't wrap my mind around it. Marsh was Adaline's grandson. The idea of it was so strange, and yet comforting somehow.

I *had* to stop thinking about Marsh. I was going out with Robert tonight and the last thing I needed was to be thinking about another man over dinner.

A small smile lit my lips as I brought Robert's face to my mind's eye. He was handsome, though in a different way from Marsh. Where Marsh had been lean and slender, Robert was broader, more muscular. He appeared to be the type who enjoyed hitting the gym. I smiled stupidly as I imagined him standing before a mirrored wall, doing arm curls with a twenty-pound weight. Shirtless.

I giggled at myself as heat filled my cheeks. I was a grown woman! It was perfectly all right for me to imagine my dinner date shirtless. Clearing my throat, I turned and crossed to my closet.

Now, on to the real issue. What am I going to wear?

Pursing my lips, I slid my closet door to the side and looked at my wardrobe. My smile turned to a frown as I flipped through my items.

"No, no, no. Boring, boring. Too old. Too young. Yikes, too slutty—wait, when did I buy this?"

I pulled out the tiny red dress in question, looking it over. I honestly did not remember ever buying the dress. It wasn't strapless, but it might as well have been with how small those straps were. I stepped back, holding it up to my chest as I turned toward the mirror.

"Huh," I mused as I looked at my reflection. The dress would fall to about mid-thigh, but wouldn't be indecent if I paired it with a pair of black leggings. I grinned brightly and danced in place. Not only was I going to have fun tonight, I was going to look *hot*.

Shoes!

The thought stopped my spinning. I needed to find shoes to match!

Tossing the dress carelessly onto my bed, I tore back to the closet and shoved my clothes aside, looking over my shoe rack with worry. I almost jumped in delight as my eyes landed on a pair of vibrant blue peep toe kitten heels adorned with delicate blue flowers with pearl centers. I pulled them out and looked them over, a broad grin on my lips.

"Perfect."

I dropped the shoes onto the bed, grabbed a towel and headed off to the shower. I spent an hour standing under the spray, slathering myself with my special body wash I reserved for dates and big events. I let the hot water sluice over my body and work the kinks out of my muscles. It felt amazing. I only turned off the taps when the water began to run cool.

Flicking off the tap, I stepped out, wrapped myself in a towel and set to drying my hair. Thoughts of Adaline crowded my mind, as the monotonous buzz of the dryer filled my ears.

I was worried about her—probably more worried than she was about herself, stubborn old thing. She might be comfortable waving off a near death experience, but neither Doctor Robins nor I were being so blasé with her health.

It took the whole remaining hour and a half to get ready. I didn't want to miss a step. My stomach was in knots as I slid my feet into my shoes and grabbed my clutch purse out of my closet, transferring my wallet and keys into it. I looked at my watch again and stomped my foot.

"Juliet! Knock it off! He'll be here when he gets here," I scolded myself. I needed to calm down or I would be a nervous wreck by the time he arrived. Taking one last look in the mirror, I admired my makeup, my artfully styled hair that had actually done what I wanted for a change.

"I look *hot.*" I chuckled at the disbelief in my voice before turning in observation of my outfit. The buzzing of the intercom made me jump. Amused at myself, I walked to the door and pressed the intercom button.

"Hello?"

"Juliet? Oh, good, I got the right number." His soft chuckle had my blood heating. "It's Robert, may I come up?"

"Yes," I squeaked, pressing the release button. I waited nervously for Robert to knock on my door, twisting my clutch until I feared I would mangle it. I forced myself to put it down, grabbing a dishtowel and wiping off my sweaty palms. At this rate, I was going to have to reapply my deodorant.

My heart jumped in my chest at the staccato knocks on my door.

Okay, you can do this, I told myself. I worked up what I hoped was a normal smile, and not the slightly crazed one I felt like I was wearing and pulled open the door.

Robert turned as the door opened, a warm and inviting smile on his lips. He looked amazing. He wore a pale yellow button down beneath a midnight blue blazer that sat nicely on his broad shoulders, and had paired them with dark slacks. I swallowed at the spicy scent of him, his cologne making my head spin in the most pleasurable of ways.

"Juliet, you look ravishing," he complimented. He smiled wider, exuding charm as he held out a single white rose to me. I blushed and took the rose, bringing it to my nose and inhaling the subtle scent.

"Thank you," I replied. "You're looking pretty sharp yourself. Let me just put this in water and grab my purse."

I stepped away from the door and moved toward the kitchen, opening a cabinet at random and plucking down a glass. My hands shook with nerves as I filled the glass with water and dropped the rose into it. I grabbed my clutch to give my hands something to do and turned, only to find myself face to face with Robert.

"Oh!" I said in a shocked little cry, taking a step back and laughing self-consciously.

"Forgive me," Robert apologized. "I was curious to see your place. I like it, it's very you."

"Oh, no, that's ... it's fine. I should have invited you in."

Robert smiled, his brown eyes bright with mirth. "Shall we?" His deep baritone was a delicious purr across my senses as he offered me his arm. He was insanely handsome, with dark close-cropped hair, and light stubble clinging to his strong jawline. I felt like my tongue had swollen to twice its normal size.

"Uh huh," I nodded stupidly, my mouth hanging slightly open, in awe of him. With effort, I swallowed and smiled back as he led me out the door and down to his sleek, black sports car. I whistled softly as I looked it over. "Wow, that's a really nice car."

Robert smiled, opening the door for me. "Thank you. I got it for a steal."

"A steal?" I chuckled as I slid into the car, curling my legs as he closed the door. I was sure his steal would pay off my car, my rent for a month and still leave me some left over. I glanced over at him as he slid into the driver's seat and started the engine. "Aren't you an EMT?"

"Yes, I am. Why?" Robert glanced at me before pulling out into traffic.

"Because if you can afford this kind of car on an

EMT's paycheck, then I need to change professions." I grinned at him as I slid my hand over the polished leather, allowing myself to dream about what it would be like to own a car like this.

Robert chuckled and shook his head, flexing his fingers on the wheel. "I normally don't admit this so early into a relationship, but I have family money."

I sighed, my dream popping and running in sad little rivulets down the window. "That must be nice."

"It has certainly come in handy. However, I do my best not to rely on it."

I snorted, "If *I* had family money, I'd be relying on it all the time."

Robert chuckled. I smiled and closed my eyes, leaning my head back as I listened to the light classical music playing from the stereo.

"Where are we going?" I asked.

"It's a surprise," he replied.

I groaned. "I really don't like surprises."

"Trust me, you'll like this one."

I pursed my lips, not entirely sure I believed him. Adaline's words came back to my mind and caused my lips to turn up into a smile. I cast a quick glance in his direction, watching him as he concentrated on the road.

He was so handsome. My mother had always warned me against handsome men, saying that you had to be even more vigilant around them. A part of me wanted to rally against her words simply because she had said them.

Dismissing thoughts of my mother, I looked out the window, enjoying the cityscape passing by in a blur of colored lights.

Secrets

The drive was pleasant and brief and I caught myself leaning forward in my seat as I looked out the window.

I gasped as the sign of the restaurant came into view. "Andina? You're seriously taking me to Andina?"

"Yes, I seriously am," Robert confirmed. "Is that a problem?"

"No. I just ... It's a really nice restaurant."

"Yes, it is. Shall we?"

Robert chuckled and exited the car. I sat in my seat, staring at the building with growing trepidation. It was only a matter of time before I said something stupid and embarrassed myself.

I smiled at Robert as he opened the car door and offered me his hand. Swallowing down my nerves, I looped my arm with his as we walked into the restaurant.

The place was beautifully decorated, with dark chocolate colored tables covered with ivory cloths. Exposed wooden beams gave it a rustic feel, while the circular cloth wrapped lights offered a modern touch.

The hostess smiled brightly as we approached the podium.

"Welcome to Andina!" she greeted us. "Do you have a reservation?"

"Yes, Robert Ahlström."

Robert smiled at me as the hostess nodded, checked off his name and led us to our table. After we were seated, I slapped my hands on the table and leaned forward.

"This is amazing," I gushed. "I've wanted to come here for months but I could never afford it, and the wait list for a reservation is as long as my leg. How did you do it? Did you have to call in a favor or throw money at them or-?"

I stopped talking abruptly, slapping my hand over my mouth in horror.

Tell me I didn't say any of that out loud.

I squeezed my eyes closed in embarrassment and lowered my hand slowly.

"I am so sorry. I talk a lot when I'm nervous and I don't know when to shut up and I just go on and on and ... Clearly this is an issue, as I'm doing it again, so I'm just going to slink under the table and die now."

I leaned back in my seat and covered my red-hot face with my hands.

To my relief, Robert laughed. I looked at him through my fingers, my heart stuttering at his grin and the light of humor in his eyes.

"Yes, this place is amazing, though I've only been here a few times. And yes, my family has a standing reservation at many of the restaurants in town, which I abuse from time to time to impress a girl. And while you have amazing legs, I don't believe the wait list is quite so long."

I laughed, dropping my hands into my lap and smiling at him.

Whew. Disaster averted.

The rest of the dinner went amazingly. Robert was charming, and easy to talk to and we spent most of the night trading off entertaining stories about patients.

"That reminds me, I wanted to ask how your patient was doing. Adaline, I believe her name was?"

"I'm honestly not sure. The doctor can't seem to figure out what's wrong with her. She ... She flat lined earlier this week, actually." I frowned, looking into my wine glass as my thoughts drifted.

"That is horrible. I'm truly sorry to hear that." Setting aside his wineglass, Robert stretched out his hand and took mine. His thumb glided over the back of my hand, causing little shivers of delight to race up and down my arm.

I pulled my hand away gently as my pulse raced. Licking my lips, I smiled at him and reached for my wine. "Thank you. I'm pretty worried about her."

Robert slowly closed his hand into a fist before pulling it back across the table. Clearing his throat, he reached for his wine glass as well. "You two are close?"

"Yes, we are."

"In that case, I hope she recovers quickly." Robert smiled at me, setting his glass aside. "I did not mean to bring up such a somber topic."

I waved my hand, offering him a reassuring smile. "No, don't worry about it. It was sweet of you to ask. She'll be thrilled to hear you took me to such a nice place."

"You spoke to her of me?" Robert asked in disbelief, his brow rising faintly.

"Only a little bit. I mean, I only mentioned we were going out. Nothing major. I don't really know anything major to tell ... except that you're rich."

I frowned, clamping down on my babbling once more.

This man is going to walk away from this confident that I am insane.

"Yet. You don't know anything major, yet." Robert mused with a grin. Lifting his hand, he signaled for the check. When it came, I craned my neck, trying to catch a glimpse of the total, but was unable to. It was probably a good thing I didn't.

Rising from his seat, Robert offered me his arm once more.

"Aren't you a gentleman?" I smiled in appreciation as I entwined my arm with his and allowed him to lead me from the restaurant.

"I do try to be. My mother would be pleased that all her hard work is paying off."

"Does your mother live nearby?" I asked as we stepped out into the night.

Robert shook his head, opening the passenger side door for me. "No, she does not. She lives in Lerwick, an island off the northern coast of Scotland."

"Oh, wow. Is that where you grew up?"

"It is indeed, yes." Robert gestured for me to get into the car and I did so, my mind reeling.

Marsh was from Ireland and Robert was from a Scottish island. What were the odds?

THE RIDE BACK to my apartment went just as smoothly as the drive to the restaurant. I closed my eyes and leaned back. The soft piano music that washed over me combined with the wine was helping to relax me. I let my head loll to the side so I was looking at Robert, allowing my eyes to trail over his form. I smiled.

"Thank you for dinner. It was amazing."

"I told you that you would enjoy the surprise," Robert grinned as he confidently directed the car into a parking spot in front of my building. "May I walk you up?" he asked after parking.

"I would like that a lot," I smiled brightly, watching him as he exited the car and crossed to open

Secrets

my door for me. I loved that he opened the doors for me. And he had pushed my chair in at the restaurant. Maybe chivalry wasn't dead after all.

"I must tell you, you look ravishing in that dress."

I blushed and giggled, leaning against him as we walked up the steps. "Why thank you, sir. I think this might be my new favorite dress."

"Well, it's definitely mine." Robert winked at me, pulling open the outer door. He pressed his hand to my lower back and guided me through the door before following me inside.

"And I think it would look smashing on you," I teased, taking painstaking care as we climbed the stairs. Aside from my earlier blunder, the night was going well and I did not want to screw it up by falling on my face.

Robert laughed and shook his head. "If only I had your legs."

I grinned at him, resting my hand on his arm. "But, you don't." I giggled once more, turning my head to point out my door. "Hey, why don't you have more of an accent?"

I stopped dead in my steps. My eyes widened, lips parting in shock as I stared at the hunched figure sitting on my doorstep.

"Oh my God," I whispered, sobering instantly as I disengaged from Robert and stepped slowly forward.

His clothes were filthy, the hem of his trench coat ragged and torn. The backpack we had purchased was also torn and covered in dirt and what I had a sinking suspicion was blood. Reaching out, I gently touched his shoulder.

"Marsh?" I whispered.

Marsh grunted softly, shifting and lifting his head

with effort. I gasped as his face came into view. The entire right side of his face was swollen and bruised, his eye nearly swollen shut. Dried blood clung to his lips and chin.

"Marsh, what happened to you?" I whispered, tears burning my eyes as I crouched down before him, momentarily forgetting about Robert. Fear filled my stomach like it had been coated with ice. Kicking off my shoes, I moved onto my knees as he groaned, opening his left eye and looking at me. His cracked lips moved into a crooked grin.

"Juliet." Marsh lifted his hand and cupped my cheek, running his thumb along my lips. His voice was rough and his lips bled as he spoke.

"Shh, I'm here. Don't talk. Let's get you inside."

Swallowing down my concern, I pushed my shoulder under his arm, straining as I tried to lift him. "Marsh, I need you to help me."

"May I be of assistance?"

My head jerked up at Robert's offer and I nodded frantically. "Yes, please. Help me get him inside?"

With Robert's help, we lifted Marsh to his feet, the motion eliciting a sharp cry of pain from Marsh. Fumbling with my purse, I yanked my keys out and shoved them into the lock. I braced my hand on Marsh's chest as I threw open the door, grunting as Robert and I carried him toward the couch.

"Okay, easy, easy," I guided. "Just set him down gently." I sighed, looking over Marsh with concern before stepping back and looking to Robert. "I'm sorry, this was unexpected."

Robert shook his head, offering a smile. "Do not worry, we can always have coffee another day."

"Of course."

Crossing my arms over my chest I walked Robert toward the door. "Thank you, for everything,"

"You're welcome," Robert replied, kneeling down and picking up my shoes, handing them to me. I smiled, opening my mouth to thank him again when he leaned in, pressing his lips to my cheek. He lingered, his hot breath sending chills dancing along my neck and shoulders.

"Another time, goodnight, Juliet."

I looked longingly after him as he stepped out of my doorway and walked down the hall. Sighing, I closed my door and set the locks, turning toward Marsh.

When did my life stop being easy?

Blowing out a breath, I walked toward the couch, biting my lower lip as I knelt down in front of Marsh.

"Marsh, can you hear me?" I asked.

I looked him over using a more critical eye than I had in the hallway. His eye looked horrible, a jagged cut ran up from just below the socket and fanned outward toward the temple. I winced as I caught sight of the bruising around his neck.

"Marsh? Marsh! Can you hear me?" I raised my voice, relieved when he jerked and groaned. "No, no, don't move. Can you tell me what happened?"

"Juliet," Marsh whispered, my name sounding like a plea. He struggled to open his eyes. "God, it hurts."

"I'll be right back." I touched his knee before rising to my feet and running into the kitchen. I filled a bowl with warm water and grabbed a towel, moving quickly but carefully back toward my patient while taking care not to spill a drop. I set the water aside and looked at him.

"Marsh, I need to get you out of those clothes."

"Words I thought you'd never say," he chuckled weakly, then coughed and groaned, grabbing at his left side.

"Okay, Romeo. No more flirting. Can you stand?"

I slid my hands along his shoulders as he shook his head in the negative. I pushed his coat off and pulled his arms free, taking care of any injuries he might have. Tossing it aside, I set about unbuttoning his shirt. I gasped in shock at the cuts and bruises that littered his chest. The left side of his body was cast in shades of ugly black and purple.

"Oh, Marsh," I breathed, gingerly running my fingertips along the mass of bruises. I instantly regretted it when he hissed and jerked away from my touch. "I'm sorry!"

Biting my lower lip, I grabbed the water and dipped the cloth into it. I rose up on my knees and lightly dabbed at his lips and the cut near his eye.

"Always ... taking care of ... me," Marsh panted, a pained smile resting on his lips.

"Well, I wouldn't have to if you would stop getting hurt," I teased lightly, keeping my tone carefree and easy. "Tell me what happened?"

"It was nothing. I was in the wrong place. I did not see them coming until it was too late."

"Them?"

"The men who beat me up."

"Men? How many were there?"

"Six," Marsh coughed and grunted, wincing as he jerked his head away from my touch.

"Six? Six guys beat you up?" I pulled back, gaping

as I let my hand fall against my knee. "What did they want?"

"To kill me."

I stared at him, shaking my head in disbelief. "What? No, I'm sure they were just ... just looking for money, or something."

"No, Juliet," he insisted. Pain and rage filled the depths of his icy blue eyes. "They were sent to kill me."

CHAPTER SEVENTEEN

"SAY WHAT NOW?" I was sure I had heard him wrong. That fear I felt earlier came back tenfold.

"They were sent to kill me. I am just glad you were not there when they came."

I licked my lips, holding up a hand, palm out. "Wait, just give me a moment." I shook my head faintly, trying to make sense of his words. "How, exactly, do you know they were sent to kill you?"

Marsh sighed and groaned, clutching his side. "Juliet, I promise I will tell you everything. But right now, it really hurts."

"Right, of course." I nodded, forcing my mind to think of him as a patient first. I dropped the towel and rose to my feet, darting into my room for my emergency kit. I checked the contents before snapping the lid closed and rushing back to Marsh.

"Okay, I'm going to take your blood pressure and listen to your breathing," I said, glancing at him as I wrapped my blood pressure cuff around his arm. I noted his numbers mentally—thankfully, they were within normal range. Setting aside the cuff, I got out my stethoscope and listened to his heart and lungs.

"Everything sounds clear. I'm going to give you something for the pain now. And I'm sorry, but I'm pretty sure your ribs are broken."

Marsh groaned as I rose, this time leaving him to fetch him a glass of water. I placed the pain pills on his lips before holding the glass to them.

"Drink it all. I'm pretty sure you're dehydrated," I instructed. I set the empty glass aside and sighed as Marsh leaned his head back against the couch, closing his eyes. I had so many questions. I wanted to demand answers, not force myself to be patient.

Marsh gave another coughing chuckle before groaning and wincing. "Damn, that hurts. I thought they were broken."

"You're filthy. You need to get into the shower and clean up before I treat you anymore. Do you think you can stand?"

Marsh nodded, and after much grunting and cursing on both our parts, we got him to his feet.

"Lean on me," I said, wrapping my arm around his waist. I grunted in a truly un-ladylike manner as his weight came down on me. I thanked my lucky stars that my apartment was small as I half led, half carried Marsh into my room and through to the bathroom. I propped him against the wall as I turned on the shower.

Swallowing hard, I looked to Marsh, a deep blush creeping up my neck and heating my cheeks. "Okay, I'm going to have to ... undress you now."

Marsh smiled crookedly at me, his head lolling to the side so he could look at me with his good eye. "I'll try not to get too excited."

I laughed softly, removing his shirt from his

shoulders and unbuttoning his pants with shaking fingers. I did my best to compartmentalize my mind. But there was no way I could keep from noticing his toned abs, the darkness of his skin. Inhaling deeply, I slid his jeans down, removing them as I set his shoes aside. His legs were lean and muscular, and devoid of any major damage.

Swallowing heavily, I reached for the waistband of his boxers. I gasped when his hand closed over mine.

"I ... tried to stop you sooner. I think I would rather be fully healed when you undress me."

I looked up at him, my breath trembling though my lips. His fingers left trails of fire wherever they touched my flesh. I had never wanted to burn so much in my life.

Slowly, I straightened, keeping my eyes locked on his. I didn't move my hands from his waist. My thumbs moved of their own volition, gliding along his flesh and eliciting a deep groan from him.

Steam filled the bathroom, lending a dreamlike haze to everything. His eyes on mine, Marsh cupped my cheek, drawing his thumb along my lower lip and causing them to tremble open.

I panted softly, unable to catch my breath. I licked my lips and tasted him. Pleasure shot through me as his hand moved from my cheek to the nape of my neck. In a fluid motion, one I wouldn't have thought possible due to his injuries, he bent his head and crushed his lips to mine.

My world exploded. Flashes of light lit like fireworks behind my eyelids. Urgency filled us both as I stepped into him, my hands gripping his hips tightly.

Using both hands now, he cupped my face, tilting

my head as he deepened the kiss.

The roughness of his lips made me gasp in pleasure. His tongue teased against mine as my lips parted, shooting arrows of desire to the deepest parts of me. His hands moved down my back, fingertips burning holes of pleasure across my skin.

My knees quaked and I moaned lustily as his lips left mine and trailed down my neck, gliding over my shoulder. Closing my eyes, I tilted my head, offering him more room to roam as I moved my hands upward, grazing them over his sides.

Marsh hissed in pain as my hand ran over his broken ribs. Cursing, he leaned away from me, both of us panting heavily.

"I'm sorry," I gasped, my eyes wide and blurred with desire. I felt bad that I had hurt him, but I selfishly wanted nothing more than for him to kiss me again. I felt more alive than I ever had before, my blood zinging through my veins.

Marsh looked down at me, a deliciously crooked smile on his lips. "It's probably for the best. I'm really in no condition to ... continue."

I blinked, not understanding at first. Then it dawned on me.

"Oh! Oh, right. Of course. I-I'm just going to ... go find you something to wear."

I backed away from him, my hormones screaming in protest. His eyes never left me, thrilling every molecule in my body. I turned abruptly and all but ran from the bathroom, grabbing the bedpost and leaning against it.

Oh my God!

I felt like I couldn't breathe. I was too hot, too

stirred up. More than anything, I wanted to march back into that bathroom and climb on top of that man. I touched my neck where his lips had been and stifled a moan of pleasure at the memory.

Blowing out a breath, I shook my head.

Focus.

I strode from the bedroom, crouching down by the couch. I reached for Marsh's backpack. Unzipping it, I was relieved to find that he'd managed to keep the clothes I'd bought for him.

Someone was trying to kill him.

I frowned as the possibility washed over me, chilling me to my core. Why would someone want to kill Marsh? Shaking off the thought violently, I pulled out a fresh pair of boxers and stood, walking back into the bedroom.

His reflection in the mirror was blurred and distorted from the condensation. I stared at that reflection, imagining the dripping water on the mirror was on his skin. My body tingled at the thought of watching those droplets roll down his stomach and along his thighs. I bit my lip hard to keep from sighing aloud.

"I brought you some clean underwear," I called out, stepping toward the bathroom and holding them out.

Marsh stepped out of the bathroom, a towel slung low over his hips. My mouth dropped open as I got my wish. A dark circle of ink rested on the left side of his chest, a blue seal breaking up the black background. I watched those crystalline droplets from his shoulders down, through the darkness of his chest hair and lower until they gave up their journey and were caught by the towel around his waist.

Marsh looked at me as he gingerly dried his hair off with a smaller towel, slowly lowering his arm as I continued to just stare at him.

"Juliet? Are you all right?"

I snapped my jaw closed with an audible click and looked away quickly. "Yeah, I'm fine. How are you?"

A seal? Why does he have a seal tattoo?

Marsh studied me a minute longer before nodding. "I'm feeling much better."

I walked toward him, taking hold of his chin and examining the cut below his eye. Relief warred with confusion as I studied the cut. It seemed smaller, as if it had already begun healing. I shook off the thought. It had probably just appeared worse than it was, and a good cleaning had revealed it for its true nature. Frowning, I looked to his ribs and blinked in shock, lightly running my fingers along them.

He flinched and grunted, but he didn't pull away. The bruises were already dissipating.

"What in the world? "I whispered in bafflement, moving my hand along the area once more.

"Something wrong?" Marsh asked, dipping his head and trying to catch my eye.

"No. Maybe. It doesn't make sense." I laughed softly in confusion before looking him dead in the eye, my expression serious. "On a scale of one to ten, ten being the worse pain you've ever felt, how are you feeling right now?"

Marsh shrugged and tossed the towel he had been using to dry his hair toward the bathroom. I watched in shock and horror as he twisted at the waist to do so.

What the hell?

"I would say a five, perhaps even a six."

"And when you first got here? When I found you?"

"That would have easily been a ten, if not higher."

I shook my head and touched my temples with my fingers as I worked to make sense of what I was seeing. A hysterical laugh bubbled up in my chest. "This makes no sense."

"Actually, it does." Marsh sighed softly before reaching out for me. "Juliet, there's something I need to tell you."

I blinked at him, lowering my hands from my head. "What?"

Marsh inhaled deeply, his eyes on me. I watched as he tensed and I panicked.

"Maybe you should get dressed first?" I asked quickly. "Yes. Get dressed. I'll go wait in the living room." My words tumbled over themselves as they raced to leave my lips. I didn't know why I was stalling, but something in his tone had me wanting to run scared.

"All right. I will be right out, then."

I nodded, dropping my eyes to the floor as I hurried from the room. My heart raced and a cold sweat coated my palms. I scrubbed them against my thighs as I struggled to regulate my breathing, feeling the hysteria clawing at my throat once more.

Breathe, Juliet. Just breathe.

How was he healing? That was the only possible explanation for what I'd seen. Was it some sort of genetic disorder?

I shook my head, brow furrowed as I paced the room. I had never heard of anything like this before.

Secrets

Not in any of the studies I'd read in nursing school, or since. And though I wasn't certain of much right now, I was positive that if someone with regenerative powers existed outside of comic books, it would have made headlines the world over.

"Juliet?"

I turned, swallowing as I looked at Marsh. My heart rate ramped up, drowning out every sound except for the steady *whoosh, whoosh* of my rapid pulse in my ears.

Marsh looked at me, shifting his feet before moving across the room to grab his backpack and draw out a pair of jeans. He looked distinctly uncomfortable.

I watched him dress before closing my eyes and releasing a shuddering breath.

Calm down. Breathe. Just breathe.

Marsh buttoned his jeans and looked to me. "We need to talk."

I nodded, shaking out my hands and walking stiffly toward the couch. I sat down, placing my hands carefully on my knees and focused on my breathing. Marsh sat beside me, allowing some distance to be kept between us. He shifted and I felt his eyes on me.

"Juliet, where did you get this?"

I looked up quickly, not having expected the question. Marsh stared at me, his expression somber. My brow furrowed before I focused on the silver circle held between his index finger and thumb.

The ring.

"I ... I found it. In the cave." I shook my head. "What does that have to do with anything?"

"And this? Did you find this in the cave as well?" Marsh demanded, holding up the strange cloth. I stared at him, my confusion mounting.

What was going on?

"Yes, I found that there as well. What is this all about, Marsh?"

Marsh gave a soft sardonic chuckle as he looked at the ring and the cloth. "More than you could possibly imagine."

I watched him slide the ring onto the third finger of his right hand, and sigh. A faint flash, there and gone, lit the room. It was so abrupt, I was positive I had imagined it.

"Those are the things you lost, aren't they? The reason you were so desperate to find the cave?"

"Yes," Marsh said as he nodded slowly, looking at the cloth stretched between his hands. "Do you know what this is?"

I shook my head in the negative, feeling my body tingle and my stomach tighten in anticipation. Finally I would get the answers I so desperately needed.

Marsh inhaled, continuing to avert his eyes from me, long enough that I began to fear he would say nothing more. I curled my hands into fists and bit my lip to keep from screaming at him, forcing myself to remain silent as I watched him intently.

"When I last saw you, you asked me a question. Do you recall what that was?"

I blinked rapidly as I shook my head. "No."

"You asked, 'What *are* you?'"

I had? A memory flashed. Our lips inches apart. My whispered question. Him walking away.

I shifted, forcing my hands to relax as I took a steadying breath. "Okay."

"I am ready to answer that question. My memories

have returned. All of them. I remember who I am. What I am."

I quaked with nervous excitement. My heart leapt to hear his memories had returned. But my joy was quickly displaced with fear of the unknown.

Marsh turned his body so he was facing me straight on, his eyes boring into me.

"I am a Selkie," he whispered.

CHAPTER EIGHTEEN

"A WHAT?"

"A Selkie. Juliet, I am entrusting you with this secret, and must entreat that you tell no one. My life, and those of my family, would be in mortal danger." Marsh lunged at me, grabbing my hands and gripping them tightly. "Please, Juliet. Swear to me that you will tell no one."

I swallowed heavily; panic fluttered in my heart like a crazed butterfly.

"I swear," I whispered, wondering what I was getting myself into.

"I am sure you have many questions." Marsh licked his lips, rubbing his palms together before looking at me and offering a nervous smile.

I ran my fingers through my hair, dropping my head into my hands. "I-I do. Uh, a Selkie? I don't ... even know what that is." I felt like I was living in an episode of the Twilight Zone.

"We are creatures of the sea. In our natural forms, we appear as seals."

"You're a seal?" I slapped a hand over my lips to stop the laugh that bubbled up from escaping.

Marsh chuckled softly, rubbing at his brow. "Sometimes, yes."

"Like, a seal, seal?"

Marsh lifted his brows and lowered his hand, his lips twitching. "Are there other kinds?"

"Well, apparently!" I slapped my hands on my thighs and shoved myself to my feet, pacing the room. I rubbed at my forehead, shaking my head against the information I was being given. "This can't be real." I could feel Marsh watching me from his spot on the couch, letting me pace, allowing me time to work through it all. "So, you're a Selkie thing. And that means that sometimes you're a seal?" I looked at him, mentally assessing everything I knew about him. He had never seemed crazy or unstable to me before. But two head wounds later, I was beginning to doubt his sanity. Best to tread carefully.

"In the very short version, yes."

I looked him in the eye, wanting nothing more than to scream, *prove it*. I gave another soft laugh and stopped my pacing.

"What is that?" I demanded, pointing at the cloth held lightly in his hands.

Marsh inhaled deeply through his nose, shoulders tensing as he looked down at his hands. "It is my skin."

"Your ... skin?"

"Yes. My sealskin. It must have been knocked free during the storm."

"Knocked free ..." I nodded, lifting my eyes to his, biting down on the hard bubble of hysteria that rose in my throat.

"Yes, which is why you found an injured man in that cave and not a seal."

I licked my lips, the action quickly becoming a nervous habit. I shivered, wrapping my arms around myself. "And the ring?"

"It is a family ring. Passed down the male line. My grandmother gave it to me after my father died."

His words resonated inside of me and I barked out a sharp laugh. "That reminds me. I know her. Your grandmother."

"What?" Marsh hissed, rising slowly from the couch, still favoring his left side.

"She's my patient."

Marsh shook his head, his expression baffled. "Why is she in Oregon?"

"She's been here before, off and on for the last couple of years. You didn't know?"

"It became harder to stay in touch after I left Ireland." Marsh dragged his hand through his hair, leaving it spiked and disheveled. "This is not good."

"It's not good for you to be near your grandmother? Why not? No, wait." I held up a hand, cutting him off. "I don't think I can process anymore."

Marsh nodded, smirking at me. "Fair enough."

I blew out a breath and looked at him for a long moment. "Prove it."

The challenge hung in the air. The words had slipped out without a thought, but now that I had spoken them I realized how badly I needed him to do just that.

"What?"

"Prove it!" I screamed, shocking us both with my outburst.

Marsh stared at me with fear and uncertainty in his eyes before he nodded. "As you wish." He reached for his pelt, lovingly stroking the soft skin as he looked up at me, appearing completely unsure. "It's really very simple, Juliet," he said, his voice barely above a whisper.

I watched as he unfurled the skin, giving it a gentle shake. He kept his eyes downcast as he unbuttoned his jeans, removing them and his boxers. I knew I shouldn't look, but I couldn't drag my eyes away.

Once nude, he draped the skin around his shoulders. As the pelt made contact with flesh, the air began to pulse.

Marsh's eyes locked on mine, growing darker as a deep, midnight blue took over the icy tone of his irises. Chills skittered down my spine, my breathing ragged.

Slowly, he spread the pelt, which seemed to grow as he caressed it. He smoothed it over his shoulders, his torso, and his arms. It clung to him, adhering to his human skin completely.

The pulse intensified, slamming into my chest with such force it stole my breath. A faint golden glow filled the space around Marsh as he worked the pelt down his legs, smoothing until no flesh could be seen. He straightened, his eyes meeting mine, latching on and holding for what felt like a lifetime. His fingers trembled as he reached behind him, gripping the pelt and pulling it over his head, covering his face.

The golden glow flashed brightly, and suddenly, Marsh was no longer standing before me.

I blinked and looked down, my breath coming in strangled gasps. A scream bubbled up in my throat as I found myself staring into the familiar ice blue eyes of a seal.

As I stared at the seal, I felt the hysteria growing.

Closing my eyes, I let my head fall back and gave into the laughter. It burst out of my lips, filling the room and shaking my body. I laughed until my sides ached and tears streamed down my cheeks.

I had been questioning his sanity and here I was, laughing like a loon. That thought only made me laugh harder. I bent at the waist, gripping my stomach and sucking in gulps of air. The air around me pulsed and I was blinded by another golden flash.

"Juliet, are you okay?"

The concern in Marsh's tone made me jerk my head up. Slowly I straightened, pressing my lips together as I stared at the ceiling and shook my head minutely, tears dripping down my cheeks.

"No. I'm not even *close* to okay," I sniffled as I scrubbed the heels of my hands across my cheeks.

Marsh cursed softly as he closed the distance between us. Taking my hand he turned me slightly and pulled me into him. I resisted at first, shaking my head before giving into the comfort he was offering.

My head fit perfectly in the space between his shoulder and neck. I couldn't help marveling at the warmth of him, yet again. His scent washed over me, calming me to the depths of my soul.

How was it that the date was the highlight of my week only a few hours ago? The date wasn't anything compared to this. I struggled to get my breathing under control as I hiccupped. Marsh crooned softly, stroking my hair and my back rhythmically.

"I'm sorry," Marsh whispered against my ear, the heat of his breath doing wonders to erase the chills the hysteria had brought about.

I nodded mutely, pulling out of his embrace. My

world had been turned upside down in a matter of moments. Yet no matter how hard it was to believe, Marsh had proven himself to me.

"Juliet?" Marsh whispered, cupping my cheek and dashing away a trailing tear with his thumb.

"Yeah?" I croaked, my voice hoarse from my earlier hysterics.

"I am sorry that I ruined your date."

The date had been the furthest thing from my mind. I shook my head, covering his hand with my own. "You didn't ruin the date, just the end of it."

I gave him a faint smile and was rewarded with his soft chuckle. It was then that it hit me that he was completely naked.

"Uh, Marsh?" I blushed and directed my eyes skyward, though they didn't stay that way for long.

"Yes?"

"You're, um, still naked."

Marsh looked down at himself before offering an apology and stepping back to get his jeans. I bit my bottom lip, stealing a glance at him and smiling softly to myself. I needed to stop being so prudish. He was gorgeous and desirable, and I certainly wanted him.

And he was a seal. Sometimes.

I laughed to myself. I was insane. I had to be. There was no other explanation for what I was feeling. I covered my lips and turned away as I giggled. I had run the gamut of emotions tonight and suddenly found myself exhausted.

My giggles quickly turned into a yawn that turned into a startled cry as Marsh touched my shoulders.

Marsh jerked his hands away and held them up, palms out. "Easy," he assured. "I will not hurt you. I said your name twice."

I pressed my hand to my heart and sighed. "I'm sorry. I was thinking."

"You have much to think about. You should get some sleep. I will gather my things and-"

"No!" I pointed at him, my eyes wide. "You are not walking out on me again."

His mouth moved to speak, but he paused, seemingly reconsidering his words. "As you wish, then. I will remain in your apartment." Marsh's lips twitched as he lowered his hands.

"Good. Okay." I exhaled, weariness washing over me in waves. My knees shook and gave out, sending me falling to the floor in a rush of dizziness.

Marsh's strong arms caught me before I hit the floor. He lifted me easily, as if I weighed nothing. I sucked in a breath, looking up at him.

"Thank you," I whispered, my head still spinning.

"You should sleep," Marsh murmured, carrying me across the living room and into my bedroom.

"Marsh! No! Your ribs! You shouldn't be carrying me!" I tapped at his chest repeatedly with my fist, rolling my eyes as he ignored me. "Marsh, I mean it!"

Marsh set me down on the bed, his hands resting lightly at my sides. "My ribs are fine, Juliet. Healing is one of the perks of my pod."

"Oh," I looked up at him. My head was pounding from exhaustion. Licking my lips, I scooted back on the bed with a heavy yawn before lying on my side. I noticed him moving to leave and I jerked upright, my hand shooting out in protest.

"Marsh, wait. Stay … stay with me?" My throat was tight as I spoke the question, fear and nerves riddling my system.

Marsh regarded me silently for a time before nodding slowly and crossing to the bed. The mattress shifted and I rolled slightly, coming to settle on my side as he moved in place behind me. I closed my eyes, listening to the sound of him breathing with a small smile. I reached blindly around myself and took his hand, pulling his arm over my side and holding his hand against my chest.

"Good night, Marsh," I whispered.

Silence followed my words and my eyelids became heavy. My breathing evened out and slowed as sleep sang its siren song. Just as I was about to fall over the edge, Marsh spoke softly:

"Good night, Juliet."

CHAPTER NINETEEN

*D*ARKNESS SURROUNDED ME. *There was no light, just darkness and fear. I opened my mouth to scream, but a flurry of bubbles came forth. I kicked and thrashed, but to no avail, I sank deeper and deeper into the darkness. The cold water pressed against me, leeching away the last vestiges of warmth from me.*

My body convulsed with spasms as the last of my air left my lungs, leaving them burning, screaming, yearning. Feebly, I stretched out my hand, fingers reaching for the dying light fluttering before my eyes. The darkness crept in, stealing my vision as the oppressive cold of the water stole my life.

"Juliet! Wake up!"

I jerked awake, reality slamming into me with enough force to leave me shaking violently. My skin was like ice and I tasted the salt of my tears on my lips. I panted for breath, the cold sweat of fear clinging to my skin.

Marsh turned my head, his eyes luminous in the darkness. His rough fingers stroked my cheeks, dashing away my tears. I reveled in his warmth, closing my eyes and releasing an unsteady breath.

"Tell me." The words were spoken softly, hanging on the air as I tried to gather myself.

Sniffling, I leaned against Marsh, needing his warmth, his comfort, him.

"I was drowning," I quivered. "Just like before. And I died. I died." I gasped and closed my eyes as my words ended on a choked sob.

I had dreamed my death. Again. After a lifetime of drowning in my dreams, you think I would be used to it.

"Shh. You did not die. You are alive and well. I will protect you."

Something clicked inside of me. I shifted in his embrace and looked into his eyes. "Guardian."

Marsh blinked, confusion crossing his eyes. "What?"

"You're the Guardian." I didn't know where any of this was coming from. It was as if someone, something, were speaking through me.

"How do you know this?" Marsh's voice was hushed, his eyes widening in shock.

"I don't know," I blubbered, shaking my head. My hair fell around me in tangles, I pushed it back and sniffled. "The dream. The dream at the beach house. I had it just before you came back. The voices told me about the Guardian. It's you, isn't it?"

Marsh looked at me intently, his breathing growing ragged as excitement flickered in his eyes. "Have you always feared the sea, Juliet?"

I furrowed my brow in confusion, not understanding. "What does that have to do with anything?"

"Answer me. Please." The urgency of his tone caused my stomach to clench.

"Yes. For as long as I can remember. I can't even take baths." I felt stupid admitting it. What adult was so afraid of water they couldn't take a bath?

Marsh cursed softly, looking away from me. "It makes sense. All of it. Why didn't I see it before?"

"Umm, excuse me? What makes sense?" My heart sped in my chest and I had a distant fear that it would forget how to beat at a regular pace.

"The Lost One. You're the Lost One."

I blinked rapidly before laughing softly in disbelief. "I'm sorry to burst your big epiphany, but I have no idea what that means."

"Red as the sunset, fearful of the sea. The Guardian will know her, his heart she will see."

Chills danced merrily up and down my spine at his words. I stared at him as his eyes found mine.

"You are the one,"

"The one?" I gave a soft, nervous laugh, my brain still muddled by sleep and fear. "Is now really the time to be spouting poetry?"

Marsh chuckled softly, shaking his head before looking to me and taking my hand. "It is not poetry, Juliet. It is a prophecy, spoken by the last Seer before she died. I never thought I would say it."

"Seer? I don't …" I shook my head, covering my eyes with one hand, leaving my other clasped in his warm grasp.

"I know you do not understand, but it is imperative you believe me."

"Believe you? How can I believe you when I have

Secrets

no idea what you're talking about? What I think is that you need to explain *everything* to me. Starting with this prophecy."

I wasn't sure I was ready to hear anything he had to say, but something inside of me urged me to listen and keep an open mind. Taking a deep breath, I shifted and looked toward him keeping my expression neutral.

Marsh gave my hand a squeeze, licking his lips and inhaling deeply through his nose. "I will do my best to explain it."

When he spoke, his voice was soft, the words coming confidently from his lips. It was like a litany from school, one you had heard so many times you could repeat it with your eyes closed. His words built a world I could never have imagined. One of faraway places and a culture no one knew existed.

I listened quietly as he spoke of his pod, the clan of Selkies he came from. They lived on the Irish coast, little groups dotting along the seashore. There was another clan, and they made their homes in the Scottish Isles and along the Swedish coast.

"Long ago, the clans were one, united under the same banner. *Teaghlach*, family. There was peace, and the clans lived in harmony. Until the Time of Storms. Two brothers, twins, were born. Mellán and Dougal ruled in peace for many years, until Dougal happened upon an ancient box while on a scouting mission. The Rune Box. Delighted with his find, Dougal brought the box to Mellán. After careful study, Mellán found the box to do extraordinary things. During the threat of famine, Mellán called on the box, and it answered. Harvests were more abundant than ever, babies were born in spades, and life was good. But Dougal grew jealous of the favor the people bestowed upon his brother, and stole the box from Mellán in the night."

I shifted, curling my legs closer to my body as I propped my head on my palm, my elbow digging into my pillow. I was completely caught up in the story. He had a way with words, with storytelling. It was as if I could see it all, playing out in my mind.

"In Dougal's hands, war broke out. Those who were allies became enemies, and Dougal rose to a crushing power, leaving a river of blood in his wake. The people cried out for peace, and Mellán answered. Rallying those loyal to him, he went to war against his brother. Defying all odds, Mellán was victorious. He took the box to the farthest reaches of his land, intent on destroying the thing that had ripped apart his family. Amidst the wind and rain, he had no hope of hearing Dougal as he snuck upon him, and ran him through with their father's sword. As Mellán's blood soaked into the ground, Dougal realized what he had done. In his grief, he swore a vow over his brother's body that he would rid the land of the box."

Marsh paused, long enough that I feared the story was done. I sat up, staring at him intently. "Did he?" I asked. "Did he destroy the box?"

Marsh shook his head. "Dougal had become ensnared by the power of the Rune Box, and he was unable to destroy it. In an attempt to hold to his vow, Dougal buried the box, praying that would restore peace in his brother's memory. But the damage had been done. The clans split in two, and the Clan Wars began. It has been chaos ever since. The Council was created to regain some peace, but it is always short lived."

Secrets

I shook my head, feeling as if I had stepped into a fairytale. "That is tragic! All of that because of a box? Where does the prophecy come in? This, 'Lost One?'"

Marsh inhaled deeply, his eyes going distant. "Twenty-two years ago, the Seer had a vision. In her vision, she saw the Lost One, the Peace Bringer. And she saw the man who would be their guide, their protector. Their Guardian. The Seer stood before the council the next day and spoke of what she had seen. That one would be born who would wield the power to bring about peace and unite the clans, and bring about harmony once more. She was laughed at."

My brow furrowed as confusion rolled through me. "Why would they laugh at her? Seems to me like that would be something they would want, you know?"

"It should have been; however war is profitable. Raising the young to be soldiers gives those with the thirst for power the feeling that they are in control. Not all on the Council disregarded her words. They fought amongst themselves, but ultimately the prophecy was deemed admissible. Soldiers were chosen and sent out to find this Lost One."

"What happened to the Seer?"

Marsh stared straight ahead, his tone deadpan. "She and her mate were killed shortly after by the sälskinn clan, leaving their son an orphan to be raised by his grandmother."

I gasped, covering my lips with my hand before setting my palm against his arm. I felt the muscles go taunt, watched a muscle twitch in his jaw as he stared at the opposite wall.

"I'm so, so sorry," I whispered, knowing the words would do nothing to ease the pain. "How old were you?"

"I was ten. My grandmother promised me their deaths were swift. But she never let me forget my mother's words. I just never expected that I would be the Guardian she spoke of."

I licked my lips, looking down to where my hand rested against his arm. It was insane, all of it. How could a sane person be expected to believe any of this was true? Yet, somewhere deep in the depths of my soul, I knew it was. I believed in him, unquestionably.

"*If* I am the Lost One, and you're the Guardian, that means ... you were looking for me, even before we met." I whispered, the romance of it making my lips curve upward.

Marsh turned his head, his eyes seeking out mine, a smile of his own warming my heart. He looked down at my hand against his arm and slid his fingers beneath mine until our palms met, our fingers entwining.

"There is no *if*, Juliet. I believe you to be the Lost One, the one I have spent years searching for. And now I have found you."

"You have," I smiled, blushing softly and biting my lower lip. "But I'm afraid there is a lot of 'if.' I've never been anyone's anything, and there's a good reason for that. So, what are you going to do with me now?"

"I am going to protect you, with my dying breath if necessary. There is much to plan. I will need to escort you to Ireland immediately. We should go see Adaline before we do anything, she will have a better idea of how to proceed."

I laughed softly, my sexy bubble burst. "Wait, wait, slow down. Go to Ireland?"

"Yes. So that you can stand before the Council and fulfill the prophecy."

"That's another thing—why would a human be able to unite your clans?"

"A human would be unable to."

"Then I'm not the one." I sighed, my heart sinking. The idea had been so nice, being needed by this man, by a whole group of people. But, like everything else in my life, it wasn't meant to be.

"You are the one, I'm certain of it."

"What makes you so sure? I'm a human, Marsh! Human. Not seal. I'm afraid of water, for crying out loud! It can't be me. I'm sorry. I am. I wanted it too."

Marsh stared at me, his eyes narrowing. I squirmed under the intensity of his gaze, suddenly reminded of the night of the storm, the danger I had felt he was capable of. Marsh's eyes widened slightly before he gave a short bark of disbelief.

"You don't know." He dragged his fingers through his hair and sighed, cursing softly. "Well, that complicates things."

"Don't know what? What are you going on about? And what the heck were you doing with your eyes, x-raying me?"

"Juliet, I am sorry, but you are not human. Not fully, anyway."

I laughed and shook my head. When Marsh didn't join in, I gulped.

"Of course I'm human!" I argued, uncertainty tingeing my voice.

"No, Juliet. You're part Selkie. I can sense it, I just didn't know what it was before."

I burst out laughing, I couldn't help it. The idea

was so absurd. "Oh, right. Sure. I'm part seal. My mother just left that little tidbit out for the last twenty-some years." I snorted and shook my head.

"Your family, what do they look like? Red haired like you?"

"Well, no. My mom and dad have dark brown hair, my sister too, actually. Dad always joked that the postman had brought me ..." I trailed off, my insides turning to ice. "What are you saying, Marsh? That my family is *not* my family?"

"What I'm saying is, maybe you should call your parents."

I stared at him, shaking my head slowly as I climbed off the bed, straightening my rumbled dress. Absently, I thought about changing before I grabbed my phone, muttering about calling my parents at three in the morning and how stupid this all was. Hair color didn't mean anything.

You've always felt like an outsider. Never living up to their expectations. Never being as perfect as Beatrice.

I clamped down on that inner voice and forced a smile into my voice as the line picked up. "Mom. Yes, I'm fine. No, I know what time it is. Because it couldn't wait until then. Because it couldn't. Mom. Mom. Mom, could you just stop a minute and let me talk, please? Thank you!"

I exhaled in frustration and uncurled my hand from the fist I had made, shaking out the nerves that filled my system. "I need my birth certificate. Because, I need to get a passport, okay? I-What? What do you mean?" I swallowed, my heart slamming against my ribs. "You have to tell me what?" I whispered, knees trembling.

Secrets

I lowered to the edge of the bed as my mother continued, her voice breaking and becoming muffled as blood pounded in my ears. My hand went numb and the phone fell to the floor, hitting the carpet with a muted thump.

I stared at my shadowed reflection in the mirror, lost in the darkness of the night. A perfect reflection of me.

The bed shifted and I felt Marsh moving closer. He said nothing, nor did he touch me, simply offering the quiet comfort of his presence. The pregnant silence stretched on before I found the strength to speak.

"You were right," I choked, tears thickening my voice. "I was adopted."

CHAPTER TWENTY

THE DOOR CLOSED behind him firmly, the lock clicking audibly. With a scowl, Robert dropped his keys into the bowl beside the door and pressed his fingers to the light pad on the wall. Each room illuminated one after the other. The apartment was lavishly furnished, dark wood and grey walls with splashes of bold colors said in no uncertain terms that it was a man's residence.

Still, the lighting was dim, moody, and romantic, and only made him scowl further.

Striding across the room, he unbuttoned his shirt until it was open, his steps carrying him toward the glass wall. Throwing open the door, he stepped out onto the balcony and looked out over the city.

The night had not gone to plan at all. He had been close—so close. And then *he* had ruined it.

How could Robert have known Marsh would show up? The men he sent should have been more than enough to finish the man off. He'd been alone, for Christ's sake.

They would have to be seen to. He could not tolerate incompetence.

Secrets

A low electronic droning filled the night and he sighed heavily, ignoring it. It persisted, and with a whispered curse, Robert spun on his heel and strode back into the apartment. His shirt and jacket flapped in the breeze he created as he briskly walked into the kitchen, pulling his phone from his pocket.

"Yes?" he growled as he answered it, yanking open the fridge and removing the bottle of wine. He popped the cork and got down a glass, filling it to capacity.

"Is it done?" the voice on the line asked sharply.

No room for pleasantries.

"I ran into some ... complications."

"Then uncomplicate them! I want this finished. Now!"

"I will finish it. You have nothing to fear," Robert snapped, gripping the delicate stem of the glass tight enough to crack it.

"You promised me you could do this. Swore I would have no reason to worry. And yet, I worry. You are not man enough for this task."

Fury rose white hot within him, a blinding mask searing across his eyes. He sent the glass flying, the golden liquid arching as it and its vessel hit the far wall and shattered into a million tiny shards, glittering like diamonds in the recess lighting.

"I am man enough!" he roared, his chest heaving in anger.

"Tsk, tsk, such temper. You have one more chance. Do not disappoint me again."

The line clicked off, leaving Robert holding the phone in a white knuckled grip. Taking extraordinary care not to break it, he set the phone down and grabbed the bottle of wine, taking a long pull from the bottle he strode across the room.

The man was a complication, one he had not planned for. But he could adjust. He was nothing if not adaptable.

His anger simmered and cooled, shifting into cold calculation. A dark smile curled his lips as he took another pull from the bottle. This was a blessing, if he played it right. And he always played to win.

CHAPTER TWENTY-ONE

"JULIET, YOU NEED to talk to me."

I stared straight ahead, my eyes unfocused, as they had been for the last fifteen minutes. I only knew how long it had been because Marsh had mentioned it moments before.

How was I supposed to talk? My heart and my brain were numb. *Why* had they never told me? For twenty-seven years, I had been Juliet Adams. Now who was I?

"Juliet."

I flinched as he spoke my name, finally looking at him. His eyes captivated me as I stared at him—they always did. My face felt tight from dried tears and I was more exhausted than I had ever been. I sniffled and lowered my eyes.

"I can't," I insisted, taking a peek back up at him to see his reaction.

Marsh sighed and pinched the bridge of his nose, clenching his jaw. I knew he was becoming frustrated, but I couldn't drum up the energy to care.

"You have to," he insisted. The steel in his voice shocked me.

"What did you say?" I asked, dumbfounded.

"I know you've been through a lot tonight, and I know it's four in the morning, but I *need* you to get it together." Marsh's eyes locked on mine, boring into me as his jaw tightened. Tension colored his voice, and I could almost feel his control slipping.

I sputtered, scoffing and crossing my arms over my chest and ... well, I pouted.

"I don't have to do anything!" I corrected. "And, I don't like you right now!" I was adopted. I wasn't even human! And he wanted me to just *deal* with it?

"I don't really care if you don't like me right now, so long as you talk to me!"

My eyes narrowed as I glared at him. Hurt shot through me, awakening me from the numbness. "I don't *want* to talk about it! What I want is some fricking compassion!"

Tears burned my eyes, surprising me. I had been positive I had cried myself out. Sniffling I scraped the back of my hand beneath my nose. "And you don't even care," I added with a snap.

Marsh sighed, moving toward me. He laced his arms around me and pulled my back against his chest, resting his chin on my shoulder. He held me like that for a time, silence filling the room.

"I do care. Is that better?"

I laughed softly, pushing at his arm. He held me tighter. "You're a jerk."

Marsh's chuckle vibrated through me, relaxing me as nothing else had. "I'm sorry," he whispered.

"Don't be. Hey, at least now I know who I am. Without you, I might never have found out. So, thank you." Blowing out a breath, I traced my fingertips

Secrets

along his forearm, drawing random patterns and shapes. After a time, I shifted my head to the side, stealing a look at him.

"You're welcome. Though, I must admit I feel odd being responsible for upsetting your life."

I gave a dry laugh and covered my face with my hands. My shoulders shook with a mixture of laughter and sobs. "And I envied Adaline her life," I muttered as I dropped my hands, pulling away and shifting to look at him. "She's one too, isn't she? A Selkie?"

Marsh nodded slowly, reaching out to tuck my hair behind my right ear. "Yes, love. She is."

"Selkies all around me." I shook my head and took a deep, shuddery breath. "Okay. I think I'm okay."

Marsh watched me closely for a time before nodding and giving my shoulder an awkward pat. "Good. I was worried about you there for a time."

"Afraid I would crack under the pressure?" I quipped.

"Yes," Marsh answered seriously.

I blew out a breath that quickly turned into a yawn. "I have not had enough sleep," I grumbled, "and I'm going to have to get up in a few hours to go to work." I groaned and pressed the heel of my hand to my eyes. I was *not* looking forward to work.

"I would like to accompany you."

Lifting my brows, I lowered my hand and looked at Marsh quizzically, an odd humor curving my lips. "To work?"

"Yes," he replied. "I would like to see Adaline. It has been years since I saw her last."

"Right. Of course you can go. But, I thought you said it wasn't safe for the two of you to be close?"

"It's not. But I still wish to see her."

"Why? I mean, why is it not safe? At first I thought there was some rule about having two Selkies too close together but," I gestured between him and myself, "apparently it won't make the world go boom."

Marsh gave a deep chuckle. "You need to sleep, lass. The lack of it is addling your brain. There'll be time enough to answer your questions."

"Hey, you were the one who wanted me to talk about it." I pointed out, sliding off the bed and crossing to my dresser. I really needed to get out of this dress. It was *not* the most comfortable thing to sleep in.

"Because I was afraid you had gone into shock. I'm not the medical professional here."

I smirked, pulling out a tank top and pajama bottoms from my drawer before facing him, my brow furrowed. "What *do* you do?"

"What do I do?"

"Yeah, you know, for work?" I stepped into the bathroom and shucked off my leggings and dress, quickly pulling on my pajamas. I walked back into the bedroom and climbed onto the bed, lying down with a sigh.

"I am a day laborer," Marsh explained. "I've worked mostly construction jobs. It's easy to find people who need help, no matter where I am."

"So, you're like a jack of all trades or something?" I asked, closing my eyes.

"Or something."

I nodded, sleep rushing up and winning over and I gave into it.

THE BLARE OF my alarm sounded all too soon.

Secrets

Groaning heavily, I reached out my hand, slapping at it until it went quiet. I buried my face in my pillow and grumbled. I needed to get up and get ready for work, but lying in my bed was so much more comfortable.

The scent of coffee made my mouth water, motivating me to get up. I scrambled from the bed, kicking at my sheets and stumbling as my foot tangled in them. I broke my fall by slapping my hands against the doorframe.

Clearing my throat, I casually walked toward the kitchen. I smiled at the sight of Marsh standing over the stove, making what smelled like eggs.

Handsome as sin and *he cooks?*

Marsh smiled to himself as he moved the eggs from pan to plates. "I saw that,"

"Saw what?" I asked with an innocent air, pouring myself a cup of coffee and sitting at the table.

Laughing softly, Marsh carried the plates to the table and set one before me.

"Thanks," I smiled at him before beginning to eat. After the emotional upheaval of the night before, I was starving.

"You did not have much available. Do you not cook often?"

I looked at Marsh with raised brows. "Did you not see my drawer of takeout menus?"

"I did."

"There's your answer then."

I laughed as Marsh smirked. It should have felt weird, sharing breakfast with him, and yet I was comfortable. He had seen me at my worst and not run for the hills. That counted for something.

A part of me would have loved nothing more than

to linger over breakfast, talking and laughing until the coffee ran dry. But that wasn't meant to be for this morning. My phone beeped, drawing a muttered curse from me as I read the time. Gulping down the rest of my coffee, I ran into my room and dressed quickly.

"If you're coming with me, we've got to go now," I called as I shoved my phone and wallet into my usual purse and raced toward the door. Marsh followed obediently, a smirk playing about his lips.

The drive to Rose Village was quiet for the most part, both of us lost in our own thoughts. More than once I glanced in Marsh's direction. His narrowed eyes; the stern set to his lips made my anxiety rise.

"Marsh?" I asked, keeping my voice extra calm as I drove.

"Yes?"

"Do I need to be worried about anything?"

"Not at the moment. Why do you ask?"

"Because I'm kind of starting to feel like I'm in a spy movie right now. You've checked the mirror like, five times." I glanced at him again, flexing my fingers on the wheel.

He didn't answer.

That can't be good.

I forced myself to relax as I pulled into the parking lot of Rose Village.

"Okay," I started, "I don't know what your plan was, but I'm on the overnight shift, so ..."

"So, I will be here with you until you leave."

"Oh, umm, okay." I licked my lips and pulled my hair back into a ponytail, not exactly sure how this was going to play out.

"I am the Guardian, Juliet. I will not leave your

side until I know you are safe."

I lowered my hands and looked up at him with wide eyes, reading the seriousness in his expression. Phantom fingers danced along my spine, making me shiver as he stared right back at me.

"You're serious, aren't you?"

Marsh nodded. "I am. It is my duty to protect you."

"... Okay," I nodded, turning to pull open the door to the building.

My own personal guard seal.

This should be fun.

CHAPTER TWENTY-TWO

I DID MY best to ignore the onslaught of giggles and stares from the receptionist and the other ladies as Marsh and I entered Rose Village. blushing furiously as I showed Marsh where to sign in and left to clock myself in and get my badge.

Titters and more giggling met me as I stepped back into the lobby. I raised my brows as I found Marsh standing near the desk, looking uncomfortable yet trying to be polite to the surrounding women.

"Are you really from Ireland?" one asked.

"That accent!" another sighed.

"I love your beard," Stacey beamed as she reached her hand toward Marsh's face. "Can I touch it?"

I cleared my throat loudly, watching as Marsh jerked away from Stacey.

"Juliet," he breathed, his eyes wide with what looked like relief. "I was just...uh ..."

"Uh huh," I muttered, nodding my head in the other direction. "Come on. I'll take you to see Adaline."

Marsh smiled at the ladies as he extricated himself from their midst. A flurry of wistful sighs followed him and I chuckled.

"He's so handsome," someone yearned.

"How did someone like her land someone like him?" one scoffed.

The last comment stung. I closed my eyes against the bitter barb and lifted my chin.

"Don't listen to 'em," Marsh said with a smile down at me, entwining his fingers with mine. "They've got nothing on you."

"Thanks," I muttered, warmth filling me and brightening my cheeks.

Adeline's door was closed. That fact stole the warmth from me quicker than an icy breeze. I swallowed, doing my best to act calm and collected as I pushed her door open. The room was dark, the curtains drawn over the window. My stomach clenched as I stepped into the room.

"Adaline?" I whispered, looking around before my eyes were drawn to the bed. Adaline lay on her back, her breathing shallow yet even. Despite the dimness of the room, I could see she was pale.

Marsh tensed before he released my hand and slowly crossed the room.

"*Seanmháthair*," he said, stopping beside her bed and taking her hand in his. She didn't move or respond at all. Marsh squeezed her hand, a muscle ticking away in his jaw. Marsh turned toward me. "What's wrong with her?"

"I don't know. She was fine yesterday." I grabbed her chart, looking it over. Lethargy, vomiting, dizziness. Her symptoms didn't add up to anything. Sighing in frustration, I slapped the chart back into its holder. "I don't know."

"You two are loud, that's what's wrong."

Adaline's voice was thin and reedy. A wracking cough shook her thin body and seemed to exhaust her. Panting softly, she lifted her hand, touching Marsh's cheek. "*Grá.* I knew you'd come."

"Aye, *Seanmháthair.* To be this close and not see your beautiful face?" Marsh chuckled and shook his head. "You would skin me."

I smiled at the greeting, crossing my arms over my chest. Feeling more than a little awkward, I stepped away from the bed. I edged toward the door as they began speaking in low tones. I didn't recognize the words, and assumed they were speaking Gaelic.

"Where do you think you're going, missy?" Adaline asked.

I paused with my hand on the doorknob. Turning, I smiled at her. "I thought you two might want to talk. I have work and stuff."

And I feel like a third wheel.

Adaline narrowed her eyes at me and crooked her finger. "Get over here and sit, child."

I couldn't help but smile at her fiery personality as I complied. I pulled the spare guest chair closer to her bed and sat. Marsh hadn't let go of her hand. The connection hit me like a ton of bricks and longing filled me. I had never had that connection with my family. The closest I had come would be Beatrice, and even then we weren't close. At least now I knew why.

"How are you feeling?" I asked her, setting my hand on her knee. She was so pale, her lips and eyes seeming overly bright.

"I feel like I got ran over by a bus," she muttered. "But they ain't killed me yet."

Secrets

Marsh tensed visibly at her words, and I watched as their eyes connected. It was as if they were sending each other silent messages. Panic fluttered in my gut.

"That ... That's just a saying, right?" I asked.

Marsh shook his head and cursed, rising from his seat. He ran his hand through his hair, the other still clutching Adaline's. "This will not stand," he growled. "They play a dangerous game."

"You don't know who you're dealing with, boy," Adaline warned. "She's crafty, and she lets nothing get in her way. Heartless, shell of a woman."

"How did she find you?" Marsh demanded.

"Sent an underling," Adaline spat out before she was consumed with a cough, the sound wet and horrible. I cringed and gripped her knee as she took a shuddery breath. Blood tinged her lips.

"Adaline!" I cried, jumping up and grabbing a tissue. Her bony hand grabbed my arm and yanked me down until we were face to face.

"Helene," she whispered hastily before her eyes rolled back and she began to convulse.

"No!" Marsh roared, shoving me aside and grabbing Adaline in his arms. He stroked her cheeks, repeating the word as she seized. As suddenly as it started, it stopped. "Adaline? Adaline? *Seanmháthair?* Grandmother!" Marsh cried, shaking her gently.

"Don't!" I ordered, pushing myself to my feet and moving to the head of the bed. I pulled my stethoscope out and pressed it to her chest as I prayed. "She's breathing," I announced with relief. "Let her rest, I'll get the doctor."

I turned from the bed and began to cross the room just as the door flew open. I blinked in shock as three men strode in. They looked alike, dressed in dark suits and mirrored sunglasses. Their only obvious differences seemed to be their size and hair colors. One man was significantly taller than the others. The man in front had brown hair, the one to his right was blond and the man on his left was black-haired.

"Excuse me!" I barked. "You can't be in here!" I threw my hand up and marched toward them with every intention of throwing them out.

"Juliet Adams?" the brown-haired one asked. His question stopped me in my tracks and I studied him, trying to place him. He had a face that wouldn't stand out in a crowd. He reminded me a lot of the agent from the Matrix, strangely enough.

"Yes?"

Everything seemed to move in slow motion. The men moved in perfect unison, reaching into their jackets. I watched, not understanding what was happening. My eyes widened as I found myself staring down the barrel of three silenced pistols.

CHAPTER TWENTY-THREE

MY MIND BLANKED as my body froze, rooting me to the spot. I knew I should do *something* but I had no idea what that was. I stumbled to the side as Marsh barreled past me, dropping his head and slamming his shoulder into the chest of the man who had spoken. He hit with enough force to send the man falling backward, knocking his partners from their feet. A sound, like the popping of a firecracker, hurt my ears, bits of the ceiling raining down around me just after.

"Juliet, *run!*" Marsh roared at me, grabbing the lead man by the collar of his shirt and jerking him up before sending a closed fist into the man's nose. He grunted as the blond grabbed him from behind, yanking him backward.

I ran.

I screamed as the black-haired man grabbed my ankle. I thrashed and kicked on instinct, my foot connecting with his face. He grunted and cursed, but released me long enough that I was able to scramble away. I got to my feet and ran, my heart lodged in my throat.

More firecrackers. The glass of a landscape print on the wall exploded and I threw my hands up to protect my face. I heard heavy footsteps, giving chase and had to fight the urge to look behind me. Screams filled the hallway and nurses and patients ran from the commotion.

I skidded around the corner into the lobby, throwing myself against the wall, panting for breath. I closed my eyes as my head spun, before forcing them open. I could hear my pursuers; I had seconds before they were on me.

The fire alarm gleamed a brilliant red and caught my eye. Moving on instinct, I grabbed it, pulled the bar down and sprinted toward the door.

Alarms blared. I slapped my hands against the exit bar as a shot sounded and the glass of the doors spider webbed. Ducking my head I screamed as I shoved the doors open and took off across the lot toward my car. My sneakers slapped against the pavement as I ran, echoing the rapid beating of my heart. My soles skidded across the wet ground, fighting for purchase as I gripped the door handle and pulled.

Locked.

I screamed in frustration and jerked frantically on the handle, to no avail. Releasing it, I moved to run around the other side and cried out in terror as a tall, dark haired figure blocked my path. His mirrored sunglasses sat askew, offering me a view of his cold, calculating eyes. His hands were covered in black leather gloves. His lower lip was broken and bled as his lips curved into a wicked grin.

"Run," he dared. "I like the chase."

I stumbled backward, my whole body shaking

with fear.

"Marsh!" I screamed.

As if I had summoned him, Marsh appeared. He slammed into the black-haired man from behind and took him down hard. The man rolled as they went down, struggling with Marsh. Fists struck flesh, pulling pained grunts and curses from both men. I watched helplessly as they grappled, each man struggling for dominance.

My fear and panic had reached a peak.

"No! Stop it! Stop it!" I screeched, my hands fluttering uselessly in the air. I didn't know what I was saying. I didn't know what to do. I couldn't think.

Marsh grunted as he hit the man again and again, his punches aimed at face, chest and stomach. His arms bulged with each strike. Blood trailed from Marsh's mouth and eye. My heart stopped as the black-haired man wedged his arms up, pressing his thumbs into Marsh's eyes.

Marsh roared in pain, his punches dying off as he grabbed at the man's arms, pulling his hands away from his eyes. A sick smile twisted the black-haired man's lips and he bucked, taking advantage of Marsh's distraction and flipping him onto his back. In a fluid motion he straddled Marsh, wrapping his thick fingers around his throat and squeezing.

Marsh wheezed as he struggled against the man's grip. The assailant had the upper hand. Marsh released his wrists and drove a punch into the man's gut. The man grunted, but squeezed tighter.

Screams and confused shouts filled the air as people poured from the building. I glanced around, but no one had noticed the three of us, too caught up in looking for the source of what they assumed was a fire.

Marsh's lips were turning blue, his punches coming weaker. I was watching him die.

"No!" I screamed, rushing forward. I did the first thing that came to me. Yanking my right leg back, I let my foot fly toward the attacker's groin. I connected solidly enough to have pain reverberating up my leg.

With a loud groan the man crumpled, releasing Marsh and falling to his side, clutching his injured manhood. Limping toward Marsh, I crouched down, grabbed his shoulders and heaved him to his feet.

"Go," he wheezed, rubbing at his throat. "We have to go now."

"I don't have my keys. Everything's inside!"

Marsh cursed, pulling away from me and aiming a hard kick at the downed man's face. Bones crunched and I winced. The man lolled to the side, unconscious. Marsh searched the man's jacket, moving with an ease that chilled me.

"You've done this before," I accused. Marsh looked up at me, his eyes darker than I'd ever seen them. His response was cut off as we were finally noticed.

"Hey!" a deep voice roared.

Our heads jerked to the side in time to see the leader of the three men shoving his way through the milling crowd, followed closely by the blond. They were coming toward us with murderous intent.

"Go. Go!" Marsh grabbed my arm and propelled me forward, shoving me along when my feet refused to move. Three loud pops followed us and screams filled the air. I ducked my head on instinct, looking around as Marsh kept me moving.

Secrets

I looked over my shoulder and gasped, slapping at Marsh's arm. "Marsh! Do something! They're coming!"

"What do you want me to do?" he grumbled, his eyes scanning the parking lot, fingers fumbling with something.

"I don't know! Get on your knees and bark like a seal!"

I was insane. Who else would make jokes at a time like this?

His hand tightened on the back of my shirt, pulling me to a stop as he pressed his thumb down on the fob. He must have taken it from the other man. A loud rumble sounded, pulling my attention away from the rapidly approaching men.

"This way," Marsh shifted his hold from my back to my arm and tugged me along, my feet skidding stupidly as he pulled me toward the idling motorcycle. It was a large, sleek looking machine. Painted a glossy black with chrome accents. It looked like a death trap.

"Oh, no!" I argued. "I am *not* getting on that thing! Do you even know how to drive it?"

"We'll find out, won't we?" Marsh flashed me a dark grin as his hands settled at my waist and lifted me onto the back of the bike. Sirens filled the air as he held out a helmet. "Put this on."

I took the helmet from him, my fingers fumbling with the straps. Marsh climbed onto the bike in front of me, revving the engine. We peeled away from the curb just as the men reached us. I screamed as more shots were fired, the sounds behind us quickly drowned out by the rush of wind in my ears. Squeezing my eyes closed, I wrapped my arms around Marsh's waist and held on for dear life.

The vibrations of the motorcycle quickly made my lower half go numb. The wind had chilled; I couldn't stop shivering as I clung to Marsh, drinking in his warmth. Once my fear left me, exhaustion hit. I zoned out as we drove, weaving in and out of traffic. My mind was blissfully numb.

We were still traveling when I zoned back in, lifting my head from where it had rested against his back. I didn't recognize anything and frowned. Marsh leaned the bike to the right, pulling off the highway and onto an exit. There wasn't much there, just a gas station and a liquor store. I looked around, blinking the sleep from my eyes as he pulled the bike into the gas station. Pulling up to the pump, he killed the engine, finding his balance and lowering the kickstand.

"Hey, you okay back there?"

"Yeah. Yeah, I'm fine." I unhooked the helmet and rubbed at my eyes. "I'm freezing."

Marsh nodded, looking around. "You need a jacket. I'll ask if there's a store around. We need gas."

"Where are we going, Marsh? What the hell was that back there? And how could we just leave Adaline like that?" Dropping the helmet I shoved at his chest, all the fear, all the panic coming back full force, robbing me of my breath.

"Juliet."

"How could you just leave her?" I shoved at his chest again, hard enough to knock him back a step. He grabbed at my wrists, yanking my arms down by my sides.

"I did it to protect you!" he snapped. "I was thinking about saving your life!" He released me with a shake, stepping away and dragging his hand down his face before sighing. "Do you really think I wanted to leave her? She's my whole life, Juliet. *Was* my whole life."

"Don't ... Don't say that. *Don't* say that!" I glared at him, tears burning my eyes. "She's *not* dead!"

"We don't know that!" he roared, whirling on me. "Those men were sent to kill you. They tried to kill me. It's not such a stretch that they killed her, too."

Grief clenched my heart and I shook my head in violent objection as I stepped away from him. With all the ups and downs in Adaline's health, I had still never thought she would actually ...

No. No. She's not. She can't be. I won't believe it.

Sniffling, I wrapped my arms around myself, turning away from him.

"Juliet?" His voice, softer now, cut through my horror. "Hey." He touched my shoulders, drew me toward him. I pressed myself against him, burying face in his chest as I wrapped my arms around him. "We need to go." His voice shuddered a bit and I looked up, saw the tears gleaming in his eyes. He offered me a weak smile, cupping my cheek. "You're not safe."

I stepped back out of his touch, shaking my head. "You're not safe! In the short time I've known you, you've almost been killed twice, and it's all because of me!"

Marsh stepped forward, grabbing my arms and halting my retreat. "If dying meant protecting you, then I would gladly do it."

I stared at him before shaking my head again. Given the tone of his voice, I figured it would be best not to argue with him. I looked around the otherwise empty station as he moved to fill up the bikes tank.

"Wait," I interrupted, "how are we going to pay for this? I don't have my wallet." Thoughts of us peeling away with a tank full of stolen gas and cops chasing us made my stomach clench.

"I'll take care of it," Marsh assured. I was about to argue when he pulled out his wallet.

"Oh." I ran my hands through my hair and sighed. My mind was running a million miles a minute. I couldn't stop thinking about Adaline and prayed she was all right.

"Stay here," Marsh commanded, jerking me from my thoughts. I lifted my brows as he stepped away from me and walked into the attached store.

I paced restlessly, chewing my thumbnail, not taking my eyes off him for long. Minutes passed before he jogged toward me, carrying a plastic bag.

"Thrill of being on the run induces the munchies, or something?" I quipped as he passed me the bag.

"Thought you might be hungry," Marsh shrugged and passed me the helmet.

My brows lifted further as I peered into the bag and pulled out a Butterfinger. Marsh ripped the bag from my hands, causing me to blink in surprise and stifle a giggle. I winced as he shoved the helmet onto my head.

"Easy, killer," I commented.

"There weren't a lot of options," he grumbled, swinging his leg over the bike and starting the engine.

I smirked, climbing awkwardly on behind him. I scooted closer, wrapping my arms around his waist as we pulled away from the station. I closed my eyes against the bright sun, ducking my head. It felt like it should be later; the fact that it was only noon was baffling to me.

Lifting my head, I directed my voice toward Marsh's ear, shouting over the wind. "Where are we going?"

Whether he didn't hear me, or he simply didn't know, I couldn't say. I received no answer. Sighing inwardly, I rested my head against his shoulder once more and watched the landscape zip past. After about an hour of travel, my lower half was once again numb. My legs ached from their cramped position, and all in all I was uncomfortable.

Sitting up, I looked around, craning my neck to catch sight of the destination sign as it whipped past.

Cannon Beach.

We were going back to where it all began.

It was fitting, I supposed. And I had to give props to Marsh for thinking of it. The house was in Beatrice and Bill's names, so anyone looking for me might not expect to find us there.

Except Marsh was attacked somewhere along the beach ...

I squirmed as my thoughts darkened, doing my best to push them aside. The long ride left too much time for thinking about the twisted direction my life had turned. I was twenty-seven years old. I was adopted. I was on the run from hired murderers. And I wasn't even human.

The wind stole my laugh, ripping it away and flinging it behind me. Closing my eyes, I tightened my arms around Marsh, smiled as I felt his hand rest above mine. He was all I had in the world now. That thought was more comforting than I might have believed possible.

Relief washed through me as we pulled off the

highway and down the quiet city streets. I rolled my neck as Marsh parked the bike in front of the beach house and killed the engine. My muscles were stiff and it hurt to move. I groaned softly as Marsh helped me off the bike, jealous of his range of motion.

Unclasping the helmet, I lamented inwardly about my hair. I was certain it was a mess. I set the helmet on the bike and stretched, looking toward Marsh.

"Do you think we'll be safe here?"

"I'm not sure we're safe anywhere." Marsh sighed, his tone heavy. Turning toward me, he offered a weak smile and reached for my hand.

I curled my fingers around his, returning the smile as we walked toward the house. It felt weird being back. So much had happened in such a short time. Had it really only been a month?

Releasing Marsh's hand, I knelt down and felt under the doorframe. "Ah ha." I pulled the key free and rose, brandishing it. "Bea always leaves a spare."

Unlocking the door, I stepped inside, glancing around the dark house. It was eerie, walking in without my sister or her family. Marsh closed the door with a snap, making me jump.

"Sorry," he muttered, running his hand restlessly through his hair before looking at me. A thousand words were held in that look. A thousand things he wanted to say, I wanted to hear.

I shook my head and looked away, laughing softly. "I'm gonna go find something to eat."

I walked into the kitchen, flicking on the light. The coffee cups we had used last time sat in the sink, ceramic reminders of a more peaceful time. Blowing out a breath, I began opening cabinets at random. I didn't even know what I was looking for. My hand stilled on a box of crackers as I felt him behind me.

Closing my eyes, I focused on my breathing.

Deep breath in, slow breath out.

So what if it was a little shaky?

Lowering my hand, I turned to look at him. He filled the doorway, just watching me, his eyes seeming to glow in the dim light. I could stare at his eyes for the rest of my life and not utter a complaint.

"Thank you. For saving me."

A smile winked to life, starting in his irises and moving down to his lips. I giggled, shaking my head and walking toward him. His arms opened for me, pulling me tightly against him. His lips brushed over my head and I smiled wider. The world might be falling apart around me, but somehow in the midst of all the chaos, I had found my home.

I looked up at him, bringing up my hand to touch his cheek. His stubble was rough against my fingers, but I liked the texture. I could feel his heart beating as frantically as my own, beneath my palm. Rising on my toes, I inched closer. I could feel the heat of his breath on my lips, still smelling faintly of the chocolate he'd eaten earlier. His hands tightened on my hips as he drew me closer, our mouths a whisper apart.

The door flew open, the wood banging against the wall with enough force to crack it. I screamed in shock, my world spinning as Marsh shoved me behind him as he turned. Men poured into the house, blotting out the afternoon light.

"Go. Go. Juliet, Go!" Marsh barked.

I tried to get a good look at the men, but Marsh pressed his hand to my back and shoved me out of the kitchen. I stumbled and tripped, bear crawling until I got my feet beneath me again. My heart hammered against my ribs as I ran for my life for the second time that day.

Marsh and I pounded across the room, shouts following us. I hit the patio door seconds before Marsh slammed into me from behind, both our hands fumbling with the latch. Marsh roared in frustration and threw the door open, shoving me out before grabbing my hand and pulling me along.

We sprinted across the sand, the men in hot pursuit. I screamed as gunfire filled the air, throwing my hand over my head in instinct. I never stopped running.

Marsh gave a pained grunt, his body jerking to the side as he stumbled and fell. I lurched as he went down, pulling me with him. Spinning on my heel, I wrapped my fingers around his arm and pulled with all my might.

"Get up, get up!" I screamed, terror filling me as a dark crimson stain bloomed along his shoulder. Marsh slumped, groaning as I tugged on him, straining to lift him.

I screamed as a hand curled around my arm, tearing me away from Marsh and throwing me to the rough sand. My palms skidded across the abrasive surface, tearing my flesh. I glared at the man and yelped as a booted foot flew toward my face. I threw myself to the side, crying out in pain as his foot connected with my spine. Pain radiated along my back, blinding me. I shook my head as he grabbed at me, rolling me over.

Thrashing and kicking, I did the first thing that

came to mind. Scooping up a hand full of sand, I let it fly. My attacker grunted and cursed as the sand filled his eyes, causing him to stumble back and offering me enough time to get to my feet.

"Marsh! Marsh! Get up! You're the Guardian!" I shrieked, my eyes drawn away by movement. Three more men crested the hill, what had delayed them I didn't know, nor did I care to find out. My attacker had cleared the sand from his eyes, and looked more pissed than ever. My heart lodged in my throat as he pulled a knife and strode toward me.

My eyes widened as a figure rose up behind the man. He noticed and whipped around. A loud crack filled the air as Marsh swung the piece of driftwood he held, catching the attacker in the throat. The man made a strangled gurgling sound, grabbing at his throat as he went to his knees. Marsh kicked him in the face before stooping to grab the knife from the man's limp fingers. Straightening, he grabbed my hand and pulled me along, moving swiftly into a jog.

He was so pale. I kept glancing at him as we ran down the beach, the ocean looming before us. We were trapped. There was no way we could escape our pursuers on open land. Another magical cave seemed like too much to hope for.

We're going to die.

The thought ran through my head, causing my eyes to burn with tears. I squeezed his hand harder, following him blindly. Terror ripped through me as he turned *toward* the ocean.

"What are you doing?" I cried, my feet inadvertently digging into the sand, causing me to skid along.

"We can escape into the sea! They're only humans, they can't follow us," Marsh insisted, jerking on my arm and pulling me forward a foot.

"No!" I screamed, fighting at his hold. Hysteria, my old friend, was back, clawing at my chest and throat. Bile rose, searing my throat and making my stomach heave. "I can't!"

Marsh dropped my hand, grabbing my arms hard enough to bring out a squeak of pain. "You will!" his voice was steel, his eyes hard and dangerous. He shoved me toward the ocean, casting a glance behind us and cursing. "Go!"

I froze. My body trembled so violently my teeth clacked together. I couldn't have moved if I'd wanted to. My gaze locked on the ocean, on that dark, rolling water. I couldn't move. Marsh ran past me, the water rising up to lap at his legs. A lover welcoming her mate, the sea pulled him in.

I watched as he turned toward me, golden glow beginning to swirl around his body as he thrust his hand out at me. "Swim with me, Juliet! Now!"

His eyes locked onto mine, fear and desperation darkening the blue depths. I took a step. Then another. And another. Until I was running toward him, gripping his hand the light intensifying, ensconcing us both. The water crashed against my legs, icy fingers drawing me deeper, deeper.

I lost my footing and panicked, the water rising to my chest. I screamed as a wave rose up, crashing down over us, filling my mouth with choking brine. My heart sped, the heat and glow of Marsh's shift blinding me as I went under.

Water was everywhere. Above my head, below my

feet. It was my nightmare come to life. Marsh's fingers slipped from my grip and I spun in the darkness, screaming for him.

The dark water rushed in, replacing my air and cutting off my breath. Panic filled me, and I grabbed at my throat, clawing at the flesh as I began to sink. My lungs screamed for air. Black spots dotted my vision, my toes twitched as I spiraled, caught in the ebb and flow of the waves. I thrust my hand upward in an act of desperation as my vision failed and I gave into the icy grip of unconsciousness.

CHAPTER TWENTY-FOUR

ROBERT WALKED INTO the plain house, flicking his gaze around at the ugly wallpaper in the bad lighting as he closed the door behind him.

Three men seated at a round table playing a game of cards rose as Robert approached. The tallest of the three looked to the others and cleared his throat.

"Sir, I-" he began.

"Which one of you is Burk?" Robert asked sharply, cutting the man off.

The three looked at each other, tension filling the room before the black haired man lifted his hand. He moved slowly away from the table, limping heavily. A bandage adorned his swollen nose and his right eye was bruised.

"I am, sir."

Robert studied the man for a moment, looking down his nose at him. Sniffing, he strode toward the tallest of the three and in a fluid motion reached into the man's jacket and drew his gun. Robert turned his wrist, studying the nickel finish on the Beretta.

"It's beautiful, isn't it? Beautiful, yet deadly."

Shifting slightly he took aim and fired a bullet. Burk's head jerked back, crimson exploding on the wall behind him as his body crumpled.

Robert cleared his throat, and re-holstered the weapon. Tugging on the sleeve of his jacket he looked at the other two.

"Get rid of him," he instructed. Without a second glance, he moved past the two stunned men to the bedroom and pulled open the door.

He closed the door securely behind him and flipped on the light. The bulb flickered and then held, illuminating the small room. Adaline lay on a twin sized bed on the far side of the room, her feet cuffed to the metal bedframe. Though she must have been uncomfortable, she didn't say a word, simply stared at the ceiling. Robert held a grudging respect for her.

"You," Adaline spat, her eyes narrowing to slits as he crossed the room. "I should have recognized you the first time I laid eyes on you. Shame on me."

"Well, in your defense, you had just suffered a major seizure. Funny how the visions manifest." Robert unbuttoned his jacket and sat, resting his ankle on his left knee. "How are you feeling today?"

"You should know. Assuming you're the one been poisoning me."

Robert lifted a brow, a soft chuckle passing through his lips. "Age has not addled your brain, I see. I admit, I was unsure it was truly you when all this began. You have taken many different names over the years. Why is that?"

Adaline turned her head, ignoring the question and watching him with wary eyes. "Are you going to talk me to death, then? Is that the plan?"

Robert chuckled, steepling his fingers and tapping them against his chin. "I could tell you, but that takes all the fun out of it."

Adaline scoffed, looking at the ceiling. "Well, can you find your balls and get on with it? If I'm going to die, I'd rather just do it already. I was never one for much patience."

Robert scowled and rose from his seat, leaning over her and gripping her chin tightly between his index finger and his thumb. "You're very glib for someone facing death."

Adaline jerked her chin from his grasp and spat in his face. "Mommy hasn't given the order for me to die. I have nothing to worry about yet. Little Robert can't take a piss without mommy's permission."

Robert snarled, his hand flying without a thought and striking Adaline across the face. The old woman cried out in shock as pain flared through her cheek, an ugly red mark marring her face.

Lightening quick, Adaline brought up her hand, raking her nails down the side of Robert's face. Her attempt to blind him failed, as he jerked his head to the side, only just sparing his eye.

"You harpy!" he roared, striking out once more, his closed fist connecting with Adaline's nose. A sickening crunch filled the room as warm blood spurted over his hand.

"That make you feel like a man, boy? Feel real in control now, don't ya?" Adaline rasped, rolling to the side and spitting out a mouthful of blood. Her pale eyes were bright with an inner rage as she stared him down.

Robert stared at her, seething. His hands curled

into tight fists and he wanted nothing more than to wipe that sneer off her face. It took everything within him to step back, to turn on his heel and march from the room, calling for someone to see to her injury. Adaline cackled at his retreat.

Only his mother's words kept him from killing her then and there. And he would not disappoint her again.

CHAPTER TWENTY-FIVE

I WAS FLOATING, borne upon a warm golden cloud. Dots of light erupted before my closed eyelids and I gasped, sucking in sweet, cool air. I shot upward, gasping and coughing, my hand flying to my throat as I looked around in panic.

I was in a room, though it was unfamiliar. My heart thundered in my chest as I took in my surroundings. The walls were a pale yellow, broken into sections by thick wooden beams that reached from floor to ceiling. The floor was composed of pretty well worn rosewood, as if many pairs of feet had walked the planks.

Lowering my hand, I flipped the quilt off me and swung my feet from its warmth. The wood was warm beneath my bare feet as I rose, the simple white nightgown I was wearing settling around my calves. My brows furrowed as I looked down at myself, surprised by my attire. When did I change? Where was I?

Where was Marsh?

Swallowing down the fear and confusion that turned my stomach sour, I crossed to the door. It was solid wood, with an old-fashioned brass handle. The antiquity of it struck me, and I smiled. The brass was worn lighter in spots, memories of countless fingers etched into the metal for all time. Touching it lightly, I inhaled and pulled the door open.

Music, a mix of what sounded like violin and flute, wafted down the narrow hallway, joined by the smell of roasting meat and fresh bread. My stomach growled loudly as I padded down the walkway, my eyes alert and body tense.

The hallway opened into a circular room where wooden panels lined the walls, and the hardwood floors were covered in thick braided rugs. Faded couches in pale green and blue plaid made a sort of L shape, defining the sitting area of the room. A fire roared in a small stone hearth, an iron bar set into slots above the flames. Meat roasted there, the fat dripping and causing the flames to spit.

Gingerly, I touched a crocheted blanket lying on the back of the couch nearest to me, marveling at the softness of the yarn. Wherever I was, I liked the decor. It felt warm, and welcoming.

"Ah, yer awake."

I yelped and jumped out of my skin, whirling around with the blanket still in my hand. I fretted with the blanket as I looked at the woman who had spoken.

She was older than me, possibly around my mother's age. Fine lines fanned from her rich brown eyes. Freckles dotted her nose and cheeks. Her red hair was lined with silver and pulled back into a puffy ponytail, and her smile was as warm and welcoming as the room I found myself in.

She was dressed in a flannel shirt, the sleeves rolled up around her elbows, a white tee shirt visible beneath it. Jeans clad her legs, the knees stained by grass and dirt. Crossing toward me, she extended a hand, offering me a coffee mug.

"More sugar than coffee, right?" she confirmed with a smile, a soft chuckle following her words.

I narrowed my eyes as I extended my hand, accepting the mug. "Right," I said slowly, pulling my hand in close to my chest. The aroma of the coffee was rich and heady, making my mouth water.

"You can drink it. There's nothing in there but coffee, sugar and a bit'o milk. You have my word. A bit'a tea always helped me settle into a new place, but I know ya American's care fer coffee." She smiled warmly, her brown eyes lightening with humor. Her accent caught my attention and I looked around once more.

"Where am I? Who are you?"

Another soft chuckle. "Where are my manners? You must be confused as a headless chicken." She held her hand out to me, her palm was wide and looked as if it was used to hard labor. "Tabitha. Tabitha Darrow."

I gaped at her. "Darrow? As in Adaline and Marsh Darrow?"

"Aye, the very same. I'll bet she's mentioned me, though not by name. Tha's usually how mum tells it. I'm the runaway, always searching for love." She winked at me, lifting her own mug to her lips. "Ah, as for the where of it, you're in Ireland, love."

My eyes widened as the world seemed to shrink around me.

Ireland?

I was in Ireland? How in the world had I gotten

here?

And where the heck was Marsh?

"I ... Aren't you supposed to be in Vienna? I'm sorry, I don't under-Where's Marsh?"

Tabitha's face fell, her smile slipping just a touch. Worry flared within me, and I sucked in a breath as my hands began to shake violently. Coffee sloshed from the mug, scalding my hand and splashing against the white dress.

"No, no," she soothed. "Calm down, love. Give me tha', there. Tha's better." Tabitha lifted the mug from my hand, setting it aside and wrapping a strong arm around me, guiding me toward the couch. "There's not a reason for ya to be fearful, now. Marsh is just fine. The lad popped down to market for me. He'll be back in a jiff. T'wasn't about him at all, I promise ya. Wasn't expectin' ya to bring up Vienna is all."

I panted, struggling for breath as I forced myself to hear her words. He was alive. He was alive and he was coming. He was coming for me again.

"I— I'm sorry, I just ... I just ..."

"All ya need to do now is breathe, love. Take a deep breath for me? There, jus' like tha'. Good girl." Tabitha smiled, lowering me to the couch and stroking my hair.

I closed my eyes, listening to her soothing words and focusing on my breathing. The tightness in my chest slowly released and I was able to draw a free breath. My shoulder sagged and I exhaled.

"I'm sorry," I shuddered.

Tabitha shook her head, crouching down in front of me. "Not a thing to be sorry for. I didn't mean to give ya such a scare."

I blew out a breath, drawing a hand over my face. "Your face. I just, thought the worst. Nothing makes sense."

Tabitha nodded and rose, pacing the living room. "I imagine ya did. Marsh is fine, a bit banged up, but nothin' a little time won't heal. I'm sorry I made ya think otherwise."

I swallowed, nodding and rubbing my hands together. My fingertips were cold, and I had to fight the urge to give into shivers despite the warmth of the room. I believed her words, but I would feel a lot better when I could see him with my own eyes.

"Why aren't you in Vienna?" I blurted.

Tabitha blinked at me, and then chuckled, her smile returning and bringing warmth back to her face. "Aye. I was for a time. It didn't work out. Seems I have my mother's streak for lost loves."

I licked my lips, lifting my eyes to hers. "You're one too, aren't you? A selkie?"

The door opened with suddenness, the sound of rain filling the room. A sodden figure lurched forward, cursing as he battled against the wind to close the door.

"It's bucketing down out there!" Marsh muttered, striding toward the kitchen and dropping two saturated bags onto the counter. He turned to face the living room, swiping his dripping hair from his face. His eyes found mine and he smiled. "Finally woke, I see."

Warmth filled me at the sight of him. His smile washed through me, and I nodded letting go a soft breath. I laughed softly. "I guess I was out for a while."

Marsh grinned, stripping off his jacket. He wore a burgundy sweater beneath it, and the damp wool clung to his body, making my mouth go dry.

"Long enough for me to swim you to Ireland. Do you remember waking up during the trip at all?"

I shook my head, rising from the couch. "Flashes, but it's muddled, like a half-remembered dream. Mostly, I just remember... you."

I rubbed my damp palms against my thighs, suddenly feeling underdressed.

Tabitha chuckled and stepped past me. "I'll see to supper."

I looked after her, but my eyes were quickly drawn back to Marsh as he crossed toward me. I found myself captivated by the way he moved. My heart awoke, thumping to life inside my chest as my chin lifted, keeping my eyes on his. He stopped before me, a crooked grin on his lips. I closed my eyes as he cupped my cheek, his thumb tracing my lips.

"Thought I lost you there for a moment, love," he murmured.

My lashes fluttered against my cheeks as I released a shuddery breath. "I thought the same thing, back on the beach."

I touched his face, his neck, his shoulders, pausing with my palm over his chest. The steady beat of his heart calmed me, filling me with reassurance. It didn't make sense, how everything was falling apart and yet I was whole when he was near me.

Reluctantly, I opened my eyes and stepped out of his embrace. I couldn't think when he was touching me, and I needed to think.

"How did we get here? You said something about swimming but ... How are we in Ireland? And where in Ireland are we?"

Marsh sighed and drew a hand through his hair, looking from me toward the kitchen where Tabitha had gone and back. "We're in Dingle to be exact. At my Aunt's house. As for the how, we swam. Well, I swam. You sort of ... floated along with me for most of it."

Floated. In the *ocean.*

I sucked in a breath as ice filled my stomach, my eyes widening. I had been *unconscious* in the ocean. The ways I could have died invaded my mind, feeding the growing anxiety until it was hard to breathe.

"I swam ... in the ocean?"

Tabitha stepped back into the living room, wiping her hands on a dishtowel. She nodded, a soft smile on her lips.

"Aye, lass," she said. "'Tis true. And to answer yer earlier question, aye, I'm a selkie as well."

"But, there's something I don't understand," I objected, pausing. "Well, there's a lot of things I don't understand." I chuckled, the sound encroaching on hysteria as I touched my fingertips to my brow.

"We'll answer anything we can, love," Marsh said, his fingers finding mine.

I smiled softly at him, nodding before licking my lips and looking to Tabitha. "Why were those men after us? How did we swim all the way to Ireland? Have we heard anything from Adaline?"

Tabitha sighed and looked down, tossing a glance to Marsh, who took on a somber expression as he released my hand and threaded his thumbs through his belt loops. They shared another look and anger rose within me.

"You look scared. Why?"

Another shared, silent look.

"Why?" I demanded, causing them both to jump. "Stop babying me!"

Marsh narrowed his eyes before blowing out a breath. "We are scared. It's Adaline," he explained.

Fear coated my stomach. I let go a shaky breath. "Is ... Is she ...?" I lifted my brows, my heart pounding in my chest, pumping frost through my veins.

"No, no," Tabitha replied. "Nothin' like tha'... yet." She sighed, stepping toward me before stopping. She focused on the towel she twisted in her hands. "We've only just learned Robert has her. We're not really sure wha' her condition is. Jus' tha' he has her."

Marsh turned away, crossing his arms over his chest as he stared out the rain lashed window. Tension rode his shoulders hard, stiffening his form. I longed to go to him, but the news kept me where I stood.

"Robert? Robert who?" I shook my head, not understanding.

"Robert Ahlström."

"The Robert I went on a date with, Robert? EMT Robert? Why in the hell would he have her?"

"Aye. Marsh tells me ya know of him, that he sought you out. It's a good thing Marsh showed up when he did, else you'd probably be dead right now."

"But why?" I shook my head in denial of her words. It didn't make sense. Robert had Adaline? Robert wanted to kill me? Nothing was adding up. I could feel the dull pain of a headache behind my eyes.

"Helene," I whispered, my voice gaining strength. "Who is Helene?"

Tabitha gasped softly, throwing a look toward Marsh's back before looking back to me. "Helene

Ahlström is Robert's mother," she explained. "How is it you've come by that name?"

"Adaline whispered it to me, just before those men showed up."

I gripped my head as the pain intensified. My knees weakened and I dropped back onto the couch, a soft groan escaping my lips.

Marsh crossed the room and knelt beside me, resting his hand on my knee.

"Juliet?" he asked with concern.

"I'm fine," I insisted. "Just a little dizzy."

"Girl needs to eat. All that traveling, not enough stops for food and rest." Tabitha muttered, turning and striding toward the hearth. She removed the roast and hurried it toward the kitchen. The smell of it made my stomach grumble loudly and my mouth water. I hadn't realized how hungry I was until that moment.

Silence ruled us as we ate. I was positive I had never tasted anything so good in my life. The bread was fresh and coarse against my tongue. I was positive the butter was fresh too, its flavor somehow richer. The meat, I soon found, was pork. It was crusted in herbs, and had a melted cheese that spilled from the center. I ate my fill, and then some.

Groaning, I leaned back, patting my stomach. The heat of the room had my eyelids drifting, though the last thing I wanted was sleep. What I wanted were answers.

"Thank you for dinner, Tabitha. It was amazing." I smiled at her, attempting to rise as she stood and began clearing plates.

"No, no," Tabitha insisted. "You sit. Ya need yer rest. I'll jus' pack this away." She beamed at me before

Secrets

disappearing into the kitchen. The sound of running water and the clink of dishware soon followed her.

Sighing softly, I looked to Marsh, anxiety gnawing at me. "Marsh, are we safe here?" I glanced toward the kitchen. "Is *she* safe with us here?"

Marsh didn't respond, his eyes downcast. It was as if he were searching for answers from the wood. His shoulders lifted and fell as he exhaled deeply, lifting his eyes to mine at long last.

"I don't know," he admitted. "I don't know much of anything right now. I'd like to think we're safe. As far as I know, no one knows Tabitha's returned. It should give us a bit of a head start at least."

"A head start? Where are we going?"

"To the Council. You have to stand before them and complete the prophecy. It's the only way I know of to end this."

I sighed and nodded, rubbing at my forehead. The pain was back, though I wasn't sure it had ever left. I was bone tired, even though from the sound of it, I'd slept the better portion of a week. Something niggled at the back of my mind and I lowered my hand.

"Marsh, did we really swim the whole way here?" I asked.

Marsh nodded, a smile twitching at his lips. "Aye, and you're a damn good swimmer."

"Me, a good swimmer? Ha. I don't remember any of it," I said in awe of myself.

"You were in and out. I was pretty worried about you." Marsh smiled at me, reaching across the table and taking my hand.

"How did I survive?" I whispered, looking down at our joined hands. "The last thing I remember, I was drowning. I died."

Marsh tightened his hold on my hand, when he spoke his voice was rough with emotion. "You shifted. The only thing I can come up with, is your selkie half took over. I've never seen anything like it. It was beautiful."

I gaped at him, my pulse hammering in my ears. "I ... 'went seal?'"

Marsh nodded, smiling. "Aye."

"Me. Juliet, the woman so petrified of water I can't even take a bath ... 'went seal?'" My voice hitched as the enormity of it sank in. Shaking my head in denial, I rose from the table, suddenly filled with a restless energy. "No, no. It's not possible. I've never ... I can't ... *You're* sure you saw me turn into a seal?"

"I pulled you to the surface, helped you get your barring. But, aye, you were a seal."

"Where's my skin thing then? Don't I have to have a skin thing to be a seal?" The very thought of having a seal skin skived me out. I remembered how Marsh's had felt in my hands, and couldn't stop the shudder that over took me. *Gross.*

"I figured it was best if I held onto it for you until you woke up. You're the first half-selkie I've ever met. I wasn't sure if maybe it worked differently for you."

Hesitantly, I turned my gaze to him, watching him silently, my heart swelling. "Thank you."

I trailed my eyes over his face, noting the shadows beneath his eyes, the dark stubble lining his jaw. When was the last time he had truly slept? My questions could wait.

"You saved me," I whispered, taking his hand. "Ever since you met me, you've done nothing but rescue me." I dropped my eyes to our hands, focusing on tracing the faint, white scar on his knuckle with my thumb. Hesitantly, I looked back to him, ready for the punch to my gut his eyes always brought.

Marsh lifted his eyes to me, a faint smile on his lips. "I'm pretty sure that's part of being the Guardian," he replied.

I laughed under my breath and nodded. "Maybe so."

We both looked up as Tabitha stepped back into the room. Her eyes moved between us, taking in our joined hands. A smirk came to her lips, threatening to bloom into a full-blown grin.

"Well, I don' know about you two, but I'm wiped. I think I'll turn in." Her eyes danced with humor as she crossed the room, bent down and kissed Marsh's head. "Good night." Tossing us a wink, she exited the room.

Heat filled my cheeks and I moved to pull my hand from Marsh's only for him to tighten his grip. My heart leapt into my throat, thumping forcefully. I didn't think my heart could beat any harder. He had to know what he was doing to me. I was pretty sure China could hear my heart from here.

"Juliet," he said, leaning toward me.

"When was the last time you slept?" I blurted. My question took us both by surprise. Marsh regarded me with confusion before shaking his head. I wanted to kick myself.

Way to kill the mood, ding dong!

"You don't have to be afraid of me, Juliet. I will not hurt you."

His words hit me and I dropped my gaze. My fingers traced patterns on the table. "I know that, I've never been afraid of that."

"Then why do you shy away from me?"

I shrugged, keeping my eyes downcast. I knew why, but I wasn't sure I was ready to admit it. I *was* scared. I was scared to my core of giving my heart away again. While I wanted to think Marsh would never break my heart, I didn't know if I was ready to take the chance.

"You should get some sleep. You really look awful," I whispered, lifting my gaze and finding myself lost in his eyes.

Marsh laughed softly, shaking his head. "You know, I'm starting to like you worrying about me."

I slanted him a look and smiled. "Yeah, well, don't get used to it."

"Why? Are you planning on stopping?"

No, a small voice inside me whispered. Marsh grinned at me, as if he knew.

"I don't understand how I slept so much, but I'm still so tired."

"I'm not sure how much rest you actually got."

I glanced at him, unreasonable nerves filling me and making me fidget. "I-I should, um, head to bed." I flicked my gaze to meet his briefly and turned to go down the hall when a thought stopped me.

"Wait, where are you sleeping?"

Marsh lifted his brows, a sexy smile flirting about his lips. "Right across from you. I won't let anything happen to you."

"I know," I replied with a small grin. I had no doubt that he would protect me.

CHAPTER TWENTY-SIX

DARKNESS SURROUNDED ME, oppressive and thick, enveloping me. I ran, my bare feet pounding against the unseen ground. My chest ached as I panted for breath. I could hear them behind me, their heavy footfalls gaining ground.

Shots sounded and bits of shadow rained down around me, white mist seeping through the holes. I screamed, weaving as I did my best to avoid the bullets. My throat burned as I sucked in a breath and glanced over my shoulder.

I could see them now, three hulking shadows, shades lighter than the surrounding darkness. Their faces were obscured; their forms were wrong, misshapen and twisted.

Facing forward, I screamed as a wall of solid mist rose up before me. The impact reverberated through my body. I flew backward, crashing down with a jarring force.

Tendrils of mist wrapped around my wrists and ankles. I thrashed and screamed to no avail, whimpering in fright.

My body stilled as a wave of cold washed over me. Looking up, I found the three men standing over me. Distance had belied the true horror of their appearance. One's head was wrong, the back of it extending outward with the dome sunken in. Another's limbs were too long, more like tentacles than arms and legs. The last was the most grotesque. Massive pools of darkness took up most of his face, leaving me to assume they were his eyes. A spiny protrusion issued from his forehead, a tiny, pulsating orb swinging before me. Their faces were twisted into perverted glee, thin lips stretched tight, thick cords of saliva dripping from jagged teeth.

As a unit, they lifted their arms, training the guns they held on me. Terror renewed my thrashing, and I screamed as they fired and the world went dark.

"Juliet! Wake up, love!"

Marsh's voice broke through the darkness, his hands strong and real against my shoulders. My eyes flew open and locked onto his, grounding me.

"Marsh!" I clawed at him, scrambling to sit up in the bed and wrap my arms around him neck. Burying my face in his chest, I let the tears come. Sobs ripped through my throat and shook my body violently. Marsh crooned to me, banding his arms tightly around me and pulling me firmly against him. His bare chest vibrated beneath my cheek and his hand stroked over my hair repetitively.

After a time, my sobs quieted. I didn't move, choosing to stay curled up against him, reveling in the warmth of him. It was then that I realized he was singing.

Secrets

His voice was a deep baritone that thrummed through me. Stilling myself, I listened to the words:

> "Dear thoughts are in my mind
> And my soul soars enchanted
> As I hear the sweet lark sing
> In the clear air of the day
> For a tender beaming smile
> To my hope had been granted
> And tomorrow she shall hear
> All my fond heart would say
>
> I shall tell her all my love,
> All my souls' adoration
> And I think she will hear
> And will not say me nay.
> It is this that give my soul
> All its joyous elation
> As I hear the sweetest lark sing
> In the clear air of the day."

"That was beautiful," I whispered. I could hear his heart thrumming steadily beneath my cheek, feel the rise and fall of his breath. Closing my eyes, I drank in the comfort he offered.

"I'm glad you liked it," His lips pressed against my temple, his breath warm across my face. "Do you want to talk about it, love?"

I shook my head, pressing my face against his chest and breathing him in. "You're calling me 'love.'"

I felt him pull back, could feel his eyes on me. Shifting my position, I tilted my head up to meet his gaze.

"Is that a problem?" he challenged.

"No," I replied, shaking my head, my gaze locked on his. Something was different between us. A shift had occurred, though I didn't know when. All I had to do was take that step. Make that leap. But was I ready to admit how I felt? I wasn't sure. And that stopped me.

His thumb moved across my cheek, brushing against the edge of my lips. "Good." He dropped his hand and pulled away from me, breaking our gaze as he rose from the bed. "I'll let you get back to sleep."

"Marsh." I bit my lower lip and looked up at him. His brows rose in silent question when I didn't speak further. Silently, I extended my hand, swallowing deeply as his fingers curled around mine. "Stay?"

I heard him inhale at my whispered request. His fingers placed pressure against mine as he moved back onto the bed. I scooted over to make room, though I didn't give him long to settle in before curling against him and exhaling softly as I rested my face against his chest.

"Sleep sweet, Juliet," Marsh crooned, wrapping his arms around me.

I lay in the circle of his arms, my eyes growing heavy. His breathing was my lullaby.

CHAPTER TWENTY-SEVEN

MARSH BLEW OUT a breath as he regarded the building before him. It was a tall, white marble structure, though time had left her imprint on the building. Three stories in height, it towered over the other buildings, most of which only managed one story. The massive front doors were painted a deep blue, the brass handles shiny and new.

Rolling his neck, he climbed the steps leading up to those doors, his heart pounding wildly in his chest. This was the first time he would go before the Council since he'd been placed in Adaline's care, and the thought of standing before those men and women filled him with a chill that seeped to his bones.

The hinges creaked as he opened the doors and stepped into the cool darkness of the entryway. His feet echoed as he walked the length of the hall. The walls were painted pale beige, the high ceilings decorated in a hundred different murals, each depicting a scene from their history. One scene in particular caught his attention and he paused, craning his neck to view it:

Two selkies, a male and female, sat on a rock, the

waves crashing around them. Each was halfway through their shift, their skins covering the lower portions of their bodies, leaving their upper halves human. Their faces were turned toward one another, locked in a passionate gaze. The woman's auburn hair flowed behind her, as if tossed by the wind.

"Mr. Darrow?"

Marsh blinked and jerked his gaze from the mural, looking to the small woman who had spoken. She was short in stature, with pale blonde hair pulled back into a bun. Square framed glasses rested on a pert nose. Her dress was business-like, a cream top with a navy-blue skirt, and she held a thick folder against her chest. "The Council will see you now."

"Aye," Marsh nodded, following the woman as she turned and pushed open a door.

He halted suddenly, his boots just outside the threshold. This was it. With another step, he would be in their chambers, and the ball would be firmly out of his court. Taking a deep breath, Marsh squared his shoulders and stepped through the door.

If he'd thought the hallway was large, it in no way compared to the Council chamber. White marble lined the floors, interspersed with diamonds of sapphire. The walls were variegated shades of blue, and thick curtains of green silk draped from the ceiling, fluttering in the artificial air. White rails blocked off the audience seats from the floor.

A raised dais sat at the back of the room, looking down over all. Six tall crimson chairs held the council members—three men, three women. Their stern faces looked down at him, weighing, judging.

Marsh shook his arms as he crossed to the podium

in the center of the room, his steps like cracks of thunder in the otherwise silent space. The chill air caused the hair on his arms to stand on end. Nerves ran rampant through his body, cold sweat beading along his brow and trickling down his spine.

He fought the urge to sneeze as a mix of perfumes wafted down toward him, borne on the currents of the AC. His eyes moved around the empty chairs, thankful the Council had granted his request to speak to them alone. The silence of the six people watching his every move was unnerving.

"Mr. Darrow, this council is quite curious as to why you have requested this meeting." The clipped tones of the High Councilor boomed in his ears as the man turned up his nose, lifting his gaze from the paper that had held his attention. Sharp green eyes looked down out of a long face. Thickly silvered black hair was shorn in a severe cut. If his goal was to give off an air of intimidation, he was nailing it.

"Councilors, I have located the Lost One," Marsh spoke loudly and clearly, doing his best to hide the tremor from his voice while looking to each member in turn.

A chorus of chuckles and soft titters echoed around the room, reverberating and surrounding him. A white-haired woman leaned forward, gripping the edge of the table and looking down at Marsh.

"The Lost One? You expect us to believe you have found them?"

"I have. And I do," Marsh nodded, resting his hands on the podium and gripping it hard, doing his best to keep his rising anger from coloring his tone. "Her name is Juliet, and she is the one the prophecy spoke of."

"Boy, many have come before this council claiming much as you are now. What makes your claim different?" a weasel faced man demanded. His dark hair formed a sharp widow's peak and his black eyes burrowed into Marsh, even from a distance.

"I am the Guardian! Foretold by the last seer!" Marsh seethed, slamming his hands down on the podium and giving each council member a steely look. The sound filled the room like a gunshot. No one spoke, and Marsh cursed himself for his outburst. He watched desperately as the members leaned back in their chairs, their hushed whispers creating an angry buzz in the room.

"What is your name, boy?" a voice called out, silencing the whispering.

"Marsh, Marsh Darrow."

The woman rose from her chair, placing her hands on the table and leaning forward. A long braid of salt and pepper hair fell over her shoulders as her eyes narrowed, searching his face. "Adaline's boy?" she asked.

Hope flared with Marsh like a summer storm. "Aye. Do you know my grandmother?"

The woman nodded, coughing roughly before sitting down. She turned to the others, muttering something before settling in her chair, her eyes returning to Marsh.

He stood at the podium as they conferred in hushed voices, low enough he couldn't make it out. They had to believe him. It all fit. His mother's prophecy had come to pass, he was certain of it. Unease tore at him, and it was all he could do to keep himself from pacing the room.

The High Councilor rose from his chair. "This Council has come to its decision."

Marsh moved around the podium, stepping closer to the dais, his heart pounding in his chest.

"We are agreed to see this woman. You'll bring her to us in one week's time. In that time, we will assess your claim that you are the foretold Guardian."

Marsh whooped in delight, punching his fist into the air before clearing his throat and regaining his composure. "Aye, I'll bring her forth. Thank you. Thank you!"

"You are dismissed."

Not even the High Councilor's tone could dim Marsh's grin. They were reviewing his claim, and they had consented to see Juliet. He knew that once they saw her, they would have no doubt of the truth of his words.

CHAPTER TWENTY-EIGHT

I WOKE ALONE the next morning, instantly missing Marsh's warmth. After dressing in a shirt borrowed from Tabitha and my jeans, I made my way toward the kitchen.

Marsh and Tabitha sat at the table, their heads close together as they spoke in heated whispers. Tabitha and I both jumped as Marsh slammed his hand on the table.

"Enough!" he hissed at her, shoving his chair back and pacing toward the window. As someone who appeared so cool and collected on the surface, it was easy to miss the storm that brewed inside of him.

I cleared my throat and stepped forward. "Good morning,"

Tabitha offered me a wan smile as she rose from the table and stepped into the kitchen. "Mornin' lass," she replied. "Will ya be wantin' some coffee?"

"I would love some, thank you."

I glanced between her and Marsh, frowning. The tension could be cut with a knife. Squaring my shoulders, I strode toward him and crossed my arms over my chest.

"What's going on, Marsh?" I asked.

Secrets

Marsh sighed heavily before tearing his gaze from the window and looking at me. My heart turned over in my chest as our eyes met. I had to force myself to focus on his words and not the movement of his lips, or the images they conjured.

"I went to the council this morn," he explained. "I'm to bring you before them for judging. Tabitha ... does not agree."

"Judging?" I gulped, ice tickling my veins.

"Aye. They'll assess our claim to the prophecy."

"And if they find the claim false?" I whispered, gratefully accepting the mug of coffee Tabitha offered me.

"They won't," Marsh replied flatly, his tone steel as his eyes drifted toward the window and the misty morning beyond.

Tabitha shook her head, muttering softly.

"What?"

"I said, 'they might,'" she explained.

"Might what?"

"Find the claim false. Boy's got it in his mind that this is it, an' I'm not saying it isn't. I'm saying he needs to prepare for the Council to be the same savage tools they've always been. Tha's all I'm sayin'."

Marsh snorted, keeping his back to us. Tabitha glowered at him, setting her mug down on the table with a thump.

"You just keep livin' in that fantasy, Marsh Darrow! But I'll tell the lass true!" Tabitha turned her attention to me, her eyes hot. "Ya know what will happen if they find the claim to be false? They'll either kill ya for knowing our secret or they'll lock ya away until the world forgets about ya. And this thick boyo

243

here? He'll be made an example of. Publicly flogged for incitin' fear and layin' false claim. And then, if he's lucky, he'll get locked away too. Tha's the cold truth of it!" Tabitha nodded sharply and bustled past us, muttering beneath her breath as she went. A moment later, her door slammed shut.

I blinked, furrowing my brow and quietly mulling over her words before looking to Marsh.

"What do we do if they find it false?" I asked, my voice quivering.

"They won't," he commanded, his eyes shifting to lock on mine.

"But Marsh-"

"I said, they won't! Have faith, Juliet. I do."

I looked down into my coffee, studying the dark liquid for a long moment. I felt Marsh shift away from me again. For all his assurance, I could feel his nerves as easily as my own.

"I have faith," I corrected. "I have faith in you."

Marsh turned toward me with a smile, reaching out and cupping my cheek with his free hand. "I'm glad."

I covered his hand with mine, smiling at him before turning my head to kiss his palm. "You should apologize to Tabitha. She's worried about you. Scared for you."

Marsh looked at me, his gaze shifting over my shoulder before nodding. His fingers squeezed mine briefly as he stepped away and disappeared down the hall.

Closing my eyes, I exhaled and leaned against the wall. What a fool I was, running around like a child in a fairytale when there was real danger all around me.

Secrets

Tabitha's words ran through my mind, carrying images of horror. I felt as if I had been blind. I must have been to not see the precipice of danger we were toeing.

Opening my eyes, I lowered myself into a chair and wrapped my fingers around my coffee cup, soaking in the warmth. So much had already gone wrong in such a short period of time. People were actively trying to kill me. Adaline was in the hands of a psycho, possibly dead. And if this council of strangers found my claim to be false ...

I couldn't think of it.

I shoved away the grim thoughts of Marsh being bound, stripped, and whipped. My body trembled with a shudder. So much rested upon me. So many lives in the hands of Juliet The Ruiner.

Gritting my teeth, I curled my hands into fists, resolve burning through me.

No. No! I will not let them down.

I was the one—Marsh had said so. He was *sure* of it. All I had to do was believe in myself half as much as he believed in me.

A peace settled over me, a warm glow of acceptance. After twenty-seven years, I finally felt like I knew who I was. Or who I was becoming, at least.

CHAPTER TWENTY-NINE

IN A DESPERATE attempt to end my ever-present worry, Marsh took me to the beach. The cool sea breeze fluttered my hair and caused my stomach to clench in pain as my mind swam with thoughts.
I had missed Kylie's birthday. Beatrice would never forgive me for that. Heck, I wasn't in the mood to forgive myself.

Wrapping my arms around myself, I looked out over the green hued ocean. Marsh walked along beside me, my silent companion. I appreciated his company, and his silence.

Maybe I could send her something.

I had seen a few handmade dolls in the shops. Though if I did that, I would have to explain why I was in Ireland. And that wasn't something I felt capable of yet. The only person who could even understand would be Adaline …

Adaline.

My heart clenched painfully as I thought of her. I missed her, more than I would have thought possible. I was certain our story had been on the news. Had she seen it? Had my parents? So many people I had just left behind. I had no idea what had happened to my phone. I hadn't thought about it before, but now that I had, I couldn't stop.

Blowing out a breath, I lifted my hands and ran my fingers through my hair.

My parents.

They had to be going out of their minds with worry. The last time we had spoken, mother had dropped the bomb that I was adopted. And then I had disappeared.

And then there was Robert—the same Robert who had lied to and deceived me, who had gone out of his way to meet me. Who was hurting someone I cared about.

I forced the thoughts from my mind, looking out over the ocean as we walked. Tabitha had been insistent that I learn everything I possibly could about the Council and Selkie history in the days before our appointment, whereas Marsh was determined to distract me from our impending peril by taking me on a tour around Dingle Bay.

And I was more than happy to be distracted.

We spent the days window-shopping, visiting pubs and taking long walks along the beach. The day before the Council meeting, Marsh took me to see Fungie the Dolphin.

Fungie was a popular attraction in Dingle, and after reading about him in the brochure the boat captain handed me, I could see why.

Cold spray brushed against my cheeks as the boat bounced and rolled over the waves. Music, piped through hidden speakers, filled the air. I gripped the rail of the boat as I stood at the bow, looking out over the green water. I smiled as Marsh moved up behind me, pressing his body to mine and warming me through to the bone.

"Have you seen him yet?" he asked; his breath washing over my neck and ear, sending shivers of delight through me.

"No," I whispered, leaning back against him.

Marsh chuckled, banding his arms around my waist. "Well, you're not going to with your eyes closed."

Laughing softly, I opened my eyes and looked out over the sea. I still saw nothing, but I didn't care. In this moment, I was safe. I was free of terror.

"There," Marsh declared suddenly, pointing. My eyes tracked the direction of his finger and a huge grin split my face as I saw him. I watched the dolphin clear the water in a mighty leap before spinning in the air and disappearing once more.

"He's beautiful," I murmured, my eyes darting about, hoping to catch sight of him once more.

"Aye, you should see him up close."

"Will he come closer to the boat?" I whipped around in his arms, childlike hope making my voice giddy.

"Aye, he might," Marsh chuckled and tucked some wayward hair behind my ear. "But I meant closer than that."

I wrinkled my nose, lifting my chin. "Closer than him coming up to the boat?"

"Oh, aye." Marsh's eyes twinkled with mischief as he leaned toward me, lowering his voice. "I'm talking about swimming with him, love."

My eyes widened and I shook my head violently.

Secrets

"Oh, no! Nope. Uh-huh. I don't think so. Last time I got in the water I drowned!"

"*Almost* drowned. And actually, you swam beautifully."

"Don't downplay it, Marsh! I could have di-eee!" I shrieked as cold water sprayed along my back, followed by the clicks and whistles of a playful dolphin.

"Fungie says hello!" the Captain called out, guffawing.

"You could have told me he was behind me!" I grumbled at Marsh, slapping his arm.

"I could have, but you're just so cute when you're mad. I was captivated."

Heat filled my cheeks at the crooked grin he gave me. "Jerk," I muttered without wrath.

Marsh chuckled, grinning broadly at me. Shaking my head, I turned my back on him, scanning the water for the dolphin. The Captain turned the music back up and I gasped as my ears caught the familiar strains. Throwing my arms out to either side, I rose on my toes and lifted my face to the wind.

"I'm the queen of the world!" I called out, before laughing at myself.

"Juliet, what are you doing?"

I whirled around, grinning like a fool. "*Titanic*! It's like we're on the *Titanic*!"

Marsh frowned at me, slipping his hands into his pockets and clearing his throat. "Uh, this is the *Gimili*, and the *Titanic* is at the bottom of the ocean, love."

"No! I mean, I know *that*. The *Titanic*, with Leo DiCaprio? You know, the scene where he ... You haven't seen *Titanic*?"

"Of course not, Juliet. It sank years ago and

currently resides at the bottom of the ocean."

"The movie, Marsh! I'm talking about the movie! How have you not seen the movie?"

Marsh's brow flattened as my meaning finally dawned on him. His face went momentarily blank before he laughed and shook his head. "Oh, a movie. I was beginning to worry about your history education."

I stared at him, before shaking my head and laughing once more. "Unbelievable."

Marsh chuckled and wrapped his arms around me again, resting his chin on my shoulder. We watched the water as the boat turned and made its way back toward the dock. Fungie followed the boat to the dock, and I smiled as he all but waved at us as we disembarked.

The throng of people milling about the wharf had thinned, and one glance held the answer. Dark clouds lined the sky, ominous peels of thunder rolling in the distance.

Glancing up, I frowned. "I'm suddenly regretting not bringing any rain gear."

Marsh laughed, wrapping an arm around my shoulders as we walked. "Don't worry, the sky's always threatening rain here. That's just Ireland."

I gave him a skeptical look, which had him snickering. My lips twitched as his laugh washed over me. I loved his laugh. It was such a warm, free sound, something I hadn't heard from him often. Our eyes met, and my stomach quivered, my heart flipping in my chest.

"Let's walk along the beach."

I lifted my brows at his suggestion, glancing up to the swollen sky. "Are you sure?"

Marsh glanced upward, his expression unsure

before he dropped his gaze and flashed me a confident smile. "Aye, I'm sure. Come on, we'll be fine. Trust me."

I held my skeptical look for a moment before laughing and nodding. "All right. I'm trusting you."

Marsh lifted his arm from my shoulders and took my hand, bringing it up and kissing the back of it. Delight skittered up my arm as we left the blacktop and walked out onto the beach.

Marsh nodded as we passed a couple of fishermen packing up their gear. The elder of the two squinted at us, before calling out.

"Ya hear tha' storm comin' don' ya, boyo? Did ya lose your marbles?"

Marsh shook his head, lifting his hand to them as we passed. My lips twitched upward as I glanced at him.

"Even strangers are questioning your sanity. Regretting this decision yet?" I teased.

"Not at all."

Thunder rippled across the sky, loud enough to still my heart. I jumped, my eyes widening as I looked around. Gripping Marsh's hand tighter, I pressed myself against him. He might not have regretted the decision, but I did.

Marsh wrapped his arm around me, pulling me closer, a chuckle rumbling through him. "If I'd known all it would take is a little bit of thunder …"

I slapped at his chest and laughed. I was being silly. Marsh knew this area better than I, and if he said we would be fine, then I needed to trust him. I blew out a breath and smiled at him.

And then, the sky opened up.

I yelped in shock as the rain pelted down, soaking me to the core in an instant. With a laughing curse Marsh grabbed my hand and ran down the beach, leaving me no choice but to follow. My jeans clung to my legs, my shirt suctioning to my body as we ran. I laughed, gripping his hand tighter as my shoes slipped against the wet sand.

Lightning slashed across the sky, rending the air with the scent of ozone, the sharp, metallic scent that follows lightning. I stumbled, clinging to Marsh as I went to a knee, laughing like a loon. With ease he hauled me up, spinning me around as the rain crashed down around us. Another peal of thunder roared, sending us lurching for cover.

"In here!" Marsh called over the cacophony of the storm. Blindly, I followed, my sodden hair plastered to my face, obscuring my vision. Sand gave way to stone, the muted light of the day dimming further as we darted into our makeshift shelter.

Panting, I slapped my hair from my eyes and laughed as I shook the water from my arms.

"Whew! That was insane!" I looked around, my brows lifting. "Are we in a ..."

"A cave, aye," Marsh confirmed. "There are a few along this beach."

I stopped and stared at Marsh, lowering my arms and licking the water from my lips.

A cave.

It was storming outside, and we had run into a cave for shelter. It was oddly-

"Fitting,"

"Did you say something?" Marsh turned to me, his brows lifted, a faint smile curving his lips.

"I said 'fitting.' Being in this cave with you, during the storm. It's fitting."

Marsh moved toward me, his smile widening as he reached out and pulled some hair from my cheek. "Fitting how?"

I looked up into his eyes, my body coming alive at his closeness. "I found you in a cave during a storm. I'll never forget it."

"Never?" Marsh asked, closing the small gap between us.

I shook my head, my voice blocked by my pounding heart, which had taken up residence there. Marsh wrapped an arm around me, pulling me tight against him. I was positive he could feel the thunderous beat of my heart.

"Marsh-"

"No," Marsh cut me off, placing a finger against my lips. "No, you're not allowed to talk right now."

Our eyes met and he grew a slow, sexy smile before lowering his finger. I licked my lips, tasting him and shivered. His hand shifted, cupping my cheek and drawing his thumb over my lips before he pressed his lips to mine.

Pleasure coursed through me as his lips moved over mine. I gasped as his teeth closed over my lower lip, sending bolts of delight through my system. I smoothed my hands over his shoulder, my fingers gliding over the wet wool of his sweater. I pressed my body against him, his heat searing through me, igniting the dormant fire within me.

Lightning cracked just beyond the entrance of the cave, illuminating our silhouettes against the back wall. I yelped at the boom of thunder that followed, jerking away from him before laughing self-consciously and covering my lips with my hand. Marsh looked at me, a delicious smile growing over his lips before he too chuckled. Our gazes locked, held.

I didn't know who moved first, but the next thing I knew I was in his arms, their strength engulfing me, binding me to him. The scent of him overwhelmed me, filling my nose until every breath was of him. Salt, leather and something else, something I couldn't identify. Something wild and reckless that I yearned for.

Strong fingers threaded through my hair, tugging my head back and causing my lips to part as I inhaled sharply.

"Juliet." His voice was a ragged growl, echoing the hunger rioting through my veins. Blue eyes locked onto mine, the icy depths piercing my soul. I saw a carnal lust written there, a primal need to be sated superimposed over my own image. My fingers flexed against his chest as I fought to steady my breathing, his heart racing beneath my hand.

"Yes?" I asked, unable to look away from him, trapped in the cage of my own desire.

Marsh slid his thumbs along my cheeks, the rough texture of them sending ripples of pleasure down my spine, igniting parts of me I'd never felt and making my blood hum with need.

Before I could utter another word, his mouth was against mine. His lips were like fire, searing my flesh. I willingly gave myself to the flames, embracing the sweet ache. My fingers slid through his hair, crushing his mouth more firmly against mine. My lips parted at the insistent probing of his tongue. He tasted like heaven. He was ambrosia personified. His touch was everything I had ever yearned for. Something awoke within me, as if my very soul was waking from a deep slumber.

The rough, cold wall of the cave bit into my spine as he pushed me back, an annoyance quickly forgotten. Driven by desire, Marsh moved his hands down my body, thumbs trailing over my nipples, dragging down my ribs and igniting a trail of flame wherever he touched. I moaned against his mouth, drawing back to suck in gulps of sweet, cool air.

My body was alight for him, burning for him as the storm raged on scant feet from us. As my desire grew, so did the intensity of our kiss. I pulled away, panting raggedly as I tugged at his sweater, wanting it off. Needing it off. I craved to feel the warm touch of his skin. I threw the sweater to the ground, barely comprehending the sound the wet wool made as it hit the stone floor. My sole focus was on him, his body and all the things I desired to do to it.

My fingers shook as I trailed them down his naked chest, pausing to trace the black and blue tattoo.

He groaned, long and low, his head dropping back as my fingers slipped lower. A shudder escaped his body as my fingers traced a line along the rim of his pants. My eyes rose to meet his and my breath caught at the fiery passion looming behind the ice.

My feet left the floor as Marsh lifted me, pressing his body firmly against mine, our lips meeting feverishly. My hands moved frantically over him, reaching between us and fumbling with his belt, grunting in frustration.

Another deep moan rose from his throat as I

moved my hands over him, scraping my nails along his lower stomach, finally freeing the wet leather. Marsh sailed his lips down my neck as he lifted my shirt. It fell to the floor, leaving me feeling exposed, though I still had my bra and jeans on.

Marsh pulled back, his gaze moving over me. His thumbs caressed my hips, a moan issuing past my lips as I arched into his touch. His eyes rose to mine as his fingers glided upward and around my back, deftly unhooking my bra. My breath hitched as it fell away, my nipples hardening in the cooler air. Our eyes remained locked as his fingertips smoothed down my ribs toward my waist, unbuttoning my jeans. My fingers echoed his actions.

In a heartbeat, we were naked. It didn't matter that I had seen his body before—excitement filled me at the sight of him. In this moment, he was mine.

Desire pooled in my stomach as his eyes roamed over my naked flesh. The cold air attacked my skin, raising gooseflesh along my arms and legs, making the hardness of my nipples intensify. Marsh continued to look at me, his expression awestruck.

"Marsh?"

His eyes snapped to mine, as if speaking his name had broken the spell. In a flash he reached for me, crushing me against him. The hard length of his desire pressed against me and I gasped.

"You're a Goddess. Beauty incarnate," he whispered against my heated flesh, guiding me down to the floor of the cave.

My breath went from steady to ragged in the span of a heartbeat. My hands moved over his shoulders as he moved over me. A moan ripped from me as his mouth closed over my nipple, running his tongue around the sensitive flesh. I threaded my fingers through his hair, holding his mouth to me as waves of pleasure assaulted me.

Every nerve came alive as if I had been electrified. My hands traced every curve, every dip, every muscle and scar on his heated flesh. My body tightened as his mouth moved lower. It was as if the storm had moved inside my head. My hands curled into fists, my back arched and my hips bucked as his mouth pressed against my aching center.

A hoarse scream echoed through the cave as I dissolved into a quaking puddle of ecstasy. He used his tongue like a weapon, leaving me whimpering and incoherent.

I could take no more. Grabbing his hair, I hauled him upward, heedless of where his mouth had been. Pressing my lips to his, I wrapped my legs around his waist.

"Juliet," Marsh groaned as I pressed myself against his hard length.

"Yes. Yes, Marsh." I caressed his cheeks before softly kissing him once more, nodding vigorously. His body pressed against mine, his length slipping into my heated center, stretching and filling me.

The ability to think left me. All I could do was feel. There was nothing in the world but me, this man, and this cave.

Lightning flashed as our bodies came together. Our breath mingled; with each inhalation, I breathed him in, until I was full of him, until he was part of me. We were one flesh, one being.

Sweat clung to our bodies as we moved together,

finally satiating our desires. Heat coursed through me, and I wrapped my legs tighter around his waist and gave in to the pleasure.

CHAPTER THIRTY

SOFT RAIN PATTERED against the sand, dripping from the arched opening of the cave. The sound of the ocean was peaceful, the storm having passed on. Watery light fought its way through the thick clouds, dotting the dark brown sand and stone with color. I sighed contentedly and snuggled deeper into Marsh's arms. His nose was pressed against my shoulder, his breath washing over me with each draw. Closing my eyes, I smiled to myself.

When Tommy had left me, I was certain my life was over. Now, I wanted nothing more than to call him and thank him for setting me free. My smile grew wider as I trailed my fingers along Marsh's tan arm.

Marsh grunted and stirred, nuzzling deeper against my neck. "That tickles."

"You're so tan. I'm jealous," I pouted playfully, continuing to trace patterns along his arm.

"You're perfect," Marsh rumbled, shifting behind me and pressing his lips against my skin. "How are you feeling?"

"I'm content, and happy." I shifted to look at him. "Happier than I've been in a long time."

Marsh grinned at me, cupping my cheek and drawing his thumb across my lips. "Good sex will do that."

I laughed, shoving at him playfully. Our laughter reverberated through the cave as we wrestled and tickled. Breathless, I grunted as Marsh pinned me beneath him, grinning broadly at me.

"I win," he grinned.

I bucked and huffed as I tried to shake him off before settling down with a disgruntled pout. "Fine! You win!"

"It's a good thing you gave up when you did. All that moving around was about to take this conversation to a whole 'nother level."

Giggling, I wrapped my arms around his neck, heat exploding from my belly and spreading through every inch of me.

"You won't hear me complaining," I whispered huskily, biting my lower lip before moaning as Marsh pressed his lips to my neck. Closing my eyes, I threw myself into the moment, swept away by passion once more.

GOLDEN AFTERNOON LIGHT greeted us as we finally exited the cave. Hand in hand, we walked down the beach, heading back to town.

"I wish I had a camera," I mused, glancing over my shoulder at the disappearing cave.

"A camera, what for?"

"Well, to capture the beauty of this place. But to also take a picture of that cave. What if it disappears too? I would hate to never see it again. Not after what we just shared in it." I blushed and glanced up at him.

Secrets

Marsh chuckled and brought my hand to his lips, a gesture I began to fall in love with.

"You don't have to worry about that, love. But we could get you a camera if you wish."

I smiled at him before looking around, frowning at the lack of people. "What time is it? We've been gone all day, I'm sure."

Marsh stopped, squinting at the sky. "Half past six, I'd say."

A stab of guilt pierced me, and I groaned, slapping my hand to my forehead.

"What is it?" Concern tinged Marsh's voice as he looked down at me.

"My family," I replied. "I haven't called them to let them know I'm okay. And I'm certain the shooting at the Village is all over the news at home. My mom is probably freaked."

Guilt filled me, twisting my stomach into painful knots. I hadn't even thought about calling them. What did that say about me?

"Hey," Marsh said, touching my shoulder. "You've been through a lot. I'm sure they'll understand."

"Understand that I ran off to Ireland with a relative stranger and didn't even give a thought to letting them know I'm alive?"

"Juliet-"

"I just…Can we go back now?"

Marsh frowned at me, but said nothing more on the subject. A short while later, I stared out the speckled window of the cab at the rolling green fields, chewing my lower lip, lost in thought as we drove back to Tabitha's.

Would my mother be happy to hear from me? Would she be furious? And Beatrice—how would she be handling the stress of my disappearance? I should have thought about calling her straight away. She was pregnant, and didn't need to be worrying about me on top of everything else she was dealing with.

Sighing, I rubbed at my brow, as if I could massage away the oncoming headache of my jumbled thoughts. How would I ever explain the crazy turn my life had taken to them? Would I be able to make them understand?

I jumped as Marsh touched my shoulder, a soft smile on his shadowed face.

"We're here." He offered me his hand as he exited the cab. Taking it, I scrambled to follow, tossing a soft thank you to the driver. I was so preoccupied with my thoughts that I walked right into Marsh.

"Ow! What are you doing?"

"Here."

My brow furrowed as Marsh held his hand out to me. Curious, I took the offered object, my eyes widening as I discovered it to be a cell phone.

"Have you had this the whole time?" I accused, brandishing the phone.

Marsh nodded, slipping his hands into his pockets in an almost sheepish manner. "Tabitha gave it to me before we left. With everything that happened, I'd forgotten all about it. At least until you brought up calling your family."

I swallowed and looked at the phone. The thought of calling my parents had my stomach souring. Anxiety laced my veins, and I blinked in surprise when Marsh pressed his lips to my forehead.

Secrets

"Take your time. I'll be just inside." Marsh smiled at me, and then headed toward the house. I reached out, grabbing his arm and halting his steps.

"Wait," I interrupted. "Thank you. For everything."

Marsh cupped my cheek, his smile lighting his eyes as his thumb traced a pattern against my skin. "You're welcome."

Our gazes held until the air heated between us, my breath coming quicker. Marsh dropped his hand, winked at me, and turned away.

I watched him retreat, fanning myself and willing my hormones to go dormant. They weren't listening. Blowing out a breath, I looked down at the phone and dialed Beatrice's number. She answered on the third ring.

"Hello?"

"Bea? It's Juliet. I just wanted to-"

I jerked the phone away from my ear as unintelligible shrieking colored the air. Wincing, I brought the phone closer to my ear, adopting a tone of calm. "Bea, calm down. Bea, Beatrice, stop crying. Please?"

Pinching the bridge of my nose, I began to pace the small stone pathway, listening to my sister sob hysterically.

"Do you have *any* idea what I've been going through?" she hiccupped. "I come home and see on the news there was a shooting at Rose Village, and then you disappear! No one was apprehended and all I could find out from anyone was they saw you getting on a motorcycle with some mystery man!"

I groaned inwardly, immediately missing the

crying in the face of her concerned anger. "Bea, I'm sorry."

"Two weeks! Two weeks, Juliet. I've been calling you, looking everywhere. We reported you missing to the police! Why didn't you call me? No, don't answer that. Just tell me where you are. I'm coming to get you."

I heard shuffling, and the jangle of keys. Bill's muffled voice came down the line, and I sighed. How selfish had I been?

"You can't come get me, Beatrice. And please calm down. All this stress can't be good for the baby."

Beatrice gave a derisive laugh, ignoring my words. "Why can't I come get you?" She sucked in a breath, her voice rising in pitch. "Is someone keeping you? Oh my God! Were you kidnapped? Bill! What do they want? Did they hurt you?"

"No! Jesus. I haven't been kidnapped, no one has hurt me. I-" I sighed heavily and leaned against a tree. The branches fluttered in the light breeze, as if encouraging me. "It's a really long story, Beatrice."

"I'm listening."

Lifting my eyes to the sky, I inhaled and let it go.

I told her everything. Everything I had learned about Marsh, about myself, about this whole new world we had never known existed. In my mind's eye, I imagined her, my perfect, logical sister, sitting at her kitchen table. Her expression would be neutral as she listened to my insane ramblings. She would be calm, and quiet, even as she Googled the closest mental health facility.

Silence met me as I finished talking. Nerves filled me as the silence stretched, quickly followed by fear that we had been disconnected.

"Bea? Are you still there?"

"So, you're in Ireland?" she asked calmly.

Too calmly.

"Yes."

"With Marsh?"

"Yes. We're staying with his aunt."

"And he's... some sort of animal-shifter-thing?"

"He's a Selkie, yes."

"And, according to him, you are as well?"

"Well, sort of. He thinks I might be a half-breed. It's kind of confusing, but if the Council accepts my claim, I think I may be able to find out more."

Silence.

Squeezing my eyes shut, I willed away the image of police cars pulling up and carting me away. I couldn't take anymore. Slapping my hand against my thigh, I blew out an exasperated breath. "Say something, Beatrice!"

"What would you like me to say, Juliet? You have to know how insane this sounds. I'm very concerned for you right now. In all of this time, have you hit your head? Could you be delusional?"

Hot tears stung my eyes as I shook my head, a mirthless laugh rising up, catching in my throat. Sniffing back the tears, I cleared my throat.

"I should have known better. I should have known you wouldn't believe me. But I thought you, out of everyone, would at least give me a chance."

"Jules, please, I'm honestly worried about you. Let me fly you home and we can sit down and talk-"

"No, Beatrice. I have to go. Just, just know that I'm okay. I'm safe. Tell the girls I love them."

"Jules, Juliet. Do not hang up on me!"

Ignoring her words, I pressed the end button. A different kind of silence surrounded me, enveloping me in the quiet of the night. Frogs chirruped, and insects sang as the stars above winked to life. I scrubbed at my cheek, wiping at the tears I didn't realize had fallen. The phone began to vibrate, but I ignored it, shoving it in my pocket and walking up the path and into the house.

CHAPTER THIRTY-ONE

MY DREAMS WERE filled with horrors. Faceless figures towered over me, judging and casting me aside. Men with distorted bodies forcing Marsh forward, onto his knees. His howls of pain echoed through my mind as the tongue of a whip cracked along his back, opening the flesh. Blood wept, like crimson tears, puddling beneath him. His eyes found mine, filled with hatred and disgust.

Look what you've done to me, they said. *I trusted you.*

Juliet The Ruiner.

I shot up in bed, gasping for air and thrashing, fighting with the sheets and blankets that bound me. Cold sweat plastered my hair to my neck and cheeks. I pressed my fist to my mouth, choking back the sobs as the room came into focus.

My hands shook as I scrubbed them over my face, willing my breathing and pulse steady. The taste of fear was bitter on my tongue.

Shivering, I threw off the blankets and padded toward the door. I was halfway down the hall before the murmur of voices registered.

Halting in place, I bit my lower lip and pressed

against the wall. I didn't know why, but something told me not to enter just yet. Holding my breath, I strained to catch the words.

"Have you heard anything more?"

"Aye, got another package this morn. Didn' want to mention it in front of the girl. She's a panicky one, ain't she?"

"Tabitha, I think she's got a right to be, don't you?"

I heard the faint rustle of cloth and Tabitha's soft chuckle. "Aye, I was only picking." She heaved a heavy sigh, and what sounded like the clink of ice in a glass. "If I have to admit it, I'm worried."

Silence met her confession. My heart clenched at the quick inhalation and mutter curse from Marsh.

"That bastard! I'll gut him myself." His voice was low, thick with emotion and barely controlled rage. The sound of it had my curiosity peaking and fear churning.

"Get in line, boyo. Tha's my mother he's torturing."

I gasped and slapped my hand over my mouth.
Adaline.

They were talking about Adaline.
Torture?

Swallowing down my unease, I crept forward, desperate to see what was causing such turmoil. As luck would have it, their backs were to me, heads bent together as they continued to speak in low tones. Biting my lower lip again, I inched forward, jumping out of my skin as my foot came down on a worn and noisy board eliciting a loud, plaintive creek.

Like a deer caught in headlights, I froze, my eyes

widening. Marsh spun to face me as Tabitha scrambled to cover something between them. She wasn't quick enough.

"Is that ... blood?" I shrieked, my stomach lodging in my throat. Bile burned my tongue as the horror of what I was seeing registered.

Lying on a snow-white linen cloth was a small, wrinkled pinky finger, flecks of pale pink polish still visible on the nail. My knees gave out as I attempted to draw breath into my constricted lungs. Tabitha cursed musically, and wrapped the finger as Marsh rounded the couch, crouching down in front of me.

The room spun as he grabbed my shoulders tightly, steadying me. "Juliet, look at me." His tone was firm, rough. It took a concerted effort to get my eyes to focus on his face.

I couldn't blink. The image of the severed digit was burned into my retinas. My stomach reeled and darkness clouded my vision.

"Juliet! You need to be strong now. Weakness will not help Adaline."

"Her finger. They cut off her finger!" I whispered harshly, my body trembling beneath his hands.

"Aye, but at least we know she's still alive." His eyes burned into mine, fingers digging into my shoulders.

Again I forced down the threatening bile and nodded. "Okay."

"Okay." His eyes searched mine, assessing my state, before nodding and pulling me to my feet. I wobbled and steadied myself against him. Looking to Tabitha, I felt the hot prick of tears behind my eyes. "I'm so sorry."

Tabitha shook her head, a tight smile coming to her lips. "Adaline's stronger than she looks. If he thinks losing a little finger is going to break her, the bastard's dead wrong."

I stared at her, utterly amazed by her strength and unwavering faith in her mother.

"What do we do?" I looked between them, twisting my fingers together.

Tabitha lifted her chin, her eyes hard, lips pressing into a firm line. "We prepare to go to the Council. There's nothin' more important that wha' they might say righ' now."

I shook my head, my hair slapping against my face. "No. No, I can't do this. I thought I could, but I can't. I'm sorry. I can't."

"Toughen up, girl! Marsh might have got ya here, but ya need to walk yer arse through the damned door!"

I flinched at her sudden anger, caught off guard. Tabitha had been solid and kind from the moment I had arrived, but I supposed everyone had his or her breaking point.

"Enough!" Marsh roared, stepping up behind me. His hands came to my shoulders, the warmth of him pressing against my spine. I took comfort in that.

Tabitha scoffed, throwing up her hands as she turned from me. I watched her walk away, my heart breaking for her. I wished I had never left the room, wished I had never pined for adventure. The reality of it was turning out to be more of a nightmare than a dream.

"I can't do this," I whispered, turning toward Marsh and placing my hands to my cheeks, shaking my head. "I want to help, you, Tabitha, Adaline ... But I can't do this. I'm not ... I can't-"

"You can," he insisted.

"No. No, I can't. I'm going to mess it all up. Ruin it. People are going to die because of me!" My voice rose in pitch as I stared at him, not really seeing him. I saw Adaline, bleeding, broken and bruised, wracked with pain. I saw Marsh on his knees, back welling with blood, face swollen, body broken. I saw my family, gunned down, taken from me. Every one hurt or dead because of me.

"Juliet! Stop it now! You *can* do this! You *will* do this. Have *faith*, love. Believe in yourself and stop letting all these doubts defeat you. Find the strength I know you have!"

I blinked as he took my hands in his, pulling them away from my face. His hands engulfed mine, making me feel small and vulnerable.

"Marsh, I'm so scared."

"There's not a reason in the world for you to be, love. I'm right here with you, every step of the way."

There were in fact a million reasons for me to be scared, but I could see what he was doing, what he was offering. Taking a deep breath, I nodded.

"Okay. Okay, I can do this." I forced a nod, lifting my eyes to his. I plastered a smile on my face, hoping he would see some truth behind the facade.

"Yes, yes you can." Marsh cupped my cheek and smiled reassuringly at me. The feel of his thumb against my skin calmed me, even as it caused my blood to stir. "How about some breakfast?"

I followed Marsh to the table, wrapping my arms around myself. Dawn was breaking, filling the sky with subtle pinks and oranges. I stared out the window, losing myself in thought. Try as I might, I couldn't see a positive end to this situation. I wanted nothing more than to buy into Marsh's belief that the Council would see me as the Lost One. The odds, however, were not in our favor.

Breakfast was a brief affair, which I was thankful for. I didn't think my stomach could hold too much. The sun had just cleared the tree line when Tabitha returned, freshly washed and dressed. She held a soft, green dress in her arms, a faint smile on her lips.

"I thought ya might want somethin' a bit more feminine to wear," Tabitha explained. "I know ya only got but the one shirt and pants, so …"

"Thank you," I replied. I accepted the dress with a wide smile. We regarded one another for a moment, each understanding the peace offering for what it was.

"I'll meet you in town. Got a few things I need to be doing." Tabitha looked between Marsh and me, her gaze lingering on her nephew. After clapping him on the shoulder, she nodded and walked out.

Marsh stepped toward me, taking my arm and pulling me against him. Closing my eyes, I breathed in the familiar scent of him, thankful for his silence. Reluctant though I was, I pulled away, lifting the dress as explanation. I wanted nothing more than to get this day over with.

I dressed quickly, wishing I had something other than my sneakers to wear. But beggars couldn't be choosers. Finger combing my hair, I stepped out into the main room and reunited with Marsh. He too had changed, dressing in a pale purple shirt the color of heather, and dark slacks.

"Are you ready?" he asked.

"As I'll ever be, I suppose." I gave him a tight, nervous smile and took his offered hand.

The ride to town was blessedly swift, affording me almost no time for thought, and even less for doubt.

"Thanks, mate," Marsh muttered to the driver, passing him a handful of bills as we exited the cab. The sun was well and truly up now, and I blinked as the light hit my face. Shielding my eyes with my hand, I took in the unfamiliar surroundings.

The buildings around us were small, quaint shops. Many were brightly colored, their doors thrown open in welcome, windows glittering in the early morning light. The streets were cobbled, giving the area an old-world feel. It was as if I had stepped back in time. I found myself half expecting to see a horse drawn carriage come down the road.

"Juliet, over here."

I turned, lowering my hand and blinking at Marsh. He stood in the entrance of what appeared to be an alley. Frowning, I moved to follow him, my eyes on the broad expanse of his shoulders. A smile quirked my lips as I watched him walk. He had such a beautiful way of moving. I giggled softly, and Marsh turned to look at me, his brow raised quizzically.

"What?" he asked.

"Nothing," I replied, pressing my lips together, my shoulders shaking with restrained amusement. I didn't even know why I was laughing, but once I had started, I found it hard to stop. Marsh shook his head, his lips curving in response to my giggles.

"Well, whatever it is, I'm glad to hear you laughing." He shifted his gaze, his shoulders stiffening as his whole demeanor changed. "We're here."

I followed his gaze and gasped. The building was huge, and more than a little intimidating. The white stone seemed glaringly bright, causing me to squint. It was easily three stories tall, towering above everything surrounding it. Thick white columns lined the breezeway, holding up the peaked roof. I was sure there was at least a twelve-foot clearance from floor to ceiling. Even the tiled porch was white. The architecture struck me as vaguely Roman.

I squared my shoulders and looked to Marsh.

"Let's do this."

CHAPTER THIRTY-TWO

I DON'T KNOW what I was expecting, but the cool, calming feel of the interior of the Council building wasn't it. My eyes darted around the room, taking in everything around me. I had only been there once, but it wasn't so different from the courthouse in Portland—enough to draw similarities. Where Portland boasted framed photographic portraits of its judges, the Council building favored paintings.

My gaze drifted upward and I gasped in awe. The murals above me had been done with a considerable amount of skill. I studied each one as best I could, considering I was still moving.

Marsh placed his fingers against my spine, drawing my attention downward. A door at the end of the hall opened, and a petite blonde stepped through, holding a clipboard to her chest. She was demurely dressed in a cream sweater and charcoal skirt. Her hair was bound in an intricate braid, worn over her shoulder.

"Mr. Darrow, Ms. Adams," she greeted us with a small nod. "They're ready for you."

Fear rooted me to the ground. I couldn't have

moved if I had wanted to, which I didn't.

My eyes locked on the doorway beyond the woman, and my anxiety peaked. Panic filled every inch of me, left every nerve in my body screaming for me to run, to go anywhere but in that room.

That room held death.

"Juliet, we need to go," Marsh encouraged softly, taking my hand and squeezing it.

With concerted effort, I took one step, and then another. My heart thundered in my chest as I drew closer to the door. The blonde smiled prettily at me as we passed. I wanted nothing more than to slap the smile from her face.

The room beyond the door was cast in darkness and shadow. The only illumination came from two spotlights—one highlighted the podium in the center of the room, the other the raised dais at the far end. Much like my dream, I could feel that the room was larger than it appeared. Like a child in the night, I wished fervently for more light.

Marsh moved his hand to my lower back and propelled me forward, our footsteps thunderous in the silent room. My skin tingled with nerves as I stepped up to the podium. Sweat beaded my brow and tickled my spine.

"Just breathe," I whispered to myself.

The sound of a chair scraping against stone filled the room like a gunshot. Cloth fluttered and I drew my gaze upward my breath catching in my throat as I looked into a stern, gaunt face. A sharp widow's peak directed my gaze to a pair of the darkest onyx eyes I had ever seen. Even Robert's eyes had held warmth. These eyes were as cold as the stone they resembled.

Secrets

A shiver danced down my spine. It was my dream made reality. The brightness of the light obscured the faces of the other five members. I whimpered and squeezed my eyes closed.

"Step forward," a stern voice boomed, causing me to physically jerk from the shock. Licking my lips, I stepped forward at Marsh's urging, twisting my fingers together. "You are Juliet Leigh Adams, of 1564 South West Broadway, Apartment 27B, Portland, Oregon? Adopted daughter of Mary Clair Lambert-Adams, and David Michael Adams, correct?"

I gaped at the black-eyed man, shock and anger rushing through me. "How do you know all that? How do you know my address?" I demanded, surging forward. Marsh grabbed my arm, halting my steps.

"Answer the questions!" Widow's Peak barked, spittle flying as his lip curled into a sneer.

Swallowing down my annoyance, I nodded. "Yes, that is correct."

The man glared down at me before lowering into his chair. Papers were shuffled and passed around. A woman with salt and pepper hair rose next.

"We have here a copy of your adoption papers, and birth certificate," she noted. "Your birth father was not listed, but we do know the identity of your birth mother."

"What?" I breathed. I felt as if all the air had been sucked from the room. My chest constricted and my knees shook, threatening to give out. Marsh was behind me in an instant, supporting me and keeping me from hitting the floor. The blonde appeared suddenly, setting a chair at my hip before disappearing again. I sank onto the cushioned seat, my pulse beating rapidly against my ears. Emotions coursed through me, leaving my mind muddled and confused.

My birth mother, they know who my birth mother is.

"Aye, child." The woman looked down at me, a sad smile on her lips. "After an in-depth investigation, we have discovered that you are indeed a half breed. Your mother was *Séala,* a selkie of Irish blood."

Was?

The word ran through me, my heart clenching as the woman took her seat and another man rose. His eyes were a bright, warm brown.

"What reason do you have in claiming the status of the Lost One?" he asked.

Confusion swirled and I closed my eyes. It was too much. I couldn't take it all in. Pressing my fingers to my forehead, I shook my head. "Reason?" I asked. "I don't have a reason."

"You must have a reason!" Widow's Peak snapped, much to the consternation of Brown Eyes.

Anger took over and I lurched out of the chair so fast I knocked it down. "What do you want from me? I just want to know who I am! My whole life I've never fit in, never belonged, I just want to know my place in this world! Is that okay with you?"

My words echoed around the space, bouncing back to me. Widow's Peak narrowed his eyes at me and I instantly regretted yelling. Marsh cursed softly beside me, and I knew without looking at him that he was shaking his head.

This was it. I had done what I most feared. I had doomed us.

Salt and Pepper rose from her seat, a reassuring smile on her face. That was when I noticed Widow's

Secrets

Peak was the only one not smiling.

"A very noble reason to do anything, Juliet," Salt and Pepper commented. "To know your place in this world, to know yourself. Both are valid reasons indeed." She cleared her throat, shuffling papers before looking at me. "Tell me, how did you meet Adaline?"

I stared at her, struggling to find an answer to her question. The abrupt change from good cop to bad cop left me reeling. Licking my lips, I cleared my throat. "I met her a few years back, at my job. I'm a nurse at an assisted living center in Portland. She was my patient."

"I see. Adaline is a wily woman, I have no doubt she placed herself in your care with purpose."

Brown Eyes rose, setting his hand on Salt and Pepper's shoulder. She nodded, and lowered into her seat as he looked to me.

"You said you have always felt out of place. Why is that?"

"I just ... did. I've never really fit in. I don't know how to explain it."

"Was this feeling only with your family? Or with others as well?"

"With everyone. Until ..."

"Until?" Brown Eyes raised his brows, leaning toward me.

"Until I met Marsh."

He nodded, and resumed his seat. I stared up at the dais as they huddled together, whispering amongst each other. Widow Peak's voice was harsh, his opinion of me obvious. The others seemed more willing to accept me and my claim, but I had no idea how any of this worked. I jumped slightly as Marsh slipped his hand into mine, smiling down at me.

"I wish Adaline were here." I muttered, squeezing his hand and leaning my head against his arm.

"Aye, as do I."

We fell silent, the whispers of the Council the only sound in the room, save for the rapid beating of my heart. I tried to calm down, to still my worries, but fear had me in its grip. What if they denied me? What if this was all a lie? What if my nightmares were to come to pass?

"Hey," Marsh whispered, drawing my gaze upward. "It will all work out. Have faith."

"We have reached our decision." Salt and Pepper rose, folding her hands before her as she looked to her companions.

Brown Eyes rose as well, clearing his throat. His eyes locked onto mine, as if looking into my soul, judging the very essence of me. "We have. Juliet Leigh Adams, this Council has judged your claim to the prophecy."

The whole world stopped. Tension filled me and I threw out my hand, grabbing wildly for Marsh, finding him and gripping his hand tightly. A spark of hope dared to flair to life within me.

Brown Eyes looked up and down the table before returning his gaze to mine. Marsh pressed against me, his hands moving to my shoulders, his grip tight. My stomach fluttered as anticipation filled me.

This was it.

"This Council has debated," Brown Eyes announced, "and have found your claim to be truthful. It is our belief that you are the Lost One of prophecy."

Relief washed over me in waves. Marsh let out a loud whoop of delight and scooped me up, spinning me around and kissing my face all over. Tears of joy dampened my cheeks as I hugged him tightly.

"I told ya!" Marsh exclaimed. "Didn't I tell ya? I knew from the moment I saw you. I knew."

Salt and Pepper leaned over the table and cleared her throat to draw our attention. "Mr. Darrow, I am sorry to interrupt your delight. However, during our investigations into Ms. Adams, we uncovered a most disturbing rumor. Please, what is the current status of Adaline?"

Marsh released me and looked up toward the dais, his shoulders sagging. "It's not good, Council Woman. She's been kidnapped, and he's torturing her. We received confirmation of that this morn, when he sent us her finger."

Bile burned my throat at the memory. Whispered conversation erupted between the Council members, the sound loud in the large space.

Salt and Pepper turned to face us. "Do you know the identity of the one who holds her?"

Marsh's face took on a look of pure, unadulterated hatred. "Robert Ahlström," he nearly growled.

Brown Eyes rose abruptly, leaning on the dais and looking directly to Marsh. "You are certain of this?" he asked.

"Aye."

"You are also certain that he means to kill her?"

Marsh stared at Brown Eyes for a long moment before nodding silently.

A collective hush filled the room. It felt like hours, but only seconds passed. There was a flutter of cloth and a man strode forward, dressed in black from head to toe. He didn't look our way as he passed, his steps silent on the stone floor. The man stopped just before me, the smell of wood and rain wafting from him. He placed his closed fist over his heart and bowed to the Council.

"Helene Ahlström," Brown Eyes said. The man in black straightened slowly, gave a curt nod to the council members, and strode from the room, disappearing as quickly and efficiently as he had appeared.

"What's going on? Who was that?" I demanded, looking from where he had disappeared to the Council table, but they too were gone. I whirled on Marsh, opening my mouth to demand an explanation when he shook his head. He looked ancient, his face drawn, as if the weight of the world was once more resting on his shoulders.

"Don't," Marsh pleaded softly. "Don't ask. You do not wish to know."

"I do wish to know! Marsh. Tell me."

"The Council believes, rather fully, in 'an eye for an eye.'"

I turned at the soft-spoken statement, my eyes widening as I found Salt and Pepper to be the speaker. She was shorter than I had expected, the dark robes she wore making her seem even smaller.

"Oh, I see."

"It is a grisly belief, tis true, but one that has served us well." Her eyes shifted between myself and Marsh before coming to rest upon mine. "Forgive my intrusion, I wanted to introduce myself. I am Laney Ahern. Adaline has been my best friend for as long as I can remember. I want you both to know, I will do whatever it takes to bring her home."

"Thank you, Mrs. Ahern. My family appreciates the Council's support in this matter." The conversation completed, Marsh took my hand and led me from the room. Glancing over my shoulder, I did what I could to commit the room to memory. I didn't want to forget how close we had come to losing everything. If they had voted the other way ...

But they hadn't. They had found truth in my claim.

I was a half-breed. I was the Lost One. Somehow, I would restore peace to their world and take my place in it.

If only I had a clue as to how I was supposed to do that.

CHAPTER THIRTY-THREE

ROBERT PULLED UP the crushed stone driveway, parking the vintage mustang in the circular drive before the main doors of the manor. The cliff house rose before him, grey against the pearl and blue sky. Tiny pockets of crystals embedded in the stone winked in the afternoon light, lending a magical quality to the home.

Home.

The word ran through Robert's mind and brought a sneer to his lips. Walls, windows, furniture, but it was not a home. Homes were filled with love, with acceptance. His memories were filled with harsh words, rough touches. This house had never been a home.

Shoving the thought from his mind, he scowled and exited the vehicle. He had made excellent time, and for that he applauded himself. He had left the old woman in the care of hired men, under orders to stay away from her at all costs. He didn't need to lose any more men. They were expensive. Nor did he wish to risk her escape by their stupidity. Seagrass swayed as a chilling breeze moved up from the beach, but he felt nothing but rage.

Robert slammed his hands against the heavy oak door, pushing it open. His steps never faltered as he marched into the foyer, a deep scowl set on his face. His long strides propelled him across the room in quick succession. His anger rose as not a soul was present to greet him.

"Where is she?" he demanded of the first servant he saw. The frightened woman stopped in her tracks, pressing a bundle of towels to her chest and stared at him, wide eyes and mouth gaping.

Having no patience for games, Robert grabbed the woman by the throat and shook her violently, slamming her back against the wall so forcefully her teeth rattled.

"Where is she?" he growled, his voice low and dangerously calm.

"The-The madam rests in her chambers, sir! Please! Don't hurt me!" the servant shrieked, fat tears staining her cheeks.

Disgusted, Robert released her, shoving her away and causing her to stumble to the floor. He had no time or inclination to care as he raced to the double staircase that lead to the upper portions of the manor, taking the steps two at a time.

Servants scurried out of his path, huddling against the walls as he strode down the long hallway. He paused only long enough to check his clothes, combing his hair back and making himself presentable.

Trepidation filled him and caused his feet to drag. The weakness fueled his rage and with force he shoved her door open, causing the wood to smack against the opposite wall. Fear gripped his heart as he moved to her bedside, just as the woman he loved most in the world lifted her hand.

"Robert, you came to me. You came. My son." Her voice was thin, reedy and whispered, as if it took insurmountable strength to speak the words.

"Of course I did, mother. You called for me and I came as soon as I could," Robert smiled, lowering to his knees beside her bed and taking his mother's hand.

Helene opened her eyes and gasped, the action causing her to choke and gag. Her voice was hoarse, vicious, when she spoke again. "What happened to your eye?"

Robert scowled, turning his head away and touching the puckered skin over his right eye. He still wasn't used to the blindness. "Complications with Adaline. Do not worry, I am more concerned about you, mother."

"Yes, yes, you were always such a good boy. Such a good man. Better even than your father." Helene sniffed and gave a derisive chuckle, shifting in the bed as she wrapped her withered fingers tighter around her son's hand. The faint laughter soon turned into a cough that wracked her frail body.

"Mother, what happened?"

Helene licked her dry lips, her breath wheezing as she rolled her eyes in his direction. "Poison."

"Poison? Who did this to you? Tell me!" Pain and tears choked his voice as his eyes moved over his mother's form. Once tall and regal, Helene had been reduced to a sack of skin and bones in a short time. Closing his eyes, he pressed her wrinkled hand to his forehead.

"The Council. Darrow. The Other," she accused,

venom lacing her soft words.

"The Council? The Other? Darrow? Darrow did this to you? Darrow sent an Other?" Robert implored, his voice rising as his fury burned through his pain and concern. Desperately, he searched her eyes. The once sapphire orbs had faded now to the palest of blues, as if the color had been leached from them, as her life was being leached from her now.

Helene could not speak, her throat constricting. It cost her too much energy. The time was coming, quicker than she would have liked. She could feel the poison rushing through her veins. Her heart, the culprit of all her pain, pumped strongly, working swiftly to kill her.

She rolled her head toward Robert, moving her eyes over his ruined face. Handsome, he had always been so handsome, so like his father. It made her heart swell and ache to look at him now. He would not disappoint her, not in her final moments.

"Darrow. It was Darrow." She condemned the man easily, a twisted smile turning up her flaking lips. She attempted to wet them, pain seizing her chest, stealing her breath and leaving her gasping. "Water. My love, water."

Robert shifted, reaching for the glass resting on her nightstand, not willing to release her hand. Turning quickly back to her, he brought the glass to her parted lips.

"Drink, mother. The healer is on the way," Robert soothed, tipping the glass slightly.

Helene did not move. The water ran down her chin and her eyes stared lifelessly at the canopy above her, the lace fluttering in the breeze.

"Mother? Mother, drink. The healer comes. Mother? No! Mother? Mother!"

With a roar of anguish, Robert pitched the glass to the side. Water sailed out as the vessel hit with force against the antique armoire, sparkling debris falling like rain to the stone floor.

Sinking to his knees, Robert gathered Helene into his arms, pressing his face against her chest with a sob. He cradled her, moving her onto the bed. Her head flopped against his shoulder, her arms hanging limply by his sides. The hot sting of grief choked him, filling his throat with the acid taste of bile. He rocked back and forth, holding his mother against him as he cried out for her in anguish, his roars echoing around the room.

Gently, ever so gently, he laid Helene back on her pillows, taking his time as he adjusted her hair into perfection, straightened her dress. Using a kerchief, he wiped the water from her chin and neck before pulling the blankets up around her. He rested her hands over her chest, one on top of the other, and with the softest of touches, he placed his fingers to her eyelids, closing them forever.

"From the sea you were born, by the sea you lived, and in death you return," he whispered, leaning down to press a lingering kiss to her forehead. "Goodbye, mother."

Straightening, he turned and strode from the room. Hatred ignited in his heart, burning away the grief and filling him with a bitter resolve. His mother was dead. The only woman he had ever loved, dead at the hands of Marsh Darrow.

She would be avenged.

CHAPTER THIRTY-FOUR

AFTER THE TENSION and excitement of the council meeting, all I wanted was to return to Tabitha's and sink myself into a hot bath. Though the thought of baths had once stopped me cold, ever since our insane swim across oceans, I had found myself craving water, longing for the touch of the sea. Marsh was more than willing to comply with my request, and we quickly caught a cab.

Tabitha was still out by the time we got back. I pressed a quick kiss to Marsh's lips and darted off to the bathroom.

How long I stayed in there, I didn't know, but it was long enough to have my fingers mimicking prunes. The water had cooled significantly when I finally climbed from the tub, wrapping a thick white towel around myself.

I smiled as I stepped into my room, closing my eyes and leaning back against the door. My skin tingled as I blew out a breath. For the first time in a long time, I felt completely relaxed, unconcerned.

Normal.

Exhaling, I rolled my neck, shaking out my arms,

enjoying the limp feeling of my body. Pushing away from the door, I crossed to the bed, my brows drawing up into a curious frown as I looked at the cluster of bags sitting on the bed. Curiosity filling me, I reached into the nearest bag and pulled out a card, a note written on it in pretty cursive:

Juliet, I know you're lacking in clothes. Hope these help.

xx, Tabitha

I turned the card over and back, a giddy joy filling me. I dropped it onto the bed and reached into the bag, pulling out shirts and jeans and even a skirt. My eyes widened as I reached back in. It was thin, and felt like silk. Hands shaking, I drew the dress out, my breath catching in my throat.

The color of the dress was the deepest blue of the ocean, with thin golden cords for straps. I knew they would fit snugly to my shoulders.

It was just as I had seen in my dream, come to life.

Shoving the bags aside, I stretched the dress out over the quilt, looking it over. Trepidation flooded me, lending a tremble to my hands as I fingered the dress. I didn't know if I believed in fate or destiny, but they apparently believed in me.

I let the towel fall to the floor, and lifted the dress, pulling it on.

The dress felt like warm water rolling over my body. It settled with something like a sigh, fitting my form perfectly, as if it had been made for me. A giggle burst from my lips as I put my arms out and spun in circles. The hem of the dress lifted, kissing along my thighs as I moved. The room blurred and I gasped in girlish glee as I stumbled, catching my balance against the bed. Panting, I pressed my hand to my heart, feeling it race.

A knock sounded at the door. My head shot up as heat rushed through me.

"Juliet? Can I come in?" Tabitha called.

"I-Yes," I called back breathlessly, padding toward the door and pulling it open.

Tabitha gasped, putting her hands to her lips as she looked me over. "Oh lass, ya look amazing. Just like he said."

"I, um, don't have any shoes." I looked down at my bare feet before jerking my eyes to hers. "Like who said?"

Tabitha stepped away from the door, letting go a wolf whistle and gave me a grin that reminded me of Marsh. Heat burned through my cheeks once more and I fought the urge to cover my chest with my arms.

"Marsh of course! And I've got shoes for ya, child. You're stunning. You're gonna be wearin' your hair down, aye?"

"Wearing my hair down? For what?"

Tabitha chuckled and crossed the room. "I knew ya'd pick the dress. Ya wouldn' be able not to."

I shook my head, looking at her in confusion. "Tabitha, I don't know what you're talking about."

"Sit, sit. I'll see to your hair." Tabitha grinned and pushed me toward the stool in front of the vanity, grabbing up a brush and attacking my hair. When she was done, it fell down my back in ruby waves, soft as the silk I was adorned with. I stared at my reflection in shock.

"Wow," I whispered, staring at myself.

Tabitha chuckled, touching my shoulder. "Well, what are ya waitin' for? Go knock him dead, child."

I walked down the hall, my borrowed shoes clicking against the wooden floor. I twisted my hands, gnawing my lower lip as I stepped into the living room, looking for Marsh. I had no idea what was going on, but anticipation rolled through me in waves.

He stood at the open door, staring out at the darkening night. He was dressed in a black velvet jacket with tails, his arms behind him, hands clasped. Corduroys the color of charcoal hung from his hips, and a shirt of similar color as my dress clung to his chest and shoulders.

He turned as I stepped toward him, his eyes moving over me like a caress. My body quickened in response. A crooked grin bloomed on his lips as he faced me fully. He looked delicious.

"Juliet, you look amazing," Marsh said as he moved toward me, offering his arm.

I smiled as I took it, heat coursing through my body. "So do you," I replied. "Where are we going?"

"A barn dance."

"A barn dance?" I stared at him, trying to wrap my head around his simple answer. A barn dance, it seemed so strange, given everything that was going on.

"Aye, a barn dance." Marsh locked his gaze with mine, as if daring me to question him. Warmth colored his eyes, and my heart swelled in my chest.

"Won't we be over dressed?"

"And if we are?" He shrugged. "It's a party, Juliet. Relax and enjoy it."

I laughed softly and nodded, freezing as Marsh

lifted his hand and traced a fingertip along my cheek. My tongue glued itself to the roof of my mouth. I couldn't have made a sound if I'd tried.

"It's a nice night," I heard Tabitha say behind us, a grin in her voice as we jerked apart. I glanced self-consciously over to her, finding her leaning against the hallway wall. "Are ya walkin', then?"

She knows.

Marsh chuckled and nodded. "Aye, that was the plan," he replied. His eyes widened and he grunted as Tabitha tossed something his direction. Marsh lifted the flashlight and chuckled. "Thanks."

"You two have fun," Tabitha said with a smirk. "An' don' worry. I won't be waiting up and I'm a deep sleeper." She winked at us before turning and heading toward her room.

Biting my lower lip, I giggled at Marsh as he took my arm and led me out of the house. The beam of the flashlight cast a yellow glow on the ground before us, though it was nothing compared to the brightness of the moon and the stars above. My feet stilled; I looked up, captivated.

"I've never seen so many stars before," I breathed.

Marsh stopped beside me. I could feel his gaze on me. I didn't need to see him to know he was smiling at me.

"Aye, Ireland is known for its beauty," he remarked. "Though I've never known it to be as beautiful as it is now."

A blush spread through me and I chuckled, eyeing him with a teasing smile on my lips. "Okay, Romeo. Are you going to take me to the ball or not?"

Marsh grinned broadly, pulling me firmly against

him.

The walk was pleasant, the night warm and devoid of the rain of the previous evenings. The scent of jasmine and honeysuckle was heavy on the air, bringing a smile to my lips.

Before long, music filled the air, mingling with the sound of laughter. Marsh flicked off the flashlight as we made our way up the road toward a large barn. Light spilled out of both ends, the doors thrown open to the night.

I widened my eyes, looking around and trying to take in everything. A group of men sat just outside the barn doors, sitting on overturned buckets and laughing as they played their instruments. A fiddler sawed on the strings, tapping his foot in time with the beat. Another swayed as his fingers flew over the holes of his flute.

"Is that ... Is that man playing spoons?" I questioned, a giggle coloring my words as I watched the man rhythmically tapping the spoons against his thigh and palm.

Marsh laughed and nodded, lifting my hand and pressing his lips to the back of it. "Aye, love. Shall we head inside?"

I nodded, fire from his gesture skating up and down my arm, the place where he'd kissed me still ignited even moments after. Swallowing thickly, I plastered a smile on my face as we stepped into the barn.

Hundreds of mason jars hung from the rafters, each with a candle flickering inside. Tables lined the sides of the barn, some filled with platters of food and others crowded with people. Laughter and the hum of conversation filled the air, mixing pleasantly with the

Secrets

aroma of the fare. The yeasty fragrance of beer filled my nose, tickling my senses.

Giddiness filled me, intensifying the further we went. People offering smiles looked over as we moved deeper into the barn, many calling out to Marsh. I smiled back at them, sticking close to Marsh as we made our way toward the food.

My stomach rumbled as I looked down at the offerings. Puddings, cakes, and tarts topped with cream and fruit; slabs of beef, racks of lamb, dozens of potato dishes and roasted vegetables called out to be sampled.

I was choosing something to eat when a portly man boasting a brilliant orange walrus mustache strode forward and wrapped Marsh in a rib-crushing hug.

"Hallo, boyo!" he beamed. "Where in the bog have you been hiding? It's been an age, an age! And who's this?" He grinned brightly as he turned to me. "Aren't you just the prettiest lass at the party?" He gave a boisterous laugh and leaned toward me, his tone shifting to a mock whisper. "Don't go tellin' that to my wife now, eh?"

Marsh chuckled and shook his head, rubbing absently at his ribs. "Angus, this is Juliet."

Angus smiled at me once again, his small eyes all but disappearing as his face crinkled in joy.

"Juliet, a rose by any other name." Angus took my hand and kissed the back of it with flourish, bringing a titter out of me.

Marsh laughed and brushed Angus aside. "Enough of that. I'll not have you stealing my lady."

"Ho ho!" Angus chuckled, winked at me and moved off to mingle.

Marsh turned to me and offered his arm. "Dance

with me?"

Anxiety gripped my stomach as I sputtered, forcing a laugh. "Oh no. You don't want to dance with me."

Marsh frowned. "Aye, that I do. Dance with me, Juliet."

I sighed, passing a hand over my brow. "Marsh ..." I glanced around, then leaned in and lowered my voice. "I-I can't dance. I mean it. When I try I dance, it's like an ostrich imitating a flamingo on the back of an elephant walking like a penguin. It's bad. Babies cry, people run in terror. Let's just watch, okay?"

Marsh narrowed his eyes slightly, determination etched across his face. "Challenge accepted."

I yelped softly as he shifted his hold on me from my arm to my waist, drawing me out onto the dance floor. Plastering on a smile, I moved along with him, lest I would be dragged.

My heart raced in my chest as the band struck up a lively tune. Beaming couples filtered out onto the dance floor, holding hands as they began to spin and move to the reel. My mouth dropped open as I watched their feet fly over the worn wood.

"You're crazy! I can't do that!" I sputtered, looking at Marsh in wide-eyed terror. To my horror, he simply smiled and tugged me forward. "Marsh, no. Marsh! No!"

My hissed pleas fell on deaf ears. Lights and faces blurred as Marsh spun me around the dance floor. His laughter washed over me, warm and free. Throwing self-doubt and caution to the wind, I let go and allowed myself to enjoy the moment.

The music swirled around me as I laughed and

danced to the beat. I was more than a little thankful when the band switched to slower ballads. Sweat beaded my brow and dripped down my spine as I pressed myself against Marsh, breathing in his scent.

Closing my eyes, I listened to the steady beat of his heart as we swayed to the gentle crooning of the singer. Marsh's fingers were warm, his grip possessive. I didn't care, for in my heart I was his.

The candles had burned down to the end of their wicks, many sputtering out, and still we danced. I could imagine no place I would rather be than on that dance floor. It was as if we were the last people in the world.

Finally, Marsh pulled away, a warm smile on his face. His fingers traced along my cheek, over my lips as he watched me.

"I knew ya could dance," he breathed, his accent thickening.

"Only because I'm with you." I looked up into his eyes, mystified by their color. So pure and clear.

Marsh chuckled and lowered his head, his hand slipping beneath my hair, gripping the back of my neck. I rose on my toes, my lips eager against his. Desire surged through me, shocking me with its intensity. Before I could stop myself, I was parting my lips, my tongue seeking the touch of his.

A moan rumbled through him, his chest vibrating beneath my hands. His breath washed over my face, warm and sweet, his thumbs caressing the apples of my cheeks as a ragged laugh left him.

"We should probably head back before we get too out of our heads," he cautioned.

I smiled up at him, my cheeks flushed with desire. Marsh took my hands, his thumbs skating over my palms, driving me wild and making my blood hum as we walked from the barn and into the star-filled night.

CHAPTER THIRTY-FIVE

OUR WALK BACK to Tabitha's was filled with teasing touches and promising looks. I felt as if I was walking on air, my body vibrating with need. By the time we reached the house, I was on the edge of exploding. Marsh touched the back of my neck, playing with my hair and sending chills down my spine. I moaned and Marsh grinned wickedly at me.

"I'm going to jump you right here if you don't stop that," I warned.

He waggled his brows. "Is that so? Not really the way to make me stop, love."

I smirked, glancing toward the door and biting my lower lip. Tabitha had said she wouldn't wait up...

All thoughts of lovemaking left my mind as I caught sight of a white box sitting on the steps of the porch.

"Hey, what is that?" I asked, catching Marsh's brief shrug as I strode toward it. The box was strangely pristine in the darkness. My frown deepened as I crouched down beside it.

"It's addressed to us. But, how? No one knows we're here," Marsh muttered.

Confusion and curiosity warred within me, and I twisted my fingers together. Marsh drew a pocketknife from his back pocket and I blinked up at him.

"Can't be too careful right now, love," he explained. I smiled softly at him and watched as he cut the tape holding the top of the box closed, his face a mask of concentration.

Anxiety bubbled to life within my stomach, and I had the sudden and insane urge to stop him. "Marsh," I whispered, touching his arm just as he lifted the lid off the box. Despite myself, I looked.

A smaller white box rested on a bed of crushed velvet, the color a deep, rich purple, so dark it was almost black. Two red roses sat on either side of the box. My name was beautifully written across the pure whiteness of the lid in a looping font, the dark ink stark against the snow-white lid.

Trepidation quaked my hands; I reached for the lid as Marsh looked over a sealed envelope he removed. As I listened to the scratch of parchment leaving its envelope, I blew out a breath, and lifted the lid.

"Juliet, no!" Marsh roared, reaching out to me.

But it was too late.

My eyes widened in horror as my brain registered what I was seeing. Adaline's head rested within the box, her neck cleanly severed from her body. Her silver hair was spread carefully around her skull. Her eyes had been pinned open, the sightless orbs staring up and burning accusingly into mine.

A scream ripped through me as I shoved away from the box, scrubbing my hands against my thighs. I couldn't stop screaming. The sound poured from me, taking over and owning me until I *was* the scream.

Marsh cursed and wrapped his arms around me, yanking me tightly against him and pressing my face to his shoulder. "Don't look," he urged. "Don't look, love."

Tears choked his words, thickening his accent. His hands, so strong and sure, shook as they moved over my back, comforting me even as he grieved.

But I had looked. I had seen, and I could never unsee.

Sobs rose up within me, jamming in my throat before ripping free, tearing me apart and leaving me shattered.

"No! No!" I shrieked, clawing at Marsh, unsure if I was struggling against his hold, or trying to become one with him. Pain laced every breath. I couldn't blink without seeing her. The scent of blood and death overpowered the sweet smell of the flowers, turning the air toxic. "Adaline!" I screamed, raking my nails down Marsh's arm as I gave into the tears. They stung as they fell, acid on my cheeks. Sobs ripped through me, wracking my body as I gasped for breath.

The hot wash of Marsh's breath burned my neck, breaking through my grief enough to recognize his own. His tears fell upon my shoulder as he struggled for composure, his hands moving over my body in a frantic, jerking fashion.

"Hush, hush now. Breathe, love, just breathe."

The porch light flicked on and the door flew open. Tabitha was backlit, her hair wild as she hastily belted her robe. Her face was obscured, but I didn't need to see it to know it would be covered in confusion and fear. I watched in silent horror as she stepped forward into view, her eyes dropping to the box, widening in shock. She crumpled in slow motion, her knees striking the porch as her hands flew to her face. Her mouth opened in silent horror. No sound escaped. It was as if someone had muted the world, or I had gone temporarily deaf.

And then it was back. The volume of grief so loud I found myself wishing for the ignorance of silence.

Tabitha let go a wail so tortured and grief filled that it was almost inhuman. Her hands fluttered over the box as she began rocking back and forth. Marsh broke away from me, rushing to his aunt. He wrapped his arms around her, covering her like a protective blanket as she wailed, his own grief etched on his features.

Eventually, she settled, arms bound around herself as if holding herself together. My vision blurred as a fresh wave of tears dripped from my lashes. I moved to them both as the tears dried, and the howls died off, leaving nothing but echoes on the wind. Numbness set in and I leaned limply against Marsh. He kept me pressed against him, his cheek resting against my head.

Something stirred in my brain and I shifted, looking up at him. "What did the paper say?" I croaked. Out of the corner of my eye, I saw Tabitha lift her head, her eyes burning in the night.

"'An eye for an eye. Mother for a mother. We are far from even. You took my life, now I shall take every one of yours,'" Marsh intoned, staring off over my shoulder. His face was frightening, eyes colder than I could have ever imagined, mouth set in a firm, hard line. Fury burned below his grief. The tracks of his tears glimmered in the moonlight.

My stomach clenched in fear—fear of the man Marsh was morphing into, fear of what this meant for all of us. Fear of what was coming. This was not over. Robert had opened a Pandora's Box of pain and torment, and this was only the beginning. As I had learned at the council building, blood was always answered with blood.

"Marsh," Tabitha spoke, her voice hoarse and quiet.

Marsh shifted, turning his head to view her, his brows lifting slightly, body tense, the muscles taut steel beneath flesh.

Tabitha lifted her chin, her eyes hardening as she looked to her nephew. "*Deireadh air.*"

End it

Marsh inhaled sharply before schooling his expression. His eyes remained on Tabitha's as he nodded, echoing her words. Their words floated on the night, a promise and a curse, chilling me.

No, this was far from over.

CHAPTER THIRTY-SIX

THE DAYS FOLLOWING our morbid discovery were laced with quiet sobs and short tempers. Tabitha walked the cottage like a wraith, barely sleeping and eating even less. Marsh stood moodily at the windows whenever he was awake, a tumbler of whiskey gripped in his fingers more often than not and a deep scowl set on his lips. The few times I had tried to talk to him, he ignored me, his eyes distant and full of the deadly promise of a storm.

With all that had transpired, it was no surprise that I, too, pulled into my own shell. I started spending more and more time locked away in my room, listening to the periodic wails of Tabitha, and the muted crashes and curses from Marsh's room. Even then, I still tried. I went to them both, to no avail. Tabitha lashed out, ripping me apart with her words. Marsh was no better. I wanted nothing more than for him to scoop me into his arms, press his lips to my forehead and tell me it would be okay.

But that would be a lie. It would never be okay.

The days dragged on, each one worse than the last. I became more and more certain that everything was

Secrets

my fault. If I had never met Marsh, Robert would never have come after Adaline. He would have had no reason to hurt her. To hurt any of them.

Grief gripped my heart as I walked toward the closet, throwing it open and grabbing an armful of the clothes that hung there. If not for me, so many would have been spared so much pain and suffering.

Sniffling, I shoved the clothes haphazardly into a canvas duffel bag I had found under the bed. I knew what my path was now. The Council had been wrong. I wasn't the Lost One. I wasn't going to bring peace and happiness to their people. All I brought was pain and ruin.

Juliet, The Ruiner. Forever.

Wiping my hands over my wet cheeks, I lifted the bag and slung it over my shoulder. I paused at the door, my hand on the knob as I looked around the room. Everything was as it had been when I'd arrived. The only things left was the blue dress and Tabitha's shoes.

I stared at the dress, my heart aching for the happiness I had felt while wearing it—a happiness now tinged with sorrow and bitterness. I had been dancing while Adaline had been dying. While I was laughing and spinning about like a careless child, her life had been snuffed out.

Squeezing my eyes closed, I sniffled and shoved all thoughts of Adaline from my mind. I couldn't. It was too soon, the wound too fresh.

I opened the door and peered into the hall. Marsh's door was closed, and no sound came from the living room, leading me to believe that Tabitha was tucked away in her room as well. Adjusting the bag on my shoulder, I stepped out of my room and paused by

Marsh's door long enough to drop a folded piece of paper at his doorstep.

Maybe leaving a note was cowardly, but it was fitting. That's what I was. A coward.

Pressing my hand to his door, I closed my eyes and bit my lip against the threatening tears. Just the thought of leaving Marsh made my heart clench. It was the only thing that broke through the grief. It hadn't been an easy decision, but as Marsh had pulled more and more away from me, I began to realize I had only one choice.

If I wanted him to be happy, then I had to leave.

I saw him in my mind's eye standing at the window and brooding, tumbler of whiskey in his hand. Leaving was the only thing that made sense in a world that had gone senseless.

I turned from the door and crept down the hallway, walking softly through the living room. A snore ripped through the silence and stopped me in my tracks. I sucked in a sharp breath and waited to be caught.

But nothing happened.

I then saw Tabitha curled on the couch, her fingers looped limply around the neck of a whiskey bottle.

Assuring myself that she was sufficiently self-medicated, I moved past her toward the door. I gripped the knob with shaking fingers, my eyes closing as a fresh wave of sadness hit me. I hadn't imagined it would be this hard. I hadn't imagined that I would find a family in such a short period of time.

I was doing the right thing. Leaving was the best option. The only option.

Secrets

So why wasn't I moving?

My breath rattled through my lips as I fought the sob backing up in my chest. Silent tears streamed down my cheeks. Steeling my resolve, I flicked my wrist, opened the door and stepped out into the night.

I had no idea where I was going. No idea what I would do or what would happen to me. I didn't even know if I cared. There was only one thing I knew for sure, as my steps carried me away from the little cottage on the hill.

I had left my heart staring out a window.

CHAPTER THIRTY-SEVEN

MARSH GROANED AS the sunlight poured through the window, stinging his eyes and rousing him. His head throbbed painfully as he sat up, and had him cursing the previous night's drinking. And the nights before that. Prying his eyes open, he scowled at the tumbler mocking him from the nightstand. With a grunt, he threw out his hand. The cut crystal spun as he hit it with a glancing blow, sending it spiraling off the nightstand. Luck kept it from shattering, and it hit the floor with a hearty clunk and rolled the length of the room.

Dragging his hand over his face, he grimaced. His mouth tasted awful, and his clothes smelled worse. When was the last time he'd taken a shower and changed his clothes? What day was it?

Heaving a sigh, he shoved off the bed and rose to his feet. This was not how his grandmother would want him to act. A faint smile tugged at his lips as her face flashed through his memory. Adaline had always been full of laughter and life. She would smack him upside the back of the head to see him sulking and drowning himself in drink. Scrubbing at his face again, he padded barefoot toward the door pulling it open with a yawn. He needed coffee, and some painkillers.

His footsteps sounded like jackhammers through his aching head and drew a whimper from him. Rubbing his temple, he set the coffee to percolating, inhaling deeply the rich aroma. Tabitha would want tea when she surfaced, so he set about preparing that as well. And Juliet, she would most likely want the coffee. It seemed like she lived off the stuff some days.

Juliet.

Her name ran through his mind, bringing about conflicting emotions. Guilt swept through him at the way he'd acted, the way he'd treated her. He had allowed himself to be so consumed by his own pain and misery, that he'd been blind to hers.

Pinching the bridge of his nose, he blew out a breath as the percolator began to pop and hiss. He would have to do something to make it up to her, something special. Though he had no idea what. Still, there was nothing wrong with starting with coffee.

He waited impatiently for the percolator to finish, and poured two mugs, heaping sugar into one and adding a dash of milk. Lifting the mugs he made his way down the hall, taking care not to spill the scalding liquid. His steps faltered as he realized he was humming the lullaby Adaline had sung to him so often throughout his childhood. Another small smile touched his lips as he stopped outside Juliet's door.

Looking down at the two mugs, he cursed softly, attempting to adjust the mugs. Unsuccessful, he grumbled and used his knee to knock on the door.

"Juliet? Are you awake, love?"

A frown crossed his face at the lack of response.

Crouching down, he set his mug down and rose, opening the door and stepping into the room.

"Mornin', love. I brought ya coffee." His smile died as his eyes fell upon the empty bed. A quick glance had his stomach tightening. The closet doors were thrown open, the hangers askew, the only thing within the blue dress. Confusion and fear washed through him with such a force it left him breathless. He spun, marching toward his room and kicked the door open, half thinking she might have gone to him, all the while aware that didn't explain the lack of clothes.

She wasn't there.

Letting go a stream of curses, Marsh threw the mug as rage filled him. The porcelain shattered against the far wall, bits of mug and coffee pattering against the floor. He was an idiot. A fool. Had he really expected her to wait around for him to wake back up?

He was awake now.

Heedless of the broken porcelain, he strode across the room, stripping off his clothes. He grabbed new clothes at random, dressing quickly and grabbing his shoes as he rushed out the door. He yelped as his foot slid on something, sending him slamming into the wall. Marsh cursed heatedly, twisting to see what he had slipped on.

"The hell?" His voice was tinged with confusion and frustration as he bent down to retrieve the folded paper. His brow furrowed before flattening out in shock as his eyes moved over the words.

Romeo,

I will probably be long gone by the time you find this, but maybe that is for the best. I've never been

Secrets

good at goodbyes. I'm sorry. For everything. I really made a mess of it, didn't I?

The Council was wrong. I'm not the Lost One. I'm not the one you were looking for. All I have brought since you met me is pain and suffering. And I'm sorry for that. I'm so, so sorry.

Now that I've begun this letter, I find there is so much I wish I could say. But I don't have the time, the sky is already beginning to lighten.

Don't come looking for me. It's better this way.
I will never forget you.

Always,
Juliet

Marsh sank back against the wall, breath eluding him. He read the letter over again, her words floating through his mind.

Don't come after me. Goodbye.
Don't come after me.

"Screw that," he growled, crushing the paper in his hand and shoving away from the wall. He stormed out of the hall and all but bowled over his aunt.

"Whoa there!" Tabitha blinked blearily at him, swaying slightly side to side, unsteady on her feet. She scrubbed at her eyes before planting her hands on her hips and narrowing her gaze at him. "What's the story?"

"I have to go." Marsh ground out, brushing past her and dropping into a chair near the door, shoving his feet into his boots.

"Go? Go where?" Tabitha questioned, her voice thick as she yawned.

"After Juliet." Marsh shoved off the chair and

marched toward the door, leaving Tabitha tottering after him once more.

"Wait just a bleedin' moment! Why do ya need to go after her? Where did she go?"

"I don't know, but I'm going to find her. And why?" His hand closed around the knob, jerking the door open. He turned toward Tabitha, a determined glint in his eyes. "Because she told me not to."

Tabitha gaped after him as Marsh turned and strode from the cottage, the bright morning light swallowing him up. A smile touched Tabitha's lips as she stepped out on the porch, leaning against the doorframe. She waited until the rumble of her old lorry filled the air, gravel spitting as the tires spun. The old truck lurched as it hit blacktop and in moments was gone. Tabitha shook her head as she turned back into the house, heading toward the kitchen and her waiting tea.

"Atta boy."

CHAPTER THIRTY-EIGHT

BY MIDDAY, MY feet and back were aching and I was kicking myself for not bringing any water. My stomach rumbled loudly, only adding to my growing list of discomforts. And I had to pee.

The day was beautiful, at least. The sky above was scattered with puffy clouds and a cool breeze kept it from being too hot. I thanked God for small mercies.

The hours of walking alone, however, left far too much time to think. I thought about Tabitha, about Adaline, about the Council, my family, the insane turn my life had taken. But no matter what I did, I couldn't stop thinking about Marsh.

I thought about how stupid I'd been in coming to my decision to leave. It was rash; I was in a land I knew nothing of. As my foot came down on yet another sharp stone, I thought about how smart calling a taxi would have been. I shifted my bag from one shoulder to the other for the millionth time and groaned as pain flared in my neck. Stopping, I lowered the bag to the ground and looked up and down the road.

Where was I? I must have been walking for miles.

I hadn't seen a street sign in hours. Not that it mattered—I couldn't read them anyway. Blowing out a breath, I lifted my arms above my head, groaning as my back stretched and popped. I was only carrying clothes, yet it felt like I was carrying one of my nieces on my back. Guilt sang through me at that thought.

Kylie.

I still felt terrible that I had missed her birthday. I hadn't even called her. How could I possibly explain how I had forgotten to call her?

Juliet the Runier strikes again.

Shielding my face with my hand, I looked up and down the road. I had seen a farm truck early that morning, but not a soul had passed by since. Had I passed the road to Dingle somehow?

Well, that would be my luck.

Sighing, I dropped my hand against my thigh and lifted my bag, settling it back onto my shoulders. I started off again, certain I would come upon a town soon. The taxi rides to Dingle had never taken very long, and even if I had missed the road, there had to be another town close by.

The sun beat down on my back, and despite the breeze, I began to sweat. Perspiration beaded my brow and I would have sold my soul for a glass of ice water. Still I saw no cars. I saw nothing except for birds and the occasional herd of sheep. I was growing more and more concerned that I had definitely taken a wrong turn somewhere.

"Way to go, Juliet. You can't even run away properly," I scoffed and gripped the strap of the bag tighter.

How long I walked after that first break, I couldn't

say for sure, but it must have been hours. The sky was beginning to darken when my feet ground to a stop. I could go no further. Bending forward, I placed my hands on my knees and sucked in deep breaths of the rapidly cooling air. The chill air stung my lungs and had gooseflesh popping up along my arms, turning my sweat to ice. Pulling the bag off my shoulder, I rifled through it until I found the sweater. I pulled it out carefully, pressing my nose to the soft red wool.

I closed my eyes, enveloped in his scent. The sting of tears pricked hotly against my eyelids, leaving me struggling to hold them back. Sniffling, I pulled the sweater over my head, snuggling into the warmth it offered. Sitting on the side of the road, I wrapped my arms around my legs and buried my face in my knees. I felt alone, small, and completely vulnerable. More than anything I regretted telling Marsh not to come looking for me. I was lost, cold, hungry, and in need of being rescued.

I must have dozed off, because the sound of a truck roused me. Blinking the sleep from my eyes, I shoved to my feet and looked down the road. The headlights cut through the growing twilight, making me blink at their unexpected brightness. My heart leapt with insane hope as the truck came closer.

Marsh, it sang.

Licking my chapped lips, I stepped to the side of the road and threw my hands into the air, waving them.

"Hey! Hey! Stop!" I called, my voice hoarse. The truck blew past me, the speed of it fluttering my hair and making me cough. I dropped my hands in defeat, my head falling back as I let go a cry of frustration. Maybe the driver hadn't seen me?

Yeah, right.

Blowing out a breath, I grabbed my bag, slung it over my shoulder and began walking again. My legs were screaming as I crested the small hill, and I vowed then and there that if I ever made it home, I would up my exercise regime from nonexistent to at least weekly.

My steps halted as my eyes fell upon the truck that had passed me. It sat on the side of the road, hood lifted and steam billowing from either side. A stream of lilting curses colored the air and I couldn't help but giggle.

Karma, she's a mean one.

"Car trouble?" I sang merrily, as if I didn't have a care in the world, as I strode past the man. I stole a glance in his direction. He was dressed in a worn flannel shirt, the color a faded blue. Dark denim jeans clung to his legs, and he had a red bandana pressed to his face as protection against the steam. He wore an eye patch over his right eye. The skin above and below the patch was puckered and angry, as if from a recent wound.

A light chuckle followed me as the man stepped away from the truck, lowering the bandana and wiping his hands on it. "Aye, guess tha's wha' I get fer not stoppin' to help a pretty lass, eh?"

I turned to face him, crossing my arms over my chest. Despite my exhaustion, I felt a smile tugging at my lips. "I guess it is. Do you know what's wrong?"

"Radiator's acting up," he replied. "Does it every now an' again. Say, why don' ya grab me tha' jug'a water from the cab and I'll give ya a lift fer yer troubles?"

I bit my lower lip, weighing my options. Visions of news reports of travelers being kidnapped or

Secrets

disappearing ran through my mind, paralleling my mother's words of stranger danger. The sad truth was, I didn't have a choice. I had no phone, no food or water, night was coming on and I was exhausted.

"Yeah, okay. Thanks." I flashed him a quick smile and started toward the truck. "Where's it at?"

"In the cab, down on the floor. Can't miss it. You an American?"

Pulling open the door, I stuck my head in the cab, scanning the area. "Yeah, I am. How'd you guess? Umm, I don't see it."

"It's in there. Might've rolled to the other side."

I frowned, climbing into the truck a bit more and searching more thoroughly. I lifted some papers and a blanket, but still didn't see the jug. There was trash and other debris that came from someone who spent time in their vehicle, but no water jug.

"Yeah, I hate to be the bearer of bad news," I sighed as I climbed out of the truck. I gasped as I came face to face with him. Jerking back, I winced as my spine connected with the doorframe. The suddenness of his appearance had my heart jackhammering in my chest. "I, uh ... I couldn't find it," I whispered, uncomfortable with his closeness.

"No? Ah, well. Not like we need it anyway."

"What?" I asked, my brow furrowing in confusion. An alarm blared in my head, my sense of danger peaking. "Okay, well then ... I'm just going to go."

I gave him a tight smile and moved to slip around him when pain lit up my shin, and I cried out as I stumbled, landing hard. Pain flared through my skull as my head bounced off the road. My hands scraped across the rough terrain as I hit my knees, spots floating before my eyes.

"No, Juliet. You're not going anywhere." His voice lost all trace of an accent and became frighteningly familiar.

Panic took root in my chest and I struggled to think. Warm liquid trickled down my neck, and it took me far too long to realize it was blood. Nausea filled me; my stomach roiled, making me gag.

"Robert," I whispered, my voice shaky with fear. How was he here? How had he found me? Was my luck so bad that he would just happen upon the same road as I?

Mustering my strength, I forced myself to my feet. The world spun violently and I swayed, groaning and choking down the urge to be sick.

"Never in my wildest imaginings did I think I would find you alone. Where is your Guardian, little girl? Did you two have a lover's spat?" Robert grinned maliciously at me, tapping the tire iron against his thigh.

I ground my teeth, my fingers curling into fists as I struggled to focus. "You ... you killed Adaline!"

"Yes, I did. The old girl put up quite the fight too," Robert sneered as he put his fingers gingerly to his badly healing eye. "It's a shame what happens to people when they lose their head."

Rage surged through me and I charged him. My assault took us both by surprise, but it offered me a much-needed advantage. The tire iron clanged to the ground as I slammed into him, throwing him back against the truck. His head thumped solidly against metal, making my violent heart sing. My fists flew,

Secrets

hitting every part of him I could reach. I wanted him in pain. I wanted his blood.

"You killed her! You bastard!" I screeched, pummeling his chest.

Robert's shock was not long lived and he soon began fighting back. Bringing his arms up, he planted his hands against my shoulders and shoved me backward. My arms pin wheeled as I fought to catch my balance. Robert seized his moment, wrapping his fingers around my flailing arm and spinning me around.

Already unsteady, the momentum of the spin knocked my feet from beneath me and sent me colliding solidly with the truck. Blackness filled my eyes and panic surged at my sudden blindness. My distress offered me no respite.

Robert pounced, shoving his hand roughly into my hair and gathering a fistful between his fingers. I yelped as he jerked my head back, my neck and shoulders screaming.

My sight returned and I braced my hands against the truck, locking my elbows and stopping his attempt to slam my head into it. Panting for breath, I lifted my right leg and brought the heel of my foot down as hard as I could onto his instep.

Robert cursed and released his grip just enough that I was about to pull away from him. I spun around, but his form blocked my escape.

I could read the murder in his eyes. Fear led me, and I lashed out, raking my nails down the sides of his face, digging deeper into the healing side. Robert roared in pain as blood welled, spilling from the ragged tracks I'd left. He staggered backward, his hands flying to his face.

I ran.

My breath tore at my chest as my feet slapped against the road. Ducking my head, I tucked my arms close to my body and put all of my focus into running. Exhaustion was my enemy, and even with the adrenaline pumping through my veins, I began to slow. I screamed as Robert slammed into me from behind, his arms wrapping around my waist and lifting me. I kicked and flailed, screaming myself hoarse as he carried me back toward the truck.

"Women are so much trouble," he growled, hefting my writhing form. I threw my hands out again, bracing them and my feet against the doorframe and shoving backward.

"No! Help! Help! Someone help me!"

Pain ripped through my body as Robert slammed his fist into my spine. I crumpled, whimpering as he shoved me into the truck. Weakly, I rolled onto my back and kicked out, my heel connecting with his nose. Blood spurted and Robert howled.

"Argh!" His eyes flashed pure hatred and I scrambled back, terror running thick through my veins. Robert grabbed my right ankle and I screamed, thrashing and kicking. A grisly smile lit his bloody lips as he wrenched my leg to the side. There was a loud pop and I shrieked as my knee dislocated, a new kind of pain slamming through me.

Despite the pain and ever-growing weakness, I struggled as he shoved me through the right-hand door, pushing me into the passenger seat and climbed in behind me. The truck rumbled to life, further proof of his ruse, and he pulled out onto the road.

Secrets

"You broke my nose. I'm going to take my time killing you," Robert growled, his eyes raking over my form. Disgust filled me as I curled into myself, tears spilling down my cheeks.

Marsh.

His name flittered through my mind, a beacon in the growing storm, as darkness crowded in and unconsciousness took over.

CHAPTER THIRTY-NINE

NIGHT WAS RAPIDLY approaching as Marsh pulled the lorry into the petrol station, slamming the gear into park. He sat motionless, staring out the windshield. Beyond the truck, people milled about. Snippets of laughter and conversation floated toward him, the sounds of cars invaded his mind.

He came alive suddenly, slamming his fist violently into the steering wheel. The horn let go a sharp beep, causing a group of women passing before him to jump and shoot him glares as they scurried past.

Marsh paid them no heed, fighting with the seatbelt as he attempted to free himself from the truck. The stubborn catch held and he snapped. Screaming curses he fought violently with the strip of nylon, his struggles such that he set the truck rocking. The belt popped free, the clip sliding upward with deadly force and smacking him in the face. Letting go a roar, he threw the belt from him and slapped his hands repeatedly against the wheel, screaming in rage.

Panting, he dropped his head against the headrest and pinched the bridge of his nose. He'd looked everywhere. Gone to every place he could think of she would have gone. No one at the bus station had seen anyone matching her description. Like a will-o-the-wisp, she had vanished, just when he needed her most.

A bone deep weariness set in, weighing him down. It was an effort just to draw breath, let alone move. She was out there, somewhere, and he wasn't going to stop looking for her. She had to know he was coming for her. He'd already crossed half the world, and he would do it again if it meant getting her back.

Opening the door, he forced himself from the cab, tugging his wallet out of his pocket and crossing to the pump. How could she have just disappeared? If she hadn't taken the bus ...

He sighed as he pulled the nozzle out. He would have to check taxi services next. Perhaps she got a ride to the airport. His thoughts flying, he filled up the tank. He would need it full to get to Dublin and back.

Replacing the nozzle, he glanced around. He didn't even know what he was looking for. Did he really expect her to be at a random gas station, just waiting for him to show up?

Life was never that easy.

Gritting his teeth, he got back into the truck and cranked the engine. The last time they'd been at a petrol station, she'd been crying. They'd been running for their lives, and he'd held her. Breathed in her scent.

His heart ached. He wanted to hold her now. To apologize, to promise he would always keep her safe.

Where the hell are ya, love?

Shaking his head, he gunned the engine, eliciting angry honks from the other drivers as he peeled out of the station. Where could she have gone? It made sense that she would have headed toward town. But she wasn't familiar with the area. She could have easily gotten turned around, gone down the wrong road. What if she was simply lost? Wandering aimlessly? Hope sparked in his chest as he pressed the old lorry for more speed. He would go back to Tabitha's and start from there. He would go down every road and goat path if he had to. Whatever it took to bring her home.

Gripping the steering wheel tightly, he maneuvered the lorry up the winding roads. This time of night, he didn't have to worry about other drivers. It was the sheep and wildlife that would do him in if he wasn't careful. Leaning forward, he squinted into the night, his eyes searching the road. Exhaustion leached at him, pulling at his eyelids. The truck pulled to the right and Marsh jerked his head up as the wheels bit into the peat and moss, causing the lorry to bounce and whine. With a muttered curse he jerked the wheel to the left, over correcting and causing the old truck to skid.

The headlights illuminated the spinning world as Marsh slammed on the breaks. The back tires screamed and jumped as they bounced along the blacktop. The truck shuddered to a stop, the engine sputtering and dying. Marsh panted, staring out the windshield, his fingers white knuckled on the steering wheel.

Too close. That had been way too close. A mistake like that on some of these roads could see to it you never woke up the next morning.

Drawing a hand over his face, Marsh let go a shuddery breath and pinched the bridge of his nose.

"Time to give up the ghost, boyo," he muttered,

lowering his hand and cranking the engine once more. A bitter chill swept through him as his eyes locked on something on the side of the road. Leaning over, he grabbed the torch from beneath the passenger seat. Flicking it on, he stepped out of the truck, shining the beam up and down the road as he jogged toward the object.

A deep frown crossed his face as he crouched down, shining the light over the bag. His heart stopped in his chest. He recognized the bag. Tabitha had given it to him for his birthday a number of years back.

Cradling the flashlight between his cheek and shoulder, he pulled the bag toward him and frantically tore at the zipper.

Her scent poured out, along with her clothes. Heart thumping, he rose to his feet, looking around.

"Juliet! Juliet, are ya here?" His voice echoed back to him. A skitter of sound and a rustle of leaves had him whipping around in time to see a frightened fox darting away. He strained his ears, ignoring the cacophony of his heart.

Nothing.

Twisting this way and that, he shined the light up and down the road once more. The white beam crossed over darker patches on the road top, bringing him to a screeching halt.

Skid marks.

His steps heavy, he crossed to the nearest mark, crouching down and examining it. For the first time in his life, he was grateful for the survival and tracking classes Adaline had forced him to take.

The marks came from a truck, the wheels bigger than his own. He was sure the vehicle would stand out.

A farm truck, or a delivery truck. Had she gotten a ride? Rising slowly to his feet, he looked around, jaw clenched. She could be anywhere. With anyone.

Cursing, he crossed back to the bag, zipped it closed and lifted it to his shoulder. The beam of light bounced wildly, catching on something that drew his attention. With cautious steps he moved toward the item, a scrap of fabric. Stooping over, Marsh scooped it up, bringing the light up to examine it. The cloth had once been white, but was now stained with dirt and blood. Squinting in confusion, Marsh clamped down on his worry, turning the cloth over in his hand.

Worry turned to a slow burning fire as he drew his thumb over the embroidered symbol, sending flakes of dried blood drifting to the ground.

The stylized A was wrapped in a blue and red circle, the tail of the A curving to form a rolling wave. He would know that symbol anywhere. All of the older houses had one.

Alström

"I'm coming, love. You just hold on now, I'm coming for ya," Marsh muttered. Clenching his fist around the cloth, he spun toward the truck, jerking the door open and throwing himself into the cab. The engine screamed as he gunned it, tires spinning and laying down lines of rubber as he sped back toward Tabitha's.

He knew who had her. If he hurt a hair on her head, he would make him pay dearly.

CHAPTER FORTY

I woke to a monotone buzzing and the flickering of a dying bulb above me. My head ached and my mouth felt as though I had been sucking on cotton. I felt like I'd been hit by a truck, backed over, and run over again.

Licking my cracked and bleeding lips, I shifted on the bed, attempting to find comfort. It felt wrong to call it that. It was little more than a cot. The mattress was thin, less than six inches thick, so I could feel every broken spring. It was stained, and smelled faintly of mildew. Pain blazed through me, rendering me blind as my right leg throbbed. I let out a shattered cry, moving my arms to hold my knee. The rattle of chains stopped me dead.

Twisting at the waist, I stared at my left hand. A metal cuff surrounded my wrist, pinning me to the wrought iron headboard. I stared at the cuff before tugging at it stupidly, hysteria bubbling in my chest. Tiny sobs and shrieks escaped my lips as I yanked and jerked at the cuff, the metal rending my wrist a bloody mess for my efforts. I slammed my hands against the headboard, stifling my sobs and squeezing my eyes closed. My lips trembled as I forced my breathing to slow, to stem the panic running rampant through my veins.

Whimpering, I leaned my head back against the headboard, wincing as the metal pressed into my tender skull. I rested my hand against my thigh, wrinkling my nose at the dull throb that had become my reality. My leg ached like nothing I had ever felt before. My knee had swollen to an alarming rate, stretching my jeans and making the injury all the more painful. Biting back a whimper at the dark burning sensation, I attempted to shift my leg.

"Ah, ah!" I shook my head violently, my hands curling into fists as fresh tears streaked down my cheeks. "*Crap!*"

I puffed out short, ragged breaths as I tried to find something else to focus on. The room was small, windowless, and dreary. The only light came from the flicking overhead bulb, and I could hear the trickle of water, though I couldn't find its source. The sound of the water only served to remind me how thirsty I was. I swallowed involuntarily and all but gagged. Swallowing hurt. It was as if my throat had turned to sand paper.

"Help! Somebody! Help! I'm in here!" I was hoping for a scream, but all that came out of me was a pathetic hoarse whisper. Frustration filled me, and I yanked and tugged on the handcuff again, but it only led to more pain.

Calm down. Use your brain!

I needed to think. Thinking was the only way I was going to get out of here.

Twisting on the bed, I examined the headboard,

running my hands along it, ferreting out any signs of weakness or loose screws. To my ill begotten luck, it appeared to be the only thing new in this room.

I blinked against the hot press of tears as despair filled me, bringing with it the acid taste of bile. I was trapped, locked up like a prisoner with no hope of escape. Even if I could free my hand, there was no way I could run with my leg the way it was. He had me. I was at the mercy of a madman. A killer.

My wet lashes kissed the apples of my cheeks as I let the tears fall. It wasn't long before my quiet tears turned into full-blown sobs. My chest heaved as I sucked in ragged breaths, my vision blurring. I was going to die. He had promised as much. But I was going to suffer for every wrong that had been dealt him.

Fear clenched my heart as the sound of metal against metal filled the room, the lock on the door sliding open. Shrinking back as best I could on the bed, I stared at the door, willing whomever it was to go away, to leave me alone. Willing the door to remain closed.

It opened.

The creaking wheels of a cart preceded him into to the room. I shifted on the bed, shrinking back and taking care not to move my leg too much. Confusion filled me as the cart came into view. I stared wide-eyed at the phonograph sitting atop the cart. It was beautifully cared for, and gleamed under the flickering light. The scrape of paper filled the air as Robert removed a glossy black record from its sleeve, taking extreme care as he placed the record onto the phonograph and positioned the needle. The needle hovered over the spinning disc and sound filled the room as metal touched vinyl.

I scoffed inwardly as Nat King Cole's soulful voice filled the dank, disgusting room, boasting the merits of love. Only then did Robert turn toward me.

"Hello, Juliet. And how are you doing? Oh, tsk, that knee doesn't look good now does it?" His voice was soft and pleasant; it made my skin crawl.

I glared at him, remaining stubbornly silent. My wrist flicked, the cuff scraping against metal and sending a bolt of agony through my system. I gritted my teeth, my breath streaming out my nose, but I didn't make a sound.

He'd changed, and washed. Gone was the old flannel and jeans, they were replaced with a fine white linen shirt and tan khakis. His face had been cleaned as well, the two fresh track marks on his cheeks gleamed with salve. His eye was a mess. The skin around it was puckered and raw, the eye itself milky. It struck me as odd that it hadn't healed.

"Why isn't your eye healing? You're one of them, aren't you? Or did your kind not get the healing gene?" I spoke without thinking.

Robert's remaining eye flashed at me, emotions darting across it. Annoyance, anger. His expression smoothed as he stepped forward, drawing a long pair of sheers off the cart.

"Normally, you would be correct. As you can see, the marks you gave me are already well on their way to disappearing. Adaline however, played dirty. Apparently the polish coating her nails contained a poison which I had no knowledge of before she raked them down my flesh. My body is constantly combating the poison. Until I can find the antidote, it will not heal."

"It sounds painful."

"Oh, it is very much so."

"Good." I lifted my chin, letting my eyes lock on his.

Robert glared at me before shaking his head and chuckling. "Oh, I will have so much fun breaking you."

I glared at him as he tapped the sheers against his palm. My heart kicked in my chest, all sound drowned out by the rush of blood in my ears. I didn't want him to see the effect he had on me. I was crippled, at the utter mercy of his will, and I seriously doubted his mercy. My eyes locked on the sheers, watching as the silver of them flashed in the light of the flickering bulb.

With no further preamble, Robert reached down and grabbed my right ankle. It took everything within me to bite back the scream, and even then, a muffled whimper escaped. I tasted blood, and my tongue dipped into the holes my teeth had left in my lip. Robert glanced at me before placing the sheers to the hem of my jeans. Humming along to the record, he began to cut. I jerked and twitched as the cold metal slid along my skin, sending chills skating up and down my spine. Unable to choke it down any more, I screamed in agony as the sheers drew closer to my swollen knee.

Robert was meticulous, his eyes narrowed in concentration as he gently snipped the fabric. The tip of the sheers brushed my thigh and I sucked in a breath, my eyes widening. Robert withdrew them, glancing to me, his eyes holding a knowing gaze. I watched as he set the blades aside and peeled the fabric away from my leg.

"Oh, now, that looks just awful." Shaking his head, he stepped toward the edge of the bed, leaning over me.

My eyes widened further as the reality of what he was about to do hit me like a ton of bricks. I threw out my hand, attempting to ward him off. "No, no!"

An inhuman scream ripped through my body as Robert placed his hands against my knee, one on each side, and jerked it fiercely. There was a loud pop as my knee was relocated and pain like nothing I had ever felt swamped me. I was certain I would black out. My vision swam, my breath left me. In the end, it was only the handcuff and his hands that kept me on the bed.

Tears leaked from the corners of my eyes. The pain was such that I couldn't even make sound. Huffing in short gasps, I curled my fingers into fists and let go a pitiful whimper.

"There. That should feel much better," Robert crooned, reaching out to stroke my hair. Mustering my waning energy, I jerked away from his touch. Anger filled the deep brown of his eyes, and fear rose within me. His hand flew as if to strike me, stopping inches from my cheek, the breeze the motion had made fluttering my hair. I squeezed my eyes closed, panting harder, prying them open as nothing happened.

Robert slowly withdrew his hand and smoothed his shirt, though not before I saw the tremble in his fingers. He was holding on by a thread, I was sure of it. With a suddenness that left me reeling he turned on his heel, slapping the needle off the record with an ear splitting shriek and stormed from the room. The room was plunged in silence and darkness and it took me a moment to realize what had happened. He'd hit the light as he left.

I stared at the spot that was the door, unable to see anything in the pitch-blackness of the room. My chest rose and fell heavily, just another pain to my over-sensitized body. I refused to blink, refused to close my eyes. Fearing that when I did, he would return, that he would catch me unaware. Vulnerable.

Time passed, though I had no idea how much, and I began to realize this was just another of his sick methods. Water trickled in a slow, steady drip, invading my mind. With nothing else to focus on, it quickly drove me mad. I thrashed on the bed, sending bolts of pain radiating up my leg. The clink of chains was agony, the metal cutting all the more deeply into my raw and bloodied wrist. Frustration, fear, and despair rose within me and I began to scream.

CHAPTER FORTY-ONE

TIME LOST ALL meaning. My world shrunk to the size of the room I inhabited. The pain in my leg gradually faded, but other pains crept up to replace it. My wrist was beginning to emit a foul smell, and I refused to look at it when the light was on, which wasn't often. Robert had taken to keeping me in darkness, only allowing the light when he was near. My conditions were horrid. The handcuff at my wrist only allowed for so much movement, and the smell of my refuse was nauseating.

My tears had long since dried. Robert gave me only enough food and water to keep me from dying. My stomach rumbled painfully, and I twisted on the bed, praying for sleep or death. I wasn't sure which. Both would be a blessing.

My skin crawled as the lock unbolted and the door opened.

"Good morning, my dear. And how did you sleep?"

Morning? It was morning already?

I kept my back to him, ignoring him as I had done every time he came in. The smell of food wafted toward me and my stomach made itself known. The one weakness I couldn't hide.

"Time to eat. You'll need your strength today."

His words sent panic fluttering in my stomach as I turned toward him. The scent of butter had me drooling, and my eyes were drawn to the cart and the plate atop it. The sight of the pancakes had me jerking up, causing pain to radiate along my arm and a whimper to pass through my lips.

"Are you hungry, Juliet?" Robert asked sweetly, lifting a glass pitcher of orange juice and pouring it carefully into a juice glass with tiny etched flowers on it. I couldn't tear my eyes away from the liquid as it sloshed in the cup.

"No," I ground out, still unable to tear my eyes from the juice.

"No? Well, then you won't be needing this." His eyes stayed on mine as he tipped the cup, letting a stream of liquid fall to the floor.

"No!" I shrieked, lunging toward the edge of the bed, ignoring the pain as I thrust my right hand out to catch the drops. The tips of my fingers caught the final drop and I brought them to my lips, sucking the sweet taste desperately.

"It does not do to lie to me, Juliet." Robert set the glass down on the cart with a sigh. I wanted to cry.

"No, no. Please. I'm so thirsty." My throat locked as tears choked me. I reached futilely for the glass, more pitiful whimpers escaping. Robert stepped away from the cart, chuckling at my pathetic attempts. The clink of metal tore at my ears, and I gasped as my left arm fell free. Ripping my gaze from the food and the juice, I looked at my wrist, at the dangling second half of the cuff before jerking my gaze to Robert.

"That wrist looks terrible. We'll have to see to that after you eat. This room is deplorable. If you're a good girl through breakfast, I'll move you to another room."

I stared at Robert skeptically, waiting for him to snatch away the glimmer of hope he was offering. My head was screaming for me to refuse him, but my stomach and the thought of having my wrist cleaned and cared for won out. A full belly. A clean room.

I braced myself to rise from the bed, my muscles weak and unsteady. Robert stepped closer, wrapping his fingers around my left arm and I flinched, my eyes widening in terror. My gaze darted toward the open door and for half a heartbeat I considered running.

Robert must have seen the thought cross my features, for his grip tightened painfully on my arm and I yelped. His lips pressed against my ear, his breath hot and wet against my neck.

"You can try to run, but you will not enjoy the consequences."

I nodded breathlessly, focusing my gaze back onto the cart and the food. Sweet food. Precious food.

Don't say a word. Don't make him take away the food. Don't ruin this too.

My feet scuffed across the short expanse of floor as I moved toward the cart. I fell against it, gripping the sides so hard my knuckles went white. Tears stung my eyes as I moved trembling fingers toward the stack of pancakes.

It was heaven in my mouth. The butter saturated fluff all but melted on my tongue. After that first bite, I couldn't stop. I tore at the pancakes, shoving them into my mouth in handfuls, bits of crumbs and syrup clinging to my chin. My hand shot out, almost knocking over the glass of juice in my haste. I gasped as the cup tottered and all but choked. Though given my current situation, death by pancake wasn't so horrible an option.

Robert chuckled behind me as I guzzled down the orange juice. The sound made my skin crawl, but he had brought the food. I would tolerate him for that.

"You have no manners, Juliet. Look at you, you're a mess. Come, I'm going to clean you up."

Dread stopped my heart as Robert extended his hand to me, as if I were a treasured guest. The pancakes turned to glue in my mouth and I forced myself to swallow. Wiping my hand across my lips, I drummed up my courage.

Marsh was coming for me. I knew he was. He couldn't stay away. He was my Guardian. I just had to stay alive long enough for him to find me.

Lifting my right hand, I placed it in Robert's, fighting down the revulsion. How had I ever been attracted to this man? I allowed him to lead me from the room. The bright lights of the hallway stung my eyes, making me blink rapidly.

"I don't know if you've noticed, but your clothes smell awful. How about a bath?"

Despite myself, my heart soared at the offer. The thought of cleansing myself, scrubbing off the grime, soaking my aching muscles, made me nod my head.

"Please," I whimpered, blinking back tears and clawing at his arm. "Please."

It was as if Robert had become another person, the charming EMT I had met in Portland, so smoothly did he shift into the role of proper gentleman. The transition was more than a little unnerving.

Robert smiled at me and I forced myself to smile back. My stomach roiled, threatening to dislodge the food I had eaten. I couldn't begin to understand the sick game he was playing, but I was smart enough to realize my need to play along.

Carefully, I looked around the space as Robert continued to lead me toward the bathroom. We appeared to be in a large house. Though it was dated, I could tell it was lovingly cared for. Silk wallpaper lined the walls, and the floors glimmered and shined with well-oiled care. I desperately wished to know where I was and craned my neck, trying to see more of the space. Robert pulled me into a large, well-lit room and I looked around in confusion, surprised to find that we had reached the bathroom.

It was the biggest bathroom I had ever seen. An old-fashioned claw foot tub rested in the middle of the room. Directly opposite was a floor to ceiling mirror, the edges gilded, the glass itself dotted with age spots. The walls were a pale pink, decorated with small yellow rosebuds. A vanity sat to the left of the tub, the chair covered in faded pink fabric. Pots and jars lined the vanity top.

"Where are we?" I whispered, my heart sinking as it all hit me. The expensive paper, the feminine touches. This house was familiar to him. Possibly home to him.

"Don't worry about that," Robert snapped, moving away from me suddenly and turning on the taps. Pipes gurgled and whined before the water gushed from the bronze faucet. Steam quickly began to rise, and my skin vibrated at the thought of being clean.

Secrets

Unsteadily, I moved forward, mentally kicking myself for the question.

Don't make him mad! Placate him! Don't ruin this! We're so close to the bath.

Robert straightened and turned to face me, a placid smile in place. "Let's get you out of those clothes."

His smile widened as he moved toward me, his eyes glowing with dark light. Heat swept through me and I shrank back. He was going to undress me. He wanted me naked. Vulnerable.

My body shook as he reached for my sweater, pulling the hem upward. Squeezing my eyes closed, I forced my arms into the air, allowing him to remove it even as my mind screamed and raged.

You're a doll. Just a doll. A doll has no feelings. No emotions. Be a doll, Juliet. Be a doll.

I squeezed my eyes tighter as he peeled away my layers, stripping me slowly until there was nothing left. Gooseflesh rose along my skin as the air hit me. My skin tightened as Robert trailed his fingertips along my ribs.

"You are so beautiful, Juliet," he whispered, his fingers drifting along my hip before taking my hand. "Into the bath now, while it's hot."

I opened my eyes as I stepped forward, lifting my foot and stepping into the tub. I gasped as the hot water hit my skin, searing the tender flesh and causing it to pinken. I didn't care. I sunk into the boiling depths, letting the heat seep into my bones, warming me. It had been so long since I had been warm.

Robert knelt beside the tub, and I felt more than saw the leering smile on his face. The water did nothing to hide my form, leaving me bare for the viewing. I struggled not to imagine what was going through his mind. He dipped his hand into the water, wetting the cloth he held. With a gentleness I could never have expected, he began to wash my shoulders. I bit my lower lip, choking down the whimpers that threatened to rise.

Be silent. Be still.

His cloth moved along my neck, below my ear, over my clavicle. Lower. A choked sob burst from me as his hand moved over my breast. Again, I squeezed my eyes closed, flinging my mind to another place. I wasn't here. This wasn't me. I was far away, tucked safely into Marsh's arms, wrapped in his warmth and safety.

"Do you like that, Juliet?" Robert's words were a harsh whisper, evidence to the effect my nakedness was having on him.

I lifted my eyes to the ceiling, ignoring his question. Desperately, I called Marsh's face to my mind. Focused on the pure blue of his eyes, the curve and shape of his lips.

Pain flared from my nipple and I gasped.

"I said," Robert snarled, "do you like that?"

No!

"Yes," I whispered, my lips trembling as a single tear leaked from the corner of my eye.

A dark chuckle filled my ears as Robert moved his hand, returning to washing. It went on like that, with him alternating bathing me and touching me. By the time the water cooled, I had nothing left. I rose from the water at his command, extending my arms for him to wrap a towel around me.

Secrets

I was openly crying, but Robert ignored my tears, leading me to the vanity and instructing me to sit. I was a doll. I didn't even recognize my reflection. He took his time drying me, paying close attention to my breasts and the space between my legs. Excited little giggles escaped him and bile burned my throat.

"She would have liked you, you know. She liked beautiful things," Robert said, drawing a mother of pearl inlaid comb through my hair. The teeth caught and tangled in my damp tresses and I winced.

Oblivious to my discomfort, Robert continued until my hair lay flat and smooth down my back. Setting the comb aside, he moved to stand in front of me, taking my left arm in his hands.

"This, she would not have liked. It's ugly. Why haven't you healed? Is it because you're a half breed?" His lips turned up in a sneer as his fingers probed the raw, infected wound.

A scream ripped from me as pain radiated up my arm. I jerked from his grasp and shot to my feet, the towel drifting to the floor. Invigorated by the food and the bath, my hand flew without thought, my palm connecting with his cheek hard enough to jerk his head to the side.

"Bastard!" I hissed, cradling my wrist against my chest.

Robert turned his head slowly, his cheek marred by the angry print of my hand. Terror gripped me as his eyes met mine. What I saw there was more than anger, more than hate. Fury heated the brown depths. His every motion was saturated in controlled rage.

Eyes wide, I scrambled backward, my feet tangling in the towel. "I'm sorry. I'm sor-"

My words were cut off as the back of his hand connected with my cheek. The blow contained such force it knocked me from my feet, sent me sprawling to the ground.

"Bastard?" Robert asked, his foot shooting out and connecting with my ribs. My body jerked from the blow and I cried out in pain, coughing and gasping for breath. Robert kicked me again and again and I felt something inside of me break.

Forcing myself up, I tried to crawl away, his next kick glancing off my hip. Pain and panic tore through me, and I screamed as he fisted a hand in my hair and jerked backward, pulling me up onto my knees.

"Bastard, am I? I'll show you just how much of a bastard I can be."

Panting for breath, I fought to get my feet beneath me as Robert dragged me from the room. My sides screamed with each ragged inhalation. I grabbed at his wrist, digging my nails into his flesh as I fought his hold. My feet slipped and scuffed across the slick floor, leaving me no purchase. My wrist screamed as I continued to fight and claw at him.

"Enough!" Robert roared, slamming his closed fist into my face. It was as if my world exploded. My body went limp and my vision blurred. Voices swam through my consciousness and I realized we weren't alone.

My hands flew from Robert's wrist as I desperately tried to cover my nakedness. The men in the room rose from the various chairs they had occupied, their eyes hungrily feasting on my exposed flesh. Panic surged as they started toward me.

"No!" I shrieked, my cry cut off as Robert shoved

me behind him. I stumbled and fell into an armchair, curling into myself and burying my face between my knees.

"Back off! No one touches her! She is mine!" Robert growled. "Get out of here! Go guard something!"

The men stayed where they were long enough to make me worry. There were four of them and only one Robert. The odds were not good.

To my relief, however, the men turned and left the room, their displeasure palpable. Robert turned toward me, adjusting his shirt and running his hands through his hair. His eyes held fury still, though it was masked by control. The cuts on his wrist were already healing.

"That is the second time you've marked me," he noted. His voice was calm, collected.

Chills raced up and down my spine as I looked up at him. My heart sped, my mind spinning.

Don't anger him. Don't provoke him further.

"Can I have some clothes, please?" I whispered, daring to meet his gaze.

Robert stared down at me, his lip curled into a sneer. I expected him to refuse, to begin hitting me again. His hands clenched, released, clenched, and released. My heart thundered in my chest, spreading pain. He turned on his heel with a suddenness that left me breathless. I uncurled myself, but only slightly, all too aware of my nakedness. My eyes darted about, searching for any sign of a guard sneaking back for a peek, or more.

"Ow," I whispered, curling my arm around myself and cradling my ribs.

My head jerked up as the soles of Robert's shoes

sounded a staccato rhythm, heralding his return. I swallowed heavily, forcing my heart from my throat into its rightful place. A gasp ripped through me as his arm shot out. I flinched, my ribs screaming from the motion as fabric rustled and fluttered into my lap. Forcing my eyes open, I stared in shock at the dress. It was a deep purple, the material as rich as the color. Silver threads lined the hemline and the edges of the sleeves.

"Put it on," he commanded.

Despite the pain it caused me, I scrambled to pull the dress over my head. The effort had me panting, but I smoothed the material over my thighs and leaned my head back against the chair. A sharp inhalation of breath had my eyes flying open.

Robert's heated gaze moved over me, his chest rising and falling with quickened breath. I was shocked and disturbed to find his body reacting to me, more so than it had when I was in the buff. His tongue darted out, wetting his lips as a terrible whine issued from his throat.

"You, you look just like her." His tone was breathless, his eyes darkening with desire. Unease filtered through me and I scrambled backward, causing the chair to scrape across the floor. I didn't know whom he was speaking of, but something inside of me told me I was going to find out.

I shook my head, crying out as Robert lurched forward and grabbed my arm, his fingers digging into my flesh. My feet scraped along the floor as I fought for traction, dragged upward by his superior strength. My eyes grew wide as I took in the look on his face seconds before he crushed his lips to mine. Bile burned an acid trail up my throat as I struggled against him. A cry of pain slipped past our joined lips as his other hand closed around my injured wrist.

Arms pinned, my mind whirling, I struggled to think, to react to his assault. With a rough jerk, he pinned my arms behind my back holding my wrists firmly in one hand. My feet tangled in the hem of the dress, keeping me from bringing my knee up.

With a grunt I fell back against the chair, Robert's weight pressing down on me. His lips left mine and trailed across my cheek, down my neck. My skin crawled at the touch and I howled in rage and despair as Robert's hands coursed over my body, sending bolts of revulsion through me. His whimpers and excited whines coalesced into words, as he fought with the buttons on the bodice of the dress.

"Oh, Mother. I've missed you so."

His words chilled me to the core and I gagged as his hand closed over my breast. I bucked and struggled beneath him, to no avail, pinned as I was between his body and the chair. Frustrated cries and grunts tore at my throat.

He had what he wanted. His fantasy was complete. He was going to rape me.

Like hell!

I jerked my knees upward catching his inner thigh. Robert hissed out a breath and brought his gaze to mine. Fury and lust battled for dominance, his expression shifting from anger to something almost like hurt.

"Why are you fighting me, Mother?" he asked. "Haven't you missed me too?"

"No!" I screamed, centering my efforts on freeing

my hands as Robert drug me from the chair. My head snapped against the floor, knocking my teeth together as he jerked the hem of the dress upward, exposing my thighs.

"No! No, don't do this. Please!"

"Shh, Mother. We're about to be together again, just how you like it."

Tears soaked my hair as he forced my legs apart, pressing his weight more firmly against me. He could take my body, but he couldn't claim me. I belonged to Marsh. He was coming for me. I just had to hold on. He was coming.

CHAPTER FORTY-TWO

THUNDER FILLED MY ears and I squeezed my eyes closed against the coming assault. Robert's scent overwhelmed me, clogging my nose with the cloying scent of desperation and sweat. I couldn't breathe.

And then he was gone.

My eyes flew open in time to see Robert fly across the room. He smacked into the opposite wall and crumpled to the floor, bits of drywall and dust raining down upon him. I stared at his still form, my brain not comprehending the scene. Blinking, I turned my head and stared in shock at the dark figure towering above me. He wore a denim jacket and dark jeans clung to his long legs. My breath caught in my throat as he turned toward me, and I recognized his face. Familiar and unfamiliar melded together.

Marsh.

I didn't have long to look. A howl of anger filled the room and Marsh turned his head, charging forward to meet Robert head on. They crashed together like the waves against the rocky shore; the force of the impact reverberated through the room. Fists flew, the sound of flesh striking flesh was drowned out only by grunts and curses.

Robert's fist arched, striking Marsh in the cheek just as Marsh swept his right foot out, sending Robert to the ground. Robert didn't stay down long as Marsh grabbed the front of his shirt and yanked him to his feet, pulling his right arm back and slamming his fist into Robert's nose. Bone cracked and blood poured freely.

Robert laughed, a deranged grin spreading across his face as his eyes flickered over Marsh's shoulder. He coughed and spat, a glob of blood and teeth hitting the floor. An insane cackle burst free of him as he jerked out of Marsh's grip and threw his arms out to the sides.

"Enter the hero! Or have you come as the villain?" Robert laughed again, the sound chilling me as he danced backward out of Marsh's reach. The two men circled, March emitting controlled rage, Robert broadcasting a broken mind.

"Which is it, Guardian?" Robert spat the title like a curse, his voice rising until he was screaming. Spittle and blood flew from his lips, his eyes wide and manic. "Have you come to rescue the precious damsel or to slay the beast?"

Marsh said nothing as they continue to circle. Robert flicked his gaze to the open doorway of the room before returning them to Marsh. A sick smile lit his eyes as he stopped, tilting his head to the side.

"You're too late to save the fair maiden, you know," Robert said casually, as if it were just another day. He leaned toward Marsh, dropping his voice to a mock whisper. "You should have heard the way she begged for more."

Secrets

Robert locked his gaze with mine and gave a wistful sigh seconds before Marsh lunged with a roar, grabbing Robert around the throat and squeezing. Robert gasped and gagged, clawing at Marsh, who bore down on him, his arms bulging with the force of his effort. Robert's eyes rolled in his head, then he grinned. His fist shot out connecting solidly with Marsh's unprotected stomach. Marsh grunted, releasing Robert as he doubled over, gasping for breath.

"The villain, then! Here to murder me too, Guardian?" Robert screeched, aiming a kick at Marsh's side. Marsh caught his foot and shoved Robert back as he rose, his eyes stormy.

"Fuck you, Ahlström. Helene's death was of her own doing."

"Don't say her name!" Robert warned, lunging at Marsh, who side-stepped and grabbed the smaller man by the shoulders, using his momentum to hurl him into the doorframe. Robert's head cracked against the wood and with a pained grunt, he collapsed.

Marsh stood over him, panting heavily. Blood leaked from his lower lip and a gash at his right eye. When Robert didn't move, he turned toward me.

The heavy thud of boots had him jerking to a halt as my eyes widened in terror. I had forgotten about the guards.

Fear clawed at my throat as I locked gazes with Marsh. A dark resolve came over his eyes as he pulled a wicked looking knife from a sheath at his side. I hadn't even noticed it.

"This ends now," Marsh ground out, his fingers flexing on the hilt.

I swallowed back my tears, keeping my eyes on his

as he gripped the blade easily, rolling his wrist while continuing to look at me. A sad smile came to his lips as the guards' shouts grew louder, closer.

"Get behind the chair, Juliet. And stay down. No matter what you see, no matter what you hear. If you see an opening, you take it. You take it and you run. Do you understand me?"

I shook my head, my heart fracturing at the thought of leaving him to die. "No. No, I can't leave you," I choked out the words. "I won't!"

"You will." He glanced over his shoulder as the guards poured into the room. Six men crowded through the door, a few bearing bruises and signs of a previous fight. Their eyes swept the room, settling on us, as one crouched down beside Robert and checked for a pulse.

"You!" a large blond growled, glaring at Marsh.

"Promise me!" Marsh demanded, his eyes never leaving the man.

"I promise!" I wailed, scrambling to my knees as Marsh nodded faintly, signaling he heard. He stepped forward, touching the tip of the blade to his brow.

"Gentlemen, we meet again," he greeted, lowering the blade and surging forward.

It was a dance to the death. Marsh moved fluidly, deflecting punches, kicks, and the slashes of the guards' blades. The blade of Marsh's knife flashed in the dim light as he brought it in a downward arc slicing the upper arm of the closest guard.

The guard howled in pain, but Marsh received no reprieve. A second man lunged, slicing at Marsh. Marsh parried the blow only to have a guard jump at him from behind, wrapping his arms around Marsh's neck, seeking to cut off his air. Marsh rolled forward, flipping the man off his back and stabbing his blade into his gut.

Horror filled me as I watched. The five remaining guards moved as a single force, washing over Marsh like a dark wave. They surrounded and pummeled him, knocking him to the ground. A gasp ripped through me as I saw Marsh's blade spin across the floor, caught flashes of his bloody face through the legs of the men.

Run.

This was the opening he had spoken of. Déjà vu washed over me, the scene eerily similar to the one on the Oregon beach. Marsh had told me to hide, to stay safe and protected.

I was done hiding.

I shoved to my feet, the sound of ripping fabric rending the air. Tossing my gaze around, I searched for anything I could use as a weapon. Stumbling forward, I grabbed a dusty vase off a nearby table and hurled it at the nearest guard. The glass shattered against the back of his head, and with a grunt, he went down.

Two down, four to go.

My delight was short-lived. I might have taken down one guard, but I had drawn attention to myself. The large blond guard broke away from the others and stormed toward me, murder in his eyes.

I ran.

The blond laughed and raced after me.

"Run! I like the chase!" His words burned through my mind, bringing up the echo of another attacker, one of the men who had tried to kill me at the Village.

I screamed as his thick arms came around my waist, lifting me and throwing me to the side. I hit the wall with a groan and crumpled to the floor, coughing as my broken ribs screamed. Blondie towered over me, fingering the tip of his dagger as he stared down at me, all but salivating.

"Your asshole boyfriend over there killed my brother. Eye for an eye, but I'm going to have fun first."

I kicked his shin as he reached for me. His legs buckled and I threw myself to my hands and knees, crawling away from him. His fingers closed over my ankle and tightened. I cried out in anguish as my fingertips brushed against the hilt of Marsh's dagger before Blondie jerked me toward him.

Flipping onto my back, I screamed and screeched, kicking and slashing with my nails. Blondie cursed loudly as I raked my nails along his cheek. Grabbing my injured wrist he pinned it above my head.

"Marsh!" I wailed as Blondie continue to overpower me.

"Got you," Blondie growled, a dark grin parting his lips as he held me down. I balked and cursed, not backing down without a fight.

Blondie's chuckle at my efforts cut off in a gurgled gasp. The tip of a blade glimmered wetly through his throat, and I stilled as warm blood spurted over my face. He released me, grabbing for his neck as the thick, red liquid pumped liberally from the wound. I scrambled back, shock coursing through me as Robert's beaten face filled my view.

"I said," Robert hissed, "she's mine!"

I stared up at Robert, fear pinning me to the spot. His shoulders heaved, blood dripped from his hand and the tip of the blade, hitting the floor in fat drops.

Secrets

His eyes were almost black when he looked at me.

"You," I sputtered, inching backward.

Robert watched me, lifting the blade and watching the crimson droplets fall. "He ruined your dress, Mother."

"I am not your mother!" I screamed.

Robert jerked, as if he had been physically hit. His eyes locked onto mine once more and he sighed.

"No. You're not."

He moved with a shocking suddenness and I screamed, raising my arms to shield my face.

"Ahlström!"

Thunder filled my ears again and I lowered my arm in time to see Marsh slam into Robert from the side. The men hit the wall hard enough to crack it. Feral snarls and grunts sounded as they grappled. Robert shoved his hand into Marsh's face, forcing his head back until his neck strained.

Marsh growled in rage, shoving Robert back and pinning him to the wall. They struggled for the knife, Robert's blood slicked fingers quickly losing grip. Marsh slammed his forehead into Robert's. The knife clattering to the ground as Robert went limp.

"It's over!" Marsh yelled, shoving Robert away from him. Robert stumbled, catching himself against the wall, panting, his face littered with cuts and bruises.

"It's over," Marsh repeated, his chest heaving as he fought for breath. "Your men are dead. Your mother is dead. It's done. You've lost. Take your life and go."

Robert's teeth ground together as he glared at Marsh, who stared him down until Robert lowered his head with a defeated sigh, covering his face with his

353

hands. He sunk to the floor, his legs stretched out before him as he sobbed.

Marsh turned toward me, ignoring the broken cries. Our gazes locked. Cuts and darkening bruises littered his neck and face. Blood soaked through his shirt, darkest at his shoulder and left side. His jacket was gone, his jeans cut to ribbons. A faint smile licked his lips as he started toward me.

Everything moved in slow motion. At the edge of my vision, I watched Robert rise, watched as he lifted the knife. Pushed himself away from the wall. Charged.

"Marsh!" I shrieked, pointing behind him.

Marsh spun, showing no fear. His hand shot up, catching Robert by the throat, his other hand blurring as it moved, sinking the unseen blade hilt deep into Robert's chest.

Robert's eyes widened, a surprised cough escaping as he looked down at the dagger protruding from his sternum. His breath hissed out, bloody foam coating his lips as the light left his eyes and his lifeless body crashed to the floor.

I huddled against the wall, utterly transfixed. Never before had I seen such a darkness in Marsh's bright blue eyes. The killing rage that burned in them terrified me. I shrank back from him—from the heat, from the clenched fists and tension filled body.

Marsh turned back to look at me, and just like that, the fire was gone. Replaced with concern, uncertainty. In two strides, he was before me, kneeling down until we were eye to eye. A shuddery breath left his lips as he reached for me.

I flinched.

He stopped instantly. I watched his fingers curl

into fists, watched the whiteness appear on his bloody knuckles, heard the slow exhalation as his eyes found mine.

"Juliet."

My name was a whispered plea that broke the spell. Relief blazed through me, like a wildfire through deadwood. I lunged forward, wrapping my arms around his neck and clinging to him. I buried my face into the hollow of his neck and shoulder and inhaled his familiar scent. His safety. His love.

Hot tears burned my eyes as I clung to him, pressing myself more firmly against his chest, as if trying to become part of him. A ragged cry broke free as his arms came around me, binding me to him. His soft words vibrated through me as his hand stroked down my hair. I could make out only a single phrase.

"I love you."

My heart swelled. He was here. He had come for me. He had killed for me. He loved me.

I was safe.

CHAPTER FORTY-THREE

THE SUN SANK behind the verdant hills, casting its dying rays over the beach. A fire flickered and popped, sending glowing sparks dancing into the air, like hundreds of tiny faeries. The waves crashed and kissed along the shore, showering it with foamy kisses.

A shrouded figure lay on a rough wooden table, the soft ocean breeze ruffling the white sheet. Voices lifted on the air, soprano mingling with tenor. The words were foreign, but the meaning was undeniable. Tears blurred my vision as their voices rose and blended, my heart breaking all over again at the images they conjured with the sorrowful dirge.

I leaned against Marsh, sniffling and wiping the tears from my cheeks as Tabitha's voice cut off in a tear filled choke, and only Marsh's remained. Deep, clear and beautiful the final notes hung hauntingly on the night.

Marsh pressed a kiss to the top of my head before he stepped away from me. Together, he and Tabitha moved in unison, Tabitha to the head of the table, Marsh at the foot. Though it must have taken effort,

Secrets

they did not let it show as they lifted the body and carried it toward the sea.

"From the sea you were born," Tabitha spoke. "By the sea you lived, and in death you return. Goodbye, mother." Tabitha cried freely, her words thick with emotion as she and Marsh stepped into the waves, releasing Adaline to the sea.

"May the road rise up to meet you. May the wind be always at your back. May the sun shine warm upon your face; the rains fall soft upon your fields and until we meet again, may God hold you in the palm of His hand." Marsh's final prayer to his grandmother carried on the wind, seeming to flow out over the ocean.

Wrapping my arms around myself, I watched as the two embraced firmly before parting. They turned, wading through the rolling waves as they made their way back up the beach. I wiped at my cheeks again and stepped into Tabitha's open arms.

"That was beautiful," I whispered.

"Aye, she would have loved it." Tabitha gave me a squeeze, gently touched the fading bruise at my cheek. "She would have been so fiercely proud of ya, love."

I gave a watery smile and hugged her fervently. Tabitha patted my shoulder roughly and moved past me, pulling a handkerchief from her back pocket as she went.

The firelight flickered over Marsh's face, burning away the shadows and darkness. A faint smile curved his lips as our eyes met, and he held his hand out to me.

I echoed his smile as I stepped forward, taking his hand and letting him pull me against him. I reveled in the closeness and warmth he offered. I opened my eyes as Marsh lifted my left hand, watched his eyes move over the jagged healing wound on my wrist. Opening my fingers, he placed a soft kiss to my palm.

"It's healing well," he remarked, his thumb caressed my pulse point and I bit my lower lip, lifting my eyes to his.

"It is. The funeral was beautiful."

Marsh nodded, his eyes drifting toward the ocean. "She's where she belongs, her soul finally at peace." He was silent for a time, watching the water when suddenly his brows shot up and he jumped as if remembering something. "I almost forgot, this belongs to you."

I glanced down at the object in his hand, my heart stilling. It was a glossy brown, and shimmered in the firelight. "Is it?"

"Aye, your seal skin. I told you I was keeping it safe."

I took the skin from him, feeling a familiar warmth rush through me. "Thank you."

I shifted in his arms, slipping my skin into my pocket as I pressed my back against his chest and looked out over the rolling waves. His arms came around me and I closed my eyes, focusing on his breathing and the gentle sound of the waves.

"I love you, Marsh."

I felt his smile, the heat of it washing over me, through me, spreading fire from my toes to the top of my head. His breath was welcomed warmth against my ear. "And I love you, Juliet."

I smiled, placing my hands on top of his as we stood, listening to the sounds of the night around us.

Secrets

The call of gulls seeking refuge, the soft humming of Tabitha.

"Juliet?"

"Hmm?" I shifted my head, watching him out of the corner of my eye as he fought to free something from his pocket.

"Marry me."

My heart stilled in my chest and I spun around. Marsh's hand hovered before me, his ring reflecting the glow of the moonlight.

My gaze jerked from the ring to his face, my heart quickening in my chest. He was serious, and scared. I could see the fear, a fear that hadn't been present even when he was fighting for our lives.

Joy bubbled and burst within me and fresh tears sprung to my eyes. "Yes. Yes, a thousand times yes!"

Marsh's face broke into a broad grin, his hands tightening on my waist as he lifted me, spinning me in a circle as we both laughed. My feet brushed the sand as his lips found mine, sealing our promise to one another.

In that moment, it didn't matter what lay behind us, or what the future may bring. I had Marsh, I had Tabitha. I had the promise of a new family. I had my parents, my sister and the knowledge of their unconditional love.

I had a new identity.

No longer was I Juliet The Ruiner; no longer was I, "The Lost One." I was Juliet, the Found One. The Survivor. The Peace Bringer.

And I was ready for anything.

EPILOGUE

NIGHT HAD WELL and truly fallen by the time the trio came together. The firelight flickered over their faces, illuminating the shock and pleasure on the older woman, the pride on the man, the glow of hope on the younger woman. Their joy drew a deep scowl from the man on the hill.

His eyes never left them, gloved hands curling into fists as an icy rage burned through him. His teeth ground together, eyes narrowing. What right did they have for celebration?

A soft growl sounded at his side as the dog moved to peer over the edge of the rise. Hackles raised, his lips curled back to reveal sharp white canines. The man chuckled coolly as he patted the dog's dark head, ran his hand over the coarse fur.

"Soon, Fuil. We'll make our move soon. Let them have this moment. It will be their last."

ABOUT THE AUTHOR

E.H. Demeter was born in Oregon City, Oregon, though she now makes her home in South Carolina, with her husband and two children, where she can be found to hate the heat and love the rain.

The written word has been a draw since her early years, and she is seldom found without a notebook in hand. Writing is her passion, and her goal is to share her words, thoughts, and opinions with the world. She is a lover of books, hot tea, and sweets – much to the dismay of her waistline.

She grew up reading fantasy and romance novels, and finds that is where most of her inspiration lies, though her love of the young adult genre has also sparked creative fires.

She has been in two anthologies to date: *Cancer Sucks!* and *Nightmares: In Writers Retreat*, both of which were released in October of 2015. She also released her own book, *Musings From Wünderland: A book of Poetry and Prose*, in November 2015.

Stay connected with E.H. Demeter to receive updates on all new works.

You may find her on Facebook:
htttps://www.facebook.com/EHDemeter

Twitter:
https://twitter.com/EH_Demeter

Instagram:
https://www.instagram.com/thedarlingwordsmith/

And her official website:
http://www.ehdemeter.weebly.com/

LOOK FOR
LIES,
THE NEXT BOOK IN
THE RUNE TRILOGY,
COMING SOON!